Tim Gautreaux

Born and raised in Louisiana, Tim Gautreaux lives there still. His work has appeared in *Harper's*, the *Atlantic Monthly*, *GQ, Zoetrope, Prize Stories: The O. Henry Awards*, and *Best American Short Stories*. Acclaimed as 'one of the best writers to have emerged in the 1990s' (*Kirkus Reviews*), he is the author of two collections of stories and the novels *The Next Step in the Dance*, which won the 1999 SEBA Book Award, *The Clearing* and *The Missing*.

Tim Gautreaux

Waiting for the
Evening News

Stories of the Deep South

SCEPTRE

These stories were first published in the United States by Picador in two volumes: *Same Place, Same Things* in 1996 and *Welding with Children* in 1999.

This edition first published in Great Britain in 2010 by Sceptre
An imprint of Hodder & Stoughton
An Hachette UK company

I

Grateful acknowledgement is made to the following publications in which these stories first appeared: *The Atlantic Monthly*: 'Same Place, Same Things', 'Died and Gone to Vegas', 'Welding with Children'; *Story*: 'People on the Empty Road', 'Waiting for the Evening News', 'Good for the Soul'; *Stories*: 'The Courtship of Merlin LeBlanc'; *The Standard*: 'Navigators of Thought'; *GQ*: 'The Bug Man', 'Little Frogs in a Ditch', 'Easy Pickings'; *The Crescent Review*: 'License to Steal'; *The Virginia Quarterly Review*: 'Floyd's Girl'; *St Anthony Messenger*: 'Returnings'; *Harper's*: 'Deputy Sid's Gift', 'The Piano Tuner'; *New York Stories*: 'Misuse of Light'; *Image Magazine*: 'The Pine Oil Writers' Conference'; *Ploughshares*: 'Resistance'; *Fiction*: 'Sorry Blood'; *Epoch*: 'Sunset in Heaven'; *Georgia Review*: 'Rodeo Parole'; *Zoetrope*: 'Dancing with the One-Armed Girl'.

A CIP catalogue record for this title is available from the British Library

ISBN 978 0 340 83455 8

Typeset in Sabon MT by Palimpsest Book Production Limited, Grangemouth, Stirlingshire

Printed and bound by Clays Ltd, St Ives plc

Hodder & Stoughton policy is to use papers that are natural, renewable and recyclable products and made from wood grown in sustainable forests. The logging and manufacturing processes are expected to conform to the environmental regulations of the country of origin.

Hodder & Stoughton Ltd
338 Euston Road
London NW1 3BH

www.hodder.co.uk

For my wife, Winborne, and our sons,
Robert and Thomas.

Contents

Same Place, Same Things

The pump repairman was cautious. He saw the dry rut in the lane and geared the truck down so he could take it through slow. The thin wheels of his ancient Ford bounced heavily, the road ridge scraping the axles. A few blackbirds charged out of the dead brush along the road and wheeled through the sky like a thrown handful of gravel. He wondered how far down the farm lane the woman lived. When she had called him at the tourist court, she had not been confident about giving directions, seeming unsure where her own house was. On both sides of the road, fields of strawberries baked in the sun. It had not rained, the locals told him, for seven weeks.

Leafless branches reached out to snatch away his headlights. Billows of dust flew up behind the truck like a woman's face powder, settling on roadside dewberry bushes that resembled thickened fountains of lava. It was an awful drought.

After a while he arrived at a weatherboard farmhouse set behind a leaning barbed-wire fence. He pulled up and got out. No one came from the house, so he slammed the door of the truck and coughed loudly. He had been in this part of the country long enough to know that the farm people did not want you on their porches unless you were a relative or a neighbor. Now, in the Depression, life was so hard for them they trusted almost nobody. Finally he blew the truck's horn and was rewarded with a movement at one of the windows. In half a minute a woman in a thin cotton housedress came out.

'You the pump man?' she asked.

'Yes, ma'am. Name's Harry Lintel.'

She looked him over as though he were a goat she might or

might not buy. Walking to the edge of her porch, she looked back toward the field behind the house. 'If you walk this trail here for a while, you'll find my husband trying to fix the pump.' He did not like the way she made a face when she said 'husband.' He was uneasy around women who did not like their men. She walked off the porch and through the fifteen feet of thistle and clover that served as a front lawn, moving carefully toward the pump repairman, who regarded her warily. Poor people made him nervous. He was poor himself, at least as far as money goes, but he was not hangdog and spiritless like many of the people he'd met in this part of the state, beaten down and ruined inside by hard times. She looked at his eyes. 'How old you think I am?'

She seemed about forty, four years younger than he was, but with farm women you could never tell. He looked at her sandy hair and gray eyes. She was thin, but something about the way she looked at him suggested toughness. 'Lady, I've come to fix a pump. What kind do you have and what's wrong with it?'

'My husband, he'll be back in a minute. He'll know what all you need to find out. What I want to know is where you're from. I ain't heard nobody around here talk like you in a while.' She had her hair tied back in a loose knot and reached up to touch it delicately. This motion caught his eye. He guessed she might be closer to thirty-five.

Harry Lintel put a hand in his right front pocket and leaned back against the door of his truck. Taking off his straw hat, he threw it over his shoulder into the front seat. 'I'm from Missouri,' he said, running a hand through a clump of short, brassy hair.

Her expression was still one of intense evaluation. 'Ain't there no pump work in Missouri?' she asked. 'Or did your woman run you off?'

'My wife died,' he said. 'As for pump work, when it's dry and the local pump repairmen can't keep up with their work, or there ain't any pump repairmen, I come around and take up the slack.' He looked around her at the peeling house and its broken panes patched with cardboard.

'So why ain't you where you belong, taking up slack?'

He looked at her hard. That last remark showed some wit, something he had not seen in a woman for a while. 'Where's your husband, lady? I've got cash jobs waiting for me up Highway Fifty-one.'

'Keep your pants on. He'll be here, I said.' She folded her arms and came a step closer. 'I'm just curious why anyone would come to this part of Louisiana from somewheres else.'

'I follow the droughts,' he said, straightening up and walking along the fence to where it opened into a rutted drive. The woman followed him, sliding her hands down her hips to smooth her dress. 'Last week I was in Texas. Was doing a good trade until an all-night rain came in from Mexico and put me out of business. Wasn't much of a pumping situation after that, and the local repairmen could keep things going.' He looked down the path as far as he could see along the field of limp plants. 'Month before that I was in north Georgia. Before that I fixed pumps over in Alabama. Those people had a time with their green peppers. Where the devil's your old man?'

'I never see anyone but my husband and two or three buyers that come back in here to deal with him.' She began to look at his clothes, and this made him uneasy, because he knew she saw that they were clean and not patched. He wore a khaki shirt and trousers. Perhaps no one she knew wore unpatched clothes. Her housedress looked like it had been made from a faded window curtain. 'Texas,' she said. 'I saw your ad in the paper and I figured you were a traveling man.'

'No, ma'am,' he said. 'I'm a man who travels.' He saw she did not understand that there was a difference. She seemed desperate and bored, but many people he met were that way. Very few were curious about where he came from, however. They cared only that he was Harry Lintel, who could fix any irrigation pump or engine ever made.

He walked into the field toward the tree line a quarter mile off, and the woman went quickly to the house. He saw a wire strung from the house into a chinaberry tree, and then through a long file of willows edging a ditch, and figured this led to an electric pump. He was almost disappointed that the woman wasn't following him.

As he walked, he looked around at the farm. It was typical of the worst. He came up on a Titan tractor stilted on wood blocks in the weeds, its head cracked. Behind it was a corroded disk harrow, which could still have been useful had it been taken care of. In the empty field to his right stood two cows suffering from the bloat.

He was sweating through his shirt by the time he reached a thin stand of bramble-infested loblolly edging the field. Two hundred feet down the row of trees, a man hunched over an electric motor, his back to the repairman. Calling out to him, Lintel walked in that direction, but the other man did not respond – he was absorbed in close inspection of a belt drive, the pump repairman guessed. The farmer was sprawled on a steel grid that hung over an open well. Harry walked up and said hello, but the farmer said nothing. He seemed to be asleep, even though he was out in the sun and his undershirt was wet as a dishcloth. Harry stooped down and looked over the pump and the way it was installed. He saw that it was bolted to the grid without insulation. Two stray wires dangled into the well. He watched for the rise and fall of the man's body, but the man was not breathing. Kneeling down, Harry touched the back of his knuckles to the steel grid. There was no shock, so he grabbed the man by his arms and pulled him off the motor, turning him over. He was dead, without a doubt: electrocuted. His fingers were burned, and a dark stain ran down his pants leg. He felt the man's neck for a pulse and, finding none, sat there for a long time, studying the man's broad, slick face, a face angry and stupid even in death. He looked around at the sorry farm as though it were responsible, then got up and walked back to the farmhouse.

The woman was sitting in a rocker on the porch, staring off

into a parched, fallow field. She looked at the repairman and smiled, just barely.

Harry Lintel rubbed his chin. 'You got a phone?'

'Nope,' she said, smoothing her hair down with her right hand. 'There's one at the store out on Fifty-one.'

He did not want to tell her, feeling that it would be better for someone else to break the news. 'You've got a lady friend lives around here?'

She looked at him sharply, her gray eyes round. 'What you want to know that for?'

'I've got my reasons,' he said. He began to get into his big dusty truck, trying to act as though nothing had happened. He wanted to put some distance between himself and her coming sorrow.

'The first house where you turned in, there's Mary. But she don't have no phone.'

'See you in a few minutes,' he said, cranking up the truck.

At the highway he found Mary and told her to go back and tell the woman that her husband was dead out by the pump. The old woman simply nodded, went back into her house, and got her son to go with her. Her lack of concern bothered him. Didn't she care about the death of her neighbor?

At the store he called the sheriff and waited. He rode with the deputies back to the farmhouse and told them what he knew. The lawmen stood over the body, looked up at the dry sky, and told the pump repairman to go back to his business, that they would take care of everything.

He and one of the deputies walked out of the field past the farmhouse, and he tried not to look at the porch as he passed, but he could not keep himself from listening. He heard nothing – no crying, no voices heavy with muted passion. The two women were on the porch step, talking calmly, as though they were discussing the price of berries. The widow watched him carefully as he got into the police car. He thought he detected a trace of perfume in the air and looked around inside the gritty sedan for its source.

That day he repaired six engines, saving little farms from turning back to sand. The repairs were hard ones that no one else could manage: broken timing gears, worn-out governors, cracked water jackets. At least one person on each farm asked him if he was the one who had found the dead man, and when he admitted that he was, each sullen farmer backed off and let him work alone. Late in the afternoon he was heating an engine head in his portable forge, watching the hue of the metal so that he could judge whether the temperature was right for brazing. He waited for the right color to rise like the blush on a woman's cheek, and when it did, he sealed a complex crack with a clean streak of molten brass. A wizened Italian farmer watched him like a chicken hawk, his arms folded across a washed-out denim shirt. 'It's no gonna work,' he said.

But when, near dusk, Harry pulled the flywheel and the engine sprang to life with a heavy, thudding exhaust, turning up a rill of sunset-tinged water into the field, the farmer cracked a faint smile. 'If you couldna fixed it, we'da run you out the parish.'

Harry began to clean his hands with care. 'Why?'

'Stranger find a dead man, that's bad luck.'

'It's better I found him than his wife, isn't it?'

The farmer poked a few bills at Harry, turned, and began walking toward his packing shed. 'Nothin' surprise that woman,' he said.

It was eight-thirty when he got back to the Bell Pepper Tourist Court, a collection of six pink stucco cabins with a large oval window embedded in each. The office, which also contained a small café, was open, but he was too tired to eat. He sat on his jittery bed, staring across the highway to the railroad, where a local passenger train trundled by, its whistle singing for a crossing. Beyond this was yet another truck farm, maybe twelve acres punctuated by a tin-roof shack. He wondered how many other women were stuck back in the woods living without husbands. The widow of the electrocuted man didn't even have children to take her mind off her loneliness. He had that. He had gotten married when he was seventeen and had raised two daughters and a son. He was now forty-four and on his own, his wife having died five years before. The small Missouri town he was raised in couldn't keep him provided with work, so he had struck out, roaming the South and the Southwest, looking for machines that nobody else could repair.

He stared through an oval window at his truck. At least he could move around and meet different people, being either sorry to leave them or glad to get away, depending. He gazed fondly at the Ford, its stake body loaded with blacksmith's tongs, welding tools, a portable forge, and boxes of parts, wrenches, sockets, coal, hardies, gasket material, all covered with a green tarp slung over the wooden sides. It could take him anywhere, and with his tools he could fix anything but the weather.

The next morning at dawn he headed out for the first job of the day, noticing that the early sky was like a piece of sheet metal heated to a blue-gray color. He pulled up to a farmhouse and a small man wearing a ponderous mustache came out from around back, cursing. Harry Lintel threw his hat into the truck and ran his hands through his hair. He had never seen people who disliked strangers so much. The little farmer spat on the Ford's tire and told him to drive into the field behind the farmhouse. 'My McCormick won't throw no spark,' he said.

Harry turned to get under way, but over the Ford's hood he saw, two hundred yards off, the back of a woman's head moving above the weeds in an idle field. 'Who's that?' he asked, pointing two fields over.

The farmer craned his neck but could not recognize the figure, who disappeared behind a brier patch between two farms. 'I don't know,' the farmer said, scratching his three-day beard, 'but a woman what walk around like that with nothing better to do is thinking up trouble.' He pointed to Harry. 'When a woman thinks too long, look out! Now, get to work, you.'

The day turned hot as a furnace and his skin flamed with sweat. By noon he had worked on three machines within a half mile of one another. From little farms up and down Highway 51 he could hear the thud and pop of pump engines. He was in a field of berries finishing up with a balky International, when he saw a woman walking along the railroad embankment with a basket in the crook of her right arm. It was the wife of the dead farmer. He waited until she was several rows away and then looked up at her. She met his gaze head-on, her eyes the color of dull nickel. He admitted to himself then and there that it scared him, the way she looked at him. Harry Lintel could figure out any machine on earth, but with women, he wished for an instruction manual.

She walked up to him and set the basket on top of his wrenches. 'You ready to eat?'

He wiped his hands on a kerosene-soaked rag. 'Where'd you come from?'

'It's not far from my place,' she said. He noticed that she was wearing a new cotton dress, which seemed to have been snagged in a few places by briers. She knelt down and opened the basket, pulling out a baby quilt and sandwiches. He sat on the parched grass next to her in a spot of shade thrown by a willow.

'I'm sorry about your man,' he said. 'I should have told you myself.'

Her hands moved busily in the basket. 'That woman and I get along all right. You did as good as you could.' They ate in silence for a while. From the distance came the deep music of a big Illinois Central freight engine, its whistle filling the afternoon, swaying up and down a scale of frantic notes. The Crimson Flyer thundered north, trailing a hundred refrigerated cars of berries, the work of an entire year for many local farmers. 'That train's off its time,' she said. 'Seems like everything's off schedule lately.' She took a bite of ham sandwich and chewed absently.

'I asked the boys that own this engine about your man. They didn't want to talk about him.' He took a bite of sandwich and tried not to make a face. It was dry, and the ham tasted like it had been in the icebox too long. He wondered if she had fed her husband any better.

'He was from New Orleans, not from around here. Nobody liked him much, because of his berries. He tried to ship bad Klondykes once, and the men at the loading dock broke his leg.'

The pump man shook his head. 'Breaking a farmer's leg's kind of rough treatment.'

'He deserved it,' she said matter-of-factly. 'Shipping bad berries gives the local farmers a bad name.' She looked at her sandwich as though she had seen it for the first time, and threw it into the basket. 'He was too damned lazy to pick early enough to ship on time.'

He was afraid she was going to cry, but her face remained as dry as the gravel road that ran along the track. He began to wonder what she had done about her husband. 'What about the services for your old man?'

'Mary's pickers helped me put him in this morning after the coroner came out and give us the okay.'

So that's it, he thought. Half your life working in the sun and then your woman plants you in back of the toolshed like a dog. He was tempted to toss his sandwich, but he was hungrier than he had been in weeks, so he bit at it again. The woman put her eyes all over him, and he knew what she was doing. He began to compare himself to her husband. He was bigger. People told him frequently that he had a pleasant face, which he figured was their way of telling him he wasn't outright ugly.

When she stared away at a noisy crow, he stole a long look at her. The dress fit her pretty well, and if she were another woman, one that hadn't just put her husband in the ground, he might have asked her for a date. A row of pale freckles fell across her nose, and today her hair was untied, hanging down over her shoulders. Something in the back of his mind bothered him.

'What's your name?' he asked.

'Ada,' she said quickly, as though she had expected the question.

'I thank you for the sandwich, but I've got to get going up the road.'

She looked along the railway. 'Must be nice to take off whenever you've a mind to. I bet you travel all over.'

'A lot travel more'n I do.' He bent down and began to pick up box-end wrenches.

'What you in such a hurry for?' she asked, stretching out her long legs into the dead grass. Harry studied them a moment.

'Lady, people around here wonder what the trees are up to when they lean with the breeze. What you think someone that sees us is going to think?'

He walked over to his truck, placed his tools in the proper boxes, row-hopped over to the engine, slung the flywheel with a cast-iron crank, and backed off to hear the exhausts talk to him. The woman watched his moves, all of them. As he was driving out of the field, he felt her eyes on the back of his neck.

That evening after supper in the Bell Pepper Tourist Court Café Harry looked up from his coffee and saw Ada walk in through the screen door. She moved across the hard-scrubbed pine floor as if she came into the place all the time, then sat across from him in a booth and put on the table a bottle of bright red strawberry wine. She had washed her hair and put on a jasmine perfume.

Harry was embarrassed. A couple of farmers watched them and Marie, the owner, lifted her chin when she saw the wine. He was at first grouchy about the visit, not liking to be surprised, but as she asked him questions about his travels, he studied her skin, which was not as rough as he'd first thought, her sandy hair, and those eyes that seemed to drink him in. He wondered how she had passed her life so far, stuck on a mud lane in the most spiritless backwater he'd ever seen. He was as curious about her static world as she was about his wandering one.

Conversation was not his long suit, but the woman had an hour's worth of questions about Arkansas and Georgia, listening to his tales of mountains as though he were telling her of China or the moon. What he wanted to talk about was Missouri and his children, but her questions wouldn't let him. At one point in the conversation she looked over at Marie and said, 'There's them around here that say if you hang around me, there's no telling what trouble you'll get into.' She put her hands together and placed them in the middle of the green oilcloth.

He looked at them, realizing that she had told him almost nothing about herself. 'You said your husband was from New Orleans, but you didn't say where you were from.'

She took a swallow of wine from a water glass. 'Let's just say I showed up here a few years ago. Nobody knows nothing much about me except I was kept back in that patch and never came in to drink or dance or nothing. Where I'm from's not so important, is it?' She took a sip and smiled at him over the rim of her glass. 'You like to dance?' she asked quickly.

'I can glide around some,' he said. 'But about this afternoon – why'd you follow me with them sandwiches out in the field?'

Ada bit her lower lip and thought a moment. 'Maybe I want to move on,' she said flatly. Harry looked out the window and whistled.

They took their time finishing off the bottle. She went to the ladies' room and he walked outside, into the dark parking lot. He stood there, stretching the kinks out of his muscles. Ada came out with him, looked up and down 51 for cars, and threw her arms around his waist, giving him a hard kiss. Then she backed off, smiling, and began walking up the dark highway toward her place.

Oh my, he thought. Her mouth had tasted of strawberry wine, hot and sweet. Oh my.

Later that night he lay in his bed with the window open, listening to the pump engines running out in the fields, which stretched away on all sides of the tourist court for miles. They throbbed, as delicate as distant heartbeats. He could tell which type each was by the sound it made. He heard an International hit-and-miss engine fire once and then coast slower and slower through several cycles before firing again. Woven into that sound was a distant Fairbanks Morse with a bad magneto throbbing steadily, then cutting off, slowing, slowing almost to stillness before the spark built up again and the engine boomed back alive. Across the road, a little McCormick muttered in a ditch. In the quiet night the engines fought the drought, popping like the musketry of a losing army. Through the screen of his window drifted the scent of kerosene exhaust.

He thought of the farmer's widow and finally admitted to himself, there in the dark, that she was good-looking. What was she doing right now? he wondered. Reading? For some reason he doubted this. Sewing? What – traveling clothes? Was she planning how to sell the patch and move back, as many women had done, to wherever she had come from? If she had any sense, he thought, she'd be asleep, and he turned over and faced the wall, listening to the springs ring under him. He tried to remember what he had done at night when he was at home, when he was twenty-four and had three children and a wife, but nothing at all came to him. Then, slowly, thoughts of rocking sick babies and helping his wife can sweet corn came to him, and before two minutes had passed, he was asleep.

The next morning the sky was as hard and expressionless as a pawnbroker's face. At eight o'clock the temperature was ninety-one, and the repairman had already welded a piston rod in Amite and was headed south. When he passed the woman's lane, he forced himself not to look down its rutted surface. He had dreamed of her last night, and that was enough, he thought. Times were so hard he could afford only his dreams. A half mile down the road he began working at pouring new babbitt bearings for an old Dan Patch engine. The owners of the farm left him alone so they could oversee a group of inexperienced pickers, and at nine-thirty, while he was turning the blower for the forge, she came out of the brush to the north, carrying a clear glass jug of lemonade.

'I'll bet you're dry,' she said, giving him the jug and a tin cup.

'You're an awful friendly lady,' he said, pouring himself a drink and looking at her slim waist, her long hair.

'I can be friendly when I want to be.' She rested her hand on his damp shoulder a moment and let it slide off slowly.

They talked while he worked the forge. He tried to tell her about his children, but she seemed not to be interested. She wanted to know where he had been and where he was going. She wanted to know how it was to live on the road, what people were like in different places. 'Do you stay in tourist courts every night?' she asked, wide-eyed.

By the time he had finished his repair, she had told him that she had just buried her third husband, that she had never been a hundred miles from the spot they were standing in, and that she didn't care if she never saw another strawberry for the rest of her days. 'Sometimes I think it's staying in the same place, doing the same things, day in, day out, that gets me down. Get up in the morning and look out the window and see that same rusty fence. Look out another window and see that same willow tree. Out another and see that field. Same place, same things, all my life.' She heard a distant train whistle and looked off toward it, caught up in the haunting sound.

Harry Lintel was at a loss in dealing with unhappy people. He remembered that putting his big arms around his young wife years ago would stop her from crying, but he had no notion why this worked. Looking at the delicate hollow of Ada's cheek, he felt sorry he didn't know what to do for her. He wondered if she would take up with him in his truck if he asked her, would just go off with him up the highway to Tennessee or Georgia, wherever the next drought was needing him to fix engines or windmills. Would this heal what was wrong?

After a local freight train racketed by, three men in overalls drove across the track, got out of their pickup, and began telling him about a big engine in a dry field six miles west, and how nobody could get it to run all week. The men ignored the woman, and as the repairman packed his tools and dumped the forge, he watched her walk off. She went south, away from her place, along the dirt lane that sidled up to the railroad, keeping her thin brown shoes out of the heaped-up dust ridge. After he loaded the truck, he cranked it and headed not west, along the route given him by the three men, but north. Turning into her lane, he bumped down along the ruts to her farmhouse. He walked to the back of the property and noticed her berries blanched by the sun as if they'd had kettles of boiling water poured over them. Returning to the house, he opened the fuse box nailed to the rear outside wall and discovered that one fuse was blown, even though it was a special heavy-duty type. He used his pocketknife to pry off the faceplate and saw where a switch wire cut into the circuit and ran from the bottom of the box through a hole into the house.

He found the front door unlocked. Walking through the house, he noticed there was little furniture: only a set of dark varnished chairs, two small, rough tables, and a rickety, curled-up sofa. The windows were dirty. In the kitchen he found the wall switch that activated the pump, and, peering close, he saw that it had been turned on. He was sure that many farms with electric pumps also had inside switches. But surely the man would have killed the circuit before he went out to work on the thing. And then he remembered that he hadn't seen any switch out in the field.

He sat down at the oilcloth-covered kitchen table and squinted out the front window. He saw a rusty fence. Looking out a side window, he saw a willow tree. My God, he thought. He turned to look through the rear window, into a field. Near the broken tractor was a freshly dug mound of dirt. He put his face down into his hands and shook like a man who had just missed being in a terrible accident.

During the next ten days he worked the whole parish. Wild animals came out of the woods looking for water. Bottoms of drainage ditches cracked open and buckled. He saw pickers brought out of the field with heatstroke. The woman found him only twice, and he was polite, listening to her tell him about her nights and what she saw through her windows. She wore the same dress but kept it clean and ironed. Once, she asked him to come over for supper, but he said he had work to do past dark.

At the tourist court he avoided the café and went to bed early, putting himself to sleep by thinking of his wife, painfully, deliberately. He remembered the kindness of her meals in their kitchen and the fondness of her touch, which was on him still, teaching him.

On a Thursday morning, before dawn, he was awakened by a drumming sound to the northwest. At first he thought it was someone at the door, but when the sound rolled down on the parish again, he knew it was thunder. By first light the rain had started in earnest, and at eight o'clock he was still in his room, staring out at sheets of wind-tortured spray welling up in puddles along the highway – three inches at least, and more to come, by the looks of the sky. It was time to move on.

In the café, for the first time Marie had no repair calls for him. He paid up, gave her a hug, and headed out north in his groaning truck, rainwater spilling off the taut new tarp covering the back.

The highway followed the railroad up through a series of small towns, and he made good time despite a traffic of small truck-loads of produce and an occasional horse-drawn farm wagon. He felt lighthearted for the first time in days, and whistled as he steered around slower vehicles navigating the rainy road. There was something good about getting out of this section of the country, he felt, something good about pointing his headlights toward Jackson or Memphis, where he would hole up in a boardinghouse and read a big-city paper until the weather reports would tell him where he'd find lots of dust, heat, worn-out pumps, and busted windmills.

About noon he pulled over at a café south of McComb. Walking to the back of the truck, he saw that one of the tarp ropes had come undone. When he raised the cloth to check inside, he saw the woman lift her face toward him, her eyes rusty and dark.

'When I heard the rain start on my roof, I knew you'd be pulling out,' she said. 'You can go somewheres. I can't.'

He stared at her for a long time, trying to figure what to say. He looked up and down the red-dirt highway lined with spindly telephone poles and then at the café, which was closed, he realized, the front door padlocked. Finally, he climbed in and sat on a toolbox lid next to her in the oily dark. 'You can't come along with me.'

'Don't say that,' she said, putting her arms loosely around his neck. 'You're the only person I ever met can go where he wants to go.' She said this not in a pleading voice but as a statement of fact. 'I can go with you. I'll be good to you, Mr Lintel.'

He looked at her eyes and guessed that she was desperate for his freedom of movement but not for him. The eyes seemed already to be looking ahead, looking at a whole world passing by a truck window. 'Where you want to go,' he said at last, 'I can't take you.'

She pulled her arms away quickly. 'What you mean by that? You just going to toss me off on the side of the road like a wore-out machine? There's something in me what needs to get away with you.'

Harry Lintel leaned toward her and took her hands, trying to remember the ways he had once brought solace to his wife. 'If I could help you, I'd bring you along for the ride,' he said. 'But I can't do a thing for you.' He half-expected her to cry when he said that, but she only shook her head.

'You've got a heart like a rock,' she told him.

'No, ma'am,' he said. 'I loved a good woman once, and I could love another. You can't come with me because you killed your old man.'

Her eyes seemed to pulse, and what softness lingered around the corners of her mouth disappeared into a flinty expression of fear and desperation.

He reached for his wallet. 'I'm going to buy a ticket and put you on the southbound. You can walk home from the station.'

She grabbed a bill from him before he offered it, then straightened up, throwing an arm in back of her as if she was searching for the handle of her cardboard suitcase. Harry stared at his empty hand for a moment and turned to climb out into the drizzle. He heard the music of a tempered wrench being picked up, and then a bomb went off in his head, and he was down on the floorboards, rolling in cinders and wire, his arms and legs uncontrolled, his eyes letting in a broken vision of the woman standing over him, looking down the way someone might examine a stunned fish. 'I've never met a man I could put up with for long,' she told him. 'I'm glad I got shut of all of mine.'

His head roared like a forge, and he tried to rise, his eyes flickering, his arms pushing him toward the woman's upraised fist, where his biggest box-end wrench glimmered like a thunderbolt. The blow was a star-giving ball of pain, and he felt the tailgate in the small of his back, the world going over like a flywheel, his face in collision with gravel and clay, a coppery rill coursing through his nose and mouth. The only thing in his head was the silver ring of a tool, and then the exhaust of a four-cylinder engine pulling away, fading into a clash of gears at the top of a hill, and then, for the longest time, nothing. Somewhere a cow bellowed, or a car passed without stopping, or wind blew through the grass around him like knowledge through an ear.

Near dusk he woke to a dove singing on the phone wires. He wondered where she would sell the truck, to what town she would ride on the train. It didn't matter. She was a woman who would never get where she wanted to go. He was always where he was going.

One eye began to work, and he watched clouds, the broken pieces of the world hanging above like tomorrow's big repair job, waiting.

Waiting for the Evening News

Jesse McNeil was running a locomotive while he was drunk, and he was doing a fine job of it, charging up the main line at fifty with the chemical train, rattling through the hot Louisiana night like a thunderstorm. He watched the headlight brighten the rails to mile-long silver spears sailing through the sandy pine wastelands of the parish. Another nameless hamlet was rolling up in the distance, one in a row of asbestos-siding-and-tin communities strung along the railroad like ticks on a dog's backbone. He had roared through it a thousand times with a hundred cars of propane and vinyl chloride and had never so much as touched the air brake, had only to blow a signal for the one crossing, and then was gone like a gas pain in the bowel, discomfort and noise for a moment, soon forgotten by the few hundred folks who lived in wherever-it-was, Louisiana. He reached for the whistle lever in the dark cab and missed it, remembering the half-pint of whiskey he had gulped behind the engine house thirty minutes earlier. He was fifty years old today, and he wanted to do something wild and woolly, like get half-lit and pull the chemical train, known by enginemen as the 'rolling bomb,' up to the Mississippi line on time for a change. He could make this run in his sleep. After he got the train stretched out and up to the speed limit, all he had to do was blow the damned whistle. The train was on tracks and couldn't get lost or wander off among somebody's cows.

Jesse looked over at his brakeman, who was watching for automobiles on his side of the train. A highway followed along the tracks and at least once every trip a noodlehead with the windows rolled up and the radio blasting would turn in front of the engine at a crossing, notice the train, maybe mess in his britches, and then shoot on across to safety. Jesse reached again for the whistle lever and pulled it, sending a five-chime-whistle note crashing off all the tin and asbestos for a mile around. The gravel crossing winked in the moonlight and was gone, the train invaded the town, and Jesse looked out his window at the black air, listening to the hollow thunder in his head and laughing at how free he felt, how nobody cared what he was doing, how lost he was in the universe. He was the anonymous taxi driver of ethylene oxide and caustic soda, chlorine and ethyl antiknock compound, a man known intimately only by his menopausal wife and the finance company.

Then with a jolt, loose wrenches and lunch boxes flew forward in a convulsion of iron, and Jesse was knocked from his seat, his thermos flying over his head and sailing out into the thundering darkness. The locomotive lurched as though a giant hand had grabbed it from behind and wiggled it like a toy. Leaning out the window and looking back along the mile-long trail of tankers, he saw a whirlwind of sparks thirty cars back, and his heart divided in two and hid up under his shoulder blades. Somewhere an air hose parted, and the brakes jammed on with a squeal. He remembered to shut off the throttle, and as the engines bucked and ground rails for a quarter mile, he saw a white tanker turn sideways in the distance. Then he knew the train was breaking apart, the rear section running in like an accordion, and here he was in the dark woods at the edge of town, more than half-drunk, witnessing a catastrophe that would have happened even if he had been stone-sober and riding the rails with a Bible in his back pocket.

The black locomotives trembled to a stop, jumping as derailing cars smacked into those tankers still on the tracks. The brakeman and conductor hit the ground, running toward all the thunder. Jesse McNeil climbed down the engine steps carefully and put his hands in his pockets, wondering what he would do, what he would tell everybody. Then the first chemical tanker exploded, pinwheeling up into the night sky, slinging its wheels and coming down into a roadside 7-Eleven, the building disappearing in an unholy orange fireball. The strange pounding Jesse heard was the sound of his own feet running north along the railroad, scattering rocks and dust until he reached a spot where he could get down to the highway and lope along the blacktop. He ran until he had no wind and his heart pounded like a fist. Then he turned and saw the sky lit up a smoky yellow. He began to stumble backward through an unnameable fear, and when an old pickup pulled out of a side road and drove north toward him, he stuck out his thumb.

Jesse hitched to the next jerkwater town up the line, and even there he could see a poisonous glow on the horizon. A log-truck driver gave him a lift to the interstate, and he was faced with the choice of going north, farther into the trash-woods sand hills where he was raised, the land of clapboard fundamentalist churches and mildewed trailers, or south toward the alien swamps and that Sodom of all Sodoms, New Orleans. He crossed the median to the southbound lane. No one would look for him in New Orleans.

After a while, a black sedan approached, and he stuck up his thumb, thinking that if he could get away long enough for his system to clear of bourbon, maybe he could tell the company officials that he'd had an attack of amnesia, or anxiety, or stupidity, and had run off like a fool to sort things out for a day. What could they do to him for being stupid? Fire him? He didn't need much money anyway. His frame house was paid for, and the only reason he worked at all was to spend time away from Lurleen, his prune-skin wife, who was always after him to paint or fix something. But if they had found him stumbling around by the engine, drunk, maybe the law would get involved. Maybe it would mean a great big fine, and if he ever did want to work for a railroad again, they wouldn't hire him to run a windup locomotive around a Christmas tree.

To his surprise the black sedan stopped, and soon he was cruising south in the company of an old Catholic priest, a Father

Lambrusco, semiretired, who was filling in for a vacationing assistant pastor at St Louis Cathedral.

'You out of work?' the priest asked, speeding past a gravel truck.

'Yeah,' Jesse said, studying the eastern sky through the windshield. 'I'm a carpenter.'

'Ah. Joseph was a carpenter.'

'Joseph who?'

The priest checked his rearview. 'Joseph, the father of Jesus.'

Jesse frowned at himself. A priest talks about Joseph the carpenter, and Jesse thinks at first that maybe he's talking about Joseph Wiggins from McComb, Mississippi. 'Oh yeah, that Joseph,' Jesse said.

'You go to church?'

'Well, some. I'm sort of a fundamentalist.'

'Isn't going to church fundamental? No, never mind. I didn't pick you up to preach. To tell the truth, I was falling asleep at the wheel.' He turned his bald head toward Jesse and smiled, keeping his mouth closed, as though he had bad teeth. 'Tell me, Mr Carpenter, do you believe Catholics worship statues?'

Jesse assured him he did not, that one friend he had made in the service had been a Catholic chaplain.

'Were you baptized by total immersion in your church?' the priest asked.

'All the way under. We got our own special tank.'

'Was your life changed?' The priest swung around a Volkswagen.

Jesse pursed his lips and looked far down the road, as if he might see his life changing up ahead. 'The minister said it might take some time in my case.'

He and the priest talked for an hour and a half about snake-handler preachers and why nuns didn't have any spare time.

At two in the morning Jesse checked into the Night O' Delight Motel on Airline Highway in New Orleans. The desk clerk, a young Asian man, asked him if he wanted a fifteen-dollar room or a sixty-dollar room with a bed warmer. 'What fool would pay sixty dollars just to sleep in a room?' he told him. He gave the man three fives, plus the tax, thankful that he had just cashed his paycheck and held back a few hundred to pay Lurleen's cousin to come over and paint the house. When he got to the room he turned on the television to check for news, flipping through channels until he reached the last station on the dial, which was showing a vividly pornographic scene. Jesse mashed the off switch and drew back his finger as though it had been burned.

He looked around at the warped paneling and the window unit, which labored without a grille in its hole near the ceiling. Tomorrow he would call in his story. Things would go fairly rough with him for running off, but he would worry about that the next day. He pulled off his coveralls and climbed into the bed, which jittered and rang, sagging badly in the middle.

The next morning his bladder woke him in time for the eight o'clock news, and as he fumbled with the dials, he wondered if the wreck would even be mentioned. The fire probably had been put out by now. The railroad would have to buy somebody's 7-Eleven, but they could have the line clear by late afternoon.

However, on Channel 4 was a helicopter view of Satan's living room, fifty tank cars crashed together and burning. Black-and-green smoke rose a mile into the air, and on both sides of the track, seed elevators, storehouses, and shops flamed in fierce amber heaps. Jesse stepped back and cupped a hand to his forehead. He tried to say something like 'What in God's name?' but he couldn't make a sound. The voice narrating the video told that the town had been evacuated and that fire-fighting teams were driven back by a mix of a dozen chemicals spilled from ruptured tankers, that the town's ditches were running with vinyl chloride and paint stripper. Then the voice told the world that Jesse P. McNeil, the train's engineer, had disappeared from the scene and it was thought that he had run off into the woods east of the derailment, where parish posse members were searching for him with teams of dogs.

When he heard his name fly out of the television, Jesse sat

down hard on the creaking bed. Hardly forty people knew he existed, and now his name had sailed out into the region like parts of his exploded train. Why, he wondered, was it important to name him at all? And sheriff's officers were in the woods searching for him like he was a criminal. When the news report ended, he turned off the television and wondered if his blood would now test free of alcohol. He decided to eat a big breakfast. Stepping out of his room, he walked over to a run-down strip of glass and blond-colored brick businesses across the highway, entered a smoky café, and sat at the counter. On a shelf over the coffee urn, a grease-stained television blinked and buzzed. A local channel was showing the wreck from ground level. A handsome announcer listed twenty evil-sounding names of chemicals that were burning, spilling, or threatening to explode. He also mentioned that the engineer was a man of average build, with red hair combed straight back, last seen hitching a ride north of the wreck site. The waitresses were absorbed in the broadcast and didn't see Jesse slowly turn away from the counter and head for the door. Outside, he stood on the curb and felt light-headed, anxious that the next person to lay eyes on him might recognize who he was. He looked up and down the neon-infested highway for escape. Next to the café was a cubbyhole-sized barbershop, and he sidled over to its door and backed inside. Jesse found an Italian-looking gentleman stropping his razor and watching a TV mounted on a rack in the corner. The engineer sat in the chair and wondered how he could ask for his hair to be combed in some new way, maybe with a part on the side, anything different from the straight-back crimson mane he sported at the moment. The barber smiled and clicked his scissors in the air twice.

'Hey, what you think of the train wreck? Some mess, right?' He ran a comb through Jesse's hair slowly, as though admiring it.

Jesse looked at him warily. He hated the big-city accent of New Orleans folks. They sounded like New Yorkers to his piney woods ear. 'I ain't heard of a wreck,' Jesse said.

The barber bobbed his head. 'Aw yeah. You just come in from

the forest, hey? You from Mississippi, right? Hay-baling time and all that shit.'

Jesse found himself nodding, glad to be given some kind of identity. Just then the television screen flashed a stern company photograph of his face. 'Look here,' he said, grabbing the barber's arm and pulling his attention away from the TV, 'can't you give me kind of a modern look? Something maybe a little younger?'

The barber sucked in his cheeks and studied Jesse's head the way an expensive artist might. 'Yeah, man. I could wash all that oil out, shorten everything up, and kinda spike it.' He clicked his scissors once. 'But your friends back in the woods gonna think you a Communist rock star or somethin'.'

Jesse took in a deep breath and watched the white-hot center of the chemical train pulse over the barber's shoulder. 'Do it to me,' he said.

After his haircut, he spent the entire morning in the café next door, reading the newspapers. The noon TV news devoted a full five minutes to the train wreck. At that point he decided he would not call in for a while, that he would wiat a few days until this was past and everyone would begin to forget, that he would lie low along Airline Highway in the Night O' Delight Motel until everyone and everything cooled off and the poisonous fumes of his train wreck had blown clear of the unlucky town. It took him a good while to decide this, because out-of-the-ordinary decisions seldom came up in his life. The engineer had been running the same routes with the same trains for so many years that lately he found it hard to pay attention to the usual telegraph poles and sweet-gum trees sailing past his cab window. In the same way, the stunted pines along the road to his house, and the little house itself, had become unseeable. Sometimes he imagined himself an unseen part of this faded, repetitive background.

The sense of being invisible made Jesse think he could not be taken seriously, which was why he never voted, hardly ever renewed his driver's license, and paid attention in church only once a year at revival time. He thought of the plywood church at the end of the dirt lane and wondered what Father Lambrusco would think of it.

During the afternoon he watched soap operas, amazed at all the little things the characters could get upset about. He laughed as he thought of Lurleen watching the same shows, a cup of coffee in her lap, a cigarette mashed in the saucer. He began to feel some of the gloom brought on by the noon newscast evaporate, and he looked forward to the five o'clock news because he knew it would tell that the crisis was over, people were returning to their homes, and the railroad would be repaired in a day or so. Waiting for the evening news, Jesse pondered life's good points, how most injuries healed up, most people changed for the better, and whatever was big news today was small potatoes on page thirty tomorrow. He lay back on his bed and studied the rain-stained ceiling and the mismatched paneling on the walls. Even this room would be remodeled someday and no one would suspect how ugly it had been. Things would improve.

But when the local news theme began to play over his scratched motel television, his face froze in a disbelieving stare. A black sky coiled and spread for miles above a crossroads town, and an evil-looking copper blaze flashed at the heart of a mountain of wreckage. The announcer stated that the train's brakeman had accused the engineer of being intoxicated at the time of the accident. Jesse balled up a fist. 'Son of a bitch,' he shouted at the television, 'that hop-head smokes weed day and night.' The announcer went on to say that the parish sheriff's department had a warrant out for the engineer's arrest and that railroad officials were hiring private investigators to locate the runaway employee. Meanwhile, firefighters were having to let the wreck burn because of an overheated propane tanker and the danger that two cars of chemicals would rupture and mix, producing mustard gas. Jesse's mouth fell open at this last awful announcement, and he began to fear that somehow everything was being blamed on him. He watched aerial shots of the fire spreading into the town, and as he did, another propane tanker went off like the end of the world, skyborne rills of fire torching a poor neighborhood of wooden houses to the east of the tracks. He sat on the floor, gathering fistfuls of cheap shag carpet, holding on, anchoring himself against the TV's revelations.

At the end of the report, he was shaking, so he snapped off the set. His name was on the air again, broadcast all over two states. And why did they want to arrest *him*? The train had come apart on its own. A wheel rim had cracked off, or a rail broke. He hadn't been speeding. Nobody knew what went wrong. Billy Graham could have been at the throttle of that locomotive and the same thing would have happened. He left the room, crossed the highway, and bought a deck of cards, returning to the little table by the window and dealing a hand of solitaire. He hoped the game would take his mind off the wreck, but after a while he began placing red eights on red nines, and he wished for his wife's face over his shoulder, telling him where he'd missed a play.

The next day he woke up and glared at the dark set a long time before deciding to shave. He refused to watch the news. Each broadcast injured his notion of who he was, and he would have no more of that. He caught a bus to the French Quarter and in Jackson Square sat on a wrought-iron bench, amazed that no one looked like his friends from his shriveled-up hometown. Jesse missed the red clay ditches and the boiled turpentine smell of Gumwood, Louisiana. He had never seen so many weak-looking men dressed in baggy, strange clothes, but he envied their anonymity, for at the moment he felt as obvious as the soaring statue of Andrew Jackson that rose before him, splattered by pigeons.

He spent all day in the Quarter, poking his sharp face into the doors of antique shops and bars, hankering for a hot charge of supermarket whiskey but holding back. Whenever he passed a newspaper vending machine, he saw a smoky photograph on the front page and felt a twinge of remorse. He wondered if he should turn himself in.

At the motel, he avoided the local news, deciding to turn the set on only for the national stuff, where, he was thinking, he would see the really important events, nothing about some local train burning a pissant town off the map. But as the CBS evening news played its intro theme over a film snippet of the main story, Jesse let out a pained yelp.

There on the screen was his wife, Lurleen, shaking her rat-gray hair and telling a reporter, 'I don't know where he run off to leaving a blowed-up train behind like that.' She sniffed and pointed a finger toward the camera. 'But it don't surprise me one bit,' she said to the world. 'No sir, not one thing that man would do would surprise a jumpy cat.' Jesse interlaced his fingers and placed his hands on top of his brushy head. On the screen, Lurleen looked powerful and almost attractive, in a dirt road kind of way. The program cut to an anchorman, and Jesse was thankful, for he half-expected Lurleen to start telling about him not paying her nephew for painting the house, and then everyone in red-white-and-blue America would know he was too lazy to paint his own damned living room. The announcer, low-voiced and serious in a blue sport coat, told how a white cloud of escaped chemical had rolled over a chicken farm and killed ten thousand hens, how three firemen were seriously injured when the wind shifted and they were overtaken by a toxic blanket.

'But the real mystery,' the announcer continued, 'is Jesse McNeil, the fifty-year-old engineer from Gumwood, Louisiana, who ran away from the scene of the accident. There are many speculations about his disappearance. Fellow workers suggest that McNeil was depressed because of his fiftieth birthday and was having marital and family problems. Whatever the reasons, he left behind a growing scene of destruction and pollution perhaps unequaled in American railroad history. Our live coverage continues from southeast Louisiana.' And there it was. Jesse's eyes widened as a camera did a slow pan of his home on Loblolly

Road, and he watched his partially bald yard, his house, which from this angle looked like a masonite-covered shoe box, and his carport, which seemed wobbly and anemic under its load of pine straw. He imagined voices all over America saying, 'Is that the best he could do after fifty years?' And there was Lurleen, sitting on the sofa in front of the big picture of the ocean surf, talking to the reporter about her husband. What could be worse than this, Jesse wondered, to be introduced to the English-speaking world by Lurleen McNeil, a chain-smoking canasta dragon whose biggest ambition in life was to have everything they owned painted sea-foam green by a dopehead nephew who never got out of the sixth grade? He listened as Lurleen told the world about him.

She leaned back on the couch and he saw her checkered shirt tighten at the shoulders. She looked thoughtful and not as dowdy as usual; he had never seen her like this. 'Sometimes he's a little out of it,' Lurleen said, blowing a stream of smoke from the side of her mouth and looking off in the opposite direction. 'I don't mean to say he's a bad man, but whenever he gets upset he tends to drink a little too much, if you know what I mean.'

Jesse jumped up straight as a rail. 'And who the hell wouldn't take a drink if they was married to a slave-driving snapping turtle?'

Lurleen looked into the camera as though she had heard the remark. 'I just wish he could put all this mess behind him and come home to help paint the living room.'

'The living room,' Jesse yelled, jerking his fists out from his sides. 'My name is on national TV and all you can think about is hiding that cheap paneling you put up last year.'

Lurleen gave the camera a wry smile and she was off; more footage of the wreck followed, more details of chemicals, casualties, government inspection teams. Agents from the Environmental Protection Agency were now looking for Jesse McNeil. The president of the local Sierra Club, a fashionably dressed thirtyish woman, stated flatly that Jesse should be hunted down like a dangerous criminal.

'What have I done to you?' he yelled, holding his outstretched palms toward the screen. 'You don't even know me. I'm nobody important.'

After the news report, Jesse went into the bathroom to splash water on his face, a face framed in the mirror by a spiked crown of hair shaped like a thistle bloom. He should have stayed at the site of the wreck, he told himself. He would have been fired and fined, but there would have been nothing like the publicity he was generating.

In his absence, what he had done was growing like a thunderstorm feeding on hot air and invisible moisture, or bigger, like a tropical storm, spinning out of control, created by TV people just because it was good business. He could not for the life of him imagine how drinking a half-pint of whiskey could generate such a hurricane of interest in who he was, or why the people of the United States had been brought into his unpainted living room to find out about him. He went back to the bed, sat down, and put his head in his hands. 'No more news for me,' he said aloud. 'Not for a while.'

For four days he avoided the newspapers and television. He rode the bus downtown, watching the faces of his fellow riders for any trace of recognition, for now he felt as famous as Johnny Carson, guilty as Hitler, and half-expected the next old lady he saw to throw up her arms and exclaim, 'It's him. It's the train wrecker.' He slouched on a bench in Jackson Square, across from the cathedral, again wondering at all the tourists, worried that even some Korean or German might recognize him. He wondered once more why a man's mistake grows with importance according to how many people know about it.

He was so deep in thought, he didn't notice when an old priest sat next to him and unfurled a fresh copy of the *Times-Picayune*. The priest, a bald man with a silver ring of hair above the ears, was on Jesse's right, so the engineer had a good view of the open front page, which carried a photo of a blazing boxcar. The priest looked over the page at Jesse. 'Are you still out of work?' It was Father Lambrusco.

'Uh, yeah. Sort of,' Jesse growled.

'Would you like a section?' he asked, shaking the paper at him.

'Uh, naw. I was just reading about the train wreck.'

The priest folded the paper half-size in his lap, studying the photograph. 'That's a big mess. I hope they get the fellow who did it.'

The phrase 'the fellow who did it' gave Jesse a brief chill. He felt obligated to mount a defense. 'The engineer was just in the cab when it happened. He might not've had anything to do with why the train came apart.'

The priest turned to him then, his dewlap flowing over his Roman collar. 'He'd been drinking and he ran away. You've got to admit that looks bad.'

Jesse scowled and kicked at a pigeon wandering too close to his shoe. 'Maybe the newspeople are blowing this thing up too much. You know, the more they yak about it, the worse it gets.'

The priest sucked a tooth and thought a moment. 'You mean, if someone does something wrong, and no one finds out, then it's not really all that wrong?'

Jesse sat back on the bench as though the priest had touched him in a sore spot. 'I didn't say that, exactly.'

'Secrecy is not innocence,' the priest said. 'If the engineer is not responsible, the facts should be brought out to that effect. But he's gone into hiding somewhere locally . . .'

Jesse lurched forward, sending two pigeons fluttering off toward General Jackson's statue. 'Does the paper say that?'

'The police think he's been sighted in New Orleans,' the priest said, picking up the paper and opening it again.

Jesse stood up then, pretending to dust off his pants, casually looking around. 'I've got to get going. So long.'

'So long,' the priest said, turning a page. 'You had lunch yet?'

'No,' he said, walking backward a couple steps. 'I've got to go.'

'Well, if you come around this time of day and I'm here, I'll buy you lunch.' The priest raised up the front page and began reading an article on the back of it.

Another day dragged by. Jesse was seated in the grim motel room, rubbing his hands together, staring at the dead television. The statement 'Secrecy is not innocence' kept running through his head, and he now wondered whether the newspeople were right in exposing his drunkenness, whether he might have noticed something wrong with his train had he been completely sober. Jesse McNeil looked back over his whole life much as a newscaster would do in a thumbnail sketch, and he shuddered to think that he had been guilty of many mistakes. He craved the television set, but he would not let himself touch the knobs that would bring him more bad news to feed his growing guilt. He pulled his wallet and saw that he was nearly out of money. He guessed it would not be long before they would find him.

Then he called his wife in Gumwood, figuring that she would tear into his shortcomings like a tent preacher. But she didn't. She was worried about him.

'Jesse,' she whispered, 'they're all around here in the woods waiting for you to come home. I know you messed up big, but please don't come back here. If you turn yourself in, find a single policeman somewhere and do it. Baby, these people think you're something awful, and I'm worried they might hurt you.' She told him what it had been like for the past few days, and he listened, moved by her care for him. For a moment he thought he had the wrong number, and then with a pang he realized that there might be more to Lurleen than he'd noticed. While she pleaded with him to be careful, he worried that she had become one of the details of his life that he no longer saw, like a telegraph pole flying by his engine window for the thousandth time. A series of clicks sounded in the background, and his wife cried for him to hang up because the line might be tapped. He slammed down the receiver and thought of her voice wavering on the wire. It took a

31

lot to shake his wife's confidence, and it scared him to think of what she had been told.

He got off a bus at midday and found the old priest reading *The Catholic Commentator* on a bench in front of the cathedral. They had lunch in a café facing the square. Jesse marveled at the hamburger he was served, a domed giant with pickle spears on the side, nothing like the flat, bland burgers he bought at the Gumwood Café. The priest made him taste one of his french fries, which was as big as a spike. 'Go on,' he said, 'have another. I love it when they leave the skin on.' He and Father Lambrusco talked vaguely about the weather and then the priest spoke about guilt, as though the two were somehow related. Eventually, Jesse twisted the conversation like a stiff wire back to the train wreck. 'Now take that poor engineer we were talking about the other day,' he told the priest. 'What he did might have been bad, all right, but the press blew the dang thing up so much, he seems like some sort of public enemy number one.'

Father Lambrusco took a sip of wine and looked off toward the square. He suddenly laughed. 'I once saw a cartoon in which someone had installed loudspeakers on top of a church and a microphone in the confessional, and all over town these sins were being broadcast.'

'Good Lord,' Jesse said, wincing.

The priest put down his glass, a strange small grin on his lips. 'Now that I think of it, I wonder what the newspapers would do with some of the things I hear in the confessional. What would the sinner's employers do, his neighbors?' He gave Jesse a piercing look with his dark, earnest eyes. 'What would you think of me if you knew what was in my heart? Would you even talk to me?'

Jesse put down his hamburger. It was so big it took away his appetite. 'I'm the one wrecked the train,' he said in a low voice, glancing quickly at the diners at a small table near them.

'The train in the paper? The burning train?'

'Yes.'

The priest sat back and sucked his lower lip. 'What are you going to do?'

Jesse wagged his head. 'I thought the longer I stayed put, the more people would forget. But it's the other way around. If I stay out one more week, I'll be right up there with Charlie Manson.'

The priest sniffed and looked again toward the square. 'You know, one of our missions burned to the ground in that little village.'

'I didn't carry a torch to it,' Jesse whined.

Father Lambrusco closed his eyes. 'When you throw a rock in a pond, you make ripples.'

Now Jesse stared off toward the cathedral, where he noticed a white pigeon perched on a gatepost. According to the priest, he was directly responsible for every poisoned and burned board in the ruined crossroads. 'What can I do?' he asked.

'Nothing,' the priest said. 'It can't be undone. Just turn yourself in. Ask forgiveness.'

Jesse scratched his jaw. Forgiveness from whom? he thought. The railroad? The crossroads town? The millions and millions who followed his mistake on television? For some reason he thought of Judas and wondered if he realized as he climbed the limbs of the fig tree, the hanging rope slung over his shoulder, how many people would come to know about him down through the years, how many would grow to hate his name. 'Do me a favor, Father. About news time tonight, ten o'clock, call somebody and turn me in.' He explained where he was staying and the priest bobbed his head, closed his eyes, and tasted a french fry. Jesse walked out onto the sidewalk and blended with the tourists. He wandered, distracted and haunted by a need for a drink, until he found a liquor store near Canal Street, where he purchased a fifth of Old Overholt rye. He told himself he needed one stiff shot to calm his nerves.

By news time that night, he was staggering drunk. He found the Gideon Bible next to the telephone and started reading Genesis for some clue to how everybody's troubles began. At news time he swayed from the bed and turned on the local station. The first story showed the train wreck. Additional cars had become involved, one new leak in a tanker of chlorine was keeping fire crews away still, and the little town was now a smudge on the map, a garden of chimneys and iron pipe rising from plots of ash. The screen showed a man in a lab coat standing a mile from the wreck, the smoke plume blossoming over his shoulder. He announced that such a deadly stew of chemicals had been spilled that the town could never be inhabited again, that all the soil for one square mile would have to be removed down to six feet, treated, and hauled off to a toxic-waste pit at a cost of tens of millions. The numbers spun slowly in Jesse's head.

There was a loud knock at the door, but he ignored it, turning the volume up high. The anchorman came back on with a somber comment: 'Rumor has it he was spotted in New Orleans, but so far he has eluded the many agencies seeking his arrest. But what kind of person is Jesse McNeil, a man who would father such devastation and disappear?' Following the question was Jesse's biography, starting with a bucktoothed photograph from his grammar school year-book and ending, after a one-minute narra- tive of the main events of his life, with a photo of him seated on a bar stool, a detached, ordinary smile given to the world at large.

He stood and slammed his palm against the side of the tele- vision, which bobbled toward the door on its wheeled rack.

'Everybody knows me,' he roared, waving his fists toward the ceiling. 'Everybody knows who I am or what happened.' He lurched to the scratched metal door of his room and pulled it open. 'You know me,' he shouted into the parking lot. Two policemen were standing a few feet away, cradling shotguns. Jesse held out his hands to them. 'I read in the Bible where Noah got drunk in his tent, yet he was the one they let run the ark.' Five men wearing suits walked in briskly from the highway. Behind Jesse, the announcer told of an upcoming live scene in a late-breaking story.

'The Lord trusted him to save our bacon,' he told them all. To the left Jesse saw men in military garb or SWAT uniforms trotting out of sight behind a building. More policemen walked stiff-legged out of the darkness. Above him, on the roof, was the sound of boots stirring gravel. He heard a helicopter somewhere and soon a spotlight lit up the parking lot, casting Jesse's hair in a bristly glow. What do they all know? he wondered. They think I'm the most dangerous man alive.

Another brutal light fired up in the parking lot and a news camera poked between two worried-looking sheriff's deputies. No one said anything and no one touched him. They seemed to be looking past him into the motel room, and he turned to see on the television most of the law officers and a pitiful figure in the center, staggering in wilted coveralls and a botched haircut like the most worthless old drunk imaginable. Everyone was frozen, watching the screen to see what would happen next. Could he say something to the world? He shook his head. Everyone knew it all, or nobody knew the first thing.

The announcer's voice was underlined with the adventure of the capture: 'Jesse McNeil has been surrounded by local, state, and federal agents at the Night O'Delight Motel on Airline Highway in New Orleans. He appears intoxicated and unable to speak now at the end of a nationwide search for the man who is at the heart of one of the largest ecological and industrial disasters the country has ever known.' For all the policemen, the truth was in the bright eye of the television. Only Jesse turned away, ashamed of the drunk on the set, yet able to stare defiantly at the crowd of officers around him. He wavered in the peeling doorway, feeling as empty-handed and innocent as every man on earth.

The cop nearest him finally touched his arm. 'Are you Jesse McNeil?' he asked.

'I feel like I'm two different people,' Jesse said feebly.

The cop began to close handcuffs around his wrists. 'Well, bud, we'll just have to put both of you in jail.' A mean-spirited crackle of laughter ringed the parking lot, and a dozen more camera lights flooded on. Jesse was pulled through the fierce blaze until he felt a policeman's moist hand on the top of his head, shoving him under the river of light and into the backseat of a cruiser, which at once moved onto the highway, bathed by strobes and headlights and stares, locked in inescapable beams.

Died and Gone to Vegas

Raynelle Bullfinch told the young oiler that the only sense of mystery in her life was provided by a deck of cards. As she set up the card table in the engine room of the *Leo B. Canterbury*, a government steam dredge anchored in a pass at the mouth of the Mississippi River, she lectured him. 'Nick, you're just a college boy laying out a bit until you get money to go back to school, but for me, this is it.' She pulled a coppery braid from under her overalls strap, looked around at the steam chests and piping, and sniffed at the smell of heatproof red enamel. In the glass of a steam gauge she checked her round, bright cheeks for grease and ran a white finger over the blue arcs of her eyebrows. She was the cook on the big boat, which was idle for a couple days because of high winter winds. 'My big adventure is cards. One day I'll save up enough to play with the skill boys in Vegas. Set up those folding chairs,' she told him. 'Seven in all.'

'I don't know how to play bourrée, ma'am.' Nick Montalbano ran a hand through long hair shiny with dressing. 'I only had one semester of college.' He looked sideways at the power straining the bronze buckles of the tall woman's bib and avoided her green eyes, which were deep set and full of intense judgment.

'Bullshit. A pet rat can play bourrée. Sit down.' She pointed to a metal chair and the oiler, a thin boy wearing an untucked plaid flannel shirt and a baseball cap, obeyed. 'Pay attention, here. I deal out five cards to everybody, and I turn up the last card. Whatever suit it is, that's trumps. Then you discard all your nontrumps and draw replacements. Remember, trumps beat all other suits; high trumps beat low trumps. Whatever card is led, you follow suit.' She ducked her head under the bill of his cap,

37

looking for his eyes. 'This ain't too hard for you, is it? Ain't college stuff more complicated than this?'

'Sure, sure. I understand, but what if you can't follow suit?'

'If nontrumps is led, put a trump on it. If you ain't got no more trumps, just throw your lowest card. Trust me, you'll catch on quick.'

'How do you win?' The oiler turned his cap around.

'Every hand has five tricks to take. If you take three tricks, you win the pot. Only on this boat, we got a special rule. If only two decide to play that hand after the draw, then it takes four tricks to win. If you got any questions, ask Sydney, there.'

Sydney, the chief engineer, a little fireplug of a man who would wear a white T-shirt in a blizzard, sat down heavily with a whistle. 'Oh boy. Fresh meat.' He squeezed the oiler's neck.

The steel door next to the starboard triple-expansion engine opened, letting in a wash of frigid air around the day fireman, pilot, deckhand, and welder who came into the big room cursing and clapping the cold out of their clothes. Through the door the angry white-caps of Southwest Pass raced down the Mississippi, bucking into the tarnished Gulf sky.

'Close that damned pneumonia hole,' Raynelle cried, sailing cards precisely before the seven chairs. 'Sit down, worms. Usual game, dollar ante, five-dollar rip if you don't take a trick.' After the rattle of halves and dollars came discards, more dealing, and then a flurry of cards, ending with a diminishing snowstorm of curses as no one took three tricks and the pot rolled over to the next hand. Three players took no tricks and put up the five-dollar rip.

The engineer unrolled a pack of Camels from his T-shirt sleeve and cursed loudest. 'I heard of a bourrée game on a offshore rig where the pot didn't clear for eighty-three passes. By the time somebody won that bitch, it had seventeen hundred dollars in it. The next day the genius what took it got a wrench upside the head in a Morgan City bar and woke up with his pockets inside out and the name Conchita tattooed around his left nipple.'

Pig, the day fireman, put up his ante and collected the next hand. 'That ain't nothin'.' He touched three discards to the top of his bald head and threw them down. 'A ol' boy down at the dock told me the other day that he heard about a fellow got hit in the head over in Orange, Texas, and didn't know who he was when he looked at his driver's license. Had amnesia. That sorry-ass seaman's hospital sent him home to his scuzzbag wife, and he didn't know her from Adam's house cat.'

'That mighta been a blessing,' Raynelle said, turning the last card of the deal to see what trumps was. 'Spades.' She rolled left on her ample bottom.

'No, it wasn't,' the day fireman said, unzipping his heavy green field jacket. 'That gal told him she was his sister, gave him a remote control and a color TV, and he was happy as a fly on a pie. She started bringing her boyfriends in at night and that fool waved them into the house. Fixed 'em drinks. Figured any old dude good enough for Sis was good enough for him. The neighbors got to lookin' at her like they was smelling something dead, so she and her old man moved to a better trailer park where nobody knew he'd lost his memory. She started into cocaine and hookin' for fun on the side. Her husband's settlement money he got from the company what dropped a thirty-six-inch Stillson on his hard hat began to shrink up a bit, but that old boy just sat there dizzy on some cheap pills she told him was a prescription. He'd channel surf all day, greet the johns like one of those old dried-up coots at Wal-Mart, and was the happiest son of a bitch in Orange, Texas.' The day fireman spread wide his arms. 'Was he glad to see Sis come home every day. He was proud she had more friends than a postman with a bagful of welfare checks. And then his memory came back.'

'Ho, ho, the *merde* hit the blower,' the engineer said, slamming a queen down and raking in a trick.

'Nope. That poor bastard remembered every giggle in the rear bedroom and started feeling lower than a snake's nuts. He tried to get his old woman straight, but the dyed-over tramp just laughed in his face and moved out on him. He got so sorry he went to a shrink, but that just cost him more bucks. Finally, you know what that old dude wound up doin'? He looked for someone would hit him in the head again. You know, so he could get back the way he was. He offered a hundred dollars a pop, and in them Orange bars most people will whack on you for free, so you can imagine what kind of service he bought hisself. After nearly getting killed four or five times, he give up and spent the rest of his settlement money on a hospital stay for a concussion. After that he held up a Pac-a-Bag for enough money to get himself hypmotized back to like he was after he got hit the first time. Wound up in the pen doin' twenty hard ones.'

They played three hands of cards while the day fireman finished the story, and then the deckhand in the game, a thick blond man in a black cotton sweater, threw back his head and laughed – *ha-ha* – as if he was only pretending. 'If that wadn' so funny, it'd be sad. It reminds me of this dumb-ass peckerwood kid lived next to me in Kentucky, built like a string bean. He was a few thimbles shy of a quart, but he sort of knew he won't no nuclear power plant repairman and got along with everybody. Then he started hanging with these badass kids – you know, the kind that carry spray paint, wear their hats backward, and pack your mailbox full of live rats. Well, they told the poor bastard he was some kind of Jesse James and got him into stealing hubcaps and electric drills. He started strutting around the neighborhood like he was bad shit, and soon the local deputies had him in the backseat for running off with a lawn mower. Dummy stole it in December.'

'What's wrong with that?' the day fireman asked, pitching in a dollar.

'Who's gonna buy a used mower in winter, you moron? Anyway, the judge had pity on him – gave him a pissant fine and sent him to bed with a sugar tit. Said he was a good boy who ought to be satisfied to be simple and honest. But String Bean hung out on the street corner crowing. He was proud now. A real gangster, happy as Al Capone, his head pumped full of swamp gas by these losers he's hanging around with. Finally, one night he breaks into a house of a gun collector. Showing how smart he is, he chooses only one gun to take from the rack, an engraved Purdy double-barrel, mint condition, with gold and ivory inlays all over, a twenty-thousand-dollar gun. String Bean took it home and with a two-dollar hacksaw cut the stock off and then most of the barrel. He went out and held up a taco joint and got sixteen dollars and thirteen cents. Was arrested when he walked out the door. This time, a hard-nut judge sent him up on a multiple bill and he got two hundred and ninety-seven years in Bisley.'

'All right,' Raynelle sang. 'Better than death.'

'He did ten years before the weepy-ass parole board noticed the sentence and pulled him in for review. Asked him did he get rehabilitated and would he go straight if he got out, and he spit on their mahogany table. He told them he won't no dummy and would be the richest bank robber in Kentucky if he got half a chance.' The deckhand laughed – *ha-ha*. 'That give everybody a icicle up the ass, and the meetin' came to a vote right quick. Even the American Civil Liberties lesbo lawyers on the parole board wanted to weld the door shut on him. It was somethin'.'

The pilot, a tall man dressed in a pea jacket and a sock cap, raised a new hand to his sharp blue eyes and winced, keeping one trump and asking for four cards. 'Gentlemen, that reminds me of a girl in Kentucky I knew at one time.'

'Why, did she get sent up two hundred and ninety-seven years in Bisley?' the deckhand asked.

'No, she was from Kentucky, like that crazy fellow you just lied to us about. By the way, that king won't walk,' he said, laying down an ace of diamonds. 'This woman was a nurse at the VA hospital in Louisville and fell in love with one of her patients, a good-looking, mild-mannered fellow with a cyst in his brain that popped and gave him amnesia.'

'Now, there's something you don't hear every day,' the engineer said, trumping the ace with a bang.

'He didn't know what planet he came from,' the pilot said stiffly. 'A few months later they got married and he went to work in a local iron plant. After a year he began wandering away from work at lunchtime. So they fired him. He spent a couple of weeks walking up and down his street and all over Louisville, looking into people's yards and checking passing buses for the faces in the windows. It was like he was looking for someone but he couldn't remember who. One day he didn't come home at all. For eighteen months this pretty little nurse was beside herself with worry. Then her nephew was at a rock concert downtown and spotted a shaggy guy in the mosh pit who looked familiar. He was just standing there like he was watching a string quartet. Between songs, he asked him if he had amnesia, which is a rather odd question, considering, and the man almost started crying because he figured he'd been recognized.'

'That's a sweet story,' the day fireman said, rubbing his eyes with his bear paw-sized hands. 'Sydney, could you loan me your handkerchief? I'm all choked up.'

'Choke this,' the pilot said, trumping the fireman's jack. 'Anyway, the little nurse gets attached to the guy again and is glad to have him back. She refreshes his memory about their marriage and all that and starts over with him. Things are better than ever, as far as she is concerned. Well, about a year of marital bliss goes by, and one evening there's a knock at the door. She gets up off the sofa where the amnesia guy is, opens it, and it's her husband, whose memory came back.'

'Wait a minute,' the deckhand said. 'I thought that was her husband on the sofa.'

'I never said it was her husband. She just thought it was her husband. It turns out that the guy on the sofa she's been living with for a year is the identical twin to the guy on the doorstep. Got an identical popped cyst, too.'

'Aw, bullshit,' the day fireman bellowed.

The engineer leaned back and put his hand on a valve handle. 'I better pump this place out.'

'Hey,' the pilot yelled above the bickering. 'I knew this girl. Her family lived across the street from my aunt. Anyway, after all the explanations were made, the guy who surfaced at the rock concert agreed it would be best if he moved on, and the wandering twin started back where he left off with his wife. Got his job back at the iron plant. But the wife wasn't happy anymore.'

'Why the hell not?' the engineer asked, dealing the next hand. 'She had two for the price of one.'

'Yeah, well, even though those guys were identical in every way, something was different. We'll never know what it was, but she couldn't get over the second twin. Got so she would wander around herself, driving all over town looking for him.'

'What the hell?' The deckhand threw down his cards. 'She had her husband back, didn't she?'

'Oh, it was bad,' the pilot continued. 'She was driving down the street one day and saw the rock-concert twin, gets out of her car, runs into a park yelling and sobbing and throws her arms around him, crying, "I found you at last. I found you at last." Only it wasn't him.'

'Jeez,' the engineer said. 'Triplets.'

'No.' The pilot shook his head. 'It was worse than that. It was her husband, who was out on delivery for the iron plant, taking a break in the park after shucking his coveralls. Mild-mannered amnesiac or not, he was pretty put out at the way she was carrying on. But he didn't show it. He pretended to be his twin and asked her why she liked him better than her husband. And she told him. Now, don't ask me what it was. The difference was in her mind, way I heard it. But that guy disappeared again the next morning, and that was five years ago. They say you can go down in east Louisville and see her driving around today in a ratty green Torino, looking for one of those twins, this scared look in her eyes like she'll find one and'll never be sure which one she got hold of.'

Raynelle pulled a pecan out of her overalls bib and cracked it between her thumb and forefinger. 'That story's sadder'n a armless old man in a room full of skeeters. You sorry sons of bitches tell the depressingest lies I ever heard.'

The deckhand lit up an unfiltered cigarette. 'Well, sweet thing, why don't you cheer us up with one of your own.'

Raynelle looked up at a brass steam gauge bolted to an I beam. 'I did know a fellow worked in an iron foundry, come to think of it. His whole family worked the same place, which is a pain in the ass, if you've ever done that, what with your uncle giving you wet willies and your cousin bumming money. This fellow drove a gray Dodge Dart, the kind with the old slant-six engine that'll carry you to hell and back, slow. His relatives made fun of him for it, said he was cheap and wore plastic shoes, and ate Spam, that kind of thing.' She turned the last card to show trumps, banging up a king. 'Sydney, you better not bourrée again. You in this pot for thirty dollars.'

The engineer swept up his hand, pressing it against his T-shirt. 'I can count.'

'Anyway, this boy thought he'd show his family a thing or two and went out and proposed to the pretty girl who keyed in the invoices in the office. He bought her a diamond ring on time that would choke an elephant. It was a *nice* ring.' Raynelle looked at the six men around the table as if none of them would ever buy such a ring. 'He was gonna give it to her on her birthday right before they got married in three weeks and meantime he showed it around at the iron foundry figuring it'd make 'em shut up, which basically it did.'

'They was probably speechless at how dumb he was,' the deckhand said out of the side of his mouth.

'But don't you know that before he got to give it to her, that girl hit her head on the edge of her daddy's swimming pool and drowned. The whole foundry went into mourning, as did those kids' families and the little town in general. She had a big funeral and she was laid out in her wedding dress in a white casket surrounded by every carnation in four counties. Everybody was crying and the funeral parlor had this lovely music playing. I guess the boy got caught up in the feeling, because he walked over to the coffin right before they was gonna screw down the lid and he put that engagement ring on that girl's finger.'

'Naw,' the engineer said breathlessly, laying a card without looking at it.

'Yes, he did. And he felt proud that he done it – at least for a month or two. Then he began to have eyes for a dental hygienist and that little romance took off hot as a bottle rocket. He courted her for six months and decided to pop the question. But he started thinking about the monthly payments he was making on that ring and how they would go on for four and a half more years, keeping him from affording a decent ring for this living girl.'

'Oh no,' the pilot said as the hand split again and the pot rolled over yet another time.

'That's right. He got some tools and after midnight went down to Heavenly Oaks Mausoleum and unscrewed the marble door on her drawer, slid out the coffin, and opened it up. I don't know how he could stand to rummage around in whatever was left in the box, but damned if he didn't get that ring and put the grave back together slick as a whistle. So the next day, he give it to the hygienist and everything's okay. A bit later they get married and're doin' the lovebird bit in a trailer down by the foundry.' Raynelle cracked another pecan against the edge of the table, crushing it with the pressure of her palm in a way that made the welder and the oiler look at each other. 'But there's a big blue blowfly in the ointment. She's showing off that ring by the minute and someone recognized the damned thing and told her. Well, she had a thirty-megaton double-PMS hissy fit and told him straight up that she won't wear no dead woman's ring, and throws it in his face. Said the thing gave her the willies. He told her it's that or a King Edward cigar band, because he won't get out from under the payments until the twenty-first century. It went back and forth like that for a month, with the neighbors up and down the road, including my aunt Tammy, calling the police to come get them to shut up. Finally, the hygienist told him she'd wear the ring.'

'Well, that's a happy ending,' the deckhand said.

Raynelle popped a half pecan into her red mouth. 'Shut up, Jack. I ain't finished. This hygienist began to wear cowboy blouses and jean miniskirts just like the girl in the foundry office did. The old boy kinda liked it at first, but when she dyed her hair the same color as the first girl, it gave him the shakes. She said she was dreaming of that dead girl at least twice a week and saw her in her dresser mirror when she woke up. Then she began to talk like the foundry girl did, with a snappy Arkansas twang. And the dead girl was a country-music freak, liked the old stuff, too. Damned if in the middle of the night the guy wasn't waked up by his wife singing in her sleep all eleven verses of "El Paso," the Marty Robbins tune.

'He figured it was the ring causing all the trouble, so he got his wife drunk and while she was asleep slipped that sucker off and headed to the graveyard to put it back on that bone where he took it. Soon as he popped the lid, the cops was on him asking him what the living hell he was doing. He told them he was putting a diamond ring back in the coffin, and they said sure, buddy. Man, he got charged with six or eight nasty things perverts do to dead bodies, and then the dead girl's family filed six or eight civil suits, and believe me, there was mental anguish, pain, and suffering enough to feed the whole county. A local judge who was the dead girl's uncle sent him up for six years, and the hygienist divorced his ass good. Strange thing was that she kept her new hair color and way of dressing, began going to George Jones concerts, and last I heard she'd quit her job at the dentist and was running the computers down at the iron foundry.'

'Raynelle, *chère*, I wish you wouldn'ta said that one.' Simoneaux, the welder, never spoke much until late in the game. He was a thin Cajun, seldom without a Camel in the corner of his mouth and a high-crowned polka-dotted welder's cap turned backward on his head. He shrugged off a violent chill. 'That story gives me *les frissons* up and down my back.' A long stick of beef jerky jutted from the pocket of his flannel shirt. He pulled it out, plucked a lint ball from the bottom, and bit off a small knob of meat. 'But that diamond shit reminds me of a old boy I knew down in Grand Crapaud who was working on Pancho Oil number six offshore from Point au Fer. The driller was puttin' down the pipe hard one day and my friend the mud engineer was takin' a dump on the engine room toilet. All at once, they hit them a gas pocket at five t'ousand feet and drill pipe come back up that hole like drinkin' straws, knockin' out the top of the rig, flyin' up in the sky, and breakin' apart at the joints. Well, my frien', he had a magazine spread out across his lap when a six-inch drill pipe hit the roof like a spear and went through and through the main diesel engine. About a half second later, another one passed between his knees, through the Playmate of the Month and the steel deck both, yeah. He could hear the iron comin' down all over the rig, but he couldn't run because his pants was around his ankles on the other side the drill column between his legs. He figured he was goin' to glory with a unwiped ass, but a worm run in the engine room and cut him loose with a jackknife, and then they both took off over the side and hit the water. My frien' rolled through them breakers, holdin' on to a drum of mineral spirits, floppin' around until a badass fish gave him a bite on his giblets, and that was the only injury he had.'

'Ouch, man.' The deckhand crossed his legs.

'What?' Raynelle looked up while posting her five-dollar bourrée.

The welder threw in yet another ante, riffling the dollar bills in the pot as though figuring how much it weighed. 'Well, he was hurt enough to get the company to pay him a lump sum after he got a four-by-four lawyer to sue their two-by-four insurance company. That's for true. My frien', he always said he wanted a fancy car. The first thing he did was to drive to Lafayette and buy a sixty-five-thousand-dollar Mercedes, yeah. He put new mud-grip tires on that and drove it down to the Church Key Lounge in Morgan City, where all his mud-pumpin' buddies hung out, an' it didn't take long to set off about half a dozen of them hard hats, no.' Simoneaux shook his narrow head. 'He was braggin' bad, yeah.'

The engineer opened his cards on his belly and rolled his eyes. 'A new Mercedes in Morgan City? Sheee-it.'

'*Mais*, you can say that again. About two, tree o'clock in the mornin' my frien', he come out, and what he saw woulda made a muskrat cry. Somebody took a number-two ball-peen hammer and dented every place on that car that would take a dent. That t'ing looked like it got caught in a cue-ball tornado storm. Next day he brought it by the insurance people and they told him the policy didn't cover vandalism. Told him he would have to pay to get it fixed or drive it like that.

'But my frien', he had blew all his money on the car to begin with. When he drove it, everybody looked at him like he was some kind of freak. You know, he wanted people to look at him – that's why he bought the car – but they was lookin' at him the wrong way, like "You mus' be some prime jerk to have someone mess with you car like that." So after a week of havin' people run off the road turnin' their necks to look at that new Mercedes, he got drunk, went to the store, and bought about twenty cans of Bondo, tape, and cans of spray paint.'

'Don't say it,' the deckhand cried.

'No, no,' the engineer said to his cards.

'What?' Raynelle asked.

'Yeah, the poor bastard couldn't make a snake out of Play-Doh but he's gonna try and restore a fine European se-dan. He filed and sanded on that poor car for a week, then hit it with that dollar-a-can paint. When he finished up, that Mercedes looked like it was battered for fryin'. He drove it around Grand Crapaud and people just pointed and doubled over. He kept it outside his trailer at night, and people would drive up and park, just to look at it. Phone calls started comin', the hang-up kind that said things like "You look like your car," *click*, or "What kind of icing did you use?" *click*. My frien' finally took out his insurance policy and saw what it did cover. It was theft.

'So he started leaving the keys in it parked down by the abandoned lumberyard, but nobody in Grand Crapaud would steal it. He drove to Lafayette, rented a motel room, yeah, and parked it outside that bad housing project, with keys in it.' The welder threw in another hand and watched the cards fly. 'Next night he left the windows down with the keys in it.' He pulled off his polka-dotted cap and ran his fingers through his dark hair. 'Third night he left the motor runnin' and the lights on with the car blockin' the driveway of a crack house. Next mornin' he found it twenty feet away, idled out of diesel, with a dead battery. It was that ugly.'

'What happened next?' The pilot trumped an ace like he was killing a bug.

'My frien', he called me up, you know. Said he wished he had a used standard-shift Ford pickup and the money in the bank. His wife left him, his momma made him take a cab to come see her, and all he could stand to do was drink and stay in his trailer. I didn't know what to tell him. He said he was gonna read his policy some more.'

'Split pot again,' the deckhand shouted. 'I can't get out this game. I feel like my nuts is hung up in a fan belt.'

'Shut your trap and deal,' Raynelle said, sailing a loose wad of cards in the deckhand's direction. 'What happened to the Mercedes guy?'

The welder put his cap back on and pulled up the crown. 'Well, his policy said it covered all kinds of accidents, you know, so he parked it in back next to a big longleaf pine and cut that sucker down, only it was a windy day and soon as he got through that tree with the saw, a gust come up and pushed it the other way from where he wanted it to fall.'

'What'd it hit?'

'It mashed his trailer like a cockroach, yeah. The propane stove blew up and by the time the Grand Crapaud fire truck come around, all they could do was break out coat hangers and mushmellas. His wife what lef' ain't paid the insurance on the double-wide, no, so now he got to get him a camp stove and a picnic table so he can shack up in the Mercedes.'

'No shit? He lived in the car?'

The welder nodded glumly. 'Po' bastard wouldn't do nothin' but drink up the few bucks he had lef' and lie in the backseat. One night last fall we had that cold snap, you remember? It got so cold around Grand Crapaud you could hear the sugarcane stalks popping out in the fields like firecrackers. They found my frien' froze to death sittin' up behind the steering wheel. T-nook, the paramedic, said his eyes was open, starin' over the hood like he was goin' for a drive.' The welder pushed his down-turned hand out slowly like a big sedan driving toward the horizon. Everybody's eyes followed it for a long moment.

'New deck,' the engineer cried, throwing in his last trump and watching it get swallowed by a jack. 'Nick, you little dago, give me that blue deck.' The oiler, a quiet olive-skinned boy from New Orleans's west bank, pushed the new box over. 'New deck, new luck,' the engineer told him. 'You know, I used to date this ol' fat gal lived in a double-wide north of Biloxi. God, that woman liked to eat. When I called it off, she asked me why, and I told her I was afraid she was going to get thirteen inches around the ankles. That must have got her attention, because she went on some kind of fat-killer diet and exercise program that about wore out the floor beams in that trailer. But she got real slim, I heard. She had a pretty face, I'll admit that. She started hitting the bars and soon had her a cow farmer ask her to marry him, which she did.'

'Is a cow farmer like a rancher?' Raynelle asked, her tongue in her cheek like a jawbreaker.

'It's what I said it was. Who the hell ever heard of a ranch in Biloxi? Anyway, this old gal developed a fancy for steaks, since her man got meat reasonable, being a cow farmer and all. She started putting away the T-bones and swelling like a sow on steroids. After a year, she blowed up to her fighting weight and then some. I heard she'd about eat up half the cows on the farm before he told her he wanted a divorce. She told him she'd sue to get half the farm, and he said go for it. It'd be worth it if someone would just roll her off his half. She hooked up with this greasy little lawyer from Waveland and sure enough he got half the husband's place. After the court dealings, he took this old gal out to supper to celebrate and one thing led to another and they wound up at her apartment for a little slap-and-tickle. I'll be damned if they didn't fall out of bed together with her on top, and he broke three ribs and ruined a knee on a night table. After a year of treatments, he sued her good and got her half of the farm.'

The deckhand threw his head back and laughed – *ha-ha*. 'That's a double screwin' if ever there was one.'

'Hey, it don't stop there. The little lawyer called up the farmer and said, "Since we gonna be neighbors, why don't you tell me a good spot to build a house?" They got together and hit it off real good, like old drinkin' buddies. After a couple months, the lawyer went into business with the farmer and together they doubled the cattle production, specially since they got rid of the critters' worst predator.'

Raynelle's eyebrows came together like a small thunderhead. 'Well?'

'Well what?' The engineer scratched an armpit.

'What happened to that poor girl?'

All the men looked around uneasily. Raynelle had permanently disabled a boilermaker on the *St Genevieve* with a corn-bread skillet.

'She got back on her diet, I heard. Down to one hundred twenty pounds again.'

'That's the scary thing about women,' the day fireman volunteered, putting up three fingers to ask for his draw. 'Marryin' 'em is just like cuttin' the steel bands on a bale of cotton. First thing you know, you've got a roomful of woman.'

Raynelle glowered. 'Careful I don't pour salt on you and watch you melt.'

The engineer released a sigh. 'Okay, Nick, you the only one ain't told a lie yet. Let's have some good bullshit.'

The young oiler ducked his head. 'Don't know none.'

'Haw,' Raynelle said. 'A man without bullshit. Check his drawers, Simoneaux, see he ain't Nancy instead of Nicky.'

Reddening, the oiler frowned at his hand. 'Well, the cows remind me of something I heard while I was playing the poker machines over in Port Allen the other day,' he said, a long strand of black hair falling in his eyes. 'There was this Mexican guy named Gonzales who worked with cows in Matamoros.'

'Another cow farmer,' the deckhand groaned.

'Shut up,' Raynelle said. 'Was that his first name or second name?'

'Well, both.'

'What?' She pitched a card at him.

'Aw, Miss Raynelle, you know how those Mexicans are with their names. This guy's name was Gonzales Gonzales, with a bunch of names in between.' Raynelle cocked her ear whenever she heard the oiler speak. She had a hard time with his New Orleans accent, which she found to be Bronx-like. 'He was a pretty smart fella and got into Texas legal, worked a few years and became a naturalized citizen, him and his wife both.'

'What was his wife's name?' the pilot asked. 'Maria Maria?'

'Come on, now, do you want to hear this or don'tcha?' The oiler pushed the hair out of his eyes. 'The cattle industry shrunk up where he was at, and he looked around for another place to try and settle. He started to go to Gonzales, Texas, but there ain't no work there, so he gets out a map and spots Gonzales, Louisiana.'

'That that rough place with all the jitterbug joints?'

'Yep. Lots of coon-asses and roughnecks, but they ain't no Mexicans. Must have been settled a million years ago by a family of Gonzaleses, who probably speak French and eat gumbo nowadays. So Gonzales Gonzales gets him a job working for two brothers who are lawyers and who run a horse farm on the side. He gets an apartment on Gonzales Street, down by the train station.' The oiler looked at a new hand, fanning the cards out slowly. 'You know how badass the Airline Highway cops are through there? Well, this Gonzales was dark and his car was a beat-up smoker, so they pulled him one day on his way to Baton Rouge. The cop stands outside his window and says, "Lemme see your license," to which Gonzales says he forgot it at home on the dresser. The cop pulls out a ticket book and says, "What's your last name?" to which he says, "Gonzales." The cop says, "What's your first name?" And he tells him. That officer leans in the window and sniffs his breath. "Okay, Gonzales Gonzales," he says real nasty, "where you live?" "Gonzales," he says. "Okay, boy. Get out the car," the cop says. He throws him against the door hard. "And who do you work for?" Gonzales looks him in the eye and says, "Gonzales and Gonzales." The cop turns him around and slams his head against the roof and says, "Yeah, and you probably live on Gonzales Street, huh, you slimy son of a bitch." "At Twelve twenty-six, apartment E," Gonzales says.'

The deckhand put his cards over his eyes. 'The poor bastard.'

'Yeah.' The oiler sighed. 'He got beat up and jailed that time until the Gonzales brothers went up and sprung him. About once a month some cop would pull him over and give him hell. When he applied for a little loan at the bank, they threw his ass in the street. When he tried to get a credit card, the company called the feds, who investigated him for fraud. Nobody would cash his checks, and the first year he filed state and federal taxes, three government cars stayed in his driveway for a week. Nobody believed who he was.'

'That musta drove him nuts,' the welder said, drawing four cards.

'I don't think so, man. He knew who he was. Gonzales Gonzales knew he was in America and you could control what you was, unlike in Mexico. So when the traffic cops beat him up, he sold his car and got a bike. When the banks wouldn't give him no checks, he used cash. When the tax people refused to admit he existed, he stopped paying taxes. Man, he worked hard and saved every penny. One day it was real hot and he was walking into

Gonzales because his bike had a flat. He stopped in the Rat's Nest Lounge to get a root beer, and they was this drunk fool from West Texas in there making life hard for the barmaid. He come over to Gonzales and asked him would he have a drink. He said sure, and the bartender set up a whiskey and a root beer. The cowboy was full of Early Times and pills, and you coulda lit a blowtorch off his eyeballs. He put his arm around Gonzales and asked him what his name was, you know. When he heard it, he got all serious, like he was bein' made fun of or something. He asked a couple more questions and started struttin' and cussin'. He pulled out from under a cheesy denim jacket an engraved Colt and stuck it in Gonzales's mouth. "You jerkin' me around, man," that cowboy told him. "You tellin' me you're Gonzales Gonzales from Gonzales who lives on Gonzales Street and works for Gonzales and Gonzales?" That Mexican looked at the gun and I don't know what was going through his head, but he nodded, and the cowboy pulled back the hammer.'

'Damn,' the welder said.

'I don't want to hear this.' Raynelle clapped the cards to her ears.

'Hey,' the oiler said. 'Like I told you, he knew who he was. He pointed to the phone book by the register, and after a minute, the bartender had it open and held it out to the cowboy. Sure enough, old Ma Bell had come through for the American way and Gonzales was listed, with the street and all. The cowboy took the gun out his mouth and started crying like the crazy snail he was. He told Gonzales that he was sorry and gave him the Colt. Said that his girlfriend left him and his dog died, or maybe it was the other way around. Gonzales went down the street and called the cops. In two months he got a six-thousand-dollar reward for turning in the guy, who, it turns out, had killed his girlfriend and his dog, too, over in Laredo. He got five hundred for the Colt and moved to Baton Rouge, where he started a postage stamp of a used-car lot. Did well, too. Got a dealership now.'

The day fireman snapped his fingers. 'G. Gonzales Buick-Olds?'

'That's it, man,' the oiler said.

'The smilin' rich dude in the commercials?'

'Like I said,' the oiler told the table, 'he knew who he was.'

'Mary and Joseph, everybody is in this hand,' the pilot yelled. 'Spades is trumps.'

'*Laissez les bons temps rouler*,' the welder sang, laying an eight of spades on a pile of diamonds and raking in the trick.

'That's your skinny ass,' Raynelle said, playing a ten of spades last, taking the second trick.

'Do I smell the ten-millionth rollover pot?' the engineer cried. 'There must be six hundred fifty dollars in that pile.' He threw down a nine and covered the third trick.

'Coming gitcha.' Raynelle raised her hand high, plucked a card, and slammed a jack to win the fourth trick. That was two. She led the king of spades and watched the cards follow.

The pilot put his hands together and prayed. 'Please, somebody, have the ace.' He played his card and sat up to watch as each man threw his last card in, no one able to beat the king, and then Raynelle leapt like a hooked marlin, nearly upsetting the table, screaming and waving her meaty arms through the steamy engine room air. 'I never won so much money in my life,' she cried, falling from the waist onto the pile of bills and coins and raking it beneath her.

'Whatcha gonna do with all that money?' the oiler asked, turning his hat around in disbelief.

She began stuffing the bib pockets on her overalls with half-dollars. 'I'm gonna buy me a silver lamé dress and one of those cheap tickets to Las Vegas, where I can do some high-class gamblin'. No more of this penny-ante stuff with old men and worms.'

Five of the men got up to relieve their bladders or get cigarettes or grab something to drink. The pilot stood up and leaned against a column of insulated pipe. 'Hell, we all want to go to Las Vegas. Don't you want to take one of us along to the holy land?'

'Man, I'm gonna gamble with gentlemen. Ranchers, not cow farmers, either.' She folded a wad of bills into a hip pocket.

Nick, the young oiler, laced his fingers behind his head, leaned back, and closed his eyes. He wondered what Raynelle would do in such a glitzy place as Las Vegas. He imagined her wearing a Sears gown in a casino full of tourists dressed in shorts and sneakers. She would be drinking too much and eating too much, and the gown would look like it was crammed with rising dough. She would get in a fight with a blackjack dealer after she'd lost all her money, and then she would be thrown out on the street. After selling her plane ticket, she would be back at the slot machines until she was completely broke, and then she would be out on a neon-infested boulevard, her tiny silver purse hanging from her shoulder on a long spaghetti strap, one heel broken off a silver shoe. He saw her at last walking across the desert through the waves of heat, mountains in front and the angry snarl of cross-country traffic in the rear, until she sobered up and began to hitch, picked up by a carload of Jehovah's Witnesses driving to a convention in Baton Rouge in an unair-conditioned compact stuck in second gear. Every thirty miles the car would overheat and they would all get out, stand among the cactus, and pray. Raynelle would curse them and they would pray harder for the big sunburned woman sweating in the metallic dress. The desert would spread before her as far as the end of the world, a hot and rocky place empty of mirages and dreams. She might not live to get out of it.

The Courtship of Merlin LeBlanc

The baby woke up after lunch, and her grandfather changed her on the sofa, spooning baby food into her until she spat it back at him. It was then he realized that his daughter had left no toys for the child. He spread out a blanket on the floor, turned on the television, and went out of the room for a minute. When he came back, the baby had the TV cord in her mouth, and he realized with a pang that he couldn't keep his eyes off her for a minute. The baby stared at him and he stared at the baby. He went into his bedroom and fumbled through a box in his closet where he kept his shotgun shells, then returned with twenty or so, giving them to the child as playthings. There were shiny red Remingtons, green Federals, yellow Winchesters, and a cheap all-plastic orange variety he had bought at Wal-Mart. They were waterproof and too big to choke on, so he figured they'd be safe.

After the ten o'clock news, he drank a shot glass of strawberry wine. He fancied that the hot medicinal charge he felt in his stomach relaxed him enough to go to sleep at once. Two hours before, he had sung to his granddaughter so she would sleep. As far as he could remember, it was the first time he had sung anything. Maybe he had sung the National Anthem once, when he was in the service, but he wasn't sure. Not knowing any lullabies, he had sung 'Your Cheating Heart.' He lay down, and after he had drifted off, the telephone on his bed table rang out. He jumped for it, thinking at once of the sleeping baby.

The voice on the phone had the sad, official sound of a state policeman. He told Merlin LeBlanc that at about four o'clock a small airplane his daughter was riding in had come down out of a cloud bank over the Gulf of Mexico and crashed next to a Monrovian freighter. The accident happened over a hundred miles from shore in a thousand feet of water.

Merlin sat up in the dark and shook his head, thinking he was having a bad dream. 'Where is my daughter?' he asked, his words husky with sleep.

'The ship's crew looked for survivors for two hours,' the voice said. 'The plane fell straight down in a dive. The crewmen got the plane number, and we found a manifest for it from Lakefront Airport here in New Orleans.' The voice dragged on for several minutes, told Merlin he would be called again in the morning and hung up. He got out of bed, turned on his lamp, and walked over to where the baby was sleeping on a pallet. He could talk until he was blue, and the baby wouldn't know that her mama was at the bottom of the Gulf at the side of some slicked-back lounge-lizard pilot who ran a plane so ratty it couldn't even stay in the sky. He was not angry or sorry, just amazed. All of his children, all three of them, were now dead. Merlin junior had run off a bridge drunk, John T. was shot dead in a poker game, and now Lucy had fallen out of the sky like a bomb in a white trash's airplane.

The loss of his first two children had saddened him, but he had denied or concealed the sorrow in his life. Now he sensed an unavoidable change coming, as though he were being drafted by the army at his advanced age. He looked at the blond head on the blanket, and a powerful fear overcame him. What would he do with her? he wondered.

He thought of the day before, when he had pulled his old tractor under the lean-to and had noticed his daughter waiting for him on the porch. He had shaken his head. Whenever she stood leaning on that post by the steps, he knew she was upset and wanted to unload on him before he got into the house. He looked away, over his fields. The strawberry harvest was finally over, the land stripped of black plastic, the played-out plants disked under, and he looked forward to a short glass of wine, an hour of TV, and the coolness of his little white wooden house. Probably not, he thought, looking over at his daughter.

Even at this distance he could tell she'd been crying. He was fifty-two years old and had never once understood crying, or at least he failed to understand how people got themselves into predicaments that made them cry. He least understood his daughter, who was his oldest child, thirty-four, and who had been married twice, abandoned by both husbands, had been an alcoholic, a drug abuser, had been detoxified twice, and now had a seven-month-old daughter by a Belgian tourist she had met in a bar in New Orleans. Merlin was a man who assumed that the world was a logical place and that people were born into it with logical minds, the way they came with the ability to breathe and eat.

He walked across the close-clipped St Augustine that grew up to the porch and looked at her. His daughter's dirty-blond hair was pulled back into a limp ponytail, and her eyes were baggy and pained. They were looking at him, but they had a faraway quality he had seen before and never tried to understand. 'You comin' by for lunch?' he asked.

'No, Daddy. I had a cup of coffee and some toast late.' She put her hands in the pockets of her jeans, not work jeans, Merlin noticed, but what she called 'preworn,' for people too lazy to wear out their own clothes. 'The baby's asleep inside on the sofa.'

'Okay,' was all he said as he pushed past her and put his hand on the screen.

'Daddy, the reason I came by was I have to get away for a couple days. I mean, I'm just going nuts hanging around Ponchatoula doing nothing.'

He stopped, his hand on the screen door handle and looked at her. 'And?' he asked. He couldn't figure his children out, but he knew there was always an 'and' in a conversation like this. He saw his daughter maybe five times a year even though she lived but three miles away in a little duplex built by the government for folks down on their luck. When she showed up, there was always an 'and.'

'And I want you to keep Susie for me while I'm gone,' she said, smiling fearfully.

He looked inside at the infant on the sofa and back at her. 'Get Mona to keep her.'

'Mona's husband couldn't find work, so they've moved to Georgia.'

'Get Doreen.'

'Doreen wants money. I don't have any money, Daddy. Look, I got all the baby food and Pampers you'll need. It'll only be two days, and I know you finished with the field today, so you'll have lots of time.'

'I can't care for a little thing that size,' he protested. But his daughter began to cry and tell him how he never really helped her out and how she met this airplane pilot in La Place who wanted to fly her to Mexico for a couple of nights and half a dozen other things, until he ran his left hand through his silver hair and told her to take off and not tell him any more. He didn't want to hear about yet another deadbeat she was going out with, and though he was tempted to tell her she was making a mistake, he held his tongue, as he always had with his children. He was a man who never offered his children advice yet always marveled at how stupidly they behaved.

In the past he had watched over Susie for three hours at a time, so he figured he could fill her mouth and mop her bottom for a couple of days. Not much more trouble than a puppy, he thought. He went inside and his daughter put her face against the screen door and peered at him. 'It'll be all right, Daddy. When I get back I'll fix you a big pot of shrimp okra gumbo like Momma used to make.'

'Awright,' he told her. He thought briefly of his wife, dead now six years, standing at the stove stirring a pot.

'Now don't get mad if she cries,' she said. 'Remember, it'll only be a couple days.'

'Awright,' he barked, walking into the dark kitchen to fix himself a lunch-meat sandwich.

The morning after the crash he got up with the baby, then fed and burped her. She smelled sour, so he put her in the big claw-footed bathtub and washed her down with Lifebuoy soap. She kept slipping out of his fingers, and he was glad finally to fish her out of the suds and rub her dry like a kitten. He dressed her in only a disposable diaper, since it was a warm day. The phone rang and it was the policeman's voice again, telling him that they were searching, but after all it was over one thousand feet of water and they weren't exactly sure where the plane had hit and other bits of unpromising news. Merlin sat in the rocker on the front porch, the baby in his lap playing with a Remington dove load, and tried to think about his daughter as a baby, but he couldn't remember a thing. His wife had tended the children just as he had tended the pigs they used to have in back of the tractor shed. He wondered if what went wrong was that he had treated his children like animals. You don't, after all, explain to an animal how to do what it's supposed to do. It goes through the gates, eats where the food is put, lies where it's proper to lie, and, when it's time, lines up to be hit or shot. He put his hand over his eyes when he thought this. Why do you have to tell children things? Why don't they do what's logical?

He was still rocking when his father pulled into the yard at ten o'clock. Etienne LeBlanc was seventy-five, feeble, and forgetful, but he had been that way for twenty years. He sat in the other porch rocker and Merlin told him about Lucy. The old man cried and mumbled into a bandanna he fished out of his overalls, and all the time Merlin looked off at his tractor, trying to remember if the oil needed changing. After a while the baby reached for her greatgrandfather, and he took her into his lap, where she pulled at the copper rivets on his bib, trying to pluck them like berries. The old man began to talk to her in French.

'Daddy,' Merlin asked, 'what am I going to do with that little thing?'

His father, a balding, straight-backed man, sun-freckled and bigboned, made a face as the baby put her thumb up his great nose. 'Only one thing to do.'

'What's that?'

'You got to get married. We got no one to give Susie to.'

Merlin blinked.

'And she's got to be a little younger than you.'

'I could use someone to cook and clean up.'

The old man tucked the baby into the crook of his left arm and looked at his son hard. 'I'm not talking about a cleanin' lady.' He said this very loudly. His upper plate fell down with a click. 'You got to find someone you can care about.'

'What?' Merlin gave his father a questioning look.

Etienne looked into his son's eyes for a while, then lay back against the rocker. 'Aw hell,' he said, shaking his head. 'I forgot who I was talking to.'

'Du,' Susie said, pulling at a tobacco tag dangling from the old man's overalls.

For two weeks, everywhere Merlin went, the baby went also, until he felt that he had somehow grown an extra uncooperative limb that he had to drag around at all times. He spoon-fed her, washed her few clothes by hand in the big bathtub, hung them out to dry, washed her, convinced her to sleep at naptime, dealt with her crying at five in the afternoon, set her on his stomach to watch the news and *Wheel of Fortune*, bought her a playpen and plastic things to chew on, and, in the evening, sang to her and bounced her on the edge of the bed to cajole her to sleep at bedtime. Only then, between eight and his own bedtime, could he read the paper, or change the air filter in the truck, or bathe himself. At six it started all over again. He thought of his dead wife and was ashamed of himself. On the fourteenth night, after he had thought long and hard on what his father had told him, he decided he would at least try to talk to a single woman. The next night was Saturday, and in the morning he called his father to come over and keep Susie. About five o'clock the old man was sprawled on the sofa, the child beating him on the head with a plastic hammer. Merlin steamed himself clean in the big tub, then dug around in the medicine cabinet for something to make himself smell good. He found a green bottle with no label and slapped on some of its contents. His face caught fire and then he remembered that the liquid was a foot liniment his wife had bought. He pictured her rubbing her white feet in the evenings after a day of working the packing shed and running the kitchen. He washed his face quickly and found an oval blue bottle, sniffed it carefully, and splashed the liquid on. There was a bottle of lard-colored hair oil plugged with a twisted piece of newspaper, and this he massaged into his hair until the silver in it shone. In his bedroom he stood in his boxer shorts before his closet and wondered what he owned that would attract the eye of a female. Other than khaki pants and shirts, he had only two pairs of green double-knit slacks, one white shirt, an orange knit shirt, and a yellow knit shirt with a little animal embroidered over the heart. Merlin pulled it off the hanger and examined it closely – the animal was a possum.

He cleared the seed catalogs and fence staples off the seat of his truck and drove into Ponchatoula, where the dim neon sign of the Red Berry Lounge caught his eye. When he walked in, Aloysius Perrin, who owned the farm next to his, spotted him from across the dance floor and yelled over the pounding jukebox, 'Hey, looka this. Clark Gable done come to the Red Berry.' Merlin grinned in spite of himself and looked down at his tight yellow shirt and green slacks. Several of his old friends were in the bar, and he settled in with them for an hour or so, keeping a weather eye out for any unattached ladies. Sure enough, around eight, two women, Gladys Boudreaux and her older sister, came in and took a table across from the jukebox. Gladys had lost her husband two years ago to heart trouble, and she was ten years younger than Merlin, so he thought that maybe she was out on the prowl. He played a slow song on the jukebox and walked over to ask her to dance. She said no, she didn't believe she would. She told him she'd just come in to drink a beer, that she and her sister were taking a break from fixing a five-gallon pot of sausage gumbo for tomorrow night's Knights of Columbus dance.

'But you can come over to my place in the next block and help me and sis ladle out the stuff into the Tupperware if you want,' she said, giving him a cute little gumbo-ladling smile. He followed the two women to their house and discovered that what they really needed was a man to wrestle the five-gallon pot off the back burners of a huge Chambers range and over to a low table. After he helped them, they gave him a bowl of gumbo and he sat there in the kitchen eating, feeling like a stray dog enjoying a handout. The gumbo was made with cheap sausage, and his bowl had a quarter inch of grease floating on top.

''Scuse me, Gladys,' he said. 'Did you fry this sausage before you put it in the gumbo?'

'No. Why? There's nothing wrong with it, is there?'

He spooned up a tablespoon of clear oil and dumped it out on the plate. 'Well, no. It's just fine. I'm just wondering if it wouldn't be quite so slick if you heated some of the fat out of the meat before you put it in the gumbo.'

'Oh, that ain't fat, Merlin. That's just juice.'

'Juice,' Merlin repeated.

'Yeah. Kind of like clear sauce. Now, don't stare at it like that. Just stick your spoon in and eat it up.' She smiled at him again in a way that made him wonder if she wanted him to scrub the big pot and put it on the top shelf in her kitchen, too.

He stared at his gumbo and understood why her husband had died from a bad heart. He ate slowly, worrying about all his friends in the Knights of Columbus.

He returned to the Red Berry Lounge, where Aloysius introduced him to a bleached blonde named Alice. They danced once or twice and sat at a table by the bar while she told him her life story, her dead husband's life story, and the problems her four sons had with the law. It occurred to Merlin that marrying someone his own age would probably make him father of several young men and women who would soon be after him for hand tools and car-insurance payments. Despite this, he told Alice about his granddaughter. She made a face and said, 'Well, let me tell you, I don't want anything to do with a kid in that yellin' and stinkin' stage. I already done my time.' When he finished his beer, Merlin excused himself and walked to the bar, standing under the rotating Schlitz sign and surveying the twenty or so folks in the room, all more or less his age. The Red Berry was known as an old folks' bar, what they called a tavern in other parts of the country. The crowd that was in here now was the same one that had started coming right after the Korean War. He spotted Gwen Ongeron, whose husband had been killed in a ferryboat collision, and she waved with one hand and adjusted the bottom of her permanent with the other. So he went over through the smoke and cowboy music to ask her to dance. They danced to two records, and in that time she asked him how much land he owned, how much he had saved up in the bank, and what year his tractor was made. He didn't follow her back to her table.

Out in the parking lot he sat in the grass-seed smell of his truck and wondered what the hell he was doing looking for a wife in a honky-tonk. It was like trying to find a good watch in a pawnshop. He tried to think back to when he had been nineteen and had asked his wife to marry him. What had he felt when he held her hand? What had he wanted thirty-three years before that he could still want now? He couldn't remember how he'd felt the day he married, couldn't remember one thing he had said to his wife. After all those years of marriage he hadn't known much about her but that she was honest and a good cook. Now, for the first time in his life, he wondered what he should look for in a wife. Whatever it was, he had had it once, didn't realize it, and was now ashamed.

He drove home and found his father asleep in an oak rocker next to the reading lamp, a photo album open in his lap. He walked up to him quietly and bent over to see what he had been studying. The old man's pointing finger was resting on a picture of Merlin's children and wife. They were all grinning like fools, Merlin thought, seated on the front bumper of a 1958 Chevrolet. He didn't think he had taken the photograph. Where had he been? Why wasn't he in it? He nudged his father and the gray eyes opened over a slow, wrinkled smile. 'Hey, boy,' he said, straightening up a bit. 'Have any luck with the ladies?'

'Nah. What you looking at, Daddy?' He bent to study the album more closely.

'It's Merlin junior, John T., and Lucy,' he said.

'And Bee.'

The old head nodded. 'And Bee. God, that woman could cook. Two minutes in the house with a fresh cut-up rabbit, and the onions and bell peppers would be a smokin' in the skillet.'

Merlin focused on the smiles in the picture. 'Makes you wonder what went wrong.' He stood up, looked down on his father's bald and spotted head. The statement hung in the air like an unanswered question. 'I was never mean to them.'

Etienne LeBlanc turned his head slowly and looked up toward the screen door as though someone was standing there. 'Maybe you should have been,' he said. 'At least that would've been something.'

On the first Monday of each month, Our Lady of Perpetual Help Nursing Home would bring Merlin's grandfather over for a daylong visit. About eight-thirty a white van pulled into the farm lot and two attendants rolled out Octave LeBlanc in his wheelchair and installed him on the porch. There wasn't much left to him. Sixty-five years before, he had been a millwright with the F. B. Williams Lumber Company in the bayous of St Mary Parish, but now he was a pale eighty-pound rack of bones. He was blind, but he could still think and talk. Etienne drew up a rush-bottomed chair on one side of him and Merlin and the baby sat on the other side in the swing. The old man blinked his dead eyes, flung a gray arm against the weatherboard of the house, and dragged his palm along the wood. 'You gonna have to paint next year, Merlin.' The voice was thin and whispery, like a broom sweeping a wood floor.

Merlin looked at the peeling paint under the eaves. 'It might last longer.'

'It might not.'

The baby moved in Merlin's arms, subsiding and yawning, dangling a naked foot over his arms, testing the air. Merlin was so full of worry about the child, he could hardly pay attention to his grandfather. He couldn't raise her. What if he died? Worse, what if he didn't do any better with her than he had with his own?

'You got a beer for me?'

'No,' Etienne said. 'You don't need no beer at eight something in the morning.'

'What,' the old man said, 'you scared it's going to kill me?'

Etienne leaned back in his chair and laughed. 'Poppa, if we give you a beer, you'll sleep through your visit.'

The old man turned his head quick as a bird. 'It's a hell of a thing you won't give me one son-of-a-bitchin' beer.' He flung a hand toward his son, who crossed his arms against his overalls and leaned back against a peeling white roof support.

The baby stuck her tongue out and blew a bubble over it. It was very warm outside, and she was in a diaper only. She made a fist with her left hand, put it into her right palm, pulled them apart, and made a noise like a laugh. Octave's head turned. 'What the hell's that?'

'A possum,' Merlin said.

'Let me see.' The old man held out two trembly arms bound with black veins. The baby went at once to him. 'Ow,' the old man said as she settled in his lap. He ran his hand over her head and over her stomach. 'Merlin,' he said fondly, a smile showing his cracked dentures, 'you tricky bastard.'

'Granpop.'

'This ain't no possum.' He put his hand between the baby's

legs and gave the diaper a quick squeeze. 'This ain't no lil' boy, either.'

Etienne leaned over to help the baby find its foot. Merlin bent down, picked up a shotgun shell, and handed it to the child.

'Whose baby is this?' Octave asked, finding the girl's nose with his fingers and gently pushing it like a button. The baby opened her mouth and sang a note.

'Lucy's,' Merlin said. 'Remember, we told you about the airplane.'

'That's right. Didn't that girl know no better than to go up in one of them damn things?' And then he turned his eyes on Merlin as though he could see, and said, 'Didn't you teach her nothin'?' and Merlin shuddered like a beef cow hit with the flat side of an ax. The old man had always told people what he thought and what they should think. Merlin feared his directness, didn't understand it. But he was ninety-three years old and all his children were still alive.

'Don't be hard on me, Granpop.'

The old man turned his head toward where he thought his son was sitting. 'Somebody shoulda,' he accused.

'Come on, now.' Etienne lost his smile.

Octave bent over and planted a shaky, slow kiss on the top of the baby's head. She looked up and burped. 'Ha-haaaa,' Octave rasped. 'You feel some better now for sure, eh, *bébé*?' His hand found the shell she was playing with and seized it. 'What's this?' He picked up his face and aimed it at Merlin.

'A play toy,' Etienne said.

'She likes it to play with.' Merlin and his father exchanged worried looks.

Octave ran his forefinger around the rim. 'Feels like a number-six play toy with a ounce-and-a-quarter shot.' He tossed it over the back of the wheelchair, where it bounced on the porch and rolled off into the grass. 'You don't give no baby a damn shot shell to play with.' His voice was little, but it spoke from a time and experience Merlin could not imagine. One of his stiff legs fell off its step on the wheelchair. 'I ought to be put in jail for causing two muskrats like you. You lying to me just because I can't move out this chair and get you.'

Etienne put a meaty hand on his father's shoulder. 'Easy, Poppa.'

''Tien, what I told you. Talk to the boy. He got no more heart than a alligator. All he cares about is his berries and his tractor.' The old man's eyes began to brim with a filmy moisture.

'Hush,' Etienne said, looking at the porch floor.

'Perrin came in the home last night. He told me about Valentino in a yellow shirt. I heard it and I believed it.'

'Hush, now. This won't do no good.'

The old man grimaced as he moved the baby over in his lap. She put four fingers in his limp green shirt pocket and pulled. 'I know what I know. Merlin in a damn barroom lookin' for a woman like a pork chop.'

Merlin put his hands together and stared at the baby. Old men made him feel weak and ignorant, because he trusted them and believed what they said about things. They had been where he was going. Here was his grandfather, ninety-three years old, his blood and his bone telling him what he was afraid to hear.

Octave coughed deeply and his whole chest caved in, his eyes closing and even his ears moving forward with the slope of his shoulders. It was a while before he got his breath back, and then his voice was weaker than ever. 'Looking for a woman like a damn toaster he can bring home and take in the kitchen and plug in. Plug in and forget it. Hot damn.' He began coughing again, but he had so little wind in him, his cough was more like a slow aspirate rattle. He seemed to be drowning in a thimbleful of liquid deep in his chest. Merlin took the baby and brought her inside while his father bent over Octave. When he came back out, Etienne's face was red, and tears were streaming down.

'What is it?' Merlin asked, holding on to the screen door handle.

'I don't know. I guess he's asleep. His heart's just like a little bird, you can't hardly hear it at all.' He sat down and began to feel for a pulse in the soft skin of his neck. 'You know,' Etienne began, 'what he said about you is true. You never felt much about your children. You never had no kind of emotions.' He placed a huge spotted hand on Octave's forehead.

Merlin sat back in his chair, pulled a handkerchief, and mopped the sweat from his face. 'Daddy, I don't know what's going on, but I'm not no rock like you and Granpop make out.'

Etienne looked over at the lean-to and the dull red tractor it sheltered. 'When you was thirteen I took you to a movie in town. Before it started up, the Movietone news come on and showed four fellows killed by a tornado, laid out next to they barn. When you saw that picture you said, "Look, Daddy, them fools nailed the seams wrong on that tin roof."' He looked down at the floor and blinked. 'I shoulda pulled you outside and talked to you right then.'

Merlin sat in the swing and put his head in his hands. A breeze slowly stirred high in the pecan tree by the porch, the way a spirit might rattle the leaves passing through. He thought about the women in town. He might try again. Maybe at church. Maybe at the KC bingo game. And he wouldn't look for a toaster.

'Merlin.' His father called his name. He was staring at the old man's face, which was the color of wood ash. 'I think he's gone at last.'

Merlin swung close. 'You want me to call the ambulance?'

'What can they do? Look.' Etienne nudged Octave's open mouth shut and pulled down his eyelids.

'Damn,' Merlin said. 'And I didn't let him have a beer.'

'They's a lot of things we didn't let him have.' Etienne turned his wet face away and looked over the disked-up fields to a group of starlings wheeling along the edge of the far tree line. 'When you first got married, you was young. We all married young. We didn't know no more about raising children than a goat knows about flying. He knew,' Etienne said, straightening up and touching his father's shoulder. 'I told you what he told me, but you looked like you . . . aw, what the hell. When I saw how you was ignoring your kids, I should have come over and whipped your ass good three or four times and thrown you in the slop with the pigs.' He put his head down and placed a hand on his father's cool leg.

It was not easy for Merlin to touch his father, but he reached over and swatted him on the shoulder.

'Damn it,' Etienne cried, 'he told me to do it, too.' He jerked his thumb at the still form in the wheelchair.

'I bet,' Merlin said. He heard the baby stirring in her new playpen and beginning to whimper. He got up and went to her, bending to pick her up the way he would lift a puppy, then changing his mind and slipping his palms under her arms. Returning to the porch, he stood next to Octave and stared down. The baby made a noise. Octave turned his head in reflex. 'Hot damn, where that baby?' he said.

Etienne sat back in his chair so hard he lost his balance and tumbled off the porch onto the grass. Merlin froze, his mouth open. Only the baby spoke, singing *laaaaaaaaa* and holding out a fist to the old man, who sensed where she was and touched her foot.

'We thought you was dead,' Merlin said at last.

Octave did not change the faraway smile on his face. 'Oh, I come and I go. The nurses said I passed away three times last week.' His hands, blue and trembly, pulled the baby toward him.

Etienne sat up on the lawn, his hand on his shoulder. 'I'm all right,' he said to Merlin. 'Just give me a minute.' He seemed to be caught between pain and laughter.

'What's this baby's name?' the old man asked in his whispery voice.

'Susie.'

He grunted. 'No, sir. Her name is Susan. Susie sounds like someone you gonna meet in the Red Berry after ten o'clock.'

'Yes, sir,' Merlin said.

'Her name is Susan. Su-san. You hear that? You gonna keep her here and raise her even if you don't find no wife.'

'Yes, sir.' Merlin sat in the swing and held on to the chain.

'You gonna talk to her every day about everything. Tell her about dogs and salesmen.'

'Yes, sir.'

'Tell her about worms and bees.' Here he wiggled his finger into Susan's belly and silver giggles rang from her round red mouth.

'Yes, sir.'

'About cooking and cars and poker and airplanes.'

'Oh sweet Jesus.' Merlin got up and went down the two steps to help his father. Making a face, Etienne reached under his bottom and pulled out the shotgun shell. He banged it upright on the edge of the porch. Octave's head wavered above the baby's bright face as he swung a foot off the wheelchair stirrup and kicked the shell back down to the ground. Merlin hugged his father under the arms and hoisted him up, keeping his hold after they were standing, trying for balance. The two of them stood there in the sunshine, chastened but determined, amazed by the smiles on the porch, where Octave and Susan whispered and sang.

Navigators of Thought

At ten-thirty Friday morning, Bert was in the wheelhouse of the company's oldest tugboat, trying to figure out its controls. The jagged squawks of the shortwave set were interrupted by Dixon's trombone voice. '*Phoenix*, come back.'

Bert turned and stared at the peeling machine, wondering why his boss was on the air instead of the dispatcher. He grabbed the microphone. '*Phoenix* by.' Please, not a towing call, he thought. Not already.

'Doc, are you cranked and hot?'

Bert made a face at the expression. 'Max had some trouble with the engines, but he's got them started now.'

'Hang by the set,' Dixon told him. 'A tanker hit the fleet above Avondale Bend and some barges are coming down. If the other tugs can't catch them, you might have to go out and lasso one.'

Bert placed a palm on the top of his bald head. 'You want us to chase a barge downriver?'

'What's the matter, Doc? Don't your speaker work?'

'You can't send the Mexican fellows after it?' Dixon's crews were hired by their captains, and the *Sonny Boy* was run by Henry Gonzales, who had employed all his relatives. The *Aspen* gleamed under the attentions of its Vietnamese operators, and the *Buddy L* twanged around the New Orleans harbor with a crew from Biloxi.

'Gonzales hung up a hawser in his prop. You might see a big grain hopper coming down in a half hour. Look out.' In a tearing snort of static, Dixon was gone, replaced by a low, whistling fabric of dismembered voices. Bert hung the mike on the set and looked upriver through the wheelhouse door. The Mississippi was a gray

73

deserted street. He sat on the stool behind the spokes of the varnished wheel and thought of how his crew had trouble tying on to drifting equipment. Like the other captains, he had been allowed to hire his own people, so he gathered men like himself, college teachers who had been fired. He wondered whether they could change form in midlife like amphibians.

He thought back to the week before, when he had been at the controls of the new *Toby*, shoving a small barge to a dock downriver from the city. He had jerked the throttle levers into reverse, and the boat had hauled back on the barge, her engines shuddering. His mouth fell open when he saw the starboard and port lines seeming to untie themselves, paying overboard as the barge charged the dock at an angle, hammering two pilings into kindling.

Several stevedores wandered over to see what had caused all the thunder. Two of them pointed at the *Toby* and laughed. Bert shoved the throttle levers up, easing the bow against the barge to keep it pinned in place. Thomas Mann Hartford and Claude McDonald, the deckhands, appeared on the push knees, and on the third try attached a rope to their tow, turning when they had finished to look warily up to the wheelhouse. Bert pushed open a window.

'Clove hitches on a barge? You've got to be kidding.' His deckhands sometimes reminded him of the cloudy-eyed freshmen in the backwoods college where he had taught for four years.

Thomas Mann lowered his small blond head to look at one of the ropes that had come undone. Bert studied his unraveling dress slacks and greasy Izod shirt, waiting for him to look up. 'I'm really sorry, Bert, but a couple of hours ago when we were picking up the barge, Claude told me about the new book on John Donne's poetry, and I went to his bunk to see it.' The deckhands had been denied tenure at a small state college and were unable to find full-time work anywhere. Thomas Mann looked up at the shattered pilings. 'We forgot to ratchet up the cables after we made the preliminary tie-off.'

Bert leaned out farther to get a better look at the damage. 'I can't believe you expected two rowboat knots to hold that thing. What the hell do you think Dixon is going to say when he finds out you two were twittering over seventeenth-century metaphors when you should have been lashing a barge?'

Claude McDonald shook the mane of dark curls clustered over his thick glasses. 'It's a formidable consideration,' he said.

At seven the next morning, the five-man crew of the *Toby* had filed onto the deep carpet of their employer's office. Dixon was the owner of two tugboat fleets, a person who could appreciate the true value of intellectuals. At sixty-six, the former deckhand still looked out of place in his fine office, his gray suit. He sat back in a tall leather chair and popped his knuckles. A series of wrinkles ran vertically across his forehead like hatchet scars. 'Please don't try to explain nothin',' he said. 'I wouldn't understand what you was talking about if you did. Last month, you ruined three hundred dollars' worth of cable, and you had me believing it was my fault, like I wrapped it around that ferryboat myself.' He looked at them hard, and Bert watched the old eyes, which were like two olives forgotten in the bottom of a jar. The crewmen kept back from the big desk, afraid for their jobs. The middle-aged cook, Laurence Grieg, was trembling, facing the loss of the first employment he had found in two years.

The engineer, a bony man with Nordic features, was Maximilian Renault, a Romantics scholar given to slow, spooky movements and inappropriate smiles. Dixon threw a hard look his way and Max backed up a step, running long fingers through his dark hair.

'You guys have tore up more machinery in six months than the other five crews put together.' Dixon looked at them carefully, his intellectuals, sorry at the expense they had caused him, but at the same time enjoying their failures. The college boys, all Ph.D.'s, would never make the money he had made. 'I realize,' he continued, turning a heavy white-gold ring on his left hand, 'that times is bad. All the good professor jobs been sucked up years ago.' He paused, letting the obvious sink in. If these had been ordinary crewmen, they might have traded glances, told Dixon to go to hell, and walked out. But discarded teachers would take anything. 'So I'm gonna keep you on, but remember this,' he said, falling forward in his chair and aiming his chopped face at them. 'I pay you damn good money – union scale. I deserve better for my boats than you been doing. If you can't do better, I got to let all of you go.'

The five men were silent. The tension had been broken, and they waited to be told to leave. Dixon sent a bored glance out over the grassy median of Carrollton Avenue, where a green-roofed streetcar clattered past. 'I can't let you stay on the *Toby*. She cost too much. Today, I'm gonna put all the Cajuns on her. I'll sell their tug and you can go on the spare.'

'The spare?' Bert looked over his shoulder at Max, who shrugged.

Mr Dixon pulled a form from his desk and began writing. 'The *Phoenix Three*,' he said.

'The old red tug tied up against the willows?'

'That's it,' Dixon said, sucking his teeth and looking up to study Max's frayed Arrow shirt. 'It was built in the twenties out of carbon steel and rivets. Even you people can't tear it up.' He looked Bert in the eye. 'Go on down to the dock and get familiar with the boat. It's got old controls. Steering it will be like dancing with a cow.'

And now Bert stood in the wheelhouse of the *Phoenix III*, pulling mud daubers' nests off the control levers and gauges. A gummy spar varnish darkened the oak cabin, and the windows were cloudy with dust and soot. He looked around at the tarnished brass, the old-fashioned curved-front cabin, worrying about the ragged machinery. Bert always suspected that Dixon had hired him as a mean joke, and now he'd played another on him.

After he'd lost his teaching appointment, his wife had to find work as a secretary, and his children were taken out of private school. During the year of fruitless applications and interviews, his family buckled down as though waiting out a stubborn malady. There were no offers of jobs, only mild interest expressed by junior colleges in Alaska, Saudi Arabia, and a fundamentalist high school in West Virginia.

Once a week he'd ridden the Jackson Avenue ferry to collect his unemployment check. He liked the gritty smell of the Mississippi that met him at the landing, and the red-and-white tugs and broad, rusty freighters sometimes floated along the channels of his dreams. The throbbing vessels moved with the power and grace of great poems.

He got the idea to apply to a towing company for work. Dixon had laughed out loud when he saw Bert's resumé. He disliked the idea of a man like Bertram Davenport so much that he hired him on the spot. He wanted to let the college man roast his brains on the steam tug *Boaz* with the backwoods savages from Arkansas he'd hired to run her. He was sure they'd throw him overboard first trip out.

However, Bert got along with the Arkansas men, who were not really savages but only easily angered farm boys from around Camden. He became an excellent harbor wheelman, learning the currents and signals as though they were in his blood. Dixon was grudgingly impressed. A smart wheelman avoided thousands of dollars in dry-dock work on smashed bows and bent propeller shafts.

Bert should have been satisfied with his success, but it only told him that he was a better river man than he had been a teacher. When he recalled how he had often bored his students and become disoriented while dealing with complex ideas in his lectures, he suspected that the English department was right in getting rid of him.

After two years, Bert was given his own small boat and was allowed to recruit men for his crew as replacements became necessary. The first scholar he'd hired was Max, his old graduate school roommate, an amiable but directionless man who worked on car engines for extra money and who had earned his final degree at forty-one after taking dozens of diverse and ill-chosen courses and then writing a seven-hundred-page dissertation on Byron and Nietzsche.

Dixon thought it a fine joke to have two scholars on one of his tugs, and he encouraged the hiring of more, so when Bert needed to employ a cook, he enlisted his old confidant, Dr Laurence Grieg, who had been fired two years before for failing too many students, and whose hobby was preparing French cuisine. The two deckhands, Thomas Mann Hartford and Claude McDonald, were hired last.

From the wheelhouse, Bert heard an old generator engine rattle alive below, and the cabin's lights came on slowly, like newly lit candles. A compressor began to chatter, and after a few minutes Max turned over one of the huge engines down in the hold, and it thundered alive, sending convulsions of black smoke from the tug's stack. Bert pulled the wheel around and saw a swirling comma of water sail out from under the stern. At least the steering worked. On the boat's long stern, he saw a deckhand making notations in a spiral-bound book. Every professor Bert knew wrote essays with the dream of earning some share of fame and a position at a well-known university. When he and his crew were languishing on the decks waiting for a towing call, most of them brought manuscripts to revise, add to, and argue over.

A month earlier, tied up in blinding fog below the Belle Chasse locks, they had met in the galley and had passed around one another's works. For hours the men sat hip-to-hip, hunched over cramped handwriting or poor typing. The conversation was stiff and polite. The pedantic, graceless ordinariness of the writing showed in the faces of the scholars gathered under the pulsing lights of the small compartment. Bert read an article in progress by Claude McDonald, a man who was a true academic, very intelligent, but so educated that he was unable to compose two coherent paragraphs in a row. After a few pages he put the paper down and wondered whether his own work was half as taxing. He smiled faintly and nodded at Claude, who was sitting two stools to the left of him, struggling with Max's enormous work on Byron. Bert turned to his right, putting his hand on Max's shoulder. 'Sometimes I think we think too much,' he told him.

Max frowned above a handwritten page. 'Thought is life.'

Bert took back his hand. 'Someone could just as well say, "Navigation is life." That's what we are now – navigators.' He liked the sound of the word.

Max turned his dark eyes on him. 'We're navigators of thought.'

Bert set the wheelhouse clock and then climbed down to the galley, where Laurence Grieg had just made coffee in a half-gallon enamel pot. Bert held a hot ironware mug in both hands and studied Laurence, how his shoulders were rounding into middle age, worn that way like a boulder in a creek by his wife, who was constantly on his back about returning to an academic job. Laurence would never work again, for his dossier contained a damning letter from his department head.

'How's Laura?' Bert asked, sitting at the counter that ran down one wall of the galley, a narrow compartment spanning the width of the boat. Laurence Grieg, who had lately begun dressing in khaki work clothes, all his polycottons and tweeds finally wearing out, adjusted the tiny gas range so the coffee would not boil.

'Laura is Laura.' He showed Bert a beleaguered smile. 'She's complaining about the smell of oil in my clothes,' he said, shaking his shiny head.

Maximilian lumbered in, got a cup of coffee, and left immediately. He seemed unware that anyone else was in the galley. Thomas Mann poked his blond head in the door. 'Bert, someone is on the radio for you.'

Bert put his cup down and went out into the wind, zipping up his corduroy jacket and climbing the flaking stairs to the wheelhouse. He picked up the receiver and spoke to the dock dispatcher, who told him that his boat might be sent to the mouth of the river to pull a ship from a sandbar. He signed off and saw that Max had followed him up. His face was weighted with embarrassment. 'Bert, Loyola has rejected my application,' he said, looking away quickly, his face growing darker. He was not a man who liked to admit that he was in trouble. None of them were.

'What about the other applications?'

'The same. Tulane's letter was very snide. The search committee said they did not employ industrial workers as professors.' He thrust his hands into his pockets. 'It's finally happened,' he said, looking down to the corrugated deck. 'I didn't tell you at first because I was ashamed.' He snuffled once, bringing a crisp new work-shirt sleeve up to his nose.

Bert imagined him in the classroom fumbling with notes. 'Why are you ashamed?'

The engineer looked past him at a small gaily painted excursion boat grinding up the river, its decks speckled with tourists pointing their cameras at the old tug. Four of them waved with enthusiasm. 'I'll never be in the classroom again.'

Bert waved back absently. 'Is that the worst that can happen?'

Max looked surprised. He replied only after he had thought fully half a minute. 'The worst is what we think it is.' He smiled quickly, catching himself. He sat down in the wheelman's chair. 'I don't think I can face it. The change, I mean. Giving up on teaching. Maybe, when my manuscript finds a publisher . . .'

'Max, you're making a good living on this job.' Bert turned away, jamming his hands into his coat pockets, feeling his ring of keys, one of which fit an office door a thousand miles away.

Max pressed a palm on the glass of the wheelhouse window. His voice was low and steady. 'Will any of us get back to where we belong?'

Bert broke another mud dauber's nest off an overhead gauge and threw it sidearm over the rail.

And then at eleven that Friday morning, there it was, Dixon's voice on the radio like a tearing tarp. '*Phoenix*, come back.'

Bert grabbed the microphone quickly. '*Phoenix* by.'

'Doc, can you move out in a flash?'

'What? Are we going down to the jetties?'

'Lord, no. It's a rodeo upriver. They're lassoing runaway barges like crazy. Somebody's chasing all but the lead barge. Go catch it.'

Bert squeezed the mike like a lemon and looked upriver. 'Couldn't you call out another boat? We're—'

'Make it smoke, Doc. I don't want to tell you twice.'

'I don't know if we can catch it. I'll have to think about—'

'Don't think. Do.' Dixon was flashing into anger. The two deckhands, hearing the broadcast, crowded into the wheelhouse, little Thomas Mann shivering and Claude McDonald squeezing one joint of a finger in his book. Bert looked upriver and saw a long grain barge nose around the bend, riding high in the water, doing about seven miles an hour.

'Doc?' Dixon's portentous voice tore through the old gray shortwave set. 'You think you got tenure here or something?'

Bert looked at Claude's arms, wondering how much was muscle. 'Okay,' he sang, 'we're heading out. *Phoenix Three* over.' Without thinking, he began to give orders. Soon, Thomas Mann was hopping about on the landing barge like a blond monkey, untying the lines. Claude rattled down the steps to the pointed foredeck, where he began making up a bowline. Bert gave four short blasts of the whistle, and Max stuck his head out of the engine room door.

'Bertram. Where're we going?' He gestured with a manuscript in his gloved hand.

'Just study your engines for a change,' he called. 'We'll need all the power they've got.'

Bert swung the steering wheel, leaned on the throttle levers hard, and felt the tug surge away from the landing barge. A cloud of black smoke billowed from the exhaust ports in the stack, the engines trembled like old horses, and Bert imagined he could hear Maximilian shouting encouragement to the machinery. He reached up for the whistle cord and blew another danger signal. The river was clear of traffic except for one ascending ore freighter, which he called to advise. The *Phoenix III* headed straight out toward the barge while Bert judged its speed and weight. Several options occurred to him instantly, not the result of deliberation. If he were to run the boat ahead and gradually slow down, letting the barge catch up to the stern and stop against it, the slanted bow might climb the rear deck and sink the tug. If he tried to tie on and control it from the side and couldn't, it might drag the *Phoenix* downriver sideways and capsize it. He decided to catch it from the rear with a bowline and yelled for Claude to tie a hundred feet of two-and-a-half-inch nylon rope to the front towing bitts and to form the free end into a loop. He could hear Maximilian below, beating on something with a hammer or wrench, and suddenly the engines, their teeth-rattling vibration gone, surged smoothly with added power.

He piloted the tug to within thirty feet of the barge, cutting the engines to half speed and following the vessel downstream, letting its rusty sides slip past. Its mooring cleats were twelve feet above Claude's head, and Bert hoped his deckhand could throw a rope that far.

As the stern of the barge slid past his bow, Bert revved the engines to keep up. Claude climbed on the hemp fender and swung the yellow hawser back and forth underhand as Thomas Mann waited behind him. He tossed the loop toward a cleat on the barge's deck, but the line tangled in itself and fell short, splashing into the churning river. Bert cut back the engines to keep from nudging the barge into a spin, then blew another series of short warning blasts to alert any boats that might be ascending Carrollton Bend.

Thomas Mann retrieved the rope and coiled it on the deck so that it would pay out smoothly. He seemed not to be thinking about anything; perhaps there was not an abstraction in Thomas Mann's head for the first time in years as he spread his legs wide, bent his back, and threw the rope into an orderly coil. When the boat rounded Carrollton Bend, Bert could see the willowy foot of

Walnut Street on the east bank, and abreast of it, three-quarters of a mile below him, two excursion vessels, a tanker in midriver, and a towboat shoving a raft of barges past the tanker on the west, all ascending.

Claude climbed high on the bow, and Thomas Mann coached him on his swing. The big man's black curls fluttered in the wind as he practiced swinging one, two, three times, and on the fourth swing, he flung his arms open like springs, tossing the noose spinning, spinning, up to the mooring cleat, where it hung on the metal like a cowboy's lariat.

'Eeeeh-haaaah,' Dr Claude McDonald yelled as Thomas Mann pulled in the slack behind him, whipping it around the double towing bitts in four quick figure eights. Bert set the engine-control levers into full reverse, and the nylon line began to tighten like an archer's bowstring. The barge slowed to a crawl as the propellers bit into the river. The hawser turned to rock, complaining on the bitts, creaking and popping on the painted iron.

'Get off!' Claude screamed at Thomas Mann, who was standing on the bitts, inspecting his knot. He jumped free and both men ran amidships as the line parted with a sound like cannon fire, whipping back to where the deckhand had stood, hitting the metal like a thunderbolt. The tug surged backward, and the barge was taken again by the current. Bert killed the engines and looked over the runaway hopper barge to the ascending tow. He saw the low profile and red vents of loaded petroleum barges. Sliding open a stubborn wheelhouse window, he yelled down, 'Get Max out of the engine room, latch the doors on the first deck, and climb to the bunk deck with Laurence.'

Looking over at the ascending towboat, Bert could see its crew coming to the rails, donning life jackets. The big boat was trapped between the freighter and the bank, and both vessels had cut their engines. The *Phoenix III* and the barge drifted down on them. Horns and whistles filled the river, and the shortwave gave off a jam of panicked voices. Bert's own crew of four watched at the rail below him as he made the old tug's engines rumble. Soon they were sloshing alongside the barge, drawing close. When the tug's bow was amidships and five feet off from the runaway's side, Bert turned the wheel, jolting into the barge and holding the bow against its flank. The *Phoenix III*'s stern swept around and the tug began to capsize. It was taking the river sideways, leaning over into the current like an old drunkard falling down slowly. The barge began to respond and move sideways into the lower bank of Nine Mile Point, but water was roaring over the tug's port rail. The crew scrambled to starboard and looked up to the wheelhouse for a signal to jump. Bert noticed that they had buckled their life vests correctly for once. They had no time to think about what they were doing.

The ascending tow was blowing shorts and the tanker contributed sonorous blasts of its steam horn. When the hopper was thirty feet from the bow of the leading petroleum barge, it swung clear into the dead water under Nine Mile Point, the *Phoenix III* heaving it toward the bank on a hard rudder. Bert looked behind, past the storm of his wheelwash, and saw the petroleum barge slide toward his stern, and he braced for the impact. The tug surged against the rusty, buckling steel, and the far side of the runaway began to rise in the air as it rode up onto a mud flat. Behind, the petroleum barge slid clear, brushing the hemp fender on the *Phoenix*'s stern. Then an empty lunch box slid off a shelf above the radio and banged to the floor and the port door swung out. A shout went up from the men at the rail as the boat went into a dying roll. Bert pulled back on the engine controls, but it was too late. The boat was heeling over, and with his crew Bert scrambled out onto the near-horizontal bunk deck wall.

Max swung down to the engine room door, pulled it open, and ducked under as it slammed like a gong. At once the crew slid toward the water and pulled at the latches on the oval steel door. They saw Max inside, struggling in a surf of brown water roiling in through the vents and up through the bilge.

'Max,' the cook shouted, leaning in. 'What are you doing?'

The engineer didn't look up. 'My manuscript,' he yelled.

The generator sucked up a charge of water and banged to a halt, the compartment falling dark. Bert jumped in, feet first, landing on the side of a stair ramp. 'Forget it. Come on.' He grabbed Max by the shirt collar and hoisted his head above the oily water, but he shook out of his grasp.

'It's the only copy,' he wailed, plunging in again, disappearing against the port wall. The river began to pour in the open door.

'It's not worth it,' Claude MacDonald yelled at Max's emerging head. 'It'll never be published.'

Thomas Mann Hartford hung upside down into the engine room. 'Max,' he pleaded. 'Give it up. It's a piece of crap.'

'No.' He rose into a shaft of water-jeweled light falling through the door. 'It will get me out of here,' he told them, going under again. Before Bert could reach him, the boat shifted to a pure horizontal, and the water reached the hot manifolds of the towering port engine, filling the engine room with steam. Bert yelped and jumped for the outstretched hands of his crew, who hauled him up through a muddy waterfall, for the boat was going down, the river storming into the open door. An explosion of steam and trapped air propelled them into deep water, the men clinging together like a raft of ants in a flood. They were swept by the current while the *Phoenix III* turned over, flashed its corroded propellers, and went down headfirst.

Bert looked over to the geysers of air breaking the river's surface and tried to think of something to say, but his mind would make no words.

Five minutes later the cook watched the Dixon fleet's crew boat approach at a chopping roar. 'I hope the old man gives us a strong cup of hot coffee before he fires us.' The hull came up to them, and Dixon himself, dressed in a wool suit and overcoat, helped pull them out of the water and hustle them into the small cabin. 'Where's that Renault guy?' he asked, his face flushed and worried.

No one could say anything for a long moment. 'He's in the engine room,' Bert finally said. Dixon turned his head and gave

the river a long, openmouthed look. Bert peered out at the dull
water while the crew boat's pilot radioed an approaching Coast
Guard cutter about the lost man. 'We tried.'

Dixon sat down and pushed the wrinkles out of one side of
his face. 'I saw what happened on radar. I heard it on the radio.'
He looked over at the rescued hopper barge. 'It's fifty feet deep
where it went down. Maybe I can have it raised.' He shook his
head once. 'Jeez, why couldn't he get out of the engine room?'

The men looked at one another, and Dr Grieg, the cook, cleared
his throat. 'I guess he got trapped.'

For a moment, Dixon hid his face in his soft, spotted hands.
'What? Did the door slam on him?'

Bert looked out at the river, which renewed itself every flowing
moment without a thought. 'Something like that,' he said,
watching a little white cutter begin to circle above the wreck, two
divers looking in the water for something to make them jump.

People on the Empty Road

Wesley and his girlfriend were parked in his father's driveway on Pecan Street, arguing in his old Pontiac Tempest. Bonita was a sulky brunette with a voice as hard as a file. She wanted him to get the forty-dollar tickets to the Travis Tritt concert, and he tried to explain that the twenty-dollar tickets were a better deal. He looked down the humpback asphalt lane to where it turned off at Le Phong's Country Boy Cash Grocery and ground his teeth. He sensed he was going to lose his temper again, the way a drunk feels in his darkened vision that he is about to fall off a stool. Bonita crossed her arms and called him the cheapest date in Pine Oil, Louisiana, and Wesley crushed the accelerator, leaving the car in neutral, letting the racket do his talking. The engine whined up into a mechanical fury until a detonation under the hood caused everything to stop dead, as if all the moving parts had welded together. Wesley cursed and got out, followed by Bonita, who spat her gum against a pin oak and put her hands on her hips. 'Now you done it,' she told him. 'When are you gonna calm down?'

Wesley examined a volcano-shaped hole in the hood of his car where a push rod had blown through like a bullet. 'You can walk home and wait for Travis Tritt to climb in your window with a bouquet of roses,' he yelled. 'But don't wait for me.'

She started down the street, then turned and shouted back to him, 'When you gonna grow up?'

'When I'm old enough to.'

Bonita continued toward her rental house in the next neighborhood. Wesley turned and went into the kitchen. The old man was at the table, home from his supermarket, sipping a glass of iced tea.

'That's the second engine this year, Wes. How many can you afford?'

'I know. She got me so damned mad.' He fell into a chair. 'I think we just broke up.'

His father ran a hand over his gray hair and then loosened his tie. 'It's just as well. She was common. Her sister who used to check for me on register six was kind of rough. What was her name, Trampoline?'

'Trammie-Aileen,' Wesley corrected. 'She works for Le Phong now.' He put his head down and his red hair fell forward like a rooster's comb.

'Know what I think?' his father asked.

'What?'

'I think you ought go come back cutting meat in the store. You were the fastest trimmer I ever had. With a rolled rump, you were an artist.'

Wesley held up the nub of his left forefinger, and his father looked out the window. 'I want to do something else for a while, Daddy.'

'I think you'll be safer cutting meat for me here in Pine Oil than off driving for that gravel company. You don't have the disposition for that.'

Wesley's face became as tight as a rubber glove. 'You mean I'm reckless, don't you?'

'You just got to find a girl who'll calm you down. Only thing'll do that is a good girl and time.'

Wesley put his head back down in his hands. 'I don't want to hear this.'

'Well, when's it gonna happen? You're twenty-four and been through eight cars.' His father took a swallow of tea and softly grabbed a fistful of his son's hair. 'That old Tempest wasn't any good, but it was transportation.'

'I can afford Lenny's rusty T-Bird. It's for sale.'

His father clamped the coppery strands in his fingers, an old game, his way of saying, 'Calm down. Come back to earth.'

Then he said, 'I'll get you a better car if you come back to work for me.'

Wesley pulled free and moved toward the window. 'I've got to go roll some gravel. I'm good at it.'

'I don't like you running those tight schedules.'

Wesley leaned on the wooden window frame and watched a wisp of oil smoke rise from the puncture in his hood. 'The construction folks want the rock quick. If we can't get it to them when they need it, someone else gets the contract.'

His father rubbed his eyes. 'Your boss is making money on your lack of patience. You need to slow down and find a girl who thinks there's more to life than fast cars and cowboy music.'

Over the next month he made more runs than any other driver at the gravel pit. His boss, old man Morris, pear-shaped, with skin like barbecued chicken, told him, 'Boy, you're a natural.'

'A natural what?' Wesley asked, stepping up into a blue Mack.

The old man spat on a wheel rim. 'A natural way to get my rock moved faster than Ex-Lax.'

Each day, his truck clipped a minute off the time to the big casino site in New Orleans, but each fast trip shaved a little off his nerves, the way the road wore down tires to the explosive air at the center of things. He couldn't help the urge to sail across the twenty-four-mile-long causeway over Lake Pontchartrain like a road-bound cargo plane weighted down with many tons of pea gravel. A big sedan might be in the right lane doing sixty-five and he would be coming up from behind at ninety, water showering up from his wheels, a loose tarpaulin flying over the forty-foot trailer wild as a witch's cape. Near his left rear mud flap there'd be another car, and the time to change lanes was exactly then or the people in the big sedan would be red pulp, so after one click of his blinker he would roll out like a fighter plane, road reflectors exploding under his tires like machine-gun bursts.

He used his recklessness like a tool to get the job done. After every twelve-hour day, he would tear out of the gravel pit in his rusty Thunderbird, spinning his wheels in a diminishing shriek for half a mile. The road turned through worthless sand bottoms and stunted growths of pine, and the car would surge into the curves like electricity, Wesley pushing over the blacktop as if he were teaching the road a lesson, straightening it out with his wheels. When he would charge off the asphalt at eighty onto a gravel road, he would force the low sedan over a rolling cloud of dust and exploding rock as though he were not in danger at every wheel skid and shimmy of slamming into a big pine like a cannonball. For Wesley, driving possessed the reality of a video game. After thirty miles, he would skid to a stop, a half ton of dust boiling in the air behind him.

His destination was a dented sea-green mobile home parked in an abandoned gravel pit. He would pull at its balky door until the whole trailer rocked like it was caught in a hurricane, and finally inside, he would sit at his little kitchen table and watch his hands shake with something beyond fatigue.

One morning at six o'clock he was awakened by an armadillo rummaging in his kitchen. The animals were all over the place and had come in before. Wesley soft-kicked it through the open door frame like a football and watched it land in a pit of green water on the other side of his car. He sat down to listen to a radio talk show coming from the AM station in Pine Oil.

'Wouldn't you say that giving a man the death penalty for stealing two cows is a bit excessive?' The host's voice was pleasant and instructive.

'If they was *your* cows, sweetie, you'd want him to fry like bacon,' a tubby voice said.

Wesley forced himself to eat breakfast, and sometime between the cereal and the orange juice, he began to relax. The woman announcer's voice was smooth as a moonlit lake, and he remembered meeting her at the store when she did a remote from the meat aisle during Pine Oil Barbecue Days. After breakfast, he sat on the galvanized step below his warped door frame, folded his hands, and rested his chin on his knuckles. He wondered how fast he would be driving in another month.

Wesley watched a lizard race from under the step. When the pit around the trailer had been operating, years before, a watchman had lived here. Spread over it for two hundred acres were green ponds shaped like almonds or moons or squares. To the south was an abandoned locomotive, its wheels sunk into the sand. Shards of machinery and cable lay about as though rained down from the clouds. He had lived in the center of the wreckage for six months and not one person had been to see him. He needed a new girl-friend – his father had said it – one who would make him go to the movies, barbecue hamburgers over a lazy fire, read magazines with no girlie pictures in them. He remembered the woman on the radio.

Turning up the ivory-colored Zenith left behind by the watchman, he listened to Janie, dealing with the farmers' wives. She ran from six to twelve, starting each program with a simple question, such as: 'Do you think people should send money to TV evangelists?' or 'Should the federal government spend more on welfare?' Many of her callers were abusive or made inflammatory statements far beyond the boundaries of simple ignorance. Most, Wesley decided after weeks of listening to the program, were people too stupid to be trusted with jobs, so they just sat around the house all day thinking up things to call the radio station about. He turned up the volume.

'Hello, you're on the air.' The voice laid hands on him.

'Miz Janie,' a high-pitched old-lady voice whined.

'Good morning.'

'Miz Janie?'

'Yes, go on. Today's topic is the library tax.' The voice was seasoned with a bright trace of kindness.

'Miz Janie, ain't it a shame what the law did those poor boys down in Manchac?'

'Ma'am, the topic is the library tax.'

'Yes, I know. But ain't it a shame that those poor boys got put in jail for killing birds?'

'You're referring to the Clemson brothers?'

'That's right.'

'They killed over two thousand Canada geese,' she said, not the least hint of outrage in her voice.

'Birds is all,' the old lady said. 'Them boys is people. You can't put people in jail for what they do to birds.'

Wesley balled up his fists and glared at the radio, remembering Elmo, his pet mallard from childhood.

'Ma'am,' the smooth voice said, 'if everybody killed all the geese they wanted to kill, soon there'd be no more geese.' Wesley searched for some bitter undercurrent in the voice but found not one molecule. The announcer gradually guided the old woman through a long channel of logic that led to the day's topic, the library tax.

'Miz Janie, everybody wants to raise our taxes. It's hard to made ends meet, you know.'

'This tax is twenty-five cents a month.' That was slick, Wesley thought.

'Well, it's the principle of the thing,' the old voice complained. 'Seems like we're paying people just to sit around and read when they ought to be out doing something else. If everybody would quit hanging around the library and get out on the highway picking up trash paper instead, we'd have a clean community, now wouldn't we?'

Wesley glared at the dusty radio. But the lady announcer continued to speak with honesty and openness until the woman on the line lost interest and hung up.

The next caller was an old man. 'What the hail we need to spend money on a damned library for? Let them what wants to read go down to Walgreen's and buy they own magazines. The old library we got's plenty enough for such as needs it.'

The next caller agreed with the millage proposal, but then a straight-gospel preacher came on the air and told that only one book ought to be in the library, and then another voice said he wouldn't mind voting for the millage if they got rid of the ugly librarian. 'I mean, if they want to renovate, let's *really* renovate and get rid of the old warthog at the front desk.' The announcer, her words like April sunshine, explained that Mrs Fulmer was a lovely person as well as a certified librarian. Wesley turned up the radio, got out the brushes and Comet, and scrubbed his trailer like a sandstorm, wondering whether the announcer was single and trying to remember what she looked like. Her voice made her seem young, in her mid-twenties maybe, like he was. Then the phone rang, and he was called for two runs to New Orleans.

Down at the pit, he drew King Rock, a vast expanse of red enamel and chrome, the soul of the gravel yard. The foreman swung his gut out of the scale shack and climbed onto the truck's step, shoving his bearded face through the window. 'If you can't push the son of a bitch to New Orleans by nine,' he said, 'you better keep going, hock the truck, and leave the country.'

Wesley pulled a steel bar from under the driver's seat, got down, and walked around the rig, beating the tires as if he was angry with them, testing for flats. It was an extra-long trailer heaped with wet gravel. Wesley drove the rig onto the twisting two-lane blacktop, stomping the accelerator at every shift of the gears. He couldn't make himself think about the danger, so he again chose to see the windshield as a big video-game screen he could roar through with the inconsequence of a raft of electrons sliding up the face of a vacuum tube. The challenge was time, and he would lose if he drove a real road. He checked his watch – five after eight. The New Orleans site had to mix cement by nine or send a shift of workers home. King Rock loped under his feet like a wolf after deer.

Wesley streaked past a speeding Greyhound bus at the bottom of a grade, cut into the right lane, hit a curve, and felt the heart-fluttering skitter of nine tires trying to leave the ground. 'Good God,' he said aloud, surprised and frightened. But when he came to a straight section, as empty and flinty as a dull lifetime, he raced down it. He turned on the radar detector and thought of the two trips he had to make. The order had come in at seven:

triple money for a load before nine in downtown. He was the only man who could make the ride.

Soon the truck was singing up to eighty. Wesley tapped his trailer brakes and drew ghosts of smoke from his rear tires. The video game had to be perfect now, for any mistake would cause a fierce yellow flash on the screen, the loss of a man.

He saw pines swarm past his window until he rose over the crest of Red Top Hill, the descending road tumbling away from him, deserted and inviting speed. He tried not to think about how fast he could go; he just rode the machinery as though it were only noise instead of iron and rock, and when he slid into the curve at the bottom of the hill, he was not really alarmed at the rear of the stopped school bus ahead with its silly tin signs flopped out and a dozen children strung across the highway.

Wesley stood on the brakes and hung on the air horn while his tires howled and a cumulus of blue smoke rolled up behind. Gravel hammered the roof of King Rock's cab, and he could hear the retreads tear off the tires. He fell out of his video game when he saw the faces of the children, real kids whose only mistake in life was to cross a road ten miles down from a greedy man's gravel pit.

The truck slid, and the trailer wagged from side to side. The hair on Wesley's arms bristled, the muscles in his legs cramped. Finally, like a child recoiling from a father's slap, he closed his eyes tight and yelled, not seeing what happened as his truck dove past the bus.

When he opened his eyes, the rig had begun to slide off the blacktop and into a roadside slough. The bumper bit a ton of mud that surfed over the windshield and roof, and the truck stopped at last. Wesley's arms and legs felt rubbery and blood-less. His head turned to the all-seeing expanse of his side mirror, which would at least miniaturize the disaster behind. No one lay in the road, though several children were cowering under the bus. Three or four heads popped up out of a roadside ditch, and he found comfort in the fact that they were looking in his direction, that perhaps there were no bodies to see. Wesley jumped to the ground, where he heard his tires hissing in the mud, and began running limp-legged to the bus. A river of powdered rubber lay on the roadway, and the air stank. The grammar school kids picked themselves up and stood silently on the grassy roadside, and he could see that no one was hurt. Standing next to the bus, trembling and accused by the young eyes, he felt a presence behind him and looked into the face of the driver, a veteran gray-haired housewife who watched him through the vent window as though he were a snake creeping on the highway. 'They'll ticket you, and you'll be back on the road again soon as you clean your pants,' she said, her face quivering with anger.

When the parish deputies showed up, they handcuffed him, and Wesley panicked, twisting against the steel loops as he sat in the backseat of the cruiser. His movement was taken, and all he could do was squirm and try not to consider what he had done. No one talked to him except to utter quick, bitten-off questions, and he longed for a helpful voice. When the deputies unlocked the gnawing cuffs at the jailhouse, Wesley shook out his arms like wings warming up for flight.

His boss claimed a favor from the sheriff and made his bail. That night about eight, Wesley drove down to Pine Oil as slowly as he could bear, found out where Janie Wiggins, the radio announcer, lived, and went to her apartment building. He was as shaky and light-headed as a convert come from a tent meeting. When he knocked on the door, a blond woman about thirty years old answered.

'Miz Janie?' he asked.

The woman examined him politely, trying to place him. She had a pleasant face that was a bit round, and bright, alert eyes. 'Do I know you?' she asked, her voice just like the one on the radio.

'I'm Wesley McBride. I met you in the meat department at McBride Mart.' He picked up his left foot and shined the top of a loafer on the back of his slacks. 'I'm one of your . . . well, fans.'

He briefly wondered if announcers on five-hundred-watt radio stations had fans. 'I've always wanted to meet you again.'

Her mouth hung open a bit, and he could see she felt complimented. 'You're the guy who does the fancy-cut rib racks. Well, I'm glad to meet you, Wesley, but I guess you ought to come by the radio station if you want to discuss advertising.'

'I don't work for the store anymore. I've got a new job, and I'd like to talk to you a little about it now, if that's all right with you. Maybe we could meet at the coffee shop down the street and sit a while.'

She looked at him harder now, studying his features. 'Talk about what?' He liked the way she ticked off her words like a northerner.

'I want to know about how you're so patient with people.' He had never once in his life thought that he would say such a thing, and he turned red.

She looked at him carefully for a moment, shrugged, and told him she would meet him for a cup of coffee in a half hour. Before she closed the door, he saw that her apartment was nearly bare, had blond paneling, cottage-cheese ceiling, rent-to-own furniture, a nubby couch.

At Slim's Coffee Hut Wesley began to tell her about himself, how he was always impatient, even as a kid, but how over the past year he'd been losing control. He showed her his shortened finger, told her about his driving and about the school bus. His hands began to sweat when he mentioned the children, and he put his palms on his knees. She reminded him of a nurse the way she listened, like someone trying to comprehend symptoms. It occurred to him that she might not be able to tell him anything.

'Let me see if I understand,' she said. 'You want to know how I can be patient with the folks that call me on the air?' He nodded. 'Well, I've got bad news for you. I was born patient. I just don't see the point in getting angry with anyone.' Wesley frowned. Was she suggesting he had some sort of birth defect? He looked down and saw grains of masonry sand in the penny slots of his loafers.

His boss, old man Morris, had given the sheriff two loads of driveway gravel to tear up Wesley's tickets, and he wanted him back on the road in a few days. Wesley wondered how long it would be before he killed someone.

'I'm sorry to bother you so late,' he said, looking into her eyes and giving her the easiest smile he could manage. 'It's just that I've been sort of waiting for things to turn around in my life. Right now, I got the feeling I can't wait any longer.'

'Oh God,' she said, her face crinkling like crepe paper, burgundy flushes coming under her eyes. 'Don't say that.'

'Say what?'

'That you're tired of waiting for things to turn around.' She put a hand palm up on the table. 'My favorite uncle used to say something close to that, over and over. Nobody knew what he really meant until we found him on his patio with a bullet in his temple.'

Wesley straightened up. 'Hey, I ain't the kind for that.'

She stood awkwardly, almost upsetting her water glass. 'I found him. You don't know how that made me feel. The missed connection.' She stared out at the street, and he saw a flash of panic in her eyes. Her expression made him think of something his father used to say: that good times never taught him one crumb of what bad times had. 'Come on,' she said, 'I want to show you something.' He followed her out, and in the middle of the block she made Wesley get into the driver's seat of her car, a boxy blue Checker, a civilian version of a taxi.

'Where'd you get this big old thing?'

'My uncle,' she explained, settling in on the passenger side. 'He said it was slow, relaxing to drive, and one of the only things that brought comfort to his life.' She rolled down the window. 'He left it to me in his will.'

'Where we going?' Wesley asked.

'Just drive around Pine Oil. I want to watch you.' So he drove down the main street a mile to the end of town as she directed. Then he drove back on a parallel street, then west again, until he had done every east-west street in the checkerboard village. She told him to pull over at the edge of town at the Yum-Yum drive-in, a cube of glass blocks left over from the fifties.

'How'd I do?'

'Awful,' she said.

Wesley thought he had never had a milder drive. The heavy Checker had floated over the city streets as though running on Valium. 'What'd I do?'

'You rode the bumper on two elderly drivers,' she told him. 'Then you signaled for dimmers from two cars who had their low beams on. And Wesley,' she said in her flutelike voice, 'six jackrabbit starts, and at the traffic light you blew your horn.'

'The old lady with the bun didn't move when the light changed.'

Her face rounded off into a tolerant smile. 'Wesley, this is Pine Oil. Nobody blows his horn at anyone else unless he spots a driver asleep on the railroad track. That woman was looking in her purse and would have noticed the light in a second. And where were *you* going? To a summit meeting?' She put her hand on his shoulder like a sister. 'You've got to pay attention to how you're doing things.' Her voice held more touch than her hand.

The fat woman wedged in the little service window of the Yum-Yum stared at them. 'Okay,' he said. 'I'll try most anything.' Janie then bought him a deluxe banana split, and even though he told her he hated bananas, she made him eat it with a flimsy plastic spoon.

Later, she made him drive the whole town, north to south, from poor brick-paper neighborhoods next to the tracks to the old, rich avenues of big drowsy houses. Janie lay back against the door, twisting a strand of hair around a finger. Finally, she asked him to take her home. When he pulled up to her apartment and turned off the motor, the quiet flowed through him like medicine.

'How do you feel, Wesley?' she asked with that voice.

'Okay, I guess. Just tired.' He felt he had dragged her huge car around town on a rope slung over his shoulder.

'You did better.' She straightened up and looked out over the long hood. 'I have no idea what's wrong with you. I just want you to know that, and I really don't think you need to see me again.' She smiled at him politely. 'Just be patient like you were when you were driving tonight. You have to wait for things to turn around.'

That's that, Wesley thought, as he helped her into the late-night air and walked her to the apartment.

The next morning he was sitting in the door of his trailer, drinking a cup of instant coffee and eating a Mars bar, wondering if he could get a job on the railroad, or even go back to work for his father. He heard the rattle and snap of gravel and saw Janie's navy-blue Checker lumber toward him through the mounds of gravel and sand. Swinging the door open quickly, she dropped from the front seat, fluffing out a full leaf-green skirt. 'Wesley, you have got to be kidding.'

'Ma'am?'

'Why're you living in a place like this? You can do better.'

He nodded slowly, taking the last bite of his candy bar and staring at her. 'My boss rented it to me the day I was hired. I guess I thought it came with the job.' In daylight, she was prettier, though he could see better the cautious cast of her eyes.

'It wasn't easy locating you, let me tell you.' She looked around at the junk as if to get her bearings, then settled her worried gaze on him. She was direct and moved precisely, unlike any woman he'd been around. 'Can you take a ride right now?' He saw the white arm move out from her side.

He put down his coffee cup. 'I reckon so. Where we going?'

She smiled. 'I like the way you say "reckon."'

Where they went was out on 51, the sluggish two-lane that bisected the parish. She had him pull up to a stop sign and wait. A pickup truck rattled by, and he started to pull out. 'Not yet,' she said.

They waited five minutes, watching lumber trucks and motor-cycles pass. Janie craned her neck and studied the southbound lane carefully. Finally she saw something that seemed to draw her interest. 'That cattle truck,' she said. 'It's perfect. Get in behind it.'

Wesley stared at the tinged sides of the slowly approaching trailer. 'Aw, no,' he pleaded.

'Follow it to Pine Oil,' she commanded as the truck packed with heaving cows rocked by. He pulled into the wall of stench and began to follow at forty miles an hour. After five miles, he begged her to let him pass.

'No,' she said. 'You'll remember this trip for the rest of your life and realize that if you can wait out this, you can wait out anything.' She turned her face to the side of the road, and the sunlight bounding off the hood brightened her high cheeks and made her beautiful. 'A road is not by itself, Wesley, even if it's empty. It's part of the people who live on it, just like a vein is part of a body. Your trouble is you think only about the road and not what might come onto it.'

He made a face but followed in silence, down through Amite, Independence, and a half a dozen redbrick and clapboard communities with countless red lights and school zones. Arriving among the low tin-and-asbestos buildings of Pine Oil, he was white-faced and nauseated.

'You look awful,' she said, leaning over, her green eyes wide. 'Does being patient upset you this much?'

'No, ma'am,' he lied.

'Well, let's see.' She had him drive to Wal-Mart and stand in the longest line to buy a can of paste wax. They went over to her apartment, where she told him to get busy waxing the car. For three hours she sat in a folding chair under a volunteer swamp maple growing by the street, watching and occasionally calling for him to go over spots he'd missed. 'Polish slower,' she called. 'Rub harder.' Wesley thought he'd like to sail the green can of wax a block down the street and tell her to go to hell, but he didn't. His face began to develop slowly in the deep blue paint of her car.

Later, she set him in a straight-back chair in her plain living room and made him read a short story in *The Atlantic* and then talk to her about it. To Wesley, this was worse than following the cattle truck. He stared down at the glossy page. What did he care about a Chinese girl who couldn't make herself look like Shirley Temple to please her mother? Then Janie drove him home and they sat in the Checker outside his trailer. He leaned over and kissed her, long and slow, once.

'Wesley,' she began, 'what did the story in the magazine mean to you?'

'Mean?' he repeated, suspicious of the word. 'I don't know.' He knew what she was doing. She was trying to make him patient enough to think.

She asked him again, this time in her nicest radio voice. He told her about the Chinese girl's guilt and about her will be independent. They talked for an hour about the story. Wesley thought he was going crazy.

The next day he did not see her, but he did listen to the radio. The topic was how to get rid of weeds in the yard. One caller, a wheezy old man, recommended pouring used motor oil along fences and sidewalks.

'But Mr McFadgin,' Janie began, using her most patient voice, 'used motor oil is full of toxic metals such as lead.'

'That's right, missy,' the old man said. 'Kills them weeds dead.'

Wesley listened to her program for three hours and did not become enraged once.

The following night she called him to meet her at the Satin Lounge, a sleepy nightclub for middle-aged locals next to the motel. In a blue dress with a full skirt, she looked like a schoolteacher, which was all right with Wesley. They talked, Wesley about his father trying to control his life and Janie about her uncle, how he had raised her, how he had left her alone. They ordered a second round of drinks, and Janie did not test him for patience for an hour. Then, someone played a slow number on the jukebox, and she stood up and asked him to dance. 'Now slow down,' she said, after they had been on the floor about ten seconds. 'This is not a Cajun two-step. Barely move your feet. Dance with your hips and shoulders.' He felt the controlling movement of her arms, of her soft voice, and realized that she was leading. After a while – he didn't know how it happened – he was leading again, but slowly. He felt like a fly struggling in sap, but he willed himself to dance like this all the way through the lengthy song.

Later on, two men sat at a table next to them. One was round and bearded, wearing a baseball cap with *Kiss My Ass* embroidered across the crown. The other, a short man with varnished blond hair, stared at Janie and once or twice leaned over to his companion, saying something behind a hand. Wesley watched him walk over to their table. The little man smiled, showing a missing tooth. He asked Janie to dance, and when she replied in a voice that made being turned down an honor, he scowled. 'Aw, come on, sweetie. I need to hug me some woman tonight.'

'I'm sorry, but I don't want to dance right now. Maybe someone at one of the other tables would enjoy your company.' She smiled, but it was a thin smile, a fence.

He grinned stupidly and leaned over the table, placing his hands down on the damp Formica. 'That sounds like a line a crap to me, sweetie.'

Wesley caught her glance but couldn't read her face. He figured that she would want him to stay calm, to avoid an argument, to sit expressionless and benign, like a divinity student. Maybe this would be another test, like polishing her mountain of a car.

'We really would like to be alone,' she said, her confident voice weakening. The man smelled of stale cigarette smoke and beer. He looked at Wesley, who did not move, who was thinking that her voice was betraying her.

'Looks like you are alone,' he said, grabbing her wrist and giving it a playful tug.

Wesley was sitting on his emotions the way he used to sit on his little brother in a backyard fight. When he saw Janie's wrist circled by a set of nubby fingers, he said in a nonthreatening voice, 'Why don't you let her go? She doesn't want to dance.'

The blond man cocked his head back like a rooster. 'Why don't you just sit there and cross your legs, little girl.'

Wesley looked down at the table as Janie was towed over to the tile dance floor. He relaxed in his fury and watched them. The little man couldn't jitterbug, his steps had nothing to do with the music, and he cramped Janie's arms on the turns. At the end of the song, he pulled her close and said something into her ear. She pushed him away, and the little man laughed.

When she stormed over to Wesley, her face was flushed, her voice a strained monotone. 'I am so embarrassed,' she said, staring straight ahead. 'Why didn't you do something instead of just sitting there like a worm?'

Wesley felt a rush of blood fill his neck. He imagined that the back of his head was ready to blow out. 'Do you know how hard it was for me to sit here and not pop him one in the face?'

She rubbed her right arm as though it hurt. 'I felt so awkward and helpless while he was limping around out there.'

'I was being patient. The only thing that would've made the little bastard happy is if I'd whipped his ass and gotten us all pitched out on the street or arrested.'

She seemed not to hear. 'I needed help and you just sat there.' She stirred her drink with a swizzle stick but did not lift it. 'I felt abandoned.' She looked down into her lap.

Wesley's face was red, even in the dim light of the Satin Lounge, and the muscles in his neck rolled and twitched. He told himself to hold back. She wanted him patient and slow. 'Hey, no harm done. It's over.'

Janie stood up, sending her chair tumbling, and slammed her purse on the table. 'Right,' she yelled. 'It's over.'

By the time he paid the tab and ran into the parking lot, all he saw were the crimson ovals of the big Checker's taillights swerving around a distant curve. In the hot night air hung the sound of her uncle's car grinding through its gears, gaining momentum as though it might never stop.

The next morning he called Janie four times at the station, and each time she hung up on him. He sat on the sun-warmed iron steps to the trailer and tried to figure out why she was so upset. He had done what he thought she'd wanted him to do. He looked over at the abandoned locomotive buried axle-deep in the sand and shook his head.

Around eight o'clock the telephone rattled. Big Morris, his boss, was on the line. 'Hey, boy. Mount that T-Bird and fly over here. We got called on a full load of masonry sand for the south shore by nine-thirty.'

Wesley stared through a cracked window at his ten-year-old car. 'It'll be a pinch.'

'C'mon. You can do it.'

'Call Ridley.'

'He went through the windshield yesterday over in Satsuma. Be out for three weeks. Listen,' Big Morris said with the cracked and weathered voice of an old politician, 'you're my man, ain't you? You're the fastest I got.'

Wesley looked at the warped and mildewed trailer, then out at the junk stacked around it. 'I think I'm going to lay off driving for a while.'

'What? You're good at speeding gravel, son.'

'I know. That's why I'd better quit.'

Two weeks later he was cutting meat in his father's grocery store, doing a fine job trimming the T-bones and round steaks, though now and then he jammed the slicer when he hurried the boiled ham. It was a new store, and the cutting room was pleasant, with lots of fluorescent lights, red sawdust on the floor to soak up the fat, and an auto-parts calendar on the wall showing Miss Rod Bearing. He always worked the one to nine P.M. shift, but today he had to cover the morning stretch. While he was in the back pulling meat out of the cooler, he noticed a familiar voice on the janitor's boom box, and he stopped, a rib cage cocked under his arm, to listen to Janie. She was dealing with Raynelle Bullfinch, a motorcycle club president from up near the Mississippi line.

'Who cares if we don't put no mufflers on our hogs, man,' Raynelle growled. 'Last time I looked, it was a free country.'

Janie's voice slid out of the radio. 'The ordinance in Gumwood is limited to neighborhood streets, Raynelle. It wouldn't affect your driving through town.'

'Yeah, well what if one of us wants to take a leak or something, and we have to buzz in off the highway? Those fat cops in Gumwood will jump on us like bottle flies.'

'You don't think anyone should mind being inconvenienced by your racket?' The voice was a little thinner, and Wesley arched an eyebrow.

'Hey, everybody has to put up with some BS.'

'Yes, but ugly noise is—'

'Aw, what the hell do you know, girlie. You never rode a Harley. You never get out of that radio station.'

'Yes, but—'

'You got a leather jacket?'

There was a second of dead air. 'Why would I want one?' The voice was flat and poisonous. Wesley leaned closer to the radio.

Raynelle shouted out, 'What?'

Another second of dead air, and then Janie's voice splintered, tantrumlike and shrill. 'Why would I want to dress like a bull dyke who thinks the highest achievement of Western civilization is a stinking motorbike that makes a sound like gas being passed?' Wesley dropped the rib cage, then caught it up quickly at his ankles and hoisted it onto the cutting table.

'You bitch,' Raynelle screamed.

Janie said something that made Wesley sit back against the meat, hold his nub, and stare at the radio. Just then, his father came through the back door, shaking rain off his hat.

'What you frownin' at, Wes? You look like somebody just had a accident.' He began pulling off a raincoat.

'Aw hell, I don't know,' he said. Janie played a commercial and then broke for the national news. Turning on the band saw, he positioned the ribs, watching the steel flash through the meat.

The next morning Wesley tuned in the local station on a new stereo in his apartment. A male voice filled his living room, an old guy with a scratchy throat who hung up on people when they disagreed with him. Wesley was surprised, the way he'd felt when something unexpected had come into the road in front of his gravel truck. He called the station and talked with the secretary, but she wouldn't tell him anything. For two mornings he listened for Janie but heard only the disgruntled voice, a sound rough and hard-nosed, a better match for the backwoods folks of the parish than Janie could make herself be. He called her at home, but the phone had been disconnected. He went to her apartment, but it was being cleaned by a Vietnamese woman who said she was getting it ready for the next occupants. Finally, he stopped at the station, which was upstairs over Buster's Dry Cleaning, and found the manager in his littered office.

'Hey, I'm Wesley, a friend of Janie. I wonder if you could tell me how to get up with her.'

The manager, a tall, square-shouldered man in his sixties, invited him to sit down. 'I'm kind of curious about her where-abouts myself. After she lost control with a caller the other day, she just jerked the headset out of her hair and threw it. She ran down the stairs with this damned angry look on her face and I haven't seen her since.'

'Does she have any relatives around here?'

The manager looked at his desk a long time before answering. 'She moved here with an uncle when she was a kid. He had to raise her, don't ask me why. She never mentioned any parents.'

Wesley bit his cheek and thought a moment. 'She told me about the uncle.'

The manager shook his head and looked across the hall to the broadcast booth. 'She was the best voice I ever had. I don't know what happened. I don't care about what she did the other day.'

'She sounded great all right.' The two men were silent a moment, savoring Janie's words as though they were polite touches remembered on the back of the neck.

'I wish I could tell you something, Wesley, but to me, at least, she was mainly a voice. It did everything for her – it was her hands and feet.' The manager leaned closer to him and narrowed his eyes. 'After she lost her uncle, I listened to her, and she didn't sound any different.' He motioned to a dusty speaker box over his door. 'But if you looked in her eyes, you could see how everything but that voice had been taken out of her. Do you know what I mean?'

'I think so,' Wesley said, standing up to go. He tried to picture her walking in and out of the studio's dowdy tiled rooms, but he couldn't see her.

The manager followed him to the door and put a hand on his back. 'She sounded like she knew it all, didn't she?'

'She could give advice,' Wesley told him, 'but she couldn't follow it.' Together they stared through the soundproof glass at a fat man scratching his bald liver-spotted skull with the eraser of a pencil, an unfiltered cigarette bobbing on his lips as he berated a caller.

He looked for her off and on for six months, writing letters and calling radio stations throughout the South. Sometimes he'd be cutting meat, hear a voice by the display cases, and go out and search the aisles. His father tried to match him with one of the cashiers, but it didn't work out. One evening he was helping the old man clean the attic of his house on Pecan Street when they found a wooden radio behind a box of canceled checks.

Wesley studied the Atwater Kent's dials and knobs. 'You stopped using this before I was born. You reckon it still works?'

His father walked over to where Wesley knelt under a rafter. 'Don't waste your time.'

'Let's plug it into the droplight there.' He stretched to the peak of the low attic.

'You won't get anything. You need a dipole antenna.'

Wesley pulled a wire from the back and attached it to an aluminum screen door propped up sideways under the rafters. 'Didn't you tell me these old sets could bring in Europe?'

His father sighed and sat Indian-style in the attic dust next to Wesley. 'You're crazy if you think you'll find her on that,' he said. They watched the Ivorine dial build its glow, heard a low whine rise as the screen door gathered sound from the air. Outside, it was sundown, and all over the country the little stations were signing off to make room for the clear-channel fifty-thousand-watt broadcasters coming from Del Rio and New Orleans, Seattle and Little Rock. Wesley turned the knob slowly, the movement of his fingers like a clock's minute hand. He passed a station in Baton Rouge, then brought in Mexico City on a rising whistle.

'This thing's got some power,' Wesley said.

His father shook his head. 'All you'll get is junk from all over the world, especially at night. What's that?'

'*Bonjour* is French. Are we getting France?'

'Maybe Canada. It's hard to tell.' For ten minutes, as the roof timbers ticked and cooled above them, they scanned the dial for used cars in Kansas City, propaganda in Cuba, Coca-Cola in someplace where children sang a clipped language they had never heard before, the voices coming clear for a moment and then fading to other tongues even as Wesley kept his hand off the dial, the radio tuning itself, drifting through a planetful of wandering signals. And then, a little five-hundred-watter from another time zone where it was not yet sundown skipped its signal for a moment over Pine Oil, Louisiana, and Wesley heard a woman's liquid voice as she ran the tail of a talk show off toward nightfall.

'Oh, it's usually not as bad as you think it is,' she was saying.

A sour voice answered, an angry sound from the inner city.

'You're not in my shoes. How do you know what I feel?' Somewhere lightning struck, and the words began to stutter and wane. Wesley grabbed the walnut box and put his head down to the speaker.

His father let out a little groan. 'It's not her. Don't be such a fool.'

'I can't know how you feel,' the announcer said. 'But are you saying there's nothing I can tell you?'

The response was lost in a rip of static, and the woman's voice trembled away from Wesley's ears, shaking like his father's dusty hand pulling back on his hair.

The Bug Man

It was five o'clock and Felix Robichaux, the Bug Man, rolled up the long, paved drive that ran under the spreading live oaks of the Beauty Queen's house. He pulled a one-gallon tank from the bed of his little white truck and gave the pump handle five patient strokes. When a regular customer was not at home and the door was unlocked, the Bug Man was trusted to spray the house and leave the bill on the counter. Her gleaming sedan was in the drive, so he paused at the kitchen door and peered through the glass. A carafe of steaming coffee was near the sink, so he knew Mrs Malone was home from the office. When he tapped on the glass with the shiny brass tip of his spray wand, she appeared, blond and handsome in her navy suit.

'Mr Robichaux, I guess it's been a month? Good to see you.' He always thought it funny that she called him Mr, since he was five years younger, at thirty-one the most successful independent exterminator in Lafayette, Louisiana.

'You been doing all right?' He gave her a wide smile.

'You know me. Up's the same as down.' She turned to place a few dishes in the sink. He remembered that a touch of sadness lingered around the edges of nearly everything she said, around the bits and pieces she had told him about herself over the years, about her dead husband. Why she told him things, the Bug Man was not sure. He noticed that most of his customers told him their life stories eventually. He began to walk through the house, spraying a fine, accurate stream along the baseboards. He treated the windowsills, the dark crack behind the piano, her secented bathroom, the closets hung with cashmere and silk. Soon he was back in the kitchen, bending behind the refrigerator and under the sink.

'Would you like a cup of coffee?' she asked. Then, as he had done off and on for five years, he sat down with her at the walnut breakfast table and surveyed her fine backyard, which was planned more carefully than some people's lives, a yard of periwinkle beds skirting dark oaks, brick walks threading through bright, even St Augustine, and in the center an empty cabana-covered pool. The Beauty Queen had been a widow for four years and had no children. He called her the Beauty Queen because she once had told him she had won a contest; he forgot which – Miss New Orleans, maybe. Each of his customers had a nickname he shared only with his wife, Clarisse, a short, pretty brunette who worked as a teacher's aide. She liked to be near children, since she couldn't have any of her own.

'Hey,' he began, 'have you seen any bugs since the last time?'

She turned three spoons of sugar into his cup and poured his cream. He stirred. 'Just a couple around the counter.'

'Little ones, big ones, or red ones?'

'Red ones, I think. Those are wood roaches, aren't they?' She looked at him with her clear cornflower blue eyes.

'They come from outside. I'll spray around the bottom of the house.' He put a hairy arm on the table and raised the cup to his mouth, sipping slowly, inhaling the vapor. 'You don't have newspaper piled up anywhere, do you?'

She took a sip, leaving a touch of lipstick on the ivory cup. 'I quit reading the newspaper. All the bad news bothers me more than it should.'

Felix looked down into his coffee. He thought it a waste for such a fine woman to live an empty life. Clarisse, his wife, kept too busy to be sad, and she read every word in the newspaper, even police reports and the legals.

'I'd rather read sad stuff than nothing,' he said.

She looked out through the large bay window into one of her many oaks. When she turned her head, the natural highlights of her fine hair spilled into his face. 'I watch TV, everybody's anesthesia. On my day off, I shop. More anesthesia.' She glanced at him. 'You've seen my closets.'

He nodded. He had never seen so many shoes and dresses. He started to ask what she did with them all, since he guessed that she seldom went out, but he held back. He was not a friend. He was the Bug Man and had his place.

In a few minutes he finished his coffee, thanked her, and moved outside, spraying under the deck, against the house, even around the pool, where he watched his reflection in a puddle at the deep end, his dark hair and eyes, his considerable shoulders rounding under his white knit shirt. He saw his paunch and laughed, thinking of his wife's supper. Turning for the house, he saw the Beauty Queen on her second cup, watching him in an uninterested way, as though he might be a marble statue at the edge of one of her walks. He was never offended by the way she looked at him. The Bug Man lived in the modern world, where, he knew, most people were isolated and uncomfortable around those not exactly like themselves. He also believed that there was a reason people like Mrs Malone opened the doors in their lives just a crack by telling him things. He was a religious man, so everything had a purpose, even though he had no idea what. The Beauty Queen's movements and words were signals to him, road signs pointing to his future.

After Mrs Malone's coffee stop came Felix's last job of the day, the Scalsons'; he had nicknamed them 'the Slugs.' As the Bug Man, he had seen it all. Most customers let him wander unaccompanied in and out of every room in the house, through every attic and basement, as though he had no eyes. He had seen filthy sinks and cheesy bathrooms, teenagers shooting drugs, had sprayed around drunken grandfathers passed out on the floor, had once bumbled in on an old woman and a young boy having sex. They had looked at him as though he were a dog that had wandered into the room. He was the Bug Man. He was not after them.

Even so, he faced the monthly spraying of the Scalsons' peeling rental house with a queasy spirit. Father Slug met him at the door, red-faced, a quart bottle of beer in his hand. 'Come on in, Frenchie. I hope you got some DDT in that tank. The sons of bitches come back a week after you sprayed last time.'

'I'll give it an extra squeeze,' Felix told him. But he realized that the entire house would have to be immersed in a tank of Spectracide to get rid of the many insects crawling over the oily paper bags of garbage stacked around the stove. When he opened the door under the sink, the darkness writhed with German roaches.

He finished in the kitchen, then walked into the cheaply paneled living room, where Mr Scalson was arguing with a teenaged son, Bruce.

'It won't my fault,' the son screamed.

Mr Scalson grabbed the boy's neck with one of his big rubbery hands and slapped him so hard with the other that his son's nose began to bleed. 'You shoulda never been born, you little shit,' he told him.

Felix Robichaux sprayed around the two men as though they were a couple of chairs and went on. He glanced out the window, to see Mrs Scalson burning a pile of dirty disposable diapers in the backyard, stirring them with a stick. In an upstairs bedroom, he found the round-shouldered daughter playing a murderous video game on an old television that was surrounded by half-eaten sandwiches and bowls of wilted cereal. In another room, the sour-smelling grandfather was watching a pornographic movie while drinking hot shots of supermarket bourbon.

The tragedy of the Scalsons was that they didn't have to be what they were. The grandfather and father held decent jobs in the oil fields. Their high school diplomas hung in the den. Yet the only thing the Bug Man ever saw them do was argue and then sulk in their rooms, waiting like garden slugs dreaming of flowers to kill.

Felix Robichaux lived on what was left of the family homestead outside of Lafayette. The house was a white frame situated a hundred yards off the highway, one big pecan tree in front and a live oak out back between the house and barn. Rafts of trimmed azaleas floated on a flat lake of grass. He thought the shrubs looked like circles of children gossiping at recess. He ate his wife's supper, a smoky chicken stew, and helped her clear the dishes from the Formica table. While she washed them under a noisy cloud of steam, he swept the tile floor and put away the spices. Then they went out on the front porch and sat on the yellow spring-iron chairs that had belonged to his father.

Clarisse and Felix lived like a couple whose children had grown and moved out. They felt accused by the absence of children, by their idleness in the afternoons, when they felt they should be tending to homework or helping at play. They had tried for all their married life, ten years, had gone to doctors as far away as Houston, and still their extra bedrooms stayed empty, their nights free of the fretful, harmless sobs of infants. They owned a big Ford sedan, which felt vacant when they drove through the country-side on idle weekends. They were short, small-boned people, so even their new motorboat seemed empty the day they first anchored in a bayou to catch bream and to talk about where their childless lives were going. Overhead, silvery baby egrets perched in the branches of a bald cypress, and minnows flashed in the dark waters, sliding like time around the boat's hull.

Clarisse stared from their porch to the pecans forming in the branches of the tree in their front yard. She slowly ran her white fingers through the dark curls at the back of her neck. Felix watched her pretty eyes, which were almost violet in the late-afternoon light, and guessed at what she would say next. She asked him whose house he had sprayed first, and he laughed.

'I started out with Boatman.'

'That's Melvin Laurent. A new one?'

He nodded. 'Then Fish, Little Neg, Mr Railroad, the Termite Twins.' He stared high into the pecan tree and flicked a finger up for each name. 'Beauty Queen and the Slugs.'

She put her hand on his arm. 'You should call them Beauty Queen and the Beasts,' she said.

'I spray the Beasts tomorrow.'

'That's right.' Clarisse crossed her slim legs and held up a shoe to examine the toe. 'It's too bad Mrs Malone doesn't get married again. Just from the couple times I saw her working down at the bank, I could tell she's got a lot to offer.'

Felix pursed his lips. 'Yeah, but she needs a lot, too. You ought to hear all the droopy-drawers talk she lays out in the afternoon. Everything's sad with her, everything gets her down. She lost too much when her husband got killed.' He thought of the Beauty Queen's eyes and what they might tell him.

'You think she's good-looking still?'

'Talk about.'

She stared off at the highway, where a truck full of hay grumbled off toward the west. 'Too bad we can't fix her up with somebody.'

He rolled his eyes at her and put his hand on hers. 'We don't know the kind of people she needs. What, you gonna get her a date with Cousin Ted?'

'Get off your high horse. Ted's all right since he's going to AA and got his shrimp boat back from the finance company.' She pulled her hand away. 'I could call names on your side, too.'

As the lawn grew long in shadow, they brewed up a playful argument until the mosquitoes drove them inside, where their good cheer subsided in the emptiness of the house.

For the rest of the month he sprayed his way through the homes of the parish, getting the bugs out of the lives of people who paid him no more attention than they would a housefly, and on the thirty-first, in the subdivision where the Beauty Queen lived, he visited a new customer, a divorced lawyer named McCall. Even though it was the first time he had sprayed there, Felix was left alone by the tall, athletic attorney, who let him wander at will through the big house he had leased. Felix took his time in the living room so he could watch McCall and size him up. He sprayed in little spurts and stopped several times to pump up. The lawyer smiled at him and asked if he followed pro football.

'Oh yeah,' the Bug Man said. 'I been following the poor Saints since day one.'

The other man laughed. 'Me too. You know, I handled a case for a Saints player once. He sued a fan who came into the stadium tunnel after a game and bit him on the arm.'

'No kidding?' Felix was fascinated at the story of a human insect, a biting football fan. He stayed a half hour and drank a beer with Dave McCall, discovering where he was from, what he did for fun, what he didn't do. After all, why wouldn't the lawyer tell him things? He was the Bug Man, who might not ever come again. The round little Cajun listened in his invisibility to things that might have significance.

'You should meet Mrs Malone,' he found himself saying. He had no idea why he said this, but it was as if a little blue spark popped behind his eyes and the sentence came out by itself, appearing like a letter with no return address. 'She's a former beauty queen and a real nice lady.' The lawyer smiled, seeming to think, What a friendly, meaningless offering. His smile was full and shining with tolerance, and Felix endured the smile, knowing he had done something important, had planted a seed, maybe.

On the fifteenth, he watered the seed when he had coffee with Mrs Malone. She seemed empty, gray around the eyes, offering him only a demitasse, as though trying to hurry him off, though she was not brusque or distant. There was no need to spend brusqueness or distance on the Bug Man.

'You know,' he began, delivering his rehearsed words carefully, 'you ought to get out more.'

She showed him a slim line of wonderful teeth. 'I guess I do what I can.'

He took a sip of coffee. 'There's a single man your age just moved in down the street. I met him the other day and he hit me as being a nice guy. He's a lawyer.'

'Are lawyers nice guys, Mr Robichaux?'

The question derailed his train of thought. 'Well, not all of them. But you know . . . uh, what was I talking about?'

'A new man in the neighborhood.'

'Single man.' He had run out of coffee; he tilted his cup

to stare into it and then looked at the carafe. She poured him another sip. 'I sprayed Buffa – I mean, Mrs Boudreaux – this morning, and she said there was gonna be a neighborhood party at the Jeansonnes' tomorrow. This guy's supposed to be there.'

'So you think I should check him out?' She wiggled her shoulders when she said 'check him out,' and Felix was worried that she was making fun of him.

'He's an awful nice man. Good-lookin', as far as I can tell.'

'Would your wife, Clarisse, think he was good-looking?'

He bit his lip at that. 'Clarisse thinks I'm good-looking,' he said at last, and the Beauty Queen laughed.

That night Clarisse and Felix sat on their porch and listened to the metallic keening of tree frogs. The neighbors had just gone home with their two young children and Felix put his hand on a damp spot near his collar where the baby had drooled. He caught the cloth between his fingers and held it as though it contained meaning. Clarisse sat with her left arm across her chest and her right fist on her lips. 'If we had had a little girl, I wonder who she would have looked like.'

'Dark curly hair and eyes deep like a well,' he said. The frogs in the yard subsided as he spoke. They sometimes did that, as though wanting to listen.

After a long while, she said, 'Too bad,' a comment that could have been about a thousand different things. One by one the frogs commenced their signals, and the moon came out from behind a cloud like a bright thought. Across the road a door opened and a mother's voice sang through the silvery light, spilling onto the lawn a two-note call – 'Ke-vin' – playful but strong, and then, 'Come out of the dark. You've got to come out of that dark.'

The next week he showed up off schedule at Mrs Malone's house, later than usual, and found her in the backyard looking at the empty pool.

'Since the weather's been so damp, I thought I'd give a few sprays around while I was in the neighborhood.'

She nodded at him as he walked by her and began spraying the cracks in the pool apron. 'I appreciate the service,' she told him, a hint of something glad lingering around her mouth.

'Uh, you been goin' out any? You know, chase the blues away?' He drew a circle in the air as if to circumscribe the blues.

'Thinking about it,' she said, hiding her mouth behind a ringless white hand.

'Yeah, but don't think too long,' he said. 'Might be time to check it out.' He wiggled his shoulders and blushed. The Beauty Queen bit a nail and turned her back on him slowly.

When he sprayed the lawyer's house, he spent an hour with him, marveling at both Mr McCall's charm and two bottles of imported beer.

Three weeks later the Bug Man went down to LaBat's Lounge for a beer after supper. As he was driving down Perrilloux Street, he passed the Coachman Restaurant, an expensive steak house. He saw a BMW parked at the curb, and stepping out of it smoothly were the long legs of Mrs Malone. The lawyer was holding her door and looking like he had been cut with scissors out of a men's fashion magazine. In the short time he had to look, Felix strained to see her face. It was full of light and the Beauty Queen was smiling, all unpleasant thought hidden for the night at least. Her blond hair spilled over her dark dress, and at the throat was a rill of pearls. The Bug Man drove on, watching them in his rearview mirror as they entered the brass door of the restaurant. When he reached LaBat's old plywood barroom, he drank a Tom Collins instead of a beer, lost three dollars in the poker machine and won four in a game of pool with two cousins from Grand Crapaud, and for the rest of the night celebrated his luck.

The next day was the fifteenth, and Mrs Malone served him coffee and no sad talk, but not one morsel of what was going on between her and the lawyer. And the Bug Man could not ask. He made himself satisfied with the big cup of strong coffee she fixed for him and the sight of the new makeup containers on the vanity in her bedroom. He finished up carefully and went to spray the Slugs'. Even the visible stench of the Slugs' bathrooms could not dampen a deep, subtle excitement Felix felt, almost the anticipation and hope a farmer feels after he has put in a crop, a patient desire for a green future.

Mr and Mrs Scalson were having an argument as Felix was trying to spray the kitchen. She got her husband down on the floor and beat at him with a flat-heeled shoe. Her lip was split and her brows and cheeks were curdled and swollen. Mr Scalson broke away from her, grabbed a pot of collard greens from the stove, and slung it, hitting her in the legs. The screaming was a worse pollutant than all the rotten food stacked against the stove. Felix watched the greens fly across the floor, the water splashing under the cabinets, a hunk of salt meat coming to rest under the table, where he knew it would stay for a week. The young daughter ran into the kitchen, a headset tangled in her hair, and began pulling ice from the refrigerator for her mother's burns. The Bug Man left without waiting to be paid, jogging down the drive toward his white truck, which waited, scoured and shiny, a reminder that some things can be kept orderly and clean.

The summer months rolled into August, and Felix Robichaux mixed his mild, subtle concoctions, spraying them around the parish in the homes of good and bad people, talking to anybody, drinking anyone's coffee, and seeing into private lives like the eye of God, invisible and judging. He began using a new mixture, which was odorless and, unlike the old formula, left no cloudy spots or drips, and now there was even less evidence that he had been in the world, had passed along the ways of people's lives, and that was all right with him.

He became even more curious about Mrs Malone, and he stepped over the understood boundary between them to ask about Mr McCall with a directness that made her eyes flick up at him. There was no doubt that for weeks she had been a happy woman, asking about Clarisse, telling him about plans for putting her pool back in service, since she'd found out that the lawyer liked to swim.

But then there was a change. In mid-August she let him in without speaking, going to the sink and doing dishes left over from the day before. While he was spraying the living room, he heard her gasp and drop one of her expensive plates to the tile floor. He put his face in the kitchen doorway.

'Let me clean that up for you,' he said. 'I know where the dustpan's at.'

'Thank you. I'm a bit shaky today.' Her color was good, he noticed, but there was a worried cast to her usually direct, clear eyes. He knelt and carefully swept the fragments into a dustpan, then he wet a paper towel and patted the floor for splinters of china.

'You want me to make you some coffee?' he asked.

She put her head down a bit and shaded her eyes. 'Yes,' she said.

The Bug Man set up the coffeemaker, then sprayed the rest of the house while the machine dripped a full pot. When he came back, she had not moved. He knew where the cups and the spoons were in hundreds of houses, and the first cabinets he opened showed him what he wanted.

'What's gone wrong?' he asked, pouring her a cup.

'Oh, it's nothing. I'm just not myself today.' She crossed her legs slowly and pulled at her navy skirt.

'Mr McCall been around?'

'Mr McCall has not been around,' she said flatly. 'He tells me he will never be around.'

The Bug Man shook his head slowly. Mrs Malone and the lawyer looked like the elegant, glittering people on the soap operas his mother watched, people he could never figure out. He was not an educated man and had never set foot in a country club unless it was having a roach problem, but he guessed that many wealthy people were complicated and refined, that those qualities made it harder for them to be happy. But he had no notion of why this was so. He thought of Clarisse, and felt lucky. 'I'm sorry to hear that,' was all he could think of to say. 'I thought you two were hitting it off real good.'

She grabbed a napkin from the table and began crying then. Embarrassed, he looked around the kitchen, raised his hands, then dropped them. 'Yes,' she said, and then she looked at him with such an intensity that he glanced away. He could have sworn that she really *saw* him. 'We've been hitting it off very well. I thought David was a little like my late husband.' She looked toward the backyard, but her gaze seemed to waver. 'I thought he was a man who carried things through.'

'Aw, Mrs Malone, these things have a way of working out, you know?'

'I'm pregnant,' she told him. 'And David wants nothing to do with me.'

Felix Robichaux took a swallow of hot coffee, opened his mouth to say something, but his mind was blasted clean by what she had said. A light seemed to come on in the back of his head. 'What are you going to do?' he said at last.

'I'm not sure, exactly.' She narrowed her gaze and watched him carefully. 'Why?' He scooted back his chair and ran his left hand down his white uniform shirt, his fingers pausing just a second on the green embroidery of his last name.

'I mean, do you think you'll keep it or give it up for adoption or what?' His eyes grew wide and he slid his round bottom to the edge of the chair.

Her voice chilled a bit with suspicion. 'I shouldn't be discussing this with you.' She looked down at the glossy tile.

'Mrs Malone, Clarisse and me, we've been trying for years to have a baby, and if you're going to give up the one you got, we'd be happy to get it, let me tell you.' The Bug Man was blushing as he said this, as though he was trying to become intimate and was unsure how to proceed.

The Beauty Queen straightened up in her chair. 'We're not talking about a cast-off sofa here, Mr Robichaux.'

'Mrs Malone, don't get mad. You know I'm just a bug man and can't talk like a lawyer or a businessman.' He opened his thick palms toward her. 'Just think about it, that's all.'

She stood and held the door open for him, and he picked up his tank and walked outside. 'I'll see you in a month,' she said. When she closed the door, the smell of her exquisite perfume fanned onto the stoop. For a moment, it overcame the smell of bug spray in Felix's clothes.

For the next month he made his rounds with a secretive lightness of spirit, not telling Clarisse anything, though it was hard in the evenings not to explain why he held her hand with a more ardent claim, why he would suddenly spring up and walk to the edge of the porch to look in the yard for something, maybe a good place to put a swing set. The closer the days wound down to the fifteenth of the month, the more hopeful and fearful he became. When he sprayed the lawyer's house, McCall let him in without looking at him, disappearing into a small office upstairs, leaving him alone in the expensive, empty house. The Bug Man decided to name him Judas.

Finally, at a little before five on the fifteenth, the Beauty Queen let him in, and he went about his business quickly, finishing, as usual, by spraying under the sink in the kitchen. He noticed that she had prepared no coffee. He looked for her in the hall and in the living room, retracing his route, giving embarrassed little shots in corners as though he was going over a poor job. He found her in the bedroom, with her back against the headboard, reading a book.

'I left a check for you on the counter,' she said.

'I saw it. How you doin', Mrs Malone?'

'I'm fine.' But the stiffness of her mouth and the deep-set hurt in her eyes said otherwise. She rested the book on top of her dress, a dark print with lilies against a black background. 'Is there something you forgot to spray?'

'Yes, ma'am. Usually I mist under your bed. Every now and then you leave a snack plate and a glass under the edge.' He got down on his knees, adjusted the nozzle on the tip of his wand, and sprayed. 'You decided what to do about the baby yet?' He wondered if she sensed the wide gulf of anticipation behind the question.

'I'm having an abortion tomorrow,' she said at once, as though she was reading a sentence from the book in her lap.

His thumb slipped off the lever of his sprayer. He was frozen on his knees at the foot of her bed. 'It would be such a fine baby,' he said, straightening his back and staring at her across a quilted cover. 'You, a beauty-contest winner, and him, a good-looking lawyer. What a baby that would make.' He began to say things that made his face burn, and he felt like a child who had set his heart on something, only to be told that he could never have what he wanted. 'Clarisse would be so happy,' he said, trying to smile.

Mrs Malone drew up her legs and glared at him. 'Mr Robichaux, what would you do with such a baby? It wouldn't be like you and Clarisse. It would look nothing like you.'

He stayed on his knees and watched her, wondering if she had planned a long time to say what she had said. He reflected on the meanness of the world and how for the first time he was unable to deal with it. 'It'd mean a lot to us' was all he could tell her.

'It would be cruel to give this child to you. Why can't you see that?' For a moment her face possessed the blank disdain of a marble statue in her backyard. 'Would you please just get out,' she said, looking down at her book and balling a white fist against her forehead.

The Bug Man left the house, forgetting to close the door, feeling his good nature bleed away until he was as hollow as a termite-eaten beam. In twenty minutes, as he pulled into the littered drive of the Scalsons', his feelings had not changed. He was late, and the Slugs were seated at their hacked table, arguing bitterly over parts of a fried chicken. Felix stood in the door, pumping up his tank, looking into the yellowed room at the water-stained ceiling, the spattered walls, the torn and muddy linoleum, the unwashed and squalling Scalsons. The grandfather dug through the pile of chicken, cursing the children for eating the livers. The mother was pulling the skins from every piece and piling them on her plate while the children gave each other greasy slaps. They tore at their food like yard animals, spilling flakes of crust and splashes of slaw under the table. 'Gimme a wing, you little son of a bitch,' Mr Scalson growled to his son.

'It doesn't have to be like this,' Felix said, and everyone turned, noticing him for the first time.

'Well, I'll be damned. It's the Frenchman. You must have water in that tank of yours, because the bugs have been all over us the past month. What'd I pay you good money for anyway, Shorty?'

Ever since he had opened the door the Bug Man had been pumping his tank, five, ten, twenty strokes. He adjusted the nozzle to deliver a sharp stream, pressed the lever, and peeled back Mr Scalson's left eyelid. The heavy man let out a yell and Felix began spraying them all in their faces, across their chests, the grandfather in the mouth with drilling streams of roach killer. The family sat stupidly for several moments, sputtering and calling out when they were sprayed again in the eyes as though being washed clean of some foul blindness. One by one the Scalsons scampered to their feet. The father swung at the Bug Man, who ducked and then cracked him across the nose with his spray wand. The grand-father came at him with an upraised chair, and the Bug Man snapped the brass wand across the top of his head, leaving a red split in the dull meat of his skull.

The next evening the weather was mild, and at dusk Felix and Clarisse were sitting in the yellow spring-iron chairs, whose backs were flattened metal flowers. He had told her everything, and together they were staring at a few late fireflies winking on the lawn like the intermittent hopes of defeated people. Across the road a mother called her child for the second time, and they watched for him as he bobbed out of a field.

In the house the telephone rang, and Felix got up slowly. It was Mrs Malone, and she sounded upset.

'What can I do for you?' he asked. He twisted the phone cord around his fist and closed his eyes.

'I was in the clinic waiting room this afternoon,' she began, her voice stiff and anesthetized, 'and I read the local newspaper's account of the attack.'

He winced when she said 'attack' and looked down at the dustless hardwood of his living room. 'I'm real sorry about that.' He thought of the expression on his wife's face when she had brought the money for his bail.

'And you did it right after you left my house,' she said, her voice rising. 'I didn't know what to think.'

'Yes, ma'am.' He listened to her breaths coming raggedly over the phone for at least a half minute, but he didn't know what else to say. He wasn't sure why he had hurt the Scalsons. At the time, he had wanted to keep them from damaging the world further.

'I don't want you to work for me anymore. I just can't have you in the house.'

'I wouldn't bother you again, Mrs Malone.'

'No.' The word came quick as a shot. 'You'll stay away.'

And that was it.

The Bug Man went back to his work at dawn, and for that day and every workday for the next ten years he walked through houses and lives. His business expanded until he had to hire three easygoing local men to spray bugs with him. He erected a small building with a storage area and office, hiring a young woman to manage appointments and payments. Clarisse attended the local college, became a first-grade teacher, and labored in her garden of children. With his spare time he began attending a local exercise club and soon lost his bulky middle, though much of his hair left with it.

Felix had been thirty-seven when the other independent exterminator in town decided to sell the business to him. These new routes were profitable, and Joe Brasseaux, Felix's best sprayer, tended them religiously, never missing an appointment for two years, except for one day when he called in sick. Felix looked over Joe's route for the afternoon, and when he saw the addresses, he decided to treat the houses himself.

About four o'clock, he pulled into the long drive that led to the Beauty Queen's house. Getting out of the truck, he looked up at the oaks, which had changed little, and at the pool in back, which swirled with bright water. The plantings were mature and lush, rolling green shoulders of liriope bordering everything.

The driveway was empty, but in the door was a key with a pair of small plastic dice hanging from it. He rang the bell and bent down to pump up his tank. When he raised his face, the door opened, and standing there was a young boy with sandy hair and blue eyes, a boy with a dimpled chin, an open, intelligent face, and, Felix noticed, big feet. 'Yes, sir?' the child said, adjusting the waistband on what appeared to be a soccer uniform.

For a moment, Felix couldn't speak. He wanted to reach out and feel the top of the boy's head, but he pointed to his tank instead. 'I've come to spray for bugs.'

'Where's Joe? Joe's the one takes care of that for us.'

The Bug Man looked inside hopefully. 'Is your mother Mrs Malone?'

'She's not here, and I'm sorry, but she told me not to let in anyone I don't know.' The boy must have noticed how Felix was staring, and stepped back.

'You don't have to be afraid of me.' Felix gave him his widest smile, all the while studying the child. 'I'm the Bug Man.'

The boy narrowed his bright eyes. 'No sir. Not to me you aren't. You'd better go away.'

At once he felt shriveled and sick, like a sprayed insect, and he wondered whether he should tell the boy that he knew his mother, that he knew who he was, but the Bug Man was by now a veteran of missed connections and could tell when a train had left a station without him. He scanned the child once more and turned away.

Pulling out of the drive, he saw in the rearview a small fair-skinned figure standing on the steps, looking after him, but not really seeing him, he guessed. He allowed himself this one glance. One glance, he decided, was what he could have.

Little Frogs in a Ditch

Old man Fontenot watched his grandson draw hard on a slim cigarette and then flick ashes on the fresh gray enamel of the front porch. The boy had been fired, this time from the laundry down the street. The old man, who had held only one job in his life, and that one lasting forty-three years at the power plant, did not understand this.

'The guy who let me go didn't have half the brains I got,' Lenny Fontenot said.

The old man nodded, then took a swallow from a warm can of Schlitz. 'The owner, he didn't like you double-creasing the slacks' was all he said, holding back. He watched a luminous cloud drifting up from the Gulf.

'Let me tell you,' Lenny said with a snarl, his head following a dusk-drawn pigeon floating past the screen, 'there's some dumb people in this world. Dog-dumb.'

The grandfather rolled his head to the side. Lenny was angry about his next paycheck, the one he'd never get.

'They was dumber back in my time,' the grandfather told him.

Lenny cocked his head. 'What you talking about? People today can't even spell *dumb*.' He pointed two fingers holding the cigarette toward the laundry. 'If it wouldn't be for dumb people, modern American business couldn't keep doing its thing selling fake fingernails and fold-up fishing rods.'

'Give it a rest,' the old man said, looking down the street to the drizzle-washed iron roof of the laundry, where a lazy spume of steam rose from the roof vent. His grandson was living with him again, complaining of the evils of capitalism, eating his food, using all the hot water in the mornings. The grandfather pulled a khaki cap over his eyes and leaned back in his rocker, crossing his arms over a tight green knit shirt. Lenny would never hold a job because he suffered from inborn disrespect for anybody engaged in business. Everybody was stupid. All businessmen were crooks. At twenty-five his grandson had the economic sense of a sixty-year-old Russian peasant.

'No. Really. Other than food and stuff you need to live, what do you really have to buy?' He took a searing drag on the last of six cigarettes he had borrowed from his girlfriend, Annie. 'A car? Okay. Buy a white four-door car, no chrome, no gold package, no nothing. But wait. Detroit wants you to feel bad if you buy a plain car. You got to have special paint. You got to have a stereo makes you feel Mr Mozart is pluckin' his fiddle in the backseat. You got to have a big-nuts engine for the road. You got to have this, you got to have that, until that car costs as much as a cheap house. If you buy a plain car, you feel like a donkey at the racetrack.'

His grandfather took a swig of Schlitz. 'If you work on your attitude a little bit, you could keep a job.'

Lenny stood up and put his nose to the screen, sniffing, as if the grandfather's statement had a bad odor. 'I can keep a job if I wanted. I'm a salesman.'

'You couldn't sell cow cakes to a rosebush.' The old man was getting tired. His grandson had been out on the porch with him for two hours now, pulling cigarettes from his baggy jeans, finding fault with everybody but his skinny, shaggy-haired self.

Lenny threw down his cigarette and mashed it with the toe of a scuffed loafer. 'As dumb as people are today I could sell bricks to a drowning man.'

Grandfather Fontenot looked at the smudge on his porch. 'No, you couldn't.'

'I could sell falsies to a nun.'

'No, you couldn't.'

'I could sell' – Lenny's mouth hung open a moment as he looked down into the cemented side yard and toward the old wooden carport at the rear of the lot – 'a pigeon.'

His grandfather picked up his hat and looked at him. 'Who the hell would buy a pigeon?'

'I could find him.'

'Lenny, if someone wanted a pigeon, all he'd have to do is catch him one.'

'A dumb man will buy a pigeon from *me*.' He pushed open the screen door and clopped down the steps to the side yard. At the rear of the lot was a broad, unused carport, swaybacked over useless household junk: window fans, a broken lawn mower, and a wheelbarrow with a flat tire. He looked up into the eaves where the ragged nests of pigeons dripped dung down the side of a beam. With a quick grab, he had a slate blue pigeon in his hands, the bird blinking its onyx eyes stupidly. He turned to his grandfather, who was walking up stiffly behind him. 'Look. You can pluck them like berries under here.'

Old man Fontenot gave him a disgusted look. 'Nobody'll eat a pigeon.'

Lenny ducked his head. 'Eat. I ain't said nothing about eat.' He smiled down at the bird. 'This is a homing pigeon.'

The grandfather put a hand on Lenny's shoulder. 'Look, let's go fix a pot of coffee and open up the *Picayune* to the employment ads. We can find something good for you to do. Come on. That thing's got fleas like a politician. Put it down.' The old man pulled at his elbow.

Lenny's eyes came up red and glossy. 'Your Ford's got a crack in the head and you can't even drive across the bayou for groceries. I'm gonna sell birds and get the damn old thing fixed.'

His grandfather sniffed but said nothing. He knew Lenny wanted the car for himself. He looked at the bird in his grandson's hands, which was pedaling the air, blinking its drop of dark eye. The old man had never owned a dependable automobile, had always driven junk to save money for his kids and grandkids. He remembered a Sunday outing to Cypress Park when his superannuated Rambler gave up in the big intersection at Highway 90 and Federal Avenue, remembered the angry horn of a cab, the yells of his son and wife as they argued about a tow truck fee while Lenny sat on the floor by a misshapen watermelon he had stolen with care from a neighbor's garden for the picnic that never happened.

'This bird,' Lenny said, turning it back into its nest, 'is gonna get your car running.'

'I told your parents I wouldn't let you get in any more trouble.' He watched Lenny make a face. Maybe his parents couldn't care less. The grandfather remembered the boy's big room in their air-conditioned brick rancher, the house they sold from under him to buy a Winnebago and tour the country. They had been gone four months and had not called once.

For two days he watched Lenny sink deeper and deeper into a red overstuffed sofa, a forty-year-old thing his wife had won at a church bingo game. It was covered with a shiny, almost adhesive plastic, broadly incised with X's and running with dark, fiery swirls. The big cushions under Lenny hissed as he moved down into the sofa's sticky grasp. For Lenny, sitting in it must have been like living with his parents again. They were hardworking types who tried to make him middle-class and respectable, who frowned on his efforts to manage the country's only Cajun punk salsa band, which was better, at least, than his first business of selling cracked birdseed to grammar school kids as something he called 'predope,' or 'pot lite.' One day Lenny had come home from a long weekend and everything he owned was stacked under the carport, a SOLD sign in front of the house. For a long while, he had lived with his friends in Los Head-Suckers, but even the stoned longhairs tired of his unproductive carping and one by one had turned him out.

Lenny folded back the classified section to the pet column and found his ad, which read 'Homing pigeons, ten dollars each. Training instructions included,' and gave the address. His grandfather read it over his shoulder, then went into the kitchen and heated two links of boudin for breakfast and put on a pot of quick grits. Lenny came in and looked over at the stove.

'You gonna cook some eggs? Annie likes eggs.'

'She coming over again?' He tried to sound miffed, but in truth, he liked Annie. She was a big-boned lathe operator who worked in a machine shop down by the river, but he thought she might be a civilizing influence on his grandson.

Lenny rumbled down the steps, and his grandfather watched him through the kitchen window. From behind the carport he pulled a long-legged rabbit cage made of a coarse screen called hardware cloth, and two-by-two's. He shook out the ancient pellets and set it next to the steps. With his cigarette-stained fingers, he snatched from the eaves a granite-colored pigeon and clapped him in the cage. Most of the other birds lit out in a *rat-tat-tat* of wings, but he managed to snag a pink-and-gray, which flapped out of its nest into his waiting hands. The old man clucked his tongue and turned up the fire under the peppery boudin.

Annie came up the rear steps, lugging a rattling toolbox. By the time Lenny came in and joined her, the old man had finished breakfast and was seated in the den beyond the kitchen. He didn't like being with both of them at the same time, because he felt sorry for the girl. He didn't understand how she could put up with Lenny's whining. Maybe he was the only man who would pay attention to her. She got a second helping and sat at the breakfast table, spooning grits and eggs into herself.

'Annie, baby.' Lenny plopped down across from her.

'I saw that ad. The one you told me about.' She broke open a loaf of French bread. 'Why would anybody buy a pigeon? They're all over the place. Our backyard shed's full of 'em.' She flipped her fluffy blond hair over her shoulders. 'What are you trying to do?' she asked. 'Prove something?' She looked up from her plate, her square jaw rising and falling under her creamy skin.

'I want to scare up some money to fix the old guy's car.'

'And what else?' She chased a lump of grits out of a cheek with her tongue and brought her large cobalt eyes to bear on his.

He bunched his shoulders. 'I don't know. It might be fun to see people throw away their money. You know. Like people do.'

'You maybe want to find out why they do it? Or maybe you're just mad you don't have any to throw away. Am I reading your mind?'

He looked down at the table, shaking his head. 'We been going out too long.'

A voice came from the den. 'I'll buy fifty shares a that.'

Lenny spoke loudly. 'I mean, she knows how I think.' He put a hand palm up on the little table. 'It's just that people throw money away on crazy stuff. It bothers the hell out of me. I could live for a year on what some people spend on a riding lawn mower or a red motorbike.'

Annie took another bite and studied him. 'You don't understand this?'

He looked away from her. 'The more they get, the more they spend.'

She put down her fork and glanced at her watch. She had to be down at Tiger Island Propeller by nine. 'Lenny, in high school this teacher made the class read a play about an old guy was a king. I mean, it was hard reading, and she had to explain it or we wouldn'ta got much out of it, but this old guy gave his kingdom away to his two bitchy daughters with the reserve that he could keep about a hundred old fishing buddies around to pass the time with. After a while one daughter gets pissed at all the racket around the castle and cuts his pile of buddies to fifty. Well, he hits the road to his other daughter's place, and guess what?'

Lenny looked at the ceiling. 'She gives him his fifty guys back and sucks the eyeballs out of the other bitch's head, right?'

Annie blinked. 'You got snakes in your skull, man.' She raised a thick hand and pretended to slap him. 'Pay attention. This second daughter cuts him back to twenty-five and the old man blows a gasket and calls her a dozen buzzards and like that. Then the first daughter shows up and says, "Look, what you want with ten, five, or even one old buddy? You don't really *need* 'em."'

Lenny snorted. 'Damned straight. What'd he say to that?'

Annie ducked her head. 'He told them even a bum had some-thing he didn't need, even if it was a fingernail clipper. That if he only had the things he needed, he'd be like a possum or a cow.'

Lenny made a face. 'What's that mean?'

The voice from the den called out, 'When's the last time you saw a possum on a red motorbike?'

'What?'

Annie put a calloused hand on one of his. 'An animal can't own nothing. Wouldn't want to. Owning things is what makes people different from the armadillos, Lenny. And the stuff we buy, even if it's one of your pigeons, sometimes is like a little tag telling folks who we are.'

He turned sideways in his chair. 'I don't believe that for a minute. If I buy a Cadillac, does that tell people I'm high-class?'

Again the voice from the den: 'You could buy a pack of weenies.'

'I said a Cadillac,' Lenny shouted.

Annie Meyer stood up and pulled on a denim cap. 'Time for work,' she announced. 'Walk me to the bus stop.' She put her arm through his. 'Hear from the parents any?'

He shook his head. 'Nothin'. Not a check, not a postcard.'

The grandfather followed them with a plastic bag of trash in his hand. When they reached the street, they saw a white-haired gentleman standing there staring at a torn swatch of newsprint. He was wearing nubby brown slacks and a green checkered cowboy shirt. He stuck out his hand palm down and Lenny wagged it.

'I'm Perry Lejeune from over by Broussard Street. About ten blocks. I saw your ad.'

Mr Fontenot gave his grandson a scowl and pulled off his cap as if he would toss it.

Lenny straightened out of his slouch and smiled, showing his small teeth. 'Mr Lejeune, you know anything about homing pigeons?'

The other man shook his head once. 'Nah. My little nephew Alvin's living at my house and I want to get him something to occupy his time. His momma left him with me and I got to keep him busy, you know?' Mr Lejeune raised his shoulders. 'I'm too old to play ball with a kid.'

'Don't worry, I'll fill you in,' he said, motioning for everyone to follow him to the back of the lot next to the junk-filled carport. He put his hand on the rabbit cage and made eye contact with Mr Lejeune. 'I've got just two left. This slate' – he nodded toward the plain bird – 'is good in the rain. And I got that pink fella if you want something flashy.'

Mr Lejeune put up a hand like a stop signal. 'I can't afford nothing too racy, no.'

'The slate's a good bird. Of course, at this price, you got to train him.'

'Yeah, I want to ask you about that.' Mr Lejeune made a pliers of his right forefinger and thumb and clamped them on his chin. Annie came around close, as though she wanted to listen to the training instructions herself. The grandfather looked at the bottom of his back steps and shook his head, wondering if this would be as bad as the fake pot debacle, when thirteen high school freshmen caught Lenny coming out of Thibaut's Store and beat him into the dusty parking lot with their knobby little fists.

Lenny put his hands in the cage and caught the pigeon. 'You got to build a cage out of hardware cloth with a one-way door.'

'Yeah, for when he comes back, you mean.'

Lenny gave Mr Lejeune a look. 'That's right. Now to start trainin', you got to hold him like a football, with your thumbs on top of him and your fingers underneath. You see?'

Mr Lejeune put on his glasses and bent to look under the pigeon. 'Uh-huh.'

'You go to your property line. Stand exactly where your property line is. Then you catch his little legs between your forefingers and your middle fingers. One leg in each set of fingers, you see?' Lenny got down on his knees, wincing at the rough pavement. 'You put his little legs on the ground, like this. You see?'

'Yeah, I got you.'

'Then you walk the bird along your property line, moving his legs and coming along behind him like this. You got to go around all four sides of your lot with him so he can memorize what your place looks like.'

'Yeah, yeah, I got you. Give him the grand tour, kinda.'

Annie frowned and hid her mouth under a bright hand. His grandfather sat on the steps and looked away.

Lenny waggled the bird along the ground as the animal pumped its head, blinked, and tried to peck him. 'Now it takes commitment to train a bird. It takes a special person. Not everybody's got the character it takes to handle a homing pigeon.'

Mr Lejeune nodded. 'Hey, you talking to someone's been married forty-three years. How long you got to train 'em?'

Lenny stood and replaced the bird in the cage. 'Every day for two weeks, you got to do this.'

'Rain or shine?' Mr Lejeune's snowy eyebrows went up.

'That's right. And then after two weeks, you take him in a box out to Bayou Park and set his little butt loose. You can watch him fly around and then go home to wait. He might even beat you there, you know?'

The man bobbed his head. 'Little Alvin's gonna love this.' He reached for his wallet. 'Any tax?'

'A dollar.'

Mr Lejeune handed him a ten and dug for a one. 'Ain't the tax rate eight percent in the city?'

'Two percent wildlife tax,' Lenny told him, reaching under the cage for a shoe box blasted with ice-pick holes.

When the man and bird had left the driveway, Lenny's grandfather cleared his throat. 'I wouldn't a believed it if I didn't see it with my own eyes.'

'That's capitalism—'

'Aw, stow it. You took that guy's money and he got nothin'.' He started up the steps, pulling hard at the railing, but stopped at the landing to look down at them.

Lenny turned to the girl and said under his breath, 'He'll feel better when I get that old Crown Vic running again.' Turning to the carport, he fished out a young pigeon from the eaves, one the color of corroded lead.

'You think what you told him will work?' she asked, bending down for her glossy pink toolbox.

'Hell, I don't know what a bird thinks. Say, you got any cigarettes on you?'

'They don't let us smoke on shift.' She looked at his back, which had begun to sag again. 'I got to get to work,' she said. 'Try not to sell one to a cop, will you?'

That day Lenny sold pigeons to Mankatos Djan, a recent African immigrant who repaired hydraulics down at Cajun Hose, Lenny's simple cousin, Elmo Broussard, who lived across the river in Beewick, and two children who showed up on rusty BMX bikes. The next morning an educated-looking man showed up, made a face at Lenny's sales pitch, and got back into his sedan without a bird. Several customers had behaved like this, but by the third day he had sold a total of twenty-three pigeons and had enough to fix the leaf-covered sedan parked against the side fence. He had given everybody the same directions on how to train the birds. He told his grandfather that after two weeks, when the birds wouldn't come back at the first trial, they would chalk things up to bad luck, or maybe a skipped day of training. Not many things could take up your attention for two weeks and cost only eleven dollars, he argued.

Thirteen days after the ad first appeared, Lenny counted his money and walked up to the front porch, where his grandfather was finishing up a mug of coffee in the heat. He looked at the cash in Lenny's outstretched hand. 'What's that?'

'It's enough money to fix the car.'

His grandfather looked away toward the laundry. 'I saw you take over twenty dollars from some children for a lousy pair of flea baits.'

'Hey.' Lenny drew back his hand as though it had been bitten. 'It's for your car, damn it.'

'That poor colored guy who couldn't hardly speak a word of English. Black as a briquette, and he believed every damned thing you told him. My grandson sticks him for eleven bucks that'd feed one of his relatives living in a grass shack back in Bogoslavia or wherever the hell he was from for a year.' He looked up at Lenny, his veiny brown eyes wavering from the heat. 'What's wrong with you?'

'What's wrong with me?' he yelled, stepping back. 'Everybody's getting money but me. I ain't even got a job, and I come up with a way, just like everybody else does, to turn a few bucks, not even for myself, mind you, and the old fart that I want to give it to tells me to shove it.'

'You don't know shit about business. You're a crook.'

'All right.' He banged the money against his thigh. 'So I'm a crook. What's the difference between me and the guy that sells a Mercedes?'

The grandfather grabbed the arms of his rocker. 'The difference is a Mercedes won't fly off toward the clouds, crap in your eye, and not come back after you paid good money for it.'

Lenny jerked his head toward the street. 'It's all how you look at it,' he growled.

'There's only one way to look at it, damn it. The right way.' His grandfather stood up. 'You get out of my house. Your parents got rid of you and now I know why. Maybe a few nights down at the mission will straighten you out.'

Lenny backed up another step, the money still in his outstretched hand. 'Gramps, they didn't get rid of me. They moved out west.'

'And it was time they did. They shoved you out the house and got you lookin' for a job, you greasy weasel.' He grabbed the money so hard he came close to falling back into his chair. 'I'll take that for the poor folks that'll start comin' round soon for their money back.'

'They'll get eleven dollars' worth of fun out the birds.'

'Get out.' The old man brought his thin brows down low and beads of sweat glimmered on his bald head. 'Don't come back until you get a job.'

'You can't put me on the street,' Lenny said, his voice softening, his face trying an ironic smile.

'Crooks wind up on the street and later they burn in hell,' the old man said.

Lenny walked to the screen door and stopped, looking down North Bertaud Street where its narrow asphalt back ran toward Highway 90, which connected with the interstate, which connected with the rest of the scary world.

He kicked the bottom of the screen and his grandfather yelled. A half hour later he was standing on the sidewalk in front, holding a caramel-colored Sears suitcase, listening to the feathery pop of wings as the old man pulled pigeons out of the rabbit cage and tossed them toward the rooftops.

He walked to Breaux's Café, down by the icehouse, drank a cup of coffee, and read the paper. Then he wandered his own neighborhood, embarrassed by the huge suitcase banging his calf, enduring the stares of the women sweeping porches. He swung by Annie's house even though she was still at work. Her father sat on the stoop in his dark gray plumber's coveralls, drinking a long-neck in the afternoon heat. He watched Lenny come to him the way a fisherman eyes a rain-laden cloud. 'Whatcha got in the suitcase, boy?'

Lenny set it down on the curb and motioned down the street with a wag of his head. 'The old man and me, we had a discussion.'

Mr Meyer laughed. 'You mean he throwed your ass in the street.'

Lenny tilted his head to the side. 'He's mad at me right now, but he'll cool down. I just got to find a place to stay for a night or two.' He glanced up at Mr Meyer, who looked like a poor woman's Kirk Douglas gone to seed. 'You couldn't put me up, you know, just for the night?'

Mr Meyer didn't change his expression. 'Naw, Lenny. What with Annie in the house and all, it just wouldn't look right.' He took a long draw, perhaps trying to finish the bottle.

'That's okay. When it gets dark, I'll just go back and sleep in his car. The backseat on that thing's plenty big enough.'

'You sell all your birds?'

'He put me out of the bird business. I was just doin' it for him. I thought it was a good idea. I didn't see no harm in it.'

'That's what got him hot.'

'What?'

'You didn't see no harm in screwing those people. I talked to Mr Danzig over by the laundry. He said you didn't see no harm in putting one, two extra creases in a pair of slacks. He told me on Mondays some pants had more pleats than a convent-school girl's skirt. The trouble with you is, you ain't seeing the harm. You see what you want to see, but you ain't seeing the harm.'

'I worked cheap for that old bastard. He could expect worse.'

Mr Meyer stood, took a last swig, then put the bottle in his hip pocket. 'You hurt his business, boy.'

'Business,' Lenny said with a snarl. 'It's bullshit. A business for people too lazy to iron their own clothes.' He kicked his suitcase and it rolled over onto the grass, flattening an old dog dropping. Mr Meyer threw back his head and laughed.

That night, the grandfather couldn't sleep, and he rolled up the shade at the tall window next to his bed, looking into the moonlit side yard at his old car parked against the fence. He thought about how Lenny was sweating and rolling like a log on the squeaky vinyl of the backseat, trying to sleep in the heat and mosquitoes. The old man knelt on the floor and folded his arms on the windowsill, thinking how Lenny should be back at the cleaners, smiling through the steam of his pressing machine. He remembered his own work down at the light plant, where he tended the thundering Fairbanks-Morse generators for forty years. Down in the yard, the Ford bobbled, and he imagined that Lenny was turning over, putting his nose in the crack at the bottom of the seat back, smelling the dust balls and old pennies and cigarette filters. The grandfather wondered if some dim sense of the real world would ever settle on Lenny, if he would ever appreciate Annie Meyer, her Pet-milk skin, her big curves. He had seen her once at her lathe, standing up to her white ankles in spirals of tempered steel as she machined pump rods and hydraulic pistons. Lenny talked with longing of her paychecks, nearly $2,400 a month, clear, all of which she saved. The grandfather climbed into bed but couldn't sleep because he began to see images of people Lenny had sold birds to – the dumb children, the African – and wondered why the boy had done them wrong. It was only eleven dollars he'd gotten. How could you sell your soul for eleven dollars?

At dawn he went down into the yard and opened the driver's door to the car. Lenny had used his key to turn on the power to the radio, the only thing in the car that still worked. He was listening to a twenty-four-hour heavy-metal station that was broadcasting a sound like the exhaust of a revving small-plane engine overlaid with an electrocuted voice screaming over and over something like 'burgers and fries.'

'That sounds like amplified puking,' the old man said.

Lenny lay back against the seat and put his arm over his blood-shot eyes. 'Aw, man.'

His grandfather pushed on his shoulder. 'You get a job yet?'

Lenny cocked up a red eye. 'How'm I gonna get a job so soon? How'm I gonna get a job smelling bad, with no shave and mosquito bites all over me?'

The old man considered this a moment, looking into his grandson's sticky eyes. He remembered the inert feel of him as a baby. 'Okay. I'll give you a temporary reprieve on one condition.'

'What's that?' Lenny hung his head way back over the seat.

'St Lucy has confessions before seven o'clock daily Mass. I want you to think about going to confession and telling the priest what you done.'

Lenny straightened up and eyed the house. The old man knew

he was considering its deep bathtub and its oversized water heater. 'Where in the catechism does it say selling pigeons is a mortal sin?'

'You going, or you staying outside in your stink?'

'What am I supposed to tell the priest?' He put his hands in his lap.

His grandfather squatted down next to him. 'Remember what Sister Florita told you one time in catechism class? If you close your eyes before you go to confession, your sins will make a noise.'

Lenny closed his eyes. 'A noise.'

'They'll cry out like little frogs in a ditch at sundown.'

'Sure,' Lenny said with a laugh, his eyeballs shifting under the closed lids. 'Well, I don't hear nothing.' He opened his eyes and looked at the old man. 'What's the point of me confessing if I don't hear nothing?'

His grandfather stood up with a groan. 'Keep listening,' he said.

After Lenny cleaned up, they ate breakfast at a café on Tulane Avenue, and later, walking back home, they spotted Annie coming up the street, carrying her toolbox, her blond hair splashed like gold on the shoulders of her denim shirt.

The old man tipped his cap. 'Hi there, Miss Annie.'

She smiled at the gesture. 'Mr F. Good morning.'

Lenny gave her a bump with his hip. 'Annie, you're out early, babe.'

She lifted her chin. 'I came to see you. Daddy told me you were wandering the street like a bum.' She emphasized the last word.

'The old man didn't like my last business . . .'

'It wasn't business,' she snapped. Annie looked down at a work boot as though trying to control her emotions. 'Lenny, yesterday morning I went walking over by Broussard Street. You know what I saw? Shut up. Let me tell you.' She put down the toolbox and held out her hands as though she was showing him the length of a fish. 'That old Mr Lejeune, on his knees with that damned bird you sold him, wobbling down his property line.'

Lenny laughed. 'That musta been a sight.'

Annie looked at the grandfather, then at Lenny's eyes, searching for something. 'You just don't get it, do you?'

'Get what?' When he saw her expression, he lost his smile.

She sighed and looked at her watch. 'Ya'll come on.' She picked up her toolbox and started down the root-buckled sidewalk toward Broussard Street. After nine blocks they crossed a wide boulevard, went one more block, and stopped behind a holly bush growing next to the curb. Across the street was a peeling weatherboard house jammed between two similar houses separated by slim lanes of grass.

'This is about the time of day I saw him yesterday,' Annie said.

'Who?' Lenny asked, ducking down as though afraid of being recognized.

'The old guy you sold the pigeon to.'

'Jeez, you want him to see me?'

She looked at him with her big, careful blue eyes. The grandfather thought she was going to yell, but her voice was controlled. 'Why are you afraid for him to see you?' She was backed into the holly bush, fresh-scrubbed for the morning shift and looking like a big Eve in the Garden.

Across the street, there was movement at the side of the house, and Mr Lejeune came around his porch slowly, shuffling on his knees like a locomotive. The grandfather stood on his toes and saw that the old man was red in the face and that the pigeon looked tired and drunk. 'Lord,' he whispered, 'he's got rags tied around his kneecaps.'

'Yesterday I saw he wore the tips off his shoes,' Annie told him. 'Look at that.' Behind Mr Lejeune walked a thin boy, awkward and pale. 'Didn't he say he had a nephew?' The boy was smiling and talking down to his uncle. 'The kid looks excited about something.'

'Two weeks,' Lenny said.

'Huh?' The grandfather cupped a hand behind an ear.

'Today's two weeks. They'll probably go to Bayou Park this afternoon and turn it loose.'

Mr Lejeune looked up and across toward where they were standing. He bent to the side a bit and then lurched to his feet, waving like a windshield wiper. 'Hey, what ya'll doing on this side the boulevard?'

The three of them crossed the street and stood on the short stretch of capsizing walk that led to a wooden porch. 'We was just out for a morning walk,' Lenny told him. 'How's the bird doin'?' The pigeon seemed to look up at him angrily, blinking, struggling. Someone had painted its claws with red fingernail polish.

'This here's Amelia,' Mr Lejeune said. 'That's what Alvin named her.' He looked at his nephew. The grandfather saw that the boy was trembling in spite of his smile. His feet were pointed inward, and his left hand was shriveled and pink.

'How you doing, bud?' the grandfather asked, patting his head.

'All right,' the boy said. 'We goin' to the park at four o'clock and turn Amelia loose.'

Lenny forced a smile. 'You and your uncle been having a good time training old Amelia, huh?'

The boy looked over to where his uncle had gone to sit on the front steps. He was rubbing his knees. 'Yeah. It's been great. The first day, we got caught out in a thunderstorm and I got a chest cold, but the medicine made me feel better.'

'You had to go to the doctor?' Annie asked, touching his neck.

'Him, too,' the boy volunteered in a reedy voice. 'Shots in the legs.' He looked up at Lenny. 'It'll be worth it when Amelia comes back from across town.'

'Why's it so important?' Lenny asked.

The boy shrugged. 'It's just great that this bird way up in the sky knows which house I live in.'

'Hey,' Mr Lejeune called. 'You want me to put on some water?'

'No thanks,' the grandfather said. 'We had coffee already.'

The old man struggled to his feet, untying the pads from his knees. 'At least come in the backyard and look at the cage.' He shook out his pants and tugged the boy toward the rear of the house to a close-clipped yard with an orange tree in the middle. Against the rear of the house was a long-legged cage shiny with new galvanized hardware cloth.

'That took a lot of work to build, I bet,' the grandfather said to Lenny, who shrugged and said that he'd told him how to do it. The corners of the cage were finished like furniture, mortised and tenoned. In the center was a ramp leading up to a swinging door. The pigeon squirted out of the old man's hand and flew into the cage, crazy for the steel-mesh freedom.

'We'll let her rest up for the big flight,' Mr Lejeune said.

Lenny glanced over at Annie's face. She looked long at the pigeon, then over at where the boy slumped against the orange tree. 'You know, if you decide you ain't happy with the bird, you can have your money back.'

Mr Lejeune looked at him quickly. 'No way. She's trained now. I bet she could find this house from the North Pole.'

Lenny smiled. 'I knew it. Another satisfied customer.'

The grandfather told Mr Lejeune how much he liked the cage.

'Aw, this ain't nothin',' he said. 'Before my back give out, I was working for Delta Desk and Chair, thirty-six years in the bookcase division. Man, you could pass your hand over my seams and it felt like glass if you closed your eyes.' He waved a flattened palm over the cage as if he was working a spell.

The grandfather touched Annie's shoulder and they said their good-byes. On the walk home, she was silent. When they got to his grandfather's, she stopped, rattled her little toolbox, and did not look at either of them. Finally, she looked back down the street and asked, 'Lenny, what's gonna happen if that bird doesn't come back to the kid?'

He shook his head. 'If she flies for the river and spots them grain elevators, she'll never see Broussard Street again, that's for sure.'

'Two weeks ago you knew he was buying Amelia as a pet for a kid.'

Lenny turned his palms out. 'Am I responsible for everything those birds do until they die?'

The grandfather rolled his eyes at the girl. She wasn't stupid, but when she looked at Lenny, there was too much hope in her eyes.

Annie clenched and unclenched her big pale hands. 'If I was a bad sort, I'd hit you with a crescent wrench.'

Lenny blinked twice, perhaps trying to figure what she wanted to hear. The grandfather knew that she paid for their dates when the boy was out of work. She bought his cigarettes and concert tickets and let him hang around her house when something good was on cable. Often she looked at him the way she studied whatever gadget was whirling in her lathe, maybe wondering if he would come out all right.

Lenny lit up a cigarette and let the smoke come out as he talked. 'I'm sorry. I'll try to think of something to tell the kid if the bird don't come back.'

She considered this for a moment, then leaned over and kissed him quickly on the side of his mouth. As he watched her stride down the sidewalk, the grandfather listened to the Williams sockets rattling in her toolbox, and he watched Lenny wipe off the hot wetness of her lips.

That night, a half hour after dark, Annie, Lenny, and his grandfather were watching a John Wayne movie in the den when there was a knock at the rear screen door. It was Mr Lejeune, and he was worried about Amelia.

'I turnt her loose about four-thirty and she ain't come back yet.' The old man combed his hair with his fingers and peered around Lenny to where Annie sat in a lounger. 'You got any hints?'

Lenny looked at a shoe. 'Look, why don't you let me give your money back.'

'Naw.' He shook his head. 'That ain't the point. The boy's gonna get a lift from seeing the bird come back.' Alvin's pale face tilted out from behind his uncle's waist.

Annie, who was wearing shorts, peeled herself off the plastic couch, and the grandfather put a spotted hand over his eyes. Lenny turned a serious face toward Mr Lejeune.

'Sometimes those birds get in fights with other birds. Sometimes they get hurt and don't make it back. What can I tell you? You want your money?' He put a hand in his pocket but left it there.

The old man sidestepped out onto the porch. 'Me and Alvin will just go and wait. If that bird'd just come back once, it'd be worth all the crawling around, you see?' He held the boy's twisted hand and went down ahead of him one step at a time. Annie moved into the kitchen and broke a glass in the sink. The grandfather tried not to listen to what happened next.

Lenny went into the kitchen to see what had caused the noise, and met a rattle of accusations from Annie.

Then Lenny began to shout. 'Why are you bitching at me like this?'

'Because you gyped that old man and the crippled kid. I've never seen you do nothing like that.'

'Well, you better get used to it.'

'Get used to what?' She used a big contrary voice better than most women, the grandfather thought.

'Get used to doing things the way I like.'

'What, like stealing from old people and kids? Acting like a freakin' slug? Now I know why your parents left your ass in the street.'

Lenny's voice came through the kitchen door thready and high-pitched. 'Hey, nobody left me. They're on vacation, you cow.'

'People on vacation don't sell their houses, leave the time zone, and never write or call. They left because they found out what it took me a long time to just now realize.'

'What's that?'

And here a sob came into her voice and the grandfather put his head down.

'That there's a big piece of you missing that'll never turn up.'

'You can't talk to me like that,' Lenny snarled, 'and I'll show you why.' The popping noise of a slap came from the kitchen and the grandfather thought, *Oh no*, and struggled to rise from the sofa, but before he could stand and steady himself, a sound like a piano tipping over shook the entire house, and Lenny cried out in deep pain.

After the grandfather prepared an ice pack, he went to bed that night but couldn't sleep. He thought of the handprint on Annie's face and the formal numbness of the walk back to her house as he escorted her home. Now, he imagined Mr Lejeune checking Amelia's cage into the night, his nephew asking him questions in a resigned voice. He even formed a picture of the pigeon hunkered down on a roof vent above the St Mary Feed Company elevator, trying with its little bird brain to remember where Broussard Street was. About one o'clock he smacked himself on the forehead with an open palm, put on his clothes, and went down to the old carport with a flashlight. In the eaves he saw a number of round heads pop into his light's beam, and when he checked the section from which Lenny had plucked Amelia, he thought he saw her. Turning off the light for a moment, he reached into the straw and pulled out a bird that barely struggled. Its claws were painted red, and the grandfather eased down into a wheelbarrow to think, holding the bird in both hands, where it pecked him resignedly. He debated whether he should just let the animal go and forget the Lejeunes, but then he imagined how the boy would have to face the empty cage. It would be like an abandoned house, and every day the boy would look at it and wonder why Amelia had forgotten where he lived. He held the bird and thought of Lenny's parents probably parked in a Winnebago in some canyon in Utah, flown off that far to escape him, his mooching and his music. Why had they really left him? The old man shook his head.

At two-fifteen the grandfather walked down the side of Mr Lejeune's house, staying close to the wall and out of the glow of the streetlight. When he turned the corner into the backyard, he was in total darkness and had to feel for the cage, and then for its little swinging gate. His heart jumped as he felt a feathery escape from his palms, and the bird squirted into the enclosure. At that instant, a backyard floodlight came on and the rear door rattled open, showing Mr Lejeune standing in a pair of mustard-colored pajama bottoms and a sleeveless undershirt.

'Hey, whatcha doing?' He came down into the yard, moving stiffly.

The grandfather couldn't think of a lie to save his soul, just stood there looking between the cage and the back door. 'I wanted to see about the bird,' he said at last.

The other man walked up and looked into the cage. 'What? How'd you get a hold of the dumb cluck? I thought she'd be in Texas by now.' He reached back and scratched a hip.

The grandfather's mouth slowly fell open. 'You knew.'

'Yeah,' Mr Lejeune growled. 'I may be dumb, but I ain't stupid. And no offense, Mr Fontenot, but that grandson of yours got used-car salesman writ all over him.'

'Why'd you come by the house asking about the bird if you knew it'd never come back?'

'That was for Alvin, you know? I wanted him to think I was worried.' Mr Lejeune grabbed the grandfather by the elbow and led him into his kitchen, where the two men sat down at a little porcelain-topped table. The old man opened the refrigerator and retrieved two frosty cans of Schlitz. 'It's like this,' Mr Lejeune said, wincing against the spray from the pull tabs, 'Little Alvin's never had a daddy and his momma's a crackhead that run off with some biker to Alaska.' He pushed a can to the grandfather, who picked it up and drew hard, for he was sweating. Mr Lejeune spoke low and leaned close. 'Little Alvin's still in fairy-tale land, you know. Thinks his momma is coming back when school takes up in the fall. But he's got to toughen up and face facts. That's why I bought that roof rat from your grandson.' He sat back and began rubbing his knees. 'He'll be disappointed about the little thing, that bird, and maybe it'll teach him to deal with the big thing. That boy's got to live a long time, you know what I mean, Mr Fontenot?'

The grandfather put his cap on the table. 'Ain't that kind of mean, though?'

'Hey. We'll watch the sky for a couple days and I'll let him see how I take it. We'll be disappointed together.' Mr Lejeune looked down at his purple feet. 'He's crippled, but he's strong and he's smart.'

The grandfather lifted his beer and drank until his eyes stung. He remembered Lenny, asleep in the front bedroom with a big knot on the back of his head and a black eye. He listened to Mr Lejeune until he was drowsy. 'I got to get back home,' he said, standing up and moving toward the door. 'Thanks for the beer.'

'Hey. Don't worry about nothing. Just do me a favor and put that bird back in its nest.' They went out and Mr Lejeune reached into the cage and retrieved Amelia, dropping her into a heavy grocery bag.

'You sure you doing the right thing, now?' the grandfather asked. 'You got time to change your mind.' He helped fold the top of the bag shut. 'You could be kind.' He imagined what the boy's face would look like if he could see that the bird had returned to the cage.

Mr Lejeune slowly handed him the bag. For a moment they held it together and listened. Inside, the bird walked the crackling bottom back and forth on its painted toes, looking for home.

License to Steal

Curtis Lado rolled out of bed slowly, pulled on his wrinkled khakis, and walked into the kitchen, yawning and scratching the back of his head with both hands. He sat down at his chrome-legged dinette table and noticed that no pots murmured on the stove and no coffee smell hung in the air. He stared down at the note left on the worn Formica. 'I had enough,' the note said. It was his wife's handwriting. He got up and shoved open the rusted-out screen door, then walked into the backyard to look for her 1969 Torino, but it was gone. He stared at the empty gravel drive and said to himself, 'What the hell?'

Curtis put on his brown vinyl bedroom slippers and walked down to the corner to use the pay phone outside the Mudbug Café to call his son, Nookey, who worked at a sausage plant in Ponchatoula.

'What you want?' Nookey yelled over the whir of a dozen grinders. 'I got a pig to do here about the size of a Oldsmobile.'

'Baby, Momma took off and I don't know where she's gone. Did she say anything to you?'

'Naw, nothing she ain't been saying since I was born. Said she was tired of living in Louisiana with somebody didn't bring home no money. Said she wanted to move to the United States.'

'What the hell's that mean?'

'I don't know,' Nookey whined. 'And I don't know where she run off to. She did say something about not paying the light bill for two months because she needed the money for a trip. Hey, this pig had to be shot with a deer rifle to bring him down. I got to get busy.'

'Just tell me where your brother is and I'll let you go.'

'Buzzy's in jail.'

'Which one?'

'Hammond.'

'Okay. Maybe he'll know something.' Curtis hung up and reached into his pocket for coins. He began dialing the jailhouse number, which he knew by heart. He got Buzzy on the phone, but his addict son didn't know what month it was, much less where his mother had driven off to that morning.

'Maybe she went to Biloxi,' Buzzy suggested in his slow, faraway voice. 'It's nice and sandy this time of year.'

'Son, why would she leave me? Answer me that? I got to know where she is.'

'Maybe she just went to the flea market.'

'No, baby. She left me a letter and everything.' His voice nearly cracked. The importance of what had happened was beginning to sink in. 'I can't understand it, Buzz. She got a refrigerator that works, she got a nice brick-paper house, and she got us.' But Buzzy, who hadn't seen his mother since he had been arrested for selling marijuana the week before, couldn't give a clue as to where she had gone. Curtis checked the coin-return slot and walked home.

He had a little folding money in his pocket from his wife's last check, but that was it. Though he had not held steady work since 1978, he knew he had to find a job fast. Without the money Inez had brought in from her job as a cashier, the power company would take his meter and Friendly Willy finance would show up to get the TV. His 1971 Dodge pickup was also not paid for. Though Curtis was convinced he had a weak heart and that work gave him a nervousness in his chest parts, he had to eat. So, in the tiny bathroom he scraped off his silver whiskers and added a shot of VO5 to his swept-back iron-gray mane. He pulled his best polyester cowboy shirt over his rounded shoulders and admired the pearly buttons in the mirror. On his way out the door, he lit up a Lucky Strike.

He drove up Highway 51 to Amite, where he saw a sign stating that a foundry was hiring. The receptionist in the main office said he would have to come back in an hour because the person who did the hiring was out, so Curtis drove back down 51 to get something to eat. At the Big Sicilian Lounge, a brown cinder-block structure huddled under a shot-up Dixie beer sign, he slid out from his truck. Inside, he hunched over the plywood bar and drank three beers quickly, as though he had come in from a two-day trip across a desert. 'Give me a pickled egg,' he said to Raynelle, the barmaid, a large redheaded woman with no eyebrows. 'I need something good to eat.'

'Why don't you try a pig lip,' she said, hoisting onto the counter a gallon jar labeled with large black letters: FIFTY CENTS A LIP. He inspected shapeless parts floating coldly under a blond gluey film.

'Fish me out one,' he told her. He finished off his meal on a paper towel, tossed down his last beer, and headed back to the foundry.

The personnel director at Deep South Metal Casting was a pretty thirty-year-old blonde who wore makeup and perfume like a cosmetics saleslady. Her name tag read TAMMY MICHELLE. She shook an application form at him, and he took it gravely, spending over an hour filling its tiny voids. Later, she read it in one minute flat. She put it down on her desk and looked at Curtis, who was seated across from her in a plastic chair. 'Mr Lado, I see you left school in the eighth grade.'

'Yes, ma'am,' he said. 'I went further than anybody in my family. I always told my own boys how important it was to get a good education. My oldest is educated more'n anybody I know.'

Tammy Michelle gave him a faint smile. 'You mean he has something like a B.A. or M.A.?'

'Yes, ma'am. He got a GED.'

The personnel director pursed her glossy lips and looked down at the smudged form on her desk. 'I see that your longest employment was at a chicken plant for three years. Is that right?'

'Yes, ma'am, I was the neck and liver man.' He gave her this information with great seriousness, as though she could not make a decision about him without it.

'Uh-huh. And you've been out of work for a number of years?'

Here, Curtis knew he had to be careful, because he didn't want to confess to the uncomfortable flutterings in his chest. Nobody hired an unhealthy man. 'You see, my wife had this wonderful job that supported us to just the upmost, and I never was a greedy man. No, ma'am, I figured to work on the every now and then and enjoy one day at a time. My daddy used to say to me, "Let the future take care of itself and never give a nail two licks when one'll make it hold." My smartest, Nookey, he's just like me. Quit school in ninth grade when he caught on that all he had to do to get a diploma was lay out four years and then take a dinky little test.'

Tammy Michelle made an unpleasant face, as if she smelled something out of the ordinary. 'Mr Lado, do you drink?'

'Not so that it affects my working, no, ma'am – just a few to wash down my meals, and at night with my podnuhs down in Hammond, but I seldom ever pop a top before breakfast.' He gave her a big leery grin just to show he wasn't offended by the question.

'You know,' Tammy Michelle began, flipping her shiny hair behind her shoulders with both hands, 'I can't see much work experience that qualifies you for an opening here at the foundry. I notice you worked for a sawmill once. What exactly did you do?'

Curtis had to close his eyes to think, it had been that long ago. 'I was a sawyer.' He looked at the young woman and knew that she didn't understand. How could he explain what a sawyer was to someone who looked and smelled the way she did?

'Could you explain?'

'I guess so,' he said. 'I used to ride the carriage, that's a five-ton iron contraption, a frame on wheels pushed and pulled by a long steam piston. It goes back and forth holding a big log, running it against a saw blade and cutting it into boards. I had a bunch of levers to wrassle with, and I rode the machine feeling like a yo-yo. That was a real job, sure enough. Me and my podnuhs all worked the same mill those days, and we sure could make the lumber fly. I was real good at it. Real good. Thirty minutes into my shift, everybody handling the new boards was hollering for me to slow down.' His voice trailed off as he thought about that first job. 'But the mill closed down after two years.'

Tammy Michelle seemed unimpressed. She gave her fluffed-out hair a toss and told him that they didn't have a job he was qualified for.

He looked back at her, unblinking. 'What about those boys that grind mistakes off the hot castings? A monkey could do that. I ain't asking for a job as a machinist.' He felt Tammy Michelle's appraising eyes on his face. She might be sweet-flavored and colored like a gumdrop, but he realized with a pang that she had hired hundreds of men. He saw her take in the bags under his eyes, the red map of veins in his eyeballs. He saw her look at his hands, soft and nicotine-stained.

'Mr Lado,' she began, a hard edge creeping into her voice, 'the casting shed is a place for young men. You're fifty-two years old.' She folded his application and placed it in a folder with dozens of others. 'You also need a high school diploma to work for us.'

'I can work steady for as long as you need me,' he said, getting up slowly. 'I know there's been some gaps when I ain't worked much, but you can't work too steady if you're a Louisiana man. You got to lay off and smell the roses a bit, drink a little beer and put some wear on your truck.'

Tammy Michelle looked down at the next application. 'So long, Louisiana man,' she said.

Curtis drove back to the Big Sicilian Lounge and drank one frosty can after another, washing down ten pickled eggs and four pig lips in three hours' time. All the while, he filled the husky barmaid's ear. Raynelle was sympathetic. 'It's a shame they ain't got no place for a good soul like you, Curtis.'

'All they're interested in is how educated a man is. They ain't interested in what all he knows that's practical.' He took a long drag on a Lucky Strike, flicking the ash on the floor.

'Education, education, education. That's all I hear,' Raynelle sang. 'Why everybody's got to be so damned smart is beyond me. I never went past six grade and look at me.' She spread her ample arms. 'Hell, I ain't lacking nothing.' Curtis looked at her sleeveless Ban-Lon shirt and agreed.

'Yeah,' Curtis began, 'used to be that all a man needed was guts and sweat to make money. All guts and sweat gets you now is laughed at.' Raynelle snorted once and adjusted her bra straps, which sank into her shoulders like steel bands on a cotton bale.

By four o'clock Curtis felt that he was beginning to be drunk, so he figured it was time to take a drive. He climbed into his truck, started it with some difficulty, and stabbed at a tuning button to bring forth country music, but grazed it with his stubby forefinger. Off in the static-filled distance he heard his favorite song, 'If You Don't Leave Me Alone, I'll Find Somebody Who Will.' He lost his temper and hit the row of buttons with a fist. There was a crunch inside the radio and the little orange indicator lurched to the left side of the dial, lodging squarely on a Public Radio station. Strains of a string quartet filled the old Dodge's cab, and Curtis made a face as though a polecat had just crawled out from under the seat. He tried the buttons and the tuning knob, but the radio was forever jammed on violins and cellos. He cursed mightily and banged on the dash until he could stand no more of the delicate, weaving melody. He snapped the switch. No music at all was better than whatever that was.

He fishtailed out onto Highway 51 and headed south under a sky filled with puffy summer rain clouds. At a traffic light in Independence, his eyes managed to focus on a hand-painted sign that read HELP WANTED. He pulled over to the mud parking lot of a small metalworking shop, went inside the rusty tin building, and spoke to the young owner, breezily telling all he knew about welding log trucks together. Finally, the owner looked up and said,

'I like you good enough, old man, but I just need someone who can read blueprints and work the math.'

Curtis cocked his head like a feisty rooster observing a big yard dog. 'Hey, I can cut iron real good. Ain't you got nobody can draw some lines on the iron what tell me where to cut?'

The owner shook his head. Curtis pleaded his case a few more minutes, but he finally gave up and left. He climbed back into his truck, but the engine only grunted twice. He got out and raised the hood. Sometimes when he let the sun shine on the battery to heat the acid, enough juice built up to start the engine. Two doors down from the metalworking shop was a bar promising a cool place to wait. Inside Anselmo's Oasis he began a lively argument with a group of strawberry farmers and pulpwood truck drivers about the value of education. One farmer told him that an education was important because you could maybe one day become a legislator and make millions of dollars. Most of the folks in Baton Rouge, he said, were real smart, lawyers even, and used what they knew to help their friends out in the construction industry by throwing an occasional bridge or firehouse job their way. 'That's what democracy is all about,' the old farmer said. 'Spreading around the gravy.'

But Curtis would not give up in the face of logic. Under the sway of six additional beers he grew cranky, grabbed the farmer by his shoulder and shook him.

'You're crazy. A Louisiana man ain't got to be a four-eyed egghead to throw away money. I could work that dog and pony show in the state capitol myself. If I had a three-hundred-dollar suit and a two-hundred-dollar secretary with a tight butt, I could steal tax money with the best of them.'

The old men carped and hollered back and forth until Anselmo and a gravel truck driver grabbed Curtis and in a clop and skitter of boots threw him out the front door. He spun and weaved back to his truck, slammed down the hood, and succeeded in starting it up, getting it in the road, and aiming it toward home.

When he got to his house, he came in through the kitchen and hit the light switch. Nothing happened. Sure enough, checking the side of the house, he found that the electric meter had been removed. Back in the darkened living room, he sat in his torn vinyl recliner and let the house spin around his head. He felt nauseated, his eyes hurt, and his heart knocked away like a big woodpecker in a hollow tree. He wondered what had gone wrong with him. Going back in memory, he saw himself as an ironclad buck that no amount of liquor, cigarettes, or wildness could ruin. When he was young, he'd planned to live forever by the strength of his body and a dab of skill he could sell for enough to keep him in fun. There was always work. He thought of his sawmill job, his favorite, riding the carriage like a cowboy on a fast horse, charging back and forth, crashing logs into the humming blade. That had been twenty-five years before. Tonight he stared at the dark outline of his television, feeling sick enough to cry, and could not for the life of him figure out what was wrong.

The next day was Friday, Nookey's day off, and as usual he came over and got his daddy out of bed. His son was thin and big-boned, his shoulders rounding under a checkered long-sleeved shirt he wore winter and summer. His polka-dot welder's cap was pulled down over a pair of patient gray eyes. Nookey woke his father by pulling one leg out of bed and dropping it toward the floor as though it might be a limb on one of the carcasses down at the sausage plant.

Everything in the refrigerator smelled bad, so they closed it up and climbed into the truck to drive to the Mudbug for breakfast. As soon as Curtis turned the key, Nookey spun on the radio. The passionate voice of a soprano shrilled from the speaker, and Nookey jumped from the truck as though it had suddenly caught fire. 'What the hail is that?' he yelled, stumbling about for a moment in the gravel.

'Aw, the damn radio is stuck on the longhair music station,' Curtis complained, turning off the voice. 'Quit fooling and come on.'

'Man,' Nookey hooted, climbing back into the Dodge. 'Sounds like a tomcat hung up in a fan belt.'

'That's just one more thing I got to pay to get fixed,' Curtis said, looking over his shoulder as he backed out onto the street. 'I got to get a job so's I can get the juice turned back on, too.'

Nookey gave a sideways nod, like a hound blinking off a horsefly. 'We'll get us some grits and eggs and I'll help you apply every place we can think of.'

And that's what they did. But the veneer mill said they needed someone who could operate a computer. The lumberyard told Curtis he was too old. The cement plant needed someone good with weights and measures. Finally, the auxiliary power plant would consider his application. They needed someone as a watchman five days a week and three hours Saturday morning. Curtis was offended when he heard the schedule and told the man doing the hiring as much.

He was cranky by the time he got there, plus somewhat drunk, having found a handy bar after each turndown to build up his courage for the next application.

Afterward, in the Big Sicilian, Nookey tugged on the bill of his cap and tried not to sound like he was complaining. 'Daddy, you shouldn'a called that man at the powerhouse a Communist just because he wanted someone to work on Saturday.'

'And why the hell not?' Curtis's indignation, usually fueled by nothing more significant than cold beer, was blazing. 'A job like that will run a man into the ground. Six days a week? When the hell will I have time for any recreation?' He knocked back half a glass of draft beer and motioned to the barmaid for another. 'Son, I'd just as soon live in Moscow and eat potato soup all day as become a pheasant worker for the power company.'

Nookey pushed back his cap, bent over the bar, and examined his fingers. 'Daddy, I work on Saturdays sometimes.'

Curtis glared at him, burgundy pools forming below his eyeballs. 'Then you got the brain of a armadillo. What you think you're gonna do, get rich? This is Louisiana, son. Ain't nobody can get rich in this state through hard work.' He threw a dollar bill at the barmaid when she brought his beer. She was an old, dark woman with hair so coarse and black it looked tarred. Leaning on her side of the bar, she listened.

'Sometimes I think you drink a little heavy, Daddy,' Nookey said, rubbing the thin blond stubble on his narrow face and looking down sorrowfully. He picked up his half-full glass, wiggled it, put it down.

Curtis swilled his beer until his eyes watered, taking down half a mug. 'You want to kill yourself working, go ahead. You'll wear your fingers off down at the weenie plant all your life for what? So you can buy some trashy piece of red dirt with a used trailer on it while some real estate fool gets most all your money and a lawyer gets the rest. You think *they* work hard? You think just because they went to parties and chased women at a college for four years that they sweat and worry every day that the sun comes up? Hell no, son. They don't have a education. They got a license to steal.' A snarl crept into his voice. He took a swig and looked at a cheerful beer poster where two girl skiers posed before an out-of-focus mountain. Curtis was confused and rueful. Something was wrong with him, but he had no idea what it was. 'If I never drank a beer or smoked a cigarette and then worked eighty hours a week for the almighty auxiliary power station, I wouldn't do better than a tar-paper house and a raggedy-ass Dodge.'

'Aw, Daddy. Come on, now.'

Curtis didn't hear his son. He was looking at the poster. 'What the hell's them girls up to anyway?' he shouted. 'Hey, one of 'em's a lawyer and the other is a politician spending our tax money at two hundred dollars a night out in Colorado.' He waved a fist at the images, as though he could shame them for both their waste and his worries.

Nookey let out a long sigh. 'I think it's time we hit the road.'

The barmaid picked up his glass. 'You want to know about a job?' she asked. 'Mr Cantrell is opening up the old sawmill in the woods back of Albany. His foreman was in here this morning. Said they're hiring.'

Curtis's eyes widened. 'That's the old Cantrell mill. I never worked there, but I worked one just like it.'

'Rode the log carriage like in the old days,' Nookey moaned, shaking his head glumly. In two minutes they were on the highway, the truck weaving between the white lines with the floating, mystical action of a street sweeper. Curtis was so drunk that Nookey tried to take the wheel from him. The old man responded by cuffing him twice across the bridge of his nose. When the truck stopped for a traffic light in Byron, Nookey jumped out. 'Go on and drive in a ditch if you want to. I believe Momma was right when she took off.' He stood on the white line at the edge of the blacktop, seeming ready to cry. He waited for his father to say something, but Curtis didn't look at him, just reached over and pulled the door shut, popping the clutch so hard that the Dodge shuddered like a horse and clods of dirt fell from under the fenders.

He pulled into the muddy lot of the Cantrell sawmill, dizzy and confident, seeing a great future ahead, full of money enough for the electric bill, cases of beer, and cartons of Lucky Strikes. That's what money was for – weekends, free time, lots of smoke, and great big barmaids.

The mill was an obsolete complex of huge wooden sheds with tin roofs bloody with rust. Curtis parked in front of the office and looked to his left across the swampy yard. The building where the main saw was stood fifty feet tall, the carriage running twenty-five feet above ground level. There was a decided lack of activity even though the boiler shed, about two hundred feet to the rear of the main saw building, gave off shimmering white streams of sawdust smoke from its three crooked stacks.

Inside the office he spoke to a man slouching behind a cluttered, greasy desk. 'You want a job?' the man asked. Curtis nodded. 'You got to see Mr Cantrell. What can you do?'

'How come there ain't no sawing going on?' Curtis slurred only two words, but the room spun slowly, like a ferry leaving shore. Inside his head something hissed and popped like bacon frying.

'We're just starting up again. This plant's been closed down for eight years, and it was wore-out when it closed.' He smiled as though his comment was funny. 'What is it you said you do?'

'I can run the carriage,' Curtis said, absently.

'We need a carriage man to run that old-time system until we get a new one set up, but we can't try you out today.'

'You got steam up.'

'Yeah, I know. But we tore out the safety bumper at the end of the carriage run because all the timbers were buggy. Say, here's Cantrell now.'

A large, ruddy man came through the door of an interior office. He wore a tailored white shirt, a narrow silk tie, and a yellow hard hat. He gave Curtis a stony, appraising look. 'What do you want?' he snapped.

'My name's Curtis Lado. I'm looking for work.' He put his hand to his chin and stroked the stubble there. Suddenly, he felt rusty and worn-out.

Mr Cantrell's face looked chiseled out of flint. He leaned forward and sniffed audibly. 'I don't hire old drunks,' he said, pushing past and into another office, rattling open a blueprint as he walked. Curtis felt as though someone had shoved him off a bar stool. He walked sideways toward the parking lot door, unable to control his movements. The door stuck in its frame and he took several moments to open it, feeling the eyes of those in the office on his back. He stumbled on the splintered steps. Out in the soggy mill yard, he leaned on his truck and stared at the building that housed the huge saw and log carriage. It looked like the one he'd worked in many years ago when he was young and sharp, a man with friends and a good job earned by his youth and raw strength only. Letting go of the truck, he set out tentatively, navigating the slop of the mill yard, climbing the long stairs that led to the big saw.

Inside, two men were welding. They glanced at him but continued to concentrate on their work. All around him, steam pipes hissed and dripped condensation. The main saw apparatus was dismantled, but the carriage was gleaming under a brush coat of linseed oil. A crew had rolled a three-foot-diameter log onto it for testing. He walked over to the carriage and stumbled, falling into the controller's seat. Tall levers stood before him and he placed his hands on them and laughed. He nudged one and the carriage trembled. Curtis smiled and felt he could control it, remembering the magical thrust of the steam-activated rod that paid out of a long cylinder and shoved the iron carriage against the saw and then pulled it away effortlessly, as though it were a puff of air. He squeezed the lever, confident that all a man needed in life was what he was born with – common sense and confidence. He gave a lever a mighty thrust.

The best view of what happened next was from the mill yard. A geyser of steam shot from a pipe in the saw shed's roof, and there was a sound like someone dynamiting a stump. The carriage and a huge oak log splintered through a wall and support beam, flying out into the mill yard and crashing down onto a late-model Cadillac, the only decent automobile for miles around. Planks, bolts, and hunks of iron rained down onto the sawmill, and an angry roar of steam rose from the punctured building. Curtis was seated on the carriage, his hands clenched white on the control levers. He stared with sober attention at the flattened Cadillac under him and tried to put his mind in motion again, but he could not think of what to do, whether to shout or run or cry, and as he studied the shiny catastrophe under him, it seemed that his mind would never start, that perhaps it had never worked at all.

Mr Cantrell walked out into the mill yard and stood next to his car, tapping a crushed fender with the clipboard he carried. He looked up at the figure seated on the carriage, who had come through a wall of timber uninjured. 'Curtis Lado. Is that what you said your name is? Well, I guess you got a little property somewhere, maybe a car, maybe your granddaddy's watch? By the time my company lawyer gets through with you, the only thing you'll have is your skin, and we'll put that in jail, and when you get out of jail, whenever you make a nickel, I'll have four cents of it for the rest of your life.' He turned his back and began yelling for a crew to go to Hammond for a crane and jacks.

Curtis climbed down and walked across to his truck, his face on fire under the derisive looks he drew from the workers hurrying about the mill yard. He was embarrassed into soberness. Going home occurred to him at once. He would hole up there like a man waiting for a hurricane.

Jamming the key into the old Dodge's ignition, he turned it, but there was only a pained grunt in response. He tried the switch again, and again, until the engine would do nothing more than utter a series of snickering clicks. Out in the yard, men watched him while they worked. Cantrell put his hands on his hips and stared, then began writing on his clipboard, his eyes now on the truck's license. Through the window of the office, Curtis could see a man on the phone, staring back at him. Deep in his chest, his heart fluttered like an engine running out of gas. He lay down out of sight on the front seat, reached up, and turned on the radio.

An announcer was speaking in a smooth, educated voice, saying that writers living in France during the seventeenth century thought Louisiana was a wasteland. There were only evil men, pestilence, and wild Indians, and no one who lived there had any hope for a bright future. Curtis closed his eyes and tried to understand the commentary, which was about an opera, but the radio voice might as well have been using the language of owls. 'A French writer,' the announcer continued, 'once introduced a section of his work by stating that it was set "in the deserts of Louisiana."' Curtis rolled onto his side and, for as long as he was able, listened to the words carefully, but they were being spoken in a tongue he had not been taught. A cloud of steam rolled past the windshield, and an orchestra filled the cab of the rusting pickup with a somber, incomprehensible music.

Floyd's Girl

T-Jean

Airborne, T-Jean's big sedan flew across the main highway, landing on a shell road like a crop duster coming down wrong. He had to find his cousin Floyd before the little girl was lost. The car hydroplaned over dips filled with rainwater, blasting muddy showers over the hood. T-Jean was afraid of the brimming roadside canals, so he watched instead the white frame house up ahead in the big field, and in a minute he swirled onto the farm road that was also the driveway, his tires spraying shells into the rice ponds. He braked, leapt from the car before it fully stopped, and charged up across the gallery and through the screen, almost knocking down Tante Sidonie.

'Floyd, where he's at?' T-Jean asked, his breath coming in little gasps.

Tante Sidonie adjusted her bifocals to look at him. 'You T-shirt is wet as a dishrag,' she said.

'Where's Floyd? The Texas man got his lil' girl.'

She had to think for one second who the Texas man was. When she remembered, she yelled, 'All the way to the tree line.' She followed him out the door, her hands on his back, pushing.

T-Jean gunned his big Ford and drove straight back until the shell drive turned to mud and rainwater. When the car settled down to its frame, he was by the old tractor shed, and he headed for it, his boots blasting the sloppy mud. Without breaking stride he ran up onto the only machine left, a heavy International M, retired because it was too old to pull and ate gas by the drum. One yank on the starter ring and the worn engine rolled twice and fired, T-Jean slamming it into second gear and taking out the rotten back wall of the shed, the big rubber cleats throwing boards in the air behind and then biting ground as the machine found high gear and waddled up on top of the mud track toward the tree line, where Floyd's big air-conditioned John Deere was stopped in the water. T-Jean stood on the seat and yelled Floyd's name over the roaring tractor, his voice cracking with effort, but he was too far away. Floyd was a short, blue-jeaned island off at the edge of two thousand acres of swamped rice field. It was five minutes before T-Jean got there.

Floyd

'What's wrong with you?' Floyd asked. The wildness in T-Jean's gray eyes was contagious, and Floyd wanted to stay calm. Since he'd turned thirty, he'd tried to cool down. He had a ten-year-old daughter to raise.

'The man from Texas, he came when you mama's at the store and got Lizette.'

Every feature of Floyd's face shifted, a movement of flesh terrible to watch. 'You mean my wife's new boyfriend?'

'Yeah, man. Grandmère saw him. She sent me. She's waitin' by the house.'

'How long?'

'Not twenty minutes.'

'Ninety west?'

'His favorite way to Texas.'

Floyd cupped his elbows in his palms, curled his upper lip, and sniffed his mustache, the whole parish road system lighting up in his mind, an aerial view of black lines against a green watery screen. He batted the other man on the knee, wheeled, and leapt up on his hulking green tractor, starting up and rolling the balloon tires north out of the field and into a trash woods of briers and saplings taller than his machine, exploding through in a scream of machinery and a rattling black column of diesel smoke. Trees snapped under his tires like breaking bones. A mile through all this was Mrs Boudreaux's little white house, closer to the main road than Tante Sidonie's, if he indeed could come out of the woods in her backyard. Floyd adjusted his cap and pushed the pedals of the frantic machine with his thin legs, trying to think, trying to stay calm. He didn't know where his wife lived. She was still his wife, because once the priest married you, you were married forever, in spite of a spiritless divorce court and a Protestant judge and a Texas lounge bum in snakeskin boots.

Floyd pictured his daughter, Lizette, her moon face and dark hair. The girl was scared of her mother, who had beaten her with a damn chinaball branch for playing with her makeup. But she was smart, smarter than Floyd, the kind of smartness that some-times got you in trouble with people. He hoped that she would not sass the Texas man. Not him.

Mrs Boudreaux

'Chick-chick-chick-chick, *venez ici. Mangez ça.*' Mrs Boudreaux scolded her white hens in the voice she long ago used to discipline her six children at breakfast. She broadcast the chicken scratch over the dirt of her backyard, then turned for the steps of her small cypress house, which shone white with rainwater. A terrific noise in the woods startled her chickens, and they raced ahead of her under the house. She turned to watch Tante Sidonie's big green machine mash three willow trees down into her yard; then she saw Floyd climb down from the cab and step over her one rosebush. He was sad-looking, she thought, like his grandpère with the big mustache. When Floyd was a baby and she held him in her lap, he was like a tough little muscle made hard by God for a hard life ahead. He was not a mean man, but determined enough to always do a thing right when it counted. It was rough, raising a young daughter with no help, having a wife who ran off with a *cou rouge*. She clucked her tongue at him when he came over to her; he was a pretty man, little, like she liked them, and dark from work.

'Hey, Misres Boudreaux, is T-man still in the service?'

She hitched her chicken-scratch bowl up under her bosom. 'What you need his car for, you?' Why else would he come here through the woods like that? she thought.

'The Texas man, he came stole Lizette just now. I got to catch him. T-Jean's grandmère is waiting to tell me.'

She looked past him toward the rattling tractor, remembering the Texas man. A fear crept up through Mrs Boudreaux's stomach as she saw the dark-haired Lizette ruined by outlanders, dragged off to the dry plains of Texas she imagined from cowboy movies. She wondered if her mother would take her to Mass or to the Stations of the Cross during Lent. She knew Texans had some kind of God, but they didn't take him too seriously, didn't celebrate him with feast days and days of penance, didn't even kneel down in their churches on Sunday.

'My old Dodge can't go fast, but you can use T-man's car if you can crank it,' she told him.

She watched Floyd run over to a plastic-covered hump next to the barn and pull bricks and tire rims off so he could get to T-man's primer-painted Z. The key was in the car and it started immediately, sounding hot and mad as a bee in a bird's beak. In ten seconds, he was on the blacktop road, and Mrs Boudreaux imagined her house as a white speck shrinking in his rearview mirror. He disappeared onto Sugarmill Highway, and she heard the exhaust storm as he accelerated toward his house three miles away, where she imagined that T-Jean's grandmère was standing in the tall grass by the mailbox, leaning against her walker, her faded cotton dress swinging at her ankles.

T-Jean's Grandmère

Potato salad. I'm going make me some potato salad and then something with gravy to pour over that and then some sweet peas.

I got a deer roast in the icebox. I could put some garlic in that and make a roux. She was always planning meals. Three a day, if not for her husband, then for her children who lived in the neighborhood. Her grandbaby, T-Jean, asked her to stand by the road and tell Floyd something. What was it? Why was she standing out in the mist? Then she remembered Lizette. What would that poor baby eat for supper?

Can she get turtle sauce piquante in Lubbock? And T-Jean's grandmère thought of the gumbos Lizette would be missing, the okra soul, the crawfish body. How could she live without the things that belong on the tongue like Communion on Sunday? Living without her food would be like losing God, her unique meal.

She heard the approaching blast of a car and the cry of brakes as Floyd stopped next to her, driving something that looked like a dull gray space capsule on wheels. He asked her what color the Texas man's car was, and she remembered why she was there. She began to talk in her creaky voice: '*Ey, Floyd, bébé, comment ça va?* Ah, it's a big man what come up you driveway wearing a John Wayne hat, a skinny man straight as a railroad, with big tall boots. An' Lizette, she was crying she wanted to take a suitcase, but he pulled her in the car like this.' Here she cranked up an arm, a bony right angle. 'This is what her arm was like.'

'*Mais*, what kind of car was he driving?' Floyd banged the backs of his hands on the steering wheel.

'Oh, yah. It was a green Chevrolet truck. A old one. At least I think it was that. Me, I don't know one from the other. I ought to have a *garde de soleil* on my head in this weather.' Floyd revved the engine, getting ready to tear off, but she reached over the rail of her walker and put a hand on the window ledge. 'How you gonna ketchum?' Her face darkened as she leaned down to Floyd's window. He told her quickly, all the while staring down the blacktop. 'Ah,' she said. 'You should take the farm roads and pass up Eunice and catch him at Poteau. Look,' she told him, 'take this. I pulled it off the dashboard of my Plimmet.'

He took a plastic statue of St Christopher from her spotted hands. 'Grandmère, the Pope said St Christopher wasn't for real.' He glanced at the magnet on the bottom.

T-Jean's grandmère gave him a scoffing look. 'If you believe in something, then it's real. The Pope's all right, but he spends too much time thinking about things instead of visiting people in grass huts like he ought.'

Floyd stuck the statue on the dash. 'There.'

She made a poking motion with her knobby forefinger. 'Turn him so he sees the road.'

Floyd twirled the plastic. '*Comme ça?*'

'*Mais oui.* Hey, Floyd?'

'*Quoi?*'

'The Texas man.'

'What?'

She smiled widely, wrinkles chasing around her face like ripples on a sun-bright pond. 'Bus' his ass.'

Floyd

The parish had just blacktopped the farm roads, so he drove hard, afraid to look at the speedometer, feeling for safety through his tires, sensing from the sway and swirl of rubber for the point at which the car would slip off the asphalt and pinwheel out into the green blur of a rice field. The image of his daughter, Mary Lizette Bergeron, her pale face and dark hair inherited from her Cancienne forebears on his side, appeared on the shimmering road ahead. He saw his daughter growing up on the windy prairie in a hard-bitten town full of sun-wrinkled geezers, tomato barbecue, Pearl beer, and country music. There was nothing wrong with West Texas, but there was something wrong with a child living there who doesn't belong, who will be haunted for the rest of her days by memories of the ample laps of aunts, daily thunderheads rolling above flat parishes of rice and cane, the musical rattle of French, her prayers, the head-turning squawk of her uncle's accordion, the scrape and complaint of her father's fiddle as he serenades the backyard on weekends. Vibrations of the soul lost for what? Because her mama wants her, too? Her mama, a LeBlanc gone bad, a woman who got up at ten o'clock and watched TV until time to cook supper. Who learned to drink beer and smoke dope, though both made her throw up the few things she ate. Who gave up French music and rock and roll for country. Who, two years ago, began to stay out all night like a cat with a hot butt, coming in after he left for work on Tante Sidonie's farm. Who disappeared like that same cat would, leaving him to rock on the porch in the evenings, wondering whether she was alive or dead, kidnapped for the nervously pretty brunette thing she was, dead in the woods, or, worse, cowboy dancing in some bar out west, laughing at him with all the *cous rouges* she thought she loved. Six months ago, she called and asked him for Lizette. He told her to come home. He heard her laugh so loud that he thought he might hang up the phone, open a window, and hear that keening laughter threading in from the west over the bending heads of the rice plants. Then she told him she would send the Texas man and that he'd never find Lizette in a place as big as Texas.

Floyd's black eyes were shiny and small, his mustache as dark as a caterpillar. There was not one ounce of fat in his 145 pounds, though he was fed by Tante Sidonie, who had already loved her husband to death with her dark gumbo. Floyd drank beer and made noise with his friends on weekends, spent his extra money on his daughter, her clothes, her Catholic school, her music lessons. Everyone in the community of Grand Crapaud knew he had good sense and would do a thing as soon as it needed doing. They knew this because he never hit a man when he was down, the grass in his yard stayed cut, he washed his car, and there were no holes in the screens of his house.

T-Man's Z seared the asphalt on the straight road south of Highway 90, spinning between the rice fields that lay swollen with steamy mirrors of rainwater. After two panic stops at intersections, he reached the turnoff to the north, blistered along for two miles, and cut a smoky bow bend onto 90 west, heading toward Texas, looking for the truck. 'What kind of man would drive a green truck?' he said aloud. He checked his watch and struggled with the math until he figured he should be close, unless, of course, the Texas man had taken another route to fool him. But he felt in his bones that the cowboy, who used to drive a cement truck on this route day in and day out, would try to escape him this way, this road.

He had gone but three miles, skimming the potholes at eighty-five, when he saw the truck, a three-quarter-ton model with steel mesh across the back of the cab. Through the window he could barely see the top of Lizette's head on one side of the cab and the Texas man's broken-brim hat on the other, not a real cowboy's hat, just a dance-hall hat. He passed them, blowing the horn and motioning them to the side of the road. In his rearview mirror, he saw the truck move onto the grassy shoulder, and Floyd smiled. It was easy, he thought. He got out and the Texas man got out. They came together, and Floyd realized that he was much smaller than his wife's new boyfriend. He looked down at his own white shrimper boots and then over at the reptile splendor of the Texas man's footgear.

'You must be the coon-ass,' the cowboy said. He had a nasty way of holding his head tilted off to the side, with his mouth belled out a bit to the left, like he was used to drooling on himself.

'I want my daughter back,' Floyd told him, looking past at the pale, wise face of Lizette in the truck. She leaned out the window on her side.

'Daddy, I want to go home,' she said. 'This man talks funny.'

'She's a-going to where she belongs, with her mama,' the cowboy said.

'No, she's not,' Floyd said, starting for the truck. The Texas man grabbed him, punched him in the mouth, and Floyd went down. He came up swinging, striking the other man in the jaw, but after a flurry of counterpunches and two sharp kicks from a set of pointed boots, Floyd found himself on his back in the roadside mud, staring at a new set of storm clouds coming up from the Gulf, listening to the green truck screeching off into the flat distance. He sat up, feeling his head spin, and thought it best to rest a while before trying to drive. A car slowed down and a farmer asked him if he needed help, but he waved him off. Then another car came along and pulled off onto the shoulder. It was a twenty-year-old Dodge driven by Mrs Boudreaux. In the front seat was T-Jean's grandmère, who pushed open the door with her tiny hands. He got in and sat next to them.

'You caught 'em and he beat you up,' the older lady said, running a cool hand over a lump on his forehead.

'*Mais*, that about sums it up.'

Mrs Boudreaux, who still had on her stretch jeans from the chicken yard, leaned over to look at him closely. 'You got to catch 'em, Floyd.'

'I'll start in a minute.' His head spun like a pirogue caught in an eddy.

'Yah,' T-Jean's grandmère began, 'you got a bump on the googoon that's gonna make you wreck for sure. Me and Alida will drive after him.' She tried to see over the dash to check the traffic.

'No, no. I've got to drive fast.'

Mrs Boudreaux clucked her tongue thoughtfully. 'It'll take an airplane to catch him now.' She and Floyd looked at each other instantly.

'Nonc René,' they said in unison.

Nonc

René Badeaux sat on his front porch steps, patching a hole in a diatonic accordion with Super Glue and a piece of oilcloth torn from an old table covering. He pulled the bellows, and the instrument inhaled a squawk. '*Merde*,' he said. He tried to play 'Allons à Lafayette,' but on the fourth note the little patch blew off and floated toward the road like a waxy leaf. Then a C button stuck.

He shook his head, thinking that he should have played a waltz until the glue dried. Looking up at a plane taking off from his strip, he remembered that the black fellow he had hired last week as a pilot was going thirty miles north to spray some worms. He waited until the drone of the engine had gone over the tree line, and then he popped the C button loose and laid the bellows of the old Monarch against his great belly and played, spraying the reedy music around the yard like nutrient for the atmosphere, breaking into whiny song. '*Mon coeur est tout casse*,' he sang, himself a wind box of lyrics playing for his own amazement.

Floyd was sitting next to him on the step before he saw him. That was one thing about Floyd – he was a quiet man, saying only what needed to be said, not yammering all sorts of bullshit when he came up. And then he said what needed to be said to his uncle. He told him about Lizette.

Nonc René had sung so many sentimental songs so badly over the years that he had become a tender man. Every woman he knew was an Evangeline bearing some great sorrow in life, and now he imagined his grand-niece dragged off to live among lizards and rock and only Mexican accordion music. How could she bear to stay there without the buzz of a fiddle and the clang of a triangle in her pretty head, the love songs sung through the nose?

'Please, Nonc,' Floyd was saying, his little eyes shining with need in the late-afternoon light. 'You know what I'm talkin' about. You know what to let me do. I can fly good.'

'You could call the police,' René teased.

'Louisiana police? Give me a break, Nonc.'

René rubbed his gray stubble and rolled his eyes toward the plane shed. 'Lollis took the good machine.'

'Even a bad plane can beat a pickup truck,' Floyd said with that smile that wasn't a smile, but a trick with those little dark eyes.

Nonc René was waiting for that smile that wasn't a smile. That's all. He wasn't hesitating for a minute. He remembered that

Floyd was still famous in the region for installing an ancient DC-3 engine in a big biplane, and when he got that Pratt & Whitney Twin Wasp tandem radial engine in the sky, it cork-screwed his homemade canvas plane through a cloud like the engine was twirling the wings instead of the propeller, and straight down he came into a rice paddy. When Nonc René and his brothers got to the field, there was just a gasoline slick on top of the mud and nothing else. They dug Floyd out with their hands and boards torn from a fence. His clothes had been ripped off by the concussion of the crash. Three brothers at once had their fingers in his mouth, digging out a pound of mud so he could breathe. They pinched clay out of his nose, washed it from under his eyelids, cleared it from his ears with twigs. When they put him on the toilet that night at the hospital – mud and six grains of rice.

Now, in eight minutes, they were in the sky, Mrs Boudreaux and T-Jean's grandmère watching them through the windshield of the old Dodge. The biplane burbled off toward the west, following Highway 90 at two hundred feet.

Lizette

It had seemed the thing to do at first. The tall bony man with the long neck – she had never seen a neck like that, with a big bump in the middle – he came into the house without knocking, took her by the arm and said, 'Let's us go see yore mama.' She could smell the raw leather of his gaudy belt. He would not let her pack a stitch, and when she protested, he jerked her along the way you pull an animal out of a hole, and her arm still hurt. She asked him where he was taking her and he said, 'God's country,' which made her wonder if he was an Arab terrorist, though she didn't think Arabs had red hair and yellow freckles up their arms. She had ridden along hoping for the best, watching the fields full of blackbirds and puddles fly by the truck's windows. Then her father had stopped them and she had screamed when she saw the tall man knock him down and kick him, and she kept on screaming when the Texas man got in the truck. He hit her then, a bone-hard backhand to the mouth, a striking-out that she had never felt before, and her teeth went into her lip and stuck. But the pain and the blood didn't bother her, just the flying scent of his hand, the pasty tinge of cigarettes, which made her think of her mother, lying on the sofa smoking one after another, staring past her at the television, always the television. She had looked back at her father as the truck tore off toward Texas, wondering when he would get up. They drove by little wood-and-tin towns, rice elevators connected by bent and rusted railroads, and she felt an empty-hearted flutter when she saw the sign that said Texas was a few miles ahead. She knew then they would pass out of the land of her blood and into some strange, inevitable place, into what must happen sooner or later. She looked over at the man in the checkered shirt, glanced at his pearl buttons, bent over and spat blood on the floor mat, looked between her knees at the blood on the floor and thought of her mother again, closed her eyes and said a Hail Mary, opened her eyes and said a second Hail Mary, but stopped after 'blessed art thou among women' when she saw a crop duster fly across the road under the phone wires about a mile ahead. The plane looped and rolled over, coming back under the wires again, flying in front of an eighteen-wheeler, drifting over the field to the south and looping again, as though the pilot and his passenger were practicing for the air circus. She saw a barrel roll, another loop, a pass over the truck, and then the plane disappeared, swallowed up by a field of tall coastal Bermuda. She looked out of all the windows, but the plane was gone. She settled down to watching the straight strip of narrow highway threading through open fields now, fields with rows freshly plowed for cotton or soybeans, some experiment the rice and cane farmers were constantly trying, those dogged Labats or Thibodeauxs, who had owned the land for more than two hundred years.

When Lizette looked west again, she saw a movement out of

a low cloud and the same plane came down over the road a mile away, flying toward the green truck, coming lower and lower until its wheels were touching the highway behind a sedan that sped up as though it were a bug being chased by a hawk. When the sedan blew past, the Texas man slammed on the brakes because the plane was taxiing now, taking up both lanes and the narrow shoulders, which sloped down into twelve-foot canals topped off with the morning's rain. Lizette began to bounce on the seat, but only a few times. Her face was rimmed with a brassy border of pain. She watched the cowboy take off his hat and place it on the seat next to her. Turning his flinty face toward hers, he told her not to move an inch. He got out, and she was glad to be rid of the smell of him, whiskey and cigarettes and some mildew-smelling aftershave.

Her daddy and uncle climbed down out of the plane, her small daddy and her old and wobbly nonc René. She knew the Texas man would beat both of them up and throw them in the canal, and she began to cry all at once with a fierce suddenness that startled her. Her father and uncle had to see her, and then it would be all right. If they did not see her, they would be beaten to pieces, so she blew the horn. She became angry when they wouldn't look, and then, as she thought would happen, the freckled, long-legged foreign thing took a swing, knocking the soft René to the ground. Her father came on punching, but in only a minute the Texas man had him down and rolling on the ground. Nonc came back up in front of the truck and fell on them both, and all three fought, her relatives taking a beating.

Ensemble

A little traffic began to back up behind the idling plane and in the westbound lane, too. A five-ton truck pulled up behind the Texas man's vehicle, and two men in coveralls got out to watch the brawl. The rolling and grunting battle went on and off the blacktop. After a good five minutes, Nonc René fell away and breathed on his back like a fish, his huge belly heaving. Floyd yelled and sat down, holding his hand between his legs. The Texas man tried to get up out of the mud, went down on one knee, and rested a while. Lizette blew the horn and tried to get someone to look at her. Out of the corner of her eye she saw a puff of silver smoke by the driver's side door, and she heard a tapping. Looking down, she saw the top of T-Jean's grandmère's head. Opening the window, she reached down for the old woman's hand and bawled. The woman looked up from her walker.

'How did you bus' you mouth?' was all she asked.

'The Texas man did it,' she whined.

T-Jean's grandmère lowered her head and worked her walker ahead of her like some sort of field machine, and when she got to where the Texas man was still down on one knee, she raised the aluminum frame and poked one of its small rubber feet an inch into his eye socket. The Texas man roared, stood up, and fell back into a muddy rut, where he wagged his head and cried aloud in pain.

'You don't come to Grand Crapaud and take no Bergeron child to drag off to no place,' she scolded, threatening him with the walker. She looked around at the fields, the thin highway. 'This child belongs with her papa. She's got LeBlanc in her, and Cancienne way back, and before that, Thibodeaux.' Her shapeless print dress swelled as she gathered the air to tell him more. She pointed her walker off at the horizon. 'You see that tree line two miles over there? Look with you good eye.'

The Texas man, one bleeding eye held shut with his left hand, obeyed.

'Them tree, they used to be right there, across that ditch. Thibodeaux boys cleared all that with axes. With *axes*. Live oak and cypress with *axes*. Two hundred acre.' She swung around to look across the road. 'Over there.' She pointed into a rice field, in the middle of which an oil-well pump drifted up and down. Nonc René rolled up on one elbow with a groan and followed the line of her walker. 'Before the Thibodeaux was more

Thibodeaux living in a house made out of dirt.' She stamped her walker into the mud and turned on the Texas man, giving him such a look that he held up his free hand. 'What you got to say, you what come to steal a Bergeron baby?'

'Yeah, man, what you got to say for yourself?' asked one of the two men who had walked up from the five-ton truck. Lizette saw that they were twins dressed in identical gray coveralls, fellows with dark, oily curls, crooked noses.

Floyd picked up his head and laughed. 'Victor. Vincent Larousse.'

'Floyd, baby. *Quoi ça dit?*'

'Tex stole my lil' girl and then broke my hand with his head.' Floyd stood up, still cradling his hand against his work jeans.

'Shut up, all you crazy Larousse,' T-Jean's grandmère told them. 'I got to hear what he's goin' to say to me.' Her small head bobbed like a fishing cork.

The Texas man rocked back in the mud a bit, a rill of muddy water beading over his thighs. 'I'm a-goin' get in my truck, head on down the road, and when it's time, I'm a-goin' come back and get that little gal for her mama.' He looked over at Mrs Boudreaux, who was leading Lizette along the shoulder of the road toward her Dodge.

T-Jean's grandmère slammed her walker into the mud again. Turning to the Larousse twins, she asked them if they were still bad boys over in Tiger Island. Vincent spat between his teeth at the Texas man, who flinched. He chucked his brother on the shoulder and they walked back to their utility truck, which had MOUTON'S SCRAPYARD painted on the doors in orange paint. Two cutting-torch rigs sat in the bed, and the twins put on goggles, ran the gauges up to eighty pounds oxygen, fifteen pounds acetylene, and walked backward to the front of the Texas man's truck, pulling gas line behind them, the torches hissing blue stars. When they cut the hood off the truck, the Texas man began yelling for the police.

Floyd looked at the little circle of farmers and truck drivers forming around the scene. 'You gonna tell a policeman you stole a little girl that was given me by a judge? You gonna tell him you punched her?'

The Texas man, who was climbing out of the rut, settled back down again, watching the Larousses burn off his fenders, the torches spitting through the thin metal as though it were paper.

'My truck,' he cried, still holding his eye.

'Hot damn,' T-Jean's grandmère said. 'Them boy is still bad, yeah.'

The Larousses cut bumper braces, motor mounts, frame members, and transmission bolts as two volunteers from the crowd rolled large pieces of truck hissing into the big ditch, where they disappeared. After fifteen minutes' work, they cut the frame and rolled the cab and the bed into the canal like boulders. Soon, all that was left on the side of the road was a puddle of oil and a patch of singed grass. The twins rolled up their lines, zeroed their gauges, and walked back to the Texas man. The one who had spoken the first time, Vincent, smiled slowly. '*Mais*, anytime you come back to Louisiana, Floyd gonna phone us,' he said, holding his palm up and pointing with his middle finger. 'An' unless you drive to Grand Crapaud in a asbestos car, you gonna wind up with a bunch of little smokin' pieces shoved up you ass.' Vincent gave him a little salute and followed Victor back to the truck, where they washed their hands with Go-Jo, pulled two Schlitzes from an ice chest, and climbed into the truck to wait.

T-Jean's grandmère gave the Texas man a long look, turned to walk off, then looked down at him again. 'You, if you woulda went off with her, all you woulda got was her little body. In her head, she'd never be where you took her to. Every day she'd feel okra in her mouth.'

Floyd began walking with her to Mrs Boudreaux's car, and Nonc René limped over to the Texas man, handing him a parachute. 'Come on,' Nonc said softly, with the voice he used to call a chicken from the coop before dinner. 'I'll take you somewhere.'

'I got to get to a hospital,' he moaned. 'That old lady like to kilt me.'

When everyone was loaded into the bobbing Dodge, Floyd pointed Mrs Boudreaux's own St Christopher statue forward and began to drive with his good hand. Several men turned the plane at a right angle to the road so it could roll over a culvert into the field, where Nonc René guided the balloon tires in the furrows. The machine splattered along until it gained the sky in a furious storm of flying mud.

Floyd drove his group west, not east to Grand Crapaud, and everyone in the car was silent. In a few minutes they pulled to the side of the road in front of the state-line marker, a rough-cast concrete slab shaped like Louisiana. In the backseat, T-Jean's grandmère laughed and clapped her hands once. Floyd turned off the engine and put his arm around Lizette, kissing the top of her head, right where her fragrant hair was parted.

'Why we stopped here?' she asked, looking at the flat fields around the car. After a few moments, a plane moaned over their heads at a hundred feet, crossing into Texas and curving rapidly upward to ten times that height. It did a barrel roll and Lizette giggled. 'Is that Nonc and the *cou rouge*?'

'Yes, baby.' They all watched through the front windshield as the plane ascended into Texas, kept watching that leaden sky until the little wings banked off to the southeast for homeland, beneath them a distant silken blossom drifting down and west on a heavy Gulf breeze.

Returnings

Elaine thought that hard work might clear her head, might not let her thoughts turn to her son. She had been coaxing the tractor through the field for four hours, turning two hundred acres into corduroy. When the rusting International was dead center in the farm, it began to miss and sputter, giving up under the April sun, far from the tractor shed. Elaine reached around the steering wheel, pulling the choke out a bit, hoping the carburetor would pass the water that she knew was in the gasoline, remembering with a pang that she had not drained the little glass water trap under the fuel tank. She hoped that her husband had been wrong when he'd told her that middle-aged women couldn't farm. Yet she had forgotten to get the water out of the line on a tractor that had been sitting up three months, its gas tank sweating on the inside. She frowned at the coughing machine. They were supposed to buy a brand-new tractor that year, a 1967 model. But there was no longer any need.

The engine fluttered and died. She checked her watch and saw that it was eleven o'clock. Climbing down, she poured a drink of water from a thermos tied under the metal seat with a strand of twine. She turned to stare at her house nearly a mile away, satisfied at the even rows of brown dirt she had heaped up. Like most women, she liked to grow things.

She was a nurturer and felt that this quality, better than any man's mechanical ability, would help her bring life to the fields of her farm. She saw a likeness between caring for a home and children and raising millions of soybeans. In her blood was a drive for generation more powerful than muscle and bone. This drive would make her a farmer.

Elaine hoped that her husband would see the tractor stalled

out and would bring her some tools. His back was hurting, and he had little to do but watch out the kitchen window or endure Lyndon Johnson talking on television about the war. A half hour after the engine died, she saw his green truck bobbing toward her very slowly across the unplowed portion of field.

'Either you're out of gas or the engine sucked up a charge of water,' he said, handing her a small toolbox through the truck window. He was tanned, clean-shaven, and strong-looking, but he winced when he raised the box up to her hands.

'Stay in the truck,' she said.

'I plan to. The ride out here's awful rough.' He ran his hand through his dark, graying curls. 'You know what to do?' He asked in a way that pleaded that she did.

'Yes. I've got plenty gas. It's water, I'm sure. You stay put.' She fixed him with a worried stare and plucked at her checked cotton blouse, which clung to her back in the heat.

Her husband blinked and rested his forearms on top of the steering wheel. 'I'm sorry that you've got to do this. I'll be better in a month or so.'

She gave him a smile as she pulled a pair of slip-joint pliers from the box. 'Joe told me how to do this. I suppose you taught him somewhere along the line.'

His eyes scanned the farm. 'It's amazing how much he did around here.'

Elaine did not answer. There was nothing to say that they did not already feel in their blood about an eighteen-year-old son who was healthy one week, plowing and fixing things, and dead the next from encephalitis. They refused to reminisce, but they talked around their son at mealtime, as though he were at the table and they were ignoring him. When they touched in any way, the message of him was on their skin, and they knew their loss. Talking could not encompass what had gone from them.

They had brought up two girls, now married and raising families in other towns, good girls, who visited. But it was to have been Joe's farm.

She made a face as she pulled the bowl of the water trap off the fuel line, spilling cold gasoline into her hands. The smell would stay in the cracks of her skin for hours, like a bad memory. Working carefully in the sun, she heard the truck start and turn for the house. She took a part out of the carburetor, cleared it of water, and put everything together, opening the gas valve once more, only to discover a leak. Twenty minutes passed before she had the tractor ready to run. Wiping her hands, she heard at the periphery of her attention the steady chop of a helicopter in the distance, a common sound in this part of the parish because of an air-training facility across the line in Mississippi. She mounted the tractor, pulled out the choke, and, with a finger in the starter ring, paused to look toward a helicopter that was passing closer than usual. A gunship, armed and camouflaged, skirted the edge of her field. It hovered a moment, approached with a whopping roar, and finally settled down in a circular dust storm seventy yards from her. She held her straw hat over her brown hair, glad at least that the machine had lit in an unplowed section. Only one person sat in the glassed-in cabin, and he watched her carefully. The pilot's stare made her uneasy. She had imagined military folk to be generally on the move, having no time for meditation. Also, something was unorthodox about the pilot's size. He appeared too small; his headphones were like cantaloupe halves clapped to his ears. He was rather dark.

After a while he kicked open a door and jumped out, the huge blades dying in speed above him. Jogging across the field in loose combat fatigues, his pistol holster flying out from his side with each leap over the bumpy soil, he trailed a partially unfolded map. Elaine squinted and saw that he was Asian and very young, maybe twenty.

'Hello,' he said, smiling mightily. 'Can you be of assistance?'

She glanced at the helicopter, wondering briefly if he had somehow stolen it. 'What's wrong? You have engine trouble, too?' she asked, pointing down at the tractor.

'No, no,' he said, smiling so that his face seemed ready to split.

He seemed desperately afraid that she would fear him. 'I need advice.'

She could see behind his smile and climbed down to the ground next to him. He was the size of a boy, his features rounded and new. 'Advice about what?'

'It is hard for me to ask,' he said, backing away, tilting his head to the left, to the right, almost crying through his grin. 'I am lost.' He unfolded a map, placing it on the ground. 'If you please could tell me where I am, I could get back to base. I am on my solo training flight and have hour to return.'

She stooped and tried to study the map, but it contained no red-lined highways and town names like the filling station maps she was used to. It was lettered in a bizarre military code. She told him she could not make heads or tails of it. She was intelligent, and her father had sent her to college for two years, but she could not deal with a map that didn't have Poireauville or Leroux spelled out on it. 'I know where the fort is over the line in Mississippi, but I couldn't tell you how to fly there. Why don't we just give them a call and have an instructor come out to fly you back?'

'No,' he wailed, his smile collapsing at last. Elaine thought of the pinched faces she saw on the newscasts in the evenings, the small people running from thatched houses, pillars of smoke in the background, the rattle of weapons. 'If I fail at pilot school, I get sent back to Vietnam as foot soldier.' He turned to look longingly at his machine, as though already it had been taken from him.

She stood and leaned against her tractor. 'Your instructor would give you another chance, wouldn't he?'

He shook his head vigorously. 'My instructor wants to see me dead in a rice paddy. He is a big American with red hair. Every day he tells me, "Le Ton, if you do not fly right, we send you home with a cheap rifle to fight VC."'

She studied him a while, looked back to the farmhouse and then to the map. Her husband could not read it, she knew. Joe probably could have.

'Le Ton. Is that your name?'

'Yes. I am from farmland, too.' He folded up his map slowly.

'You flew out of Fort Exter?' The more she looked at him, the younger he appeared, some mother's favorite, she guessed, noticing something in his eyes. Why else would he be trying so hard to stay alive?

'That is so. I fly by map and directions given by my instructor at base. No radio.' His face darkened. 'My instructor gives me bad directions.'

'You have an hour left to get back?'

He nodded. 'Thank you for trying to help me.'

She wiped her palms on her jeans. 'I'll tell you what, son. I can't judge anything from that map, but if you take me up in that machine of yours, I might be able to show you where the fort is, and then you could drop me back off here. I don't think it's more than thirty miles or so.' She could hardly believe what she'd said. She might be doing something illegal or unpatriotic. He took to the idea instantly. 'Ah, that would be good. I fly you a few miles outside of base and return here. Plenty time to get back to base.' She hung her straw hat on the breather pipe of the tractor and stepped over the big unplowed clods of earth to the gunship, climbing in next to him as he flipped overhead switches, manipulated foot pedals, and lifted hand levers at his side. The craft surged and vibrated like a toolshed in a tornado. In a moment they were whanging through the sky.

'Go east,' she yelled. Elaine watched for the water tower in Poireauville but could hardly keep her eyes off the running fields below her feet, the sugarcane, bayous, levees, and willow brakes that flew by as in a dream or a wide-screened movie at a world's fair. It was difficult to concentrate on any one landmark when the giant oaks and longleaf pines were sailing just a few feet below. Le Ton glanced at her for direction. The water tower she saw in the distance had to be Poireauville's, and she pointed toward it, but when the craft came within two miles of the round silver tank, she felt disoriented and panicky. It was too small to be

186

Poireauville's, too freshly painted. Le Ton flew a wide circle around it and she wished that all little towns still painted their names on the tanks as they had when she was a child.

'Which way?' he asked.

She scanned the ground. There were too many trees. Poireauville was a cut-over hamlet and did not support such a welter of sycamores. Perhaps they had veered a few miles northeast and were over Rodeaux. Looking to her left, she spotted a set of smokestacks and suddenly wished her husband was with her. An area man could look at a factory's stack from three miles away and tell the type of mill, the name of the owner, and the ages of his children. But she was lost.

She spotted a rusty thread of railroad and pointed down to it. 'That's the Missouri Pacific branch line. Follow it.' Her son had loved railroads and had shown her maps of the region's lines enough times that she had a vague notion of where the local tracks went. Before he was old enough to drive, she would take him on long rides so he could take pictures of stations and engines. She remembered telling him that he should photograph people, not only objects. People are what have to be remembered. She looked down at an abandoned crossroads grocery, its windows boarded up. Places are nothing.

Le Ton swirled above the railroad for six miles, looking down and then checking his compass. 'Lady, we fly north? You are sure of the railroad?' He had lost his smile completely. His face shone with a nervous sweat. It worried her that he was more frightened than she was. Looking down, she thought that perhaps this was the old north track instead of the branch that led east. Everywhere were oaks and occasionally a flat field of sugarcane she did not recognize. She saw a barn she had never seen before, a large white home, and two rows of tenant houses. She felt like a child lost in a thousand acres of razor-leafed cane.

'Go that way,' she yelled, pointing to her right. Studying the ground, she saw a cornfield slip under her and a tenant house that seemed to be empty, its iron roof bloody with rust. She was looking for a laundry line full of drying clothes, which would tell the presence of a woman. A full laundry line behind a house where the truck was gone would be a lucky find. She did not want to risk landing in the yard of a stiff-necked sharecropper who would call the sheriff before he heard her out.

A weathered cypress house passed below, and she asked Le Ton for field glasses, which he produced from a rack under his seat. She focused on the backyard. A string of laundry danced on the line, but there were many cumbersome checkered shirts, and in the front yard, two trucks.

A mile and a half across the field was a poorer house, the chimney broken at the top, the roof swaybacked. She motioned to it when she saw on its clothesline the wink of towels and sheets. She thought back to the days when she still hung out the wash, the clean damp smell of the pillowcases, and the breezy mornings her son chased his sisters through the laundry, the bright cotton licking their faces.

Le Ton was shouting, 'The house is behind. Keep going?'

Looking back with the glasses, she saw no car and no electric meter on the wires leading along the side of the house. 'Put down in the field across the road from that shack.' There was no need to soil the laundry.

The helicopter descended slowly into a pasture as several bony, fly-bitten cows lurched away into a grove of wild plum trees. As the craft touched down, she looked across the gravel road to a porch where a stout black woman sat in a rocker and shaded her eyes.

Le Ton stopped the engine. 'Why do we stop here?' He looked around at the sickly fields and the paintless tenant shack.

'I've got to ask directions from somebody who won't call a newspaper.' She jumped to the ground and he followed her to the road, where she instructed him to wait.

Once on the porch she sidestepped a gap in the flooring.

'Don't bust a leg,' the black woman sang, touching the kerchief that bound her hair. 'My man supposed to fix that when he can find a right board.'

'How you doing? I'm Elaine Campbell from down in Burkhalter community. Do you know where that is?'

The other woman stood, adjusted her apron, and stared at the floor. 'No, ma'am,' she said. 'Don't you?'

'Well, of course I know where it is when I'm there. But this boy and I seem to be lost.'

The black woman looked across the road at Le Ton, who stood like a frail post against the slack barbed wire. 'How come you ain't got on your uniform?'

'I'm not in the army. He is. He got lost over my place in Burkhalter and I was trying to show him the way to Fort Exter when we got lost again.'

'I don't know where Burkhalter is.'

'It's not far from Poireauville.'

'Law.' She sat down. 'That's twenty miles off with the crow. The roads don't hardly run thataway.' She peered across the gravel lane again. 'They left that little Chinaman run that big machine?'

Elaine turned, looked at Le Ton, and grinned. 'He's on a training mission. If they find out at the fort that he got lost, they'll send him back to Vietnam as a foot soldier. I'm just trying to help him out.'

'Vietnam,' the other woman repeated. 'I heard that word a lot. My onliest boy been sent over there. I got three girls, but only one boy. He use to be at Exter, too. Name's Vergil Bankston.' She smiled as she said the name. 'My name's Mary Bankston.'

Elaine sat in a straight-back chair and motioned for Le Ton to cross the road.

As he walked up to the porch, Mary Bankston examined him, then let out a gentle, high-pitched whine. 'If he ain't just a baby, though. Is all Vietnam peoples easy lost like you?'

Le Ton smiled defensively, considering the question. He sat on the porch floor between the women, facing them, and folded his legs. 'I am very stupid to Americans. Most trainees are farm people. We know how to plow with ox, how to use hoe.' He made a little hoeing movement with his arms. 'It is very hard to learn vectors and compression ratios, how to make big, fast helicopters run right.' He looked from one woman's face to the other. 'My cousin, Tak Dok, came to fly Corsair airplanes. In training flight, his cockpit shield blows off and he radios back what happens. Man in the tower says land at once. Tak Dok brings his plane down in the field of corn and lands without much damage. Instructors send him back to be foot soldier because they mean for him to come back to his airfield to land at once.' He looked over his shoulder toward his craft. 'Last month, Tak Dok is killed. My young cousin was a good pilot but could not always understand your way with words.'

Mary Bankston passed a long mother's look to Elaine, the expression a woman owns at night when she sits up listening to a child cough and rattle, knowing there is nothing she can do but act out of her best feelings. 'I got a pot of hot water on the stove. I can drip coffee in a minute.' She smiled at Le Ton. 'Got a tea bag somewhere, too.'

'We don't have a whole lot of time,' Elaine said, looking down on Le Ton's camouflage cap. She pulled it off a moment to look at the thick, close-cropped hair and the young brassy skin at the roots. Everything about him was small and young, laden with possibilities. 'Do you have any idea how far we are from the Mississippi line?'

'You wants to go to Exter, don't you?'

'Yes.'

'Then tell him to fly straight east to that brand-new interstate about thirty miles, then take a right and follow it down to that big green sign what say Fort Exter.'

Elaine placed her left palm on her forehead. 'I should have remembered that. I've never been on it, but I knew it was there.'

'Sure enough,' Mary Bankston said. 'Even a farmer Chinaman can find a four-lane highway. I been on it twice to go see Vergil.'

Elaine returned Le Ton's cap. 'Didn't you pass over that interstate to get into this region?'

He thought about this for a moment, and then with the

expression of an old man wise to betrayal, he answered her. 'Instructor says fly over Gulf and then come inland.'

'Let's go, then.' Mary Bankston offered to let them have two fried-apple pies for their trip, but they declined.

'He ain't never going to get no bigger if he don't eat,' she yelled after them as they crossed the fence.

Elaine called back. 'Don't tell anybody about us, especially your son.'

She nodded from her paintless porch. 'Who gonna believe me?'

Le Ton started the engine and the big gunship whirled off into the sky. She looked below and saw the old railroad they had followed earlier. 'Why aren't you heading east? You could let me off on a highway outside of base, and I could figure a way to get home.'

'That would not be right,' he said. 'You have been too helpful. I should not put you out in the middle of a wilderness.' He glanced back to the tenant house, where Mary Bankston was probably watching him as she would a young child crossing the street. 'I also have been on the big highway the black lady speaks of. I did not know it ran north-south. It is not on the map the instructor gives me.'

With the field glasses, she found the correct water tower, a larger structure to the south emblazoned with SENIORS '66, a spray-paint legend her son had helped create one moonless night. She remembered how Sammy, the local deputy, had caught him, bringing him to the house, revealing what her son had done, working a wink into his speech while Joe stood behind him in the front door, repentant and fearful.

She had never told her husband. He wouldn't have punished their son severely, but Elaine let her instinct to protect him over-power her need to discipline him. She had been so glad that he had been brought home safe. Now as the painted words swam in the field glasses, she couldn't say whether she would ever tell her husband. She forced her eyes away, over to the highway, and in a minute found the blacktop that crawled to her farm. She had no idea that the place appeared so drowsy, the roofs tired with rust, the crystal green ponds oval like the sleepy eyes of children. Le Ton circled to the rear of the farm to avoid buzzing the house and set down where he had earlier.

'I hope your tractor starts now,' he said, ducking his head, forcing a smile.

She reached over and grabbed his neck, kissing him on the cheek. 'Call Ralph Campbell in Poireauville and tell me how you did,' she said.

He was surprised, but he nodded, understanding her order. After seeing her jump down and clear the blades, he gave a broad wave, then mounted the sky.

She watched until the craft disappeared over a distant neighboring farmhouse, the home of John Thompson, whose blond daughter had loved her son. She listened to the clamor of the machine pounding into the eastern sky.

When she turned, she noticed her husband's truck lurching out toward her. Quickly, she reached under the tank and turned off the gasoline valve. He arrived, getting out this time, holding his back and walking over like someone much older. She held her breath, then asked the question. 'What brings you out here?'

'I been sleeping,' he said, rubbing his smooth jaw. 'Something woke me up. I just looked out and saw you still hadn't started the tractor.' He gave her a questioning look. 'Why didn't you walk in and get me?'

'How's your back?'

He straightened up slowly, as if to test himself. 'Feels better this afternoon.'

'That's good. No, I've taken everything apart and blown out the water. It just won't start.'

He walked up to the controls, pulled the starter ring twice, and listened. He reached up under the tank. 'You forgot to reopen the gas line,' he said.

She kicked at a clod of dirt. 'I can't believe I forgot that.'

'Women farmers,' he said, smiling that cool, wrinkled smile of his.

'I suppose you've never done the same.'

He thought a bit. 'One morning I tried and tried to start this thing. I ran down a battery before Joe – he was about nine then – came out to the shed and turned on the gas for me. He said, "Daddy, what would you ever do without me?"'

She walked over and stood next to him, the skin on her arms prickling. The empty quiet of the field was oppressive, and she pulled the starter ring. The tractor chuckled alive, but as soon as it did, he reached over and pushed the kill switch, the quiet settling on them like a memory. 'We've got to get away for a while,' he said, his voice so shaky it scared her. 'Leave the tractor here. Let's get cleaned up and drive into town.' He glanced up into the sky. 'Let's drive two towns over and get a fancy meal. You need it. You never get off this place.' He pounded the dull red tractor once with a fist.

She looked at the eastern horizon, then put her arm easily around his back and hugged him, her freckled cheek pressing against the fresh khaki of his shirt. Slipping a hand up to the hot skin of his neck, she felt his blood coursing away, knowing it to be her blood as well. They stood together in the half-plowed field, in the middle of all they had lost. He took her hand and led her to the passenger door of the truck, opening it for her as though they were on a date.

An hour later she was clipping small gold circles to her earlobes, and her husband was shaving. In the den the telephone began its slow rattle, and she bolted past the bathroom door for it. At first she was afraid to pick it up.

'Yes?' she answered, then said, 'I see. Yes.' Her expression remained neutral. 'I understand you perfectly. Sure. And thank you for calling.' She replaced the receiver and put a hand over a smile.

They got into the shimmering sedan and drove out onto the unlined road, heading through the hot afternoon toward town.

In a month the land around her would bear cornstalks growing like children. She cast a long admiring gaze at the field she'd been plowing, at the straightness of her rows where they glimmered under the sun, rails of dirt running east under a safe and empty sky.

Deputy Sid's Gift

I'm going to tell you about the last time I went to confession. I met this priest at the nursing home where I work spoon-feeding the parish's old folks. He noticed I had a finger off, and so he knew I was oil field and wanted to know why I was working indoors. This priest was a blond guy with eyes you could see through and didn't look like nobody inside of two hundred miles of Grand Crapaud, Louisiana. He didn't know that when sweet crude slid under twelve dollars a barrel, most oil companies went belly-up like a stinking redfish, and guys like me had to move out or do something else. So I told him I took a night class in scrubbing these old babies, and he said I had a good heart and bull like that and invited me to come visit at the rectory if I ever needed to.

One day I needed to, yeah. Everybody's got something they got to talk about sometime in their life. I went to the old brick church on LeBlanc Street on a Saturday morning and found him by himself in his little kitchen in the old cypress priest house, and we sat down by the table with a big pot of coffee.

So I told him what had been going through my head, how I used to have a 1962 Chevrolet pickup truck, a rusty spare I kept parked out by the road just to haul off trash. It was ratty and I was ashamed to drive it unless I was going to the dump. One day after Christmas my wife, Monette, told me to get rid of the tree and the holiday junk, so I went to crank the truck. Well, in a minute I'm standing by the road with a key in my hand, looking at a long patch of pale weeds where the truck used to be. I'm saying to myself that the truck coulda been gone a hour or a week. It's just a thing you don't look at unless you need it.

So I called Claude down at his little four-by-four city jail and he said he'd look for it the next day, that he had more expensive stuff to worry about. Ain't that a hell of a note. Then I called the sheriff's office down at the parish seat, and when I told them the truck's over thirty years old, they acted like I'm asking them to look for a stole newspaper or something. It was my truck and I wanted it back.

The priest, he just nodded along and poured us our first cup of coffee from a big aluminum dripolator. When he finished, he put the pot in a shallow pan of water on the gas stove behind his chair and stared down at his shoe, like he was hearing my confession, which I guess he was. He even had his little purple confession rag hanging on his neck.

I told the priest how the cops searched a lil' bit, and how I looked, but that old truck just disappeared like rain on a hot street. Monette, she was glad to get it out the yard, but I needed something for hauling, you know? So after not too long I found a good old '78 Ford for a thousand dollars and bought that and put it right where the other one was.

One day my little girl Lizette and me, we was at the nursing home together because of some student-visit-the-parent-at-work deal at her school. She was letting the old folks hug her little shoulders and pat her dark hair. You know how they are. They see a child and go nuts to get at them, like the youngness is going to wear off on their old bodies. At the end of my shift, one of the visitors who was there to see his dried-up wife – I think he was a Canulette, kind of a café au lait dude from out by Prairie Amère – his truck won't crank, so me and Lizette decided to bring him home. Me in my smocky little fruit uniform and Lizette with her checkerboard school suit went off in my shiny thirdhand Buick, old man Canulette sitting between us like a fence post. We rolled down the highway and turned off into the rice fields and went way back into the tree line toward Coconut Bayou. We passing through that poor folks' section on the other side of Tonga Bend when Lizette stuck her head out the window to make her pigtails go straight in the wind. Next thing I knew, she yelled, daddy, there's your truck, back in the woods. I turned the car around in that little gravel road and sure enough – you couldn't hardly see it unless you had young eyes – there was my old Chevy parked up under a grove of live oaks maybe 150 yards away.

We walked up on it, and judging from the thistles that had growed up past the bumper, it'd been there three months. I held back and asked Monsieur Canulette if anybody lived around there, and he looked at the truck and said the first word since town: Bezue. He said here and there in the woods a Bezue lived and they all had something wrong in they heads. I told him I'd put me a Bezue in jail if he stole my truck, but he just looked at me with those silver eyes of his in a way that gave me *les frissons*. I brought the old man to his little farm and then came back to Tonga Bend Store to call the deputy, who took most of a hour to get out there.

They sent Sid Touchard, that black devil, and he showed up with his shaggy curls full of pomade falling down his collar, the tape deck in his cruiser playing zydeco. He got out with a clipboard, like he knows how to write, and put on his cowboy hat. He asked me if I was the Bobby Simoneaux what called, and even Lizette looked behind her in the woods for maybe another Bobby Simoneaux, but I just nodded. He looked at the truck and the leaves and branches on it and asked me do I still want it. *Mais*, yeah, I told him. Then Sid walked up and put his hand on the door handle like it was something dirty, which I guess it was, and pulled. What we saw was a lot of trash paper, blankets, and old clothes. I looked close and Lizette stepped back and put her little hands on her mouth. The air was nothing but mildew and armpit, and by the steering wheel was a nappy old head.

He's living in it, Deputy Sid said. His eyebrows went up when he said that. Even he was surprised, and he works the poor folks of the parish. He asked again do I still want it. Hell yeah, I said. He spit. He's a tall man, yeah, and it takes a long time for his spit to hit the ground. Then he reached in and woke the man, who sat up and stared at us. He was black – back-in-the-country black. He wasn't no old man, but he had these deep wrinkles the old folks call the sorrow grooves, and he looked like he was made out of Naugahyde. His eyeballs was black olives floating in hot sauce, and when Sid tried to get out of him what he was doing in the truck, he took a deep breath and looked over the rusty hood toward the road.

Finally he said, I'm Fernest. Fernest Bezue. My mamma, she lives down that way. He pointed, and I could see he been drunk maybe six years in a row. The old cotton jacket he had on was eat up with battery acid and his feet was bare knobs. Sid give me that look like he got on bifocals, but he ain't. Hell no, I told him. I want my truck. He stole it and you got to put him in jail. So Sid said to him, you stole this truck? And Fernest kept looking at the road like it was something he wasn't allowed to see, and then he said he found it here. When he said that, I got hot.

Deputy Sid tugged Fernest out into the sunlight, slow, like he was a old cow he was pulling out a tangle of fence. He put him in the cruiser and told me and Lizette to get in the front seat. He said where Fernest's mamma lived, my Buick can't go. So we rolled down the gravel a mile, turned off on a shell road where the china-ball and sticker bushes about dragged the paint off that beat-up cruiser. Lizette, she sat on my lap, looking at Deputy Sid's candy bar wrappers on the floor, a satsuma on the seat, and a rosary around the rearview. The road gave out at a pile of catbrier and we turned left into a hard-bottom coulee full of rainwater next to Coconut Bayou. The water come up to the hubcaps and Lizette wiggled and told Deputy Sid we on a ferryboat for sure, yeah.

There's this little shotgun shack up on brick piers with the tar paper rotting off it, stovepipe stub sticking out the side wall, no steps to the door, cypress knees coming up in the yard, egg cartons and water jugs floating around on the breeze. Deputy Sid leaned on the horn for maybe fifteen seconds until the front door opened and a woman look like a licorice stick stood there dressed in some old limp dress. He rolled down the window and asked if it's her son in the backseat. She stooped slow, squinted a long time. That Fernest, she said to the water. She sure wasn't talking to us. Sid stepped out on a walk board and told me to follow. I jacked up my legs, slid over all the junk, and brought out that satsuma with me. Can't leave this with Lizette, I told him. She loves these things. Sid took it from me, tossed it to her, and she caught that with one hand.

While he talked to the woman I looked in the house. All this while, my shoes was filling up with water. The first room had nothing but a mattress and a kerosene lamp on the floor and some bowls next to it. The walls was covered with newspaper to keep the wind out. In the second and last room, the floor had fell in. The whole place was swayback because the termites had eat out the joists and side beams. It didn't take no genius to tell that the roof rafters wasn't gonna last another year. A wild animal would take to a hole in the ground before he lived in a place like that.

Deputy Sid asked the woman did she know about the truck, and she said he was living in it. He turned to me and said, look around. You want me to put him in jail?

Hell yeah, I told him, and Sid looked at me hard with those oxblood eyes he got, trying to figure a road into my head. He told me if I file charges and put him in jail, that'd cost the parish. My tax money was gonna pay to feed him and put clothes on him. He said let him stay with his mamma. The old woman stooped down again, and Fernest stared at her like maybe she was a tractor or a cloud. I looked around again and saw that putting him in jail would be a promotion in life, yeah.

Sid took off the bracelets and walked him to the house. The old lady said he could stay. Then we left, that cruiser bottoming out and fishtailing from the yard, its mud grips digging down to the claypan. Back at my truck I threw all his stuff in a pile, old coats with cigarette holes burnt through, medicine bottles from the free clinic in town, dirty drawers I handled with a stick, fried chicken skin and bones, a little radio with leaking batteries. I put my key in but the engine didn't make a sound. When I opened up the hood, all I saw was a pile of a thousand sticks and three long otter-looking animals that took off for the woods. The sheriff's tow truck brought the thing back to my house and that was that. My wife took one look at it and one smell of it and told me it had to be gone. I already had one truck.

A rainy spell set in and the truck sank down in the backyard for a couple weeks with the crawfish chimneys coming up around it till I got a nice day and scrubbed it inside and out. Down at the home we got five new poor helpless folks from the government without nobody dying to make room for 'em, so another week passed before I could get to the hardware and buy me a nice orange FOR SALE sign.

Now this was when the priest kind of leaned back against the window frame and made a faraway smile and looked out to the rose garden Father Scheuter put in before they transferred him to Nevada. Priests try not to look you in the eye when you telling stuff. Scared maybe you won't tell it straight, or tell it all. So I told him straight that the second night that old truck was parked back out on the street wearing that sign, it got stole. I called up Deputy Sid direct this time and told him what happened. He said, you want me to look for that truck again? I told him hell yeah. He said, don't you got a truck already? I think that pomade Sid been smearing on his head all these years done soaked in his brain, and I told him that. He said, you got a nice brick house, a wife, three kids, and two cars. He said, you might quit at that. He said he didn't feel like burning fifty dollars' gas looking for a forty-dollar truck. I told him I would talk to the sheriff, and he said okay, he'd look.

I wound up at the home helping out for music day, when Mr Lodrigue brings his Silvertone guitar and amp to play songs the old folks recognize. Man, they love that rusty stuff like 'As Time Goes By,' 'The Shrimp Boats Is A-Coming,' and such 78 rpm tunes they can tap their feet to. I get a kick out of them people – one foot in the grave and still trying to boogie. And Mr Lodrigue, who has wavery silver hair and kind of smoky gray eyes, he looks like Frank Sinatra to them old gals.

I got through with music day and went out to where my car was at behind the home, and there, big as a hoss, was Sid sitting on the hood of his muddy police car. I walked up and saw his arms was crossed. He said, I found it. I asked him where it was, and he said, where it was before. I said, you mean Fernest Bezue got it back in Prairie Amère? Man, that made me hot. Here I let him go free and he comes back on me like that. I cursed and spit twice. Deputy Sid looked at me like I was the thief. I asked him why didn't he haul him in, and he looked away. Finally, he said, he's alcoholic. That got me hotter. Like *I* could go down to Generous Gaudet's used-car lot drunk and steal me a car and somebody would let *me* off. Deputy Sid nodded, but he said, Simoneaux, you play with those old people like they your own *grandpère* and *grandmère*. You don't know what they done wrong in they time. I sat down next to him when he said that. The hood metal popped in and shook loose a thought in my head that kind of got me worried. It was about the folks in the home. Maybe I was nice to the old people because I was paid for that. Nobody was paying me to be nice to a drunk Bezue from Prairie Amère. I spit on the sidewalk and wondered if Deputy Sid's as dumb as he looks. Then I thought about Fernest Bezue out under the oaks, staring at the road. So I said, okay, get the tow truck to pull it in, and he says, no, I can't make a report because they'll pick him up.

What you think about that? I got to go get my own stole truck, yeah. That's my tax dollars at work.

The pot on the range gave a little jump like a steam bubble got caught under its bottom, and the priest turned and got us another cup. He was frowning a little now, like his behind's hurting in that hard-bottom chair, but he didn't say anything, still didn't look.

I went on about how I wanted to do the right thing, how me

and Monette got out on the gravel past Prairie Amère, trying to beat a big thunderstorm coming up from the Gulf. When we got to where the truck was, the wind was twisting those live oaks like they was rubber. Monette stayed in the Buick and I walked up to the old red truck, and in the bed was Fernest, sitting down with a gallon of T&T port between his legs, just enjoying the breeze. You stole my truck again, I told him. He said he had to have a place to get away. He said it like he was living in a vacation home down on Holly Beach. He was staring up into the black cloud bank, waiting for lightning. That's how people like him live, I guess, waiting to get knocked down and wondering why it happens to them. I looked at his round head and that dusty nap he had for hair and started to walk off. But he had what was mine and he didn't work for it, and I figured it would do him more harm than good to just give him something for nothing. I said if he could get two hundred dollars he could have the truck. I didn't know where that come from, but I said it. He said if he had two hundred dollars he wouldn't be sitting in the woods with a five-dollar gallon of wine. I wondered for a minute where he wanted to go, but just for a minute, because I didn't want to get in his head. So I looked in the cab where he'd hot-wired the ignition, and I sparked up that engine. I pulled out his blankets and some paper bags of food and threw them in a pile. Then I jumped into the bed and put down the tailgate. I had to handle him like the real helpless ones at the home, he was that drunk, and even in that wind he smelled sour, like a wet towel bunched up in the trunk. I put the truck in gear and left him in the middle of that clearing under them oaks, him that wouldn't pay or work. When I rolled up on the road ahead of Monette in the Buick, the rain come like a water main broke in the sky. I looked back at Fernest Bezue and he was standing next to his pile of stuff, one finger in that jug by his leg and his head up like he was taking a shower. Then a big bolt come down across the road and the rain blew sideways like busted glass, and I headed back for town.

All that night I rolled like a log in the bed. I thought the weather would blow over, but the storm set on Grand Crapaud like a flat iron and dropped big welding rods of lightning almost till dawn. On the way to work I got tempted to drive back to Prairie Amère, but I didn't, and all that day I was forgetting to change bed linen and was slopping food on the old babies when I fed 'em. It took me a week to relax, to get so I could clean the truck some more without seeing Fernest looking up at the sky, waiting. I got it ready and put it on the lawn, but this time I took the battery and left it in the carport. Nobody looked at it for about a week. One morning Lizette, she kissed me bye and went out to wait for the bus. A minute later I heard the screen door open and Lizette said the old truck was trying to run. She said it was making running noise. So I went out and looked through the glass. Fernest Bezue was in there snoring on his back like a sawmill. When Lizette found out it was a big drunk man she yelled and ran for the house. She was scared, yeah, and I didn't like that. I opened the driver door and it took me five minutes to convince him I wasn't Mr Prudhomme, a cane farmer he used to work for ten years back. When he sat up, his left eye capsized, then come back slow, and it was weak, like a lamp flame at sunup. He stared out the windshield at a place I couldn't see.

I told Fernest that I ought to pull him out and turn the hose on him for scaring my little girl like he did. He mumbled something I didn't catch, and I told him to get the hell away. But he just sat there in the middle of that old sprung bench seat like he half-expected me to get in and drive him somewhere to eat. Finally he told me the house had fell in and his mamma went off somewhere and didn't tell him. Man, I let him have it. Told him to stop that drink and get a job. He said that his drinking was a disease, and I told him yeah, it was a *lazy* disease. He said if he could help it, he would. That his daddy was the same way and died in a wreck. I told him he was in a slow wreck right now. I looked back at my house and them wilting camelias Monette planted under the windows. Then I told him if he could stay dry for a week I'd see if I could get him a mopping job at the rest home. He could save up and buy my truck. Then he put his head down and laughed. I can't stop, man, he said to me. That pissed me off so bad I went in and called the cops. After a while Claude come up in the town's cruiser, took one look at Fernest, then looked over where I'm standing by my Japan plum tree. How they made a gun belt skinny enough for that man, I don't know. He asked me, *mais*, what you 'spec us to do with him? Claude is real country, can't hardly talk American. He said Fernest can't do nothing to that truck he can arrest him for. If he steal it again the mayor gonna give him the town beutimfication award. I said arrest him, and I could see in Claude's eyes that nobody was on the night shift to keep a watch on Fernest down at that one-cell jail. Do something, I told him. He's scaring Lizette sleeping out here.

What Claude did is put him in the squad car, stop by Bug's café and buy him a ham sandwich, and drop him off at the town limits, by the abandoned rice mill buildings. They told me that when I called the station later on.

This was when the priest got up and stretched. He pointed to my cup and I shook my head. He fixed himself one more with lots of cream, got a glass of water from the tap, and sat down again, looking at me just once, real quick.

That made me feel like I could keep going, so I told him how that night and a couple nights more I couldn't sleep without dreaming something about that no-good drunk. I mean, lots of people need help. My one-legged uncle needs his grass cut, and I'd do it, but he says he don't want me to mess with it. Says I got better things to do with my time. Other people deserve my help, and that Fernest didn't deserve nothing, yet when I went to sleep, there he was in my head. When I read a newspaper, there he was in a group picture, until I focused real good. But after a while he started to fade again, you know, like before. I settled into business at the home, putting ointment on the bald men's heads, putting Band-Aids on the old ladies' bunions so they can wear shoes, though there's no place for them to walk to.

Then one morning here she come, in with three poor folks the government paid us to take, Fernest's mamma, all dried up like beef jerky. She had herself a stroke out on Mr Prudhomme's farm, where she was staying for free in a trailer, and one side of her wouldn't work. I stayed away from her for three days, until it was time for Mr Lodrigue, the music man, when everybody gets together in the big room. I was just walking by to get Mr Boudreaux his teeth he left in the pocket of his bathrobe when her good arm stuck out and grabbed my fruity little uniform. I didn't want to look in her eye, but I did. She slid out her tongue and wet her lips. The mailbox is the onliest thing standing, she told me. The house fall in. I told her it's a shame and I wanted to walk away, but she got hold of my little smock and balled it in her fist.

She told me his government check come in the mailbox, then he walk five miles for the wine. She told me he was gonna die of the wine and couldn't I help. I looked at her and I felt cold as a lizard. I asked her why me. She said, you the one. I told her he was past all help. He had the drinking disease and that was that. I pulled away and went got old man Boudreaux's choppers, and when I come back I saw her across the room, pointing at me with the one finger what would still point. You the one, that finger said. I laughed and told myself right then and there I wasn't going to help no black drunk truck thief that couldn't be helped.

The priest, he made to swat a mosquito on his arm, but he changed his mind and blew it away with his breath. I didn't know if he was still listening good. Who knows if a priest pays a lot of attention. I think you supposed to be talking to God, and the man in the collar is just like a telephone operator. Anyway, I kept on.

I told him how after work I used the phone out in the parking lot to call Deputy Sid to help me find Fernest. Yeah, I was ashamed of myself. I didn't know what I was going to do if Sid found him for me, but I had to do something to get the old lady's pointing finger out my head. I went home, and about a hour before sundown

Deputy Sid pulled up in my front yard and I went out to him, carrying Lizette, who had a cold and was all leechy like a kid gets when she's feeling bad. Sid had him a long day. His pomade hair hung down like a thirsty azalea. He said we got to go out to Prairie Amère, and so I put my little girl down, got in the old truck, and followed him out.

We went through the pine belt and past the rice fields those Thibodeaux boys own, and by them poor houses in Tonga Bend, then we broke out into Prairie Amère, which is mostly grass and weed flowers with a live oak every now and then, but no crops. The old farmers say everything you plant there comes up with a bitter taste. All of a sudden the cruiser pulled off into the clover on the side of the road, so I rolled up behind. There ain't a thing around, and I walked up and Deputy Sid said empty land is a sad thing. He stretched and I could hear his gun belt creaking. I asked why we stopped and he pointed. Maybe a hundred yards in the field, eat up by weeds, was a little barn, the kind where a dozen cows could get in out the sun. We jumped the ditch and scratched through the buttonbush and bull tongue. Deputy Sid stopped once and sneezed. He said I told him to find Fernest and he did. It wasn't easy, but he did. He asked what did I want with him, and I said his mamma wanted me to check, but that wasn't it, no. It was the people at the home what made me do it. I was being paid to be nice to them. I wanted to do something without being paid. I didn't give a damn about some black truck thief, but I wanted to help him. I couldn't tell Deputy Sid this.

We got to the tin overhang on the barn, and we wasn't able to see much inside. The sun was about down. We stepped in and waited for our eyes to get used to the place. I could smell that peppery-sweet cypress. A building can be a hundred years old – if it's made of cypress, you going to smell that. Along the side wall was a wooden feed rack three feet off the ground, and sleeping in there was Fernest, his face turned to that fine-grain wall. Deputy Sid let out a little noise in his throat like a woman would make. He said Fernest was trying to sleep above the ground so the ants couldn't get to him. He said one time two years before, Fernest passed out on the ground and woke up in blazes with a million fire ants all over him like red pepper in a open wound. He stayed swole up for three weeks with hills of running pus all over him, and when his fever broke, he was half blind and mostly deaf in one ear.

I went over to the feed trough and shook him. He smelled strong and it took five minutes before he opened his eyes, and even in the dark you could see them glowing sick. I asked him was he all right and he asked me if I was his mamma, so I waited a minute for his head to get straight. Deputy Sid came close and picked up a empty bottle and sniffed it. I reached through the slats and bumped Fernest's arm and asked him why he drank so damn much when he knew it would kill him. He looked up at me like I was stupid. He said the booze was like air to him. Like water. I told him maybe I could get him in the home with his mamma, and he stared up at the tin roof and shook his head. I asked Sid if maybe his mamma could get him picked up and put in the crazy house, and Sid told me no, he's not crazy, he's just drunk all the time. The state thinks there's a difference. Fernest sat up in the trough, hay all stuck in his hair, and he started coughing deep and wet, like some of the old folks do at the home late in the evening. Night shift is scary because them babies sail away in the dark. Anyway, Fernest's face got all uneven, and he asked me what I wanted. That stopped me. I opened my dumb mouth just to see what would come out, and I told him that Deputy Sid bought my truck and was giving it to him so he could stay in it sometime. I held up the key and gave it to him. He nodded like he expected this, like people wake him up all the time and give him cars. I looked at Sid and I could see a gold star on a tooth, but he stayed quiet. Then I told Fernest I knew he couldn't drive it, and I was going take the insurance off anyway, but he could use it to sleep out of the weather like he done before. He looked at Sid and reached out and gave him some kind of boogaloo handshake. In a minute I had the truck up in the grass by the

barn, and I pulled the battery out just in case, and Deputy Sid
brought me and the battery toward home. We pulled away from
all that flat, empty land, and after about five miles Sid asked why
I told Fernest *he* gave him the car. I looked at a tornado-wrecked
trailer on the side the road and said I didn't want nothing for
what I did. The cruiser rattled past the poor folks in Tonga Bend,
and Sid tuned in a scratchy zydeco station. Clinton Rideau and
the Ebony Crawfish started pumping out 'Sunshine Can't Ruin
My Storm,' but I didn't feel like tapping my foot.

I went home and expected to sleep, but I didn't. I thought I
did something great, but by two A.M., I knew all I did was give
away a trashy truck with the floor pans rusting out and all the
window glass cracked. I gave up the truck mostly to make myself
feel good, not to help Fernest Bezue. And that's what I told the
priest I come there to tell him.

The priest looked at me in the eyes then, and I could see something coming, like a big truck or a train. Then he leaned in and
I could smell the soap on him. He told me there's only one thing
worse than what I did. I looked at the linoleum and asked, what's
that? And he said, not doing it.

I like to fell out the chair.

About a month later Fernest's mamma died in the night, and I
called up Deputy Sid at dawn. He went out to look but he couldn't
find Fernest nowhere. Sid brought his big black self to my house,
and I saw him bouncing up my drive like he got music in his
veins instead of blood. He got on a new khaki uniform tight as
a drumhead, knife creases all over. He told me the liquor store
past Coconut Bayou said they ain't seen him. The mailbox at the
old place been eat down by termites. None of the farmers seen
him. I said it's a shame we can't tell him about his mamma, and
Deputy Sid looked at me sidewise and kissed his lips like he's
hiding a smile. I told him to come inside, and Monette fixed us
all a cup of coffee, and we sat down in the kitchen and cussed
the government.

Summer come and the weather turned hot as the doorknob to hell. The old babies at the home couldn't roll around outside, so we had to keep 'em happy in the big room by playing cards and like that. I had to play canasta with six ladies who couldn't remember the rules between plays, so I would spend three hours a day explaining rules to a game we'd never finish.

I guess it was two months after Fernest's mamma passed. I got home and sat in my easy chair by the air condition when Lizette come by and give me a little kiss and said Deputy Sid wanted me on the phone. So I went in the kitchen, and he told me he's in his cruiser out at Mr Thibaut's place in the north end of the parish, west of Mamou. He found Fernest.

I couldn't say nothing for half a minute. I asked him was he drunk, and he said no, he was way past that, and I said when, and he said he died about yesterday in the truck. I got a picture of Fernest Bezue driving that wreck on the back roads, squinting through the cracked windshield, picking his spot for the night. I told Deputy Sid I was sorry and he said, don't feel like that. He said, we couldn't do nothing for him but we did it anyway.

Welding with Children

Tuesday was about typical. My four daughters, not a one of them married, you understand, brought over their kids, one each, and explained to my wife how much fun she was going to have looking after them again. But Tuesday was her day to go to the casino, so guess who got to tend the four babies? My oldest daughter also brought over a bed rail that the end broke off of. She wanted me to weld it. Now, what the hell you can do in a bed that'll cause the end of a iron rail to break off is beyond me, but she can't afford another one on her burger-flipping salary, she said, so I got to fix it with four little kids hanging on my coveralls. Her kid is seven months, nicknamed Nu-Nu, a big-head baby with a bubbling tongue always hanging out his mouth. My second-oldest, a flight attendant on some propeller airline out of Alexandria, has a little six-year-old girl named Moonbean, and that ain't no nickname. My third-oldest, who is still dating, dropped off Tammynette, also six, and last to come was Freddie, my favorite because he looks like those old photographs of me when I was seven, a round head with copper bristle for hair, cut about as short as Velcro. He's got that kind of papery skin like me, too, except splashed with a handful of freckles.

When everybody was on deck, I put the three oldest in front the TV and rocked Nu-Nu off and dropped him in the Portacrib. Then I dragged the bed rail and the three awake kids out through the trees, back to my tin workshop. I tried to get something done, but Tammynette got the big grinder turned on and jammed a file against the stone just to laugh at the sparks. I got the thing unplugged and then started to work, but when I was setting the bed rail in the vise and clamping on the ground wire from the welding machine, I leaned against the iron and Moonbean picked the electric rod holder off the cracker box and struck a blue arc on the zipper of my coveralls, low. I jumped back like I was hit with religion and tore those coveralls off and shook the sparks out of my drawers. Moonbean opened her goat eyes wide and sang, 'Whoo. Grendaddy can bust a move.' I decided I better hold off trying to weld with little kids around.

I herded them into the yard to play, but even though I got three acres, there ain't much for them to do at my place, so I sat down and watched Freddie climb on a Oldsmobile engine I got hanging from a willow oak on a long chain. Tammynette and Moonbean pushed him like he was on a swing, and I yelled at them to stop, but they wouldn't listen. It was a sad sight, I guess. I shouldn't have that old greasy engine hanging from that Kmart chain in my side yard. I know better. Even in this central Louisiana town of Gumwood, which is just like any other red-dirt place in the South, trash in the yard is trash in the yard. I make decent money as a now-and-then welder.

I think sometimes about how I even went to college once. I went a whole semester to LSU. Worked overtime at a sawmill for a year to afford the tuition and showed up in my work boots to be taught English 101 by a black guy from Pakistan who couldn't understand one word we said, much less us him. He didn't teach me a damn thing and would sit on the desk with his legs crossed and tell us to write nonstop in what he called our 'portfolios,' which he never read. For all I know, he sent our tablets back to Pakistan for his relatives to use as stove wood.

The algebra teacher talked to us with his eyes rolled up like his lecture was printed out on the ceiling. He didn't even know we were in the room, most of the time, and for a month I thought the poor bastard was stone-blind. I never once solved for X.

The chemistry professor was a fat drunk who heated Campbell's soup on one of those little burners and ate it out the can while he talked. There was about a million of us in that classroom, and I couldn't get the hang of what he wanted us to do with the numbers and names. I sat way in the back next to some fraternity boys who called me 'Uncle Jed.' Time or two, when I could see the blackboard off on the horizon, I almost got the hang of something, and I was glad of that.

I kind of liked the history professor and learned to write down a lot of what he said, but he dropped dead one hot afternoon in the middle of the pyramids and was replaced by a little porch lizard that looked down his nose at me where I sat in the front row. He bit on me pretty good because I guess I didn't look like nobody else in that class, with my short red hair and blue jeans that were blue. I flunked out that semester, but I got my money's worth learning about people that don't have hearts no bigger than bird shot.

Tammynette and Moonbean gave the engine a long shove, got distracted by a yellow butterfly playing in a clump of pigweed, and that nine-hundred-pound V-8 kind of ironed them out on the backswing. So I picked the squalling girls up and got everybody inside, where I cleaned them good with Go-Jo.

'I want a Icee,' Tammynette yelled while I was getting the motor oil from between her fingers. 'I ain't had a Icee all day.'

'You don't need one every day, little miss,' I told her.

'Don't you got some money?' She pulled a hand away and flipped her hair with it like a model on TV.

'Those things cost most of a dollar. When I was a kid, I used to get a nickel for candy, and that only twice a week.'

'Icee,' she yelled in my face, Moonbean taking up the cry and calling out from the kitchen in her dull little voice. She wasn't dull in the head; she just talked low, like a bad cowboy actor. Nu-Nu sat up in the Portacrib and gargled something, so I gathered everyone up, put them in the Caprice, and drove them down to the Gumwood Pak-a-Sak. The baby was in my lap when I pulled up, Freddie tuning in some rock music that sounded like hail on a tin roof. Two guys I know, older than me, watched us roll to the curb. When I turned the engine off, I could barely hear one of them say, 'Here comes Bruton and his bastardmobile.' I grabbed the steering wheel hard and looked down on the top of

Nu-Nu's head, feeling like someone just told me my house burned down. I'm naturally tanned, so the old men couldn't see the shame rising in my face. I got out, pretending I didn't hear anything, Nu-Nu in the crook of my arm like a loaf of bread. I wanted to punch the older guy and break his upper plate, but I could see the article in the local paper. I could imagine the memories the kids would have of their grandfather whaling away at two snuff-dripping geezers. I looked them in the eye and smiled, surprising even myself. Bastardmobile. Man.

'Hey, Bruton,' the younger one said, a Mr Fordlyson, maybe sixty-five. 'All them kids yours? You start over?'

'Grandkids,' I said, holding Nu-Nu over his shoes so maybe he'd drool on them.

The older one wore a straw fedora and was nicked up in twenty places with skin cancer operations. He snorted. 'Maybe you can do better with this batch,' he told me. I remembered then that he was also a Mr Fordlyson, the other guy's uncle. He used to run the hardwood sawmill north of town, was a deacon in the Baptist church, and owned about 1 percent of the pissant bank down next to the gin. He thought he was king of Gumwood, but then, every old man in town who had five dollars in his pocket and an opinion on the tip of his tongue thought the same.

I pushed past him and went into the Pak-a-Sak. The kids saw the candy rack and cried out for Mars Bars and Zeroes. Even Nu-Nu put out a slobbery hand toward the Gummy Worms, but I ignored their whining and drew them each a small Coke Icee. Tammynette and Moonbean grabbed theirs and headed for the door. Freddie took his carefully when I offered it. Nu-Nu might be kind of wobble-headed and plain as a melon, but he sure knew what an Icee was and how to go after a straw. And what a smile when that Coke syrup hit those bald gums of his.

Right then, Freddie looked up at me with his green eyes in that speckled face and said, 'What's a bastardmobile?'

I guess my mouth dropped open. 'I don't know what you're talking about.'

'I thought we was in a Chevrolet,' he said.

'We are.'

'Well, that man said we was in a—'

'Never mind what he said. You must have misheard him.' I nudged him toward the door and we went out. The older Mr Fordlyson was watching us like we were a parade. I was trying to look straight ahead. In my mind, the newspaper bore the head-line, LOCAL MAN ARRESTED WITH GRANDCHILDREN FOR ASSAULT. I got into the car with the kids and looked back out at the Fordlysons where they sat on a bumper rail, sweating through their white shirts and staring at us all. Their kids owned sawmills, ran fast-food franchises, were on the school board. They were all married. I guess the young Fordlysons were smart, though looking at that pair, you'd never know where they got their brains. I started my car and backed out onto the highway, trying not to think, but to me the word was spelled out in chrome script on my fenders: BASTARDMOBILE.

On the way home, Tammynette stole a suck on Freddie's straw, and he jerked it away and called her something I'd only heard the younger workers at the plywood mill say. The words hit me in the back of the head like a brick, and I pulled off the road onto the gravel shoulder. 'What'd you say, boy?'

'Nothing.' But he reddened. I saw he cared what I thought.

'Kids your age don't use language like that.'

Tammynette flipped her hair and raised her chin. 'How old you got to be?'

I gave her a look. 'Don't you care what he said to you?'

'It's what they say on the comedy program,' Freddie said. 'Everybody says that.'

'What comedy program?'

'It comes on after the nighttime news.'

'What you doing up late at night?'

He just stared at me, and I saw that he had no idea of what *late* was. Glendine, his mamma, probably lets him fall asleep in front of the set every night. I pictured him crumpled up on that smelly shag rug his mamma keeps in front of the TV to catch the spills and crumbs.

When I got home, I took them all out on our covered side porch. The girls began to struggle with jacks, their little ball bouncing crooked on the slanted floor, Freddie played tunes on his Icee straw, and Nu-Nu fell asleep in my lap. I stared at my car and wondered if its name had spread throughout the community, if everywhere I drove people would call out, 'Here comes the bastardmobile.' Gumwood is one of those towns where everybody looks at everything that moves. I do it myself. If my neighbor Miss Hanchy pulls out of her lane, I wonder, Now, where is the old bat off to? It's two-thirty, so her soap opera must be over. I figure her route to the store and then somebody different will drive by and catch my attention, and I'll think after them. This is not all bad. It makes you watch how you behave, and besides, what's the alternative? Nobody giving a flip about whether you live or die? I've heard those stories from the big cities about how people will sit in an apartment window six stories up, watch somebody take ten minutes to kill you with a stick, and not even reach for the phone.

I started thinking about my four daughters. None of them has any religion to speak of. I thought they'd pick it up from their mamma, like I did from mine, but LaNelle always worked so much, she just had time to cook, clean, transport, and fuss. The girls grew up watching cable and videos every night, and that's where they got their view of the world, and that's why four dirty blondes with weak chins from St Helena Parish thought they lived in a Hollywood soap opera. They also thought the married pulpwood truck drivers and garage mechanics they dated were movie stars. I guess a lot of what's wrong with my girls is my fault, but I don't know what I could've done different.

Moonbean raked in a gaggle of jacks, and a splinter from the porch floor ran up under her nail. 'Shit dog,' she said, wagging her hand like it was on fire and coming to me on her knees.

'Don't say that.'

'My finger hurts. Fix it, Paw-Paw.'

'I will if you stop talking like white trash.'

Tammynette picked up on fivesies. 'Mamma's boyfriend, Melvin, says *shit dog.*'

'Would you do everything your mamma's boyfriend does?'

'Melvin can drive,' Tammynette said. 'I'd like to drive.'

I got out my penknife and worked the splinter from under Moonbean's nail while she jabbered to Tammynette about how her mamma's Toyota cost more than Melvin's teeny Dodge truck. I swear I don't know how these kids got so complicated. When I was their age, all I wanted to do was make mud pies or play in the creek. I didn't want anything but a twice-a-week nickel to bring to the store. These kids ain't eight years old and already know enough to run a casino. When I finished, I looked down at Moonbean's brown eyes, at Nu-Nu's pulsing head. 'Does your mammas ever talk to y'all about, you know, God?'

'My mamma says *God* when she's cussing Melvin,' Tammynette said.

'That's not what I mean. Do they read Bible stories to y'all at bedtime?'

Freddie's face brightened. 'She rented *Conan the Barbarian* for us once. That movie kicked ass.'

'That's not a Bible movie,' I told him.

'It ain't? It's got swords and snakes in it.'

'What's that got to do with anything?'

Tammynette came close and grabbed Nu-Nu's hand and played the fingers like they were piano keys. 'Ain't the Bible full of swords and snakes?'

Nu-Nu woke up and peed on himself, so I had to go for a plastic diaper. On the way back from the bathroom, I saw our little book rack out the corner of my eye. I found my old Bible stories hardback and brought it out on the porch. It was time somebody taught them something about something.

They gathered round, sitting on the floor, and I got down amongst them. I started into Genesis and how God made the earth, and how he made us and gave us a soul that would live forever. Moonbean reached into the book and put her hand on God's beard. 'If he shaved, he'd look just like that old man down at the Pak-a-Sak,' she said.

My mouth dropped a bit. 'You mean Mr Fordlyson? That man don't look like God.'

Tammynette yawned. 'You just said God made us to look like him.'

'Never mind,' I told them, going on into Adam and Eve and the Garden. Soon as I turned the page, they saw the snake and began to squeal.

'Look at the size of that sucker,' Freddie said.

Tammynette wiggled closer. 'I knew they was a snake in this book.'

'He's a bad one,' I told them. 'He lied to Adam and Eve and said not to do what God told them to do.'

Moonbean looked up at me slow. 'This snake can talk?'

'Yes.'

'How about that. Just like on cartoons. I thought they was making that up.'

'Well, a real snake can't talk, nowadays,' I explained.

'Ain't this garden snake a real snake?' Freddie asked.

'It's the devil in disguise,' I told them.

Tammynette flipped her hair. 'Aw, that's just a old song. I heard it on the reddio.'

'That Elvis Presley tune's got nothing to do with the devil making himself into a snake in the Garden of Eden.'

'Who's Elvis Presley?' Moonbean sat back in the dust by the weatherboard wall and stared out at my overgrown lawn.

'He's some old singer died a million years ago,' Tammynette told her.

'Was he in the Bible, too?'

I beat the book on the floor. 'No, he ain't. Now pay attention. This is important.' I read the section about Adam and Eve disobeying God, turned the page, and all hell broke loose. An angel was holding a long sword over Adam and Eve's downturned heads as he ran them out of the Garden. Even Nu-Nu got excited and pointed a finger at the angel.

'What's that guy doing?' Tammynette asked.

'Chasing them out of Paradise. Adam and Eve did a bad thing, and when you do bad, you get punished for it.' I looked down at their faces and it seemed that they were all thinking about something at the same time. It was scary, the little sparks I saw flying in their eyes. Whatever you tell them at this age stays forever. You got to be careful. Freddie looked up at me and asked, 'Did they ever get to go back?'

'Nope. Eve started worrying about everything and Adam had to work every day like a beaver just to get by.'

'Was that angel really gonna stick Adam with that sword?' Moonbean asked.

'Forget about that darned sword, will you?'

'Well, that's just mean' is what she said.

'No it ain't,' I said. 'They got what was coming to them.' Then I went into Noah and the Flood, and in the middle of things, Freddie piped up.

'You mean all the bad people got drownded at once? All right!'

I looked down at him hard and saw that the Bible was turning into one big adventure film for him. Freddie had already watched so many movies that any religion he would hear about would nest in his brain on top of *Tanga the Cave Woman* and *Bikini Death Squad*. I got everybody a cold drink and jelly sandwiches, and after that I turned on a window unit, handed out Popsicles, and we sat inside on the couch because the heat had waked up the yellow flies outside. I tore into how Abraham almost stabbed Isaac, and the kids' eyes got big when they saw the knife. I hoped that they got a sense of obedience to God out of it, but when I asked Freddie what the point of the story was, he just shrugged and looked glum. Tammynette, however, had an opinion. 'He's just like O. J. Simpson!'

Freddie shook his head. 'Naw. God told Abraham to do it just as a test.'

'Maybe God told O. J. to do what he did,' Tammynette sang.

'Naw. O. J. did it on his own,' Freddie told her. 'He didn't like his wife no more.'

'Well, maybe Abraham didn't like his son no more neither, so he was gonna kill him dead and God stopped him.' Tammynette's voice was starting to rise the way her mother's did when she'd been drinking.

'Daddies don't kill their sons when they don't like them,' Freddie told her. 'They just pack up and leave.' He broke apart the two halves of his Popsicle and bit one, then the other.

Real quick, I started in on Sodom and Gomorrah and the burning of the towns full of wicked people. Moonbean was struck with Lot's wife. 'I saw this movie once where Martians shot a gun at you and turned you into a statue. You reckon it was Martians burnt down those towns?'

'The Bible is not a movie,' I told her.

'I think I seen it down at Blockbuster,' Tammynette said.

I didn't stop to argue, just pushed on through Moses and the Ten Commandments, spending a lot of time on number six, since that one give their mammas so much trouble. Then Nu-Nu began to rub his nose with the backs of his hands and started to tune up, so I knew it was time to put the book down and wash faces and get snacks and play crawl-around. I was determined not to turn on TV again, but Freddie hit the button when I was in the kitchen. When Nu-Nu and me came into the living room, they were in a half circle around a talk show. On the set were several overweight, tattooed, frowning, slouching individuals who, the announcer told us, had tricked their parents into signing over ownership of their houses, and then evicted them. The kids watched like they were looking at cartoons, which is to say, they gobbled it all up. At a commercial, I asked Moonbean, who has the softest heart, what she thought of kids that threw their parents in the street. She put a finger in an ear and said through a long yawn that if the parents did mean things, then the kids could do what they wanted to them. I shook my head, went in the kitchen, found the Christmas vodka, and poured myself a long drink. I stared out in the yard to where my last pickup truck lay dead and rusting in a pile of wisteria at the edge of the lot. I formed a little fantasy about gathering all these kids into my Caprice and heading out northwest to start over, away from their mammas, TVs, mildew, their casino-mad grandmother, and Louisiana in general. I could get a job, raise them right, send them to college so they could own sawmills and run car dealerships. A drop of sweat rolled off the glass and hit my right shoe, and I looked down at it. The leather lace-ups I was wearing were paint-spattered and twenty years old. They told me I hadn't held a steady job in a long time, that whatever bad was gonna happen was partly my fault. I wondered then if my wife had had the same fantasy: leaving her scruffy, sunburned, failed-welder husband home and moving away with these kids, maybe taking a course in clerical skills and getting a job in Utah, raising them right, sending them off to college. Maybe even each of their mammas had the same fantasy, pulling their kids out of their parents' gassy-smelling old house and heading away from the heat and humidity. I took another long swallow and wondered why one of us didn't do it. I looked out to my Caprice sitting in the shade of a pecan tree, shadows of leaves moving on it, making it wiggle like a dark green flame, and I realized we couldn't drive away from ourselves. We couldn't escape in the bastardmobile.

In the pantry, I opened the house's circuit panel and rotated out a fuse until I heard a cry from the living room. I went in and pulled down a storybook, something about a dog chasing a train. My wife bought it twenty years ago for one of our daughters but never read it to her. I sat in front of the dark television.

'What's wrong with the TV, Paw-Paw?' Moonbean rasped.

'It died,' I said, opening the book. They squirmed and complained, but after a few pages they were hooked. It was a good book, one I'd read myself one afternoon during a thunderstorm.

But while I was reading, this blue feeling got me. I was thinking, What's the use? I'm just one old man with a little brown book of Bible stories and a doggy-hero book. How can that compete with daily MTV, kids' programs that make big people look like fools, the Playboy Channel, the shiny magazines their mammas and their boyfriends leave around the house, magazines like *Me*, and *Self*, and *Love Guides*, and rental movies where people kill one another with no more thought than it would take to swat a fly, nothing at all like what Abraham suffered before he raised that knife? But I read on for a half hour, and when that dog stopped the locomotive before it pulled the passenger train over the collapsed bridge, even Tammynette clapped her sticky hands.

The next day, I didn't have much on the welding schedule, so after one or two little jobs, including the bed rail that my daughter called and ragged me about, I went out to pick up a window grate the town marshal wanted me to fix. It was hot right after lunch, and Gumwood was wiggling with heat. Across from the cypress railroad station was our little redbrick city hall with a green copper dome on it, and on the grass in front of that was a pecan tree with a wooden bench next to its trunk. Old men sometimes gathered under the cool branches and told one another how to fix tractors that hadn't been made in fifty years, or how to make grits out of a strain of corn that didn't exist anymore. That big pecan was a landmark, and locals called it the 'Tree of Knowledge.' When I walked by going to the marshal's office, I saw the older Mr Fordlyson seated in the middle of the long bench, blinking at the street like a chicken. He called out to me.

'Bruton,' he said. 'Too hot to weld?' I didn't think it was a friendly comment, though he waved for me to come over.

'Something like that.' I was tempted to walk on, but he motioned for me to sit next to him, which I did. I looked across the street for a long time. 'The other day at the store,' I began, 'you said my car was a bastardmobile.'

Fordlyson blinked twice but didn't change his expression.

Most local men would be embarrassed at being called down for a lack of politeness, but he sat there with his face as hard as a plowshare. 'Is that not what it is?' he said at last.

I should have been mad, and I was mad, but I kept on. 'It was a mean thing to let me hear.' I looked down and wagged my head. 'I need help with those kids, not your meanness.'

He looked at me with his little nickel-colored eyes glinting under that straw fedora with the black silk hatband. 'What kind of help you need?'

I picked up a pecan that was still in its green pod. 'I'd like to fix it so those grandkids do right. I'm thinking of talking to their mammas and—'

'Too late for their mammas.' He put up a hand and let it fall like an ax. 'They'll have to decide to straighten out on their own or not at all. Nothing you can tell those girls now will change them a whit.' He said this in a tone that hinted I was stupid for not seeing this. Dumb as a post. He looked off to the left for half a second, then back. 'You got to deal directly with those kids.'

'I'm trying.' I cracked the nut open on the edge of the bench.

'Tryin' won't do shit. You got to bring them to Sunday school every week. You go to church?'

'Yeah.'

'Don't eat that green pecan – it'll make you sick. Which church you go to?'

'Bonner Straight Gospel.'

He flew back as though he'd just fired a twelve-gauge at the dog sleeping under the station platform across the street. 'Bruton, your wild-man preacher is one step away from taking up serpents. I've heard he lets the kids come to the main service and yells at them about frying in hell like chicken parts. You got to keep them away from that man. Why don't you come to First Baptist?'

I looked at the ground. 'I don't know.'

The old man bobbed his head once. 'I know damned well why not. You won't tithe.'

That hurt deep. 'Hey, I don't have a lot of extra money. I know the Baptists got good Sunday-school programs, but . . .'

Fordlyson waved a finger in the air like a little sword. 'Well, join the Methodists. The Presbyterians.' He pointed up the street. 'Join those Catholics. Some of them don't put more than a dollar a week in the plate, but there's so many of them, and the church has so many services a weekend, the priests can run the place on volume like Wal-Mart.'

I knew several good mechanics who were Methodists. 'How's the Methodists' children's programs?'

The old man spoke out of the side of his mouth. 'Better'n you got now.'

'I'll think about it,' I told him.

'Yeah, bullshit. You'll go home and weld together a log truck, and tomorrow you'll go fishing, and you'll never do nothing for them kids, and they'll all wind up serving time in Angola or on their backs in New Orleans.'

It got me hot the way he thought he had all the answers, and I turned on him quick. 'Okay, wise man. I came to the Tree of Knowledge. Tell me what to do.'

He pulled down one finger on his right hand with the forefinger of the left. 'Go join the Methodists.' Another finger went down and he told me, 'Every Sunday, bring them children to church.' A third finger, and he said, 'And keep 'em with you as much as you can.'

I shook my head. 'I already raised my kids.'

Fordlyson looked at me hard and didn't have to say what he was thinking. He glanced down at the ground between his smooth-toe lace-ups. 'And clean up your yard.'

'What's that got to do with anything?'

'It's got everything to do with everything.'

'Why?'

'If you don't know, I can't tell you.' Here he stood up, and I saw his daughter at the curb in her Lincoln. One leg wouldn't straighten all the way out, and I could see the pain in his face.

I grabbed his arm, and he smiled a mean little smile and leaned in to me for a second and said, 'Bruton, everything worth doing hurts like hell.' He toddled off and left me with his sour breath on my face and a thought forming in my head like a rain cloud.

After a session with the Methodist preacher, I went home and stared at the yard, then stared at the telephone until I got up the strength to call Famous Amos Salvage. The next morning, a wrecker and a gondola came down my road, and before noon, Amos loaded up four derelict cars, six engines, four washing machines, ten broken lawn mowers, and two and one-quarter tons of scrap iron. I begged and borrowed Miss Hanchy's Super-A and bush-hogged the three acres I own and then some. I cut the grass and picked up around the workshop. With the money I got from the scrap, I bought some aluminum paint for the shop and some first-class stuff for the outside of the house. The next morning, I was up at seven replacing screens on the little porch, and on the big porch on the side, I began putting down a heavy coat of glossy green deck enamel. At lunch, my wife stuck her head through the porch door to watch me work. 'The kids are coming over again. How you gonna keep 'em off of all this wet paint?'

My knees were killing me, and I couldn't figure how to keep Nu-Nu from crawling where he shouldn't. 'I don't know.'

She looked around at the wet glare. 'What's got into you, changing our religion and all?'

'Time for a change, I guess.' I loaded up my brush.

She thought about this a moment, then pointed. 'Careful you don't paint yourself in a corner.'

'I'm doing the best I can.'

'It's about time,' she said under her breath, walking away.

I backed off the porch and down the steps, then stood in the pine straw next to the house, painting the ends of the porch boards. I heard a car come down the road and watched my oldest daughter drive up and get out with Nu-Nu over her shoulder.

When she came close, I looked at her dyed hair, which was the color and texture of fiberglass insulation, the dark mascara, and the olive skin under her eyes. She smelled of cigarette smoke, stale smoke, like she hadn't had a bath in three days. Her tan blouse was tight and tied in a knot above her navel, which was a lardy hole. She passed Nu-Nu to me like he was a ham. 'Can he stay the night?' she asked. 'I want to go hear some music.'

'Why not?'

She looked around slowly. 'Looks like a bomb hit this place and blew everything away.' The door to her dusty compact creaked open, and a freckled hand came out. 'I forgot to mention that I picked up Freddie on the way in. Hope you don't mind.' She didn't look at him as she mumbled this, hands on her cocked hips. Freddie, who had been sleeping, I guess, sat on the edge of the car seat and rubbed his eyes like a drunk.

'He'll be all right here,' I said.

She took in a deep, slow breath, so deathly bored that I felt sorry for her. 'Well, guess I better be heading on down the road.' She turned, then whipped around on me. 'Hey, guess what?'

'What?'

'Nu-Nu finally said his first word yesterday.' She was biting the inside of her cheek. I could tell.

I looked at the baby, who was going after my shirt buttons. 'What'd he say?'

'Da-da.' And her eyes started to get red, so she broke and ran for her car.

'Wait,' I called, but it was too late. In a flash, she was gone in a cloud of gravel dust, racing toward the most cigarette smoke, music, and beer she could find in one place.

I took Freddie and the baby around to the back steps by the little screen porch and sat down. We tickled and goo-gooed at Nu-Nu until finally he let out a 'Da-da' – real loud, like a call.

Freddie looked back toward the woods, at all the nice trees in the yard, which looked like what they were now that the trash had been carried off. 'What happened to all the stuff?'

'Gone,' I said. 'We gonna put a tire swing on that tall willow oak there, first off.'

'All right. Can you cut a drain hole in the bottom so the rain-water won't stay in it?' He came close and put a hand on top of the baby's head.

'Yep.'

'A big steel-belt tire?'

'Sounds like a plan.' Nu-Nu looked at me and yelled, 'Da-da,' and I thought how he'll be saying that in one way or another for the rest of his life and never be able to face the fact that Da-da had skipped town, whoever Da-da was. The baby brought me in focus, somebody's blue eyes looking at me hard. He blew spit over his tongue and cried out, 'Da-da,' and I put him on my knee, facing away toward the cool green branches of my biggest willow oak.

'Even Nu-Nu can ride the tire,' Freddie said.

'He can fit the circle in the middle,' I told him.

Misuse of Light

The store's electric bell rang, and Mel DeSoto saw the young woman come in out of the heat with something under her arm. She looked shyly at the tripods ranked along a shelf, at the racks holding the latest cameras lined up like gleaming robotic eyes, and then she spotted his counter, the one that held the classics.

'Hello,' she said. 'Someone told me you buy old cameras.'

He realized that though she was tall and blond, and wearing a very serious and knowing expression, she was only about eighteen, at least twenty years younger than he was and a whole lifetime away. 'What do you have?'

She raised a cracked leather case to the counter. 'My grandfather died and my parents are getting rid of his things.' Her eyes slid across his face and bounded off to the back of the store. He suddenly felt big and soft and old.

Mel opened the case and began to examine a fifties-era Rolleiflex, checking the slower shutter speeds, opening the back and looking for fungus on the lenses. It was a clean camera, the mechanics crisp, almost perfect. He set it on the counter between them and listened to the timer buzz like a wasp until the shutter fired with a snap. He opened it again and pulled out an exposed roll of 120 film. 'You want this?' he asked.

She made a face. 'No.'

He looked at her and wondered about her sense of family history. 'Well, this is in pretty good shape. I can let you have two hundred dollars for it.'

She moved her hips from side to side, a girl's motion. 'I didn't know if you'd even want it.'

'This was a fine camera in its day.' He pulled out a form and asked her to sign it. 'Some dealers would try to steal it from you. Your parents will be proud you got a fair price.'

'Nobody cares what I do,' she told him. He paid her from the register, and then she was gone out into the steamy New Orleans afternoon. Mr Weinstein walked over and handled the camera.

'Dust it, and it'll be good as new. This one'll sell.' Mr Weinstein owned the store. He was a bald man with lardy skin and a dark brush of hair above his ears. His eyes flicked toward the door. 'She seemed kind of sad.'

Mel shrugged. 'This was her grandfather's.' He sat at his little workbench and began to work with Lilliputian brushes and screwdrivers. He knew old cameras and how to deal with their shiny arms and eyes, their little spring-fed brains. As a young man, he had tried his hand at art photography and took courses at Tulane, but his work was not promising, and his professor would write on his projects, sometimes on the photographs themselves, 'Misuse of light.'

At lunchtime, he walked down the street for a hamburger, and when he reached into his pants pocket for change, he found the old roll of film the girl had left with him. It was wound on a metal spool, and the backing paper dated to the fifties. He decided to try to develop it at home. Mel enjoyed the bad photography of amateurs and always tried to develop the exposed film left in old cameras he'd purchased. Sometimes the film had faded out to nothing; sometimes the emulsion would be cracked and corroded, showing only a dried lake of skin, a quarter-moon of birthday cake. But then there would be the roll that had sat in some dark closet, locked in a Kodak Tourist, or an old Zeiss folder, kept dry by air-conditioning in an upper-middle-class house, and he could develop whatever was there: backyard picnic, lakeside fish fry, the trip to the fat aunt's house. Now and then, he'd find something artful or otherwise interesting, and he'd put it in a scrapbook he kept for the purpose. He'd try to figure out what was in the minds of the people in the photographs, but he never could. Sometimes he'd try to imagine himself in one of the pictures, and when he would do this and look at the person standing next to him, he'd find only another stranger, like anyone he'd bump into on the street.

One of his prizes seemed to have been taken in the fifties. It was a color shot of a vacation to the Grand Canyon, three weeping little girls in razory focus lined up against the pipe barrier at the edge of a cliff, the canyon itself a Mercurochrome smudge in the background. Another of his favorite images came out of an ancient Leica and was a fairly close shot of a German battleship sitting in an inner-city canal, firing its huge deck guns straight down a boulevard, oil drums on the bank jumping fifty feet in all directions from the concussion, and one woman in a dark coat in the shadow of the cannon barrels, leaping from a dock, taking flight over the water like a crow. The entire image somehow rippled with the shock of the guns, as though the negative had picked up sound as well as light.

He showed the photo of the little girls to his wife. She told him that she saw merely tired children at the end of a long ride in a car without air-conditioning. His daughter thought the little girls were spoiled and had just been denied an ice-cream cone. Mel suspected an apoplectic father unaware of his irony of driving two thousand miles to record the misery of his offspring against a gorgeous but ignored background. He thought the man was either missing the point of photography or was a very bad person, uncaring about his children's misery and mocking them with a record of it. The photo had meaning, but it was closed. The figures in the paper would not talk.

One evening after his wife and daughter had gone to bed, Mel went into his home darkroom, mixed up some Microdol-X in a deep bath, and plugged in a green safelight. He dropped an ice cube into the developer and watched the thermometer in the solution fall to 68°F. In total darkness, he unwound the strip of negatives he'd gotten out of the girl's Rolleiflex and put it down into the bath, shaking it free of bubbles, then picking the long ribbon of film up by its ends and rocking it through the developer. This was a terrible way to develop film, but with forty-plus-year-old exposures, he needed to see what the images were doing. After a few minutes, he reached up in the dark and hit the button for the green light, and he saw that the film was just beginning to show images, so he rocked the wet strand through the chemical again until the emulsion began to crowd with persons and railings and what looked like deck chairs.

The next day, he sold three expensive press cameras, and right before lunch a woman came in carrying an old Brownie in its original box. He was going to turn it down, but when he pulled the cartridge from the bottom, he saw an exposed roll of 127. The woman took his offer of five dollars, did not want a receipt, and left without a word. On his way to lunch, he decided to drop the color film off around the corner at a drugstore that had one-hour service. After his meal, he picked up the photographs and went outside to lean against the building in the sun and look at what he had. The images were blue-toned and dull, barely focused: There were eleven shots of a man sitting in various pointless attitudes on a dirty cloth sofa, drinking bottled beer. He was wearing a sleeveless undershirt and had very hairy shoulders. The wall and a curtain behind the sofa were sooty, and Mel guessed the man was poor and lived in the North, in a house heated with a coal stove. The last photo was of a smiling little girl wearing a Communion dress, her hands folded in front. Her nose resembled that of the man on the sofa. Mel considered the images separately and as a suite and found nothing interesting about them either way, so he tossed them into a trash can on his way back to the shop.

That night, he went in to print the roll he'd gotten out of the sad girl's Rolleiflex. The first print in the tray showed a lovely woman in her mid-thirties, a truly lovely woman whose image kept Mel's face startled above the tray until her features began to overdevelop and darken. He printed the negative again, this time in eight-by-ten format, and a pair of eyes looked up at him as if to say, You're the one. The woman resembled Ingrid Bergman, but taller, and with an easier smile. She wore a simple full skirt of a soft-looking material, and it hung beautifully on her, without a wrinkle. The next frame was taken from farther away; she was standing next to what seemed to be a pillar, and scattered behind her were flimsy wooden folding chairs. Another shot revealed that she was on the upper open deck of some type of large vessel. The pillar was a smokestack. Blurred in the background was a railing of some sort, and behind that, a dark looming blot. Every photo was carefully composed. In one, only the woman was in focus; in another, everything was sharp, the chairs assuming a welcoming chorus of angles and shadows behind her. There were other shots, taken with the sun over the photographer's shoulder and seemingly a few minutes apart, and in these Mel could see a resemblance to the sad girl, in the cheekbones and nose. The background of frames nine and ten contained a dark boat, perhaps a navy vessel of some sort. The eleventh frame was taken with the woman leaning her back against the rail of what now, he realized, was an old excursion steamer. In this shot, the woman's expression was jarred and she was saying something. It was the only photo in which she was just a bit out of focus, and in the lower-right corner was a blurred foot, as though someone had just run in front of her before the shutter tripped. The twelfth frame had not been exposed.

In the store the next day, Mel took in a pair of Leicas and three old Voightlanders from a pawnbroker. Mr Weinstein examined his purchases and nodded. Then he noticed the photos of the woman on Mel's workbench.

'What's this?'

'She was in that Rollei I bought.'

Weinstein picked up a print and sucked a tooth. 'Those were the days when women looked like women.' He shook his shiny head. 'What're you going to do with these?'

'Well, just look at the composition. They're sort of "found art," I guess, and for the first time I have a live person connected with a roll of film of this quality. I was going to call that girl to see if she wanted them. Might be a relative.'

Weinstein arched an eyebrow. 'And?'

'You know, ask her some questions. Get into the photograph.' He looked down. 'I wish I knew where this was.'

Weinstein sniffed. 'Even I know that. See that one print? That's the Mississippi, and that blurred thing across it is Algiers Courthouse. This is some old harbor excursion boat I don't recognize. God, we used to have fun on those things.'

'You got a guess as to what year?'

'Hell, I don't know. It's not the regular boat. The *President* was at the foot of Canal Street for fifty years. This boat I don't recognize at all.' He looked down at Mel, who was sitting with a Graflex on his lap. 'Still got the scrapbook, huh? What do you get out of looking at that old stuff?'

Mel picked up a photo of the woman. 'I like trying to figure out what I'm looking at.'

Weinstein raised a hand. 'Then look at it.'

'No. I like to interpret what's there.'

'You confusing art with reality? There's a difference, you know.'

Mel looked to his left into the street. 'Life can't be art?'

Mr Weinstein put a hand on his shoulder. 'Mel, this is not art. It's a person in a photograph. When you try to think about these common images, you're not interpreting; you're being . . . well, nosy.'

Mel was offended. 'You think so?' he said, looking the Graflex uncomfortably in the eye.

He called the girl and found that she lived off Carrolton Avenue, more or less on his way home. He told her he'd drop off copies of the photographs, and she sounded polite and uninterested. In the back of his mind, he thought the woman might still be alive, and he could offer to photograph her.

The girl who'd sold the camera lived in a modern apartment building, and she met him in the lobby. After several moments of examining the prints, she touched her hair with a white hand and said slowly, 'Wait a minute,' and he watched her face descend into an unhappy place. 'This is probably my grandmother. I never knew her because she died when my mother was young – a baby, really. I feel I know her, though, because my grandfather had photographs of her on his desk all his life. She was Amanda Springer.' The girl took the set of photos Mel offered and cradled them at her waist. 'He really loved her. Everyone said that.'

'Do you know when she passed away?'

'Sometime in the fifties, I think. Grampa wouldn't talk about how she died.'

'She must have been a wonderful person.'

'I'm sure. But like I said, I never met her. And it's strange, but no one in the family ever said much specific about her, not even Grampa.' She pulled out one of the photographs, a close-up, and handed him the rest. 'This one's nice. She looks really happy. I don't need the others. I can't stand things cluttering up my apartment.' She looked at him. 'Can I pay you something?'

'No, no,' he said, backing toward the door. 'If you want any of these, I'll have them at the shop.'

Mel left feeling as though he knew less than when he'd arrived. He sat in the car looking at the prints; he wondered what Amanda Springer's voice had sounded like, how she'd danced, if the well-composed pictures were accidents, and, most intriguing of all, what would have been on the last, blank negative.

Mel's father-in-law's father, Captain McNabb, was propped on the sofa in the game room of the nursing home. The old man was a retired harbor tug pilot, and Mel had remembered this in the middle of the night as he lay awake trying to put the photographs out of his mind. Captain McNabb was wearing khaki Dockers and a blue button-down shirt. A bentwood cane rested between his legs.

'Who did you say you was?' The old man turned his white head and blinked.

'Leonard's son-in-law.'

'How is Leonard?'

'He's fine. Just bought another filling station.'

The old man chuckled. 'That little bastard.'

Mel inched closer on the sofa. 'He told me you worked the harbor in the thirties and forties.'

'What? Yeah. We ran ships down to the mouth.'

Mel pulled a photo from a folder, one that showed the deck area of the boat, a corner of the pilothouse. 'Do you recognize anything about this?'

The old man drew a pair of glasses from his shirt pocket and took the print, turning it toward the light. 'Who's the honey?'

Mel frowned. 'The boat. Can you tell me anything about the boat?'

The captain glanced up at him a moment. 'See that steel mesh over the wooden balusters? The short stacks? It's the *Lakeland*.'

'Any idea when the photo was taken?'

'She was an upriver boat – that's why she's got short stacks. They got so many damned bridges up north. She spelled the *President* now and again after the war, so this was probably late 1945 or '46.' He squinted at the photo and looked up. The captain licked his lips and rubbed his fingertips together. 'Ah, God Almighty,' he cried. 'You got another picture taken in the same direction?'

Mel handed him the folder, and the old man thumbed through the photos slowly, stopping and shaking his head at the last one. 'Ah, Lordy,' he said almost under his breath.

'What?'

'This was a spring trip. Nineteen fifty-two. I don't know, must have been March. Anyway, it was during high water. The *Lakeland* was a big antique of a dance boat nearly three hundred feet long. All wood, stern-wheeler. Steam, of course.'

'How can you tell the date?' Mel looked down at the photo in the captain's lap, and the old man put a veined finger on a gray arrow of iron blurred behind the deck railing. 'Mister, the *Lakeland* was cut in two against the dock by a U.S. Navy cruiser that'd lost its steering. It went down in less than a minute.' He handed the photo back to Mel. 'I think sixty or seventy people drowned,' he said, taking off his glasses, as though clear vision was a burden.

The next day, Mel spent two hours in the library, scanning microfilm of the *Times-Picayune* for early 1952. The paper had run articles for three days about the disaster. The collision occurred when the Barlow Brothers' excursion steamer *Lakeland* was about to cast off for an afternoon harbor tour. Mel read the main story, and then all the spin-off tales of bravery and heartbreak. At the time of the collision, the *Lakeland* was still tied to the dock at Canal Street. The USS *Tupelo* was coming downstream with a navy pilot at the helm when the ship's steering went out, and the current sent her to the bank. Some of the passengers saw the ship right before the collision and jumped over the rails to the dock. There was a side story about a deckhand who swam three children to safety, and another of a tug-boat plucking people off a section of shattered bulkhead two miles downriver. In the second day's paper were more stories and a list of the dead and injured. Amanda Springer's name was at the lower end of the column. In the third day's paper, the reporters were interviewing people in hospitals. Tales of less-than-heroic activity began to surface: how a brace of oyster fishermen were catching bodies downriver and relieving them of their wallets. There was another article that quoted the injured chief engineer as saying that the doddering *Lakeland* had had a soft hull and that the owners had had no business operating her in a busy harbor. And then Mel's mouth fell open at the microfilm machine when he read a short article beginning with the headline MAN SAVES CAMERA, LOSES WIFE. It was a terrible story about a cowardly villain named Leland Springer.

Mel went through the next week trying not to think about the meaning of snapshots. When he opened up a camera that had been traded in and found an old roll of exposed film, he pulled a latch and dumped the spool into the trash. He spent the week polishing up the cobalt optics of Graflexes and Retinas and adjusting shutter speeds, trying at least to give others the possibility of clear views and sharp scenes. He thought about the meanings of images: how art can interpret beauty or terror, but ordinary photographs could show only beautiful or terrible *fact*. He'd had copies of the newspaper article made and put them in a manila folder with the photographs, filing them with the part of his collection he kept at the store. He planned one day to put the pictures next to the article and try to reconcile the two. But not soon.

In the middle of the next week, Mel was trying to take the lenses out of an Ikoflex when the bell rang on the door and he looked up and saw the girl shimmering in out of the glare, wearing a short dress and white sandals.

'I decided to take you up on your offer of the photographs,' she said. 'I showed the one to my mom and she wanted to see the others.'

Mel pulled out a file drawer and retrieved the folder, placing it open on the glass counter. The girl saw the photocopied article at once and picked it up before he could think. She was a fast reader.

'Oh, wow,' she said. She kept reading as he told her how he'd found the article. She finished it, and he watched her read it again, as though she'd misunderstood something. He arranged the photographs twice and stacked them neatly in the folder. When he looked up again, the girl was crying. 'He abandoned my grandmother for a camera?' She said this to herself, then walked to the door, where as she passed through, she turned a pinched red face toward Mel, a face incapable of speech.

Mr Weinstein walked over and peered at Mel through his bifocals. 'You sick?'

'No. Why?'

'You look like an underdeveloped negative. What's wrong?'

Mel shook his head slowly at the old joke, watching the door.

* * *

The next afternoon, Mr Weinstein came up to Mel's counter accompanied by a beautiful woman of about fifty, tall, blond, wearing a cream-colored linen blouse and long pleated skirt.

'This is Mrs Lebreton,' Mr Weinstein said, both eyebrows raised. 'She would like to have a little talk with you.' He then turned and walked back to the chemicals section of the store, which was in the rear.

'Are you interested in classic cameras?' Mel asked hopefully.

'No,' she said coldly. 'I am not. I came here to find out why you dug up that old news article.'

Mel looked at the alligator purse that hung from her shoulder on a wide strap. 'Oh, that.' He gave her a smile reserved for people buying the most valuable cameras. He labored behind this smile, telling her about the old film that sometimes came in with the antiques, about his scrapbook.

'Don't you think that's a bizarre tendency? You're spying on strangers, for God's sake. On dead people.'

'Oh, no,' he said, truly stung. 'I'm an art photographer. I enjoy nontraditional techniques and approaches, and I'm also interested in how amateurs achieve the same effects, kind of by accident.'

The woman raised her chin. 'Do some of your nontraditional techniques include destroying a young woman's faith in her grandfather?'

Mel straightened up. He was not used to people who were deliberately offensive. 'I think that the more you know about a photograph or an image, the more you can appreciate it.'

The woman frowned down to her shoes, and Mel took a step back from the counter. 'Think of the Mona Lisa, Mr DeSoto. If we knew her smile was because she had just been unfaithful to her husband, would that knowledge make the painting greater art?'

'What?'

'I've never laid eyes on you, but I can tell you're a certain kind of idiot, and you know nothing about my father. My daughter worshiped him. He was the family anchor, so to speak. I don't know what happened the day my mother died, but now my daughter, who is prone to depression anyway, is distraught, really distraught about what you dredged up. You've done a very bad thing.'

Mel felt as if he were capsized on the bottom of the river. 'I thought the article was accurate. Otherwise, I wouldn't have gone—'

'It took me all night, Mr DeSoto, all night, and my father's memory is still not patched up in Leslie's mind. And now I'd like for you to stay away from us.'

He picked up his hands. 'Of course.'

She turned for the door, but then she glanced back at him. 'When you look at one of these images you find in a used camera, what do you see?'

'Meaning?' he said without thinking.

She thought about this a moment, then said, 'Why don't you just look at it?'

That night, Mel had a dream that he was trying to develop a photo of his wife. The first image in the tray was supposed to be her on their honeymoon, but instead, the figure of a little girl in a white Communion dress bloomed under the chemical. He put a different negative in the enlarger, one of his daughter, and again the little Italian girl appeared in the tray. One after another, no matter what negative he exposed on the easel, the little girl smiled up at him from the steps of a church, hands clasped. He woke up, the child's face razored into his brain, and tried to figure what the image meant, but he could not. He remembered the photo of the hairy father sprawled on the sofa and tried to imagine a connection, but no meaning came to him. He went into his darkroom and clicked on the enlarger, watching the face of Amanda Springer reversed in every way on the white background of his easel. He made a print.

Two months passed, and then a smiling man came into the shop, handing over a card telling that he was a deaf-mute. The man placed a Crown Graphic on the counter, pulled out a pad, and wrote that he could lip-read and that he wanted two hundred dollars for the camera. Mel examined the bellows and noted the make of the lens.

He aimed his mouth at the man. 'I can let you have one seventy-five, tops.'

The man wrote in a neat, fast hand, 'I've been offered a hundred ninety dollars for it.' He put three negative carriers on the counter. 'These go with it,' he wrote.

Mel looked the man in the eye. He didn't appear to be any different from anyone else, just more attentive. 'In that case, we'll do one ninety,' he told the deaf-mute. He pulled out an invoice and began writing, then asked the man for his signature. The man read his lips and nodded. A little light came on in Mel's head, and when the deaf-mute looked up, he asked, 'Can you read lips on television?'

The man wrote 'Some' on his pad.

'Can you tell what syllable someone is saying in a photograph?'

'Don't know,' the man wrote.

Mel went to the filing cabinet and pulled out an eight-by-ten print of the last photo taken of Amanda Springer, her mouth open, the ominous bow of the navy vessel at her back.

The deaf-mute lowered his head. 'Ga,' he wrote.

Mel put his finger next to her mouth. 'Could she be saying "Ca" as in *camera*?'

The deaf-mute furrowed his brow and bent down, and now he did look different, like an animal on a scent. He picked up his pen. 'Yes,' he scribbled. Glancing at the photo again, he wrote, 'Pretty.'

'Pretty,' Mel agreed, forming his lips around the word.

The obituary column at the library had stated that Amanda Johnsons Springer was survived by a younger brother, Malcolm Z. Mel found a Malcolm Z. Johnsons living in Metairie and called him. A scorched old voice boiled out of the phone, telling him that Leland Springer was a coward who wouldn't save his sister's life. 'I'll never forgive him for not at least trying to pull her to safety. She had a lot to live for with her daughter and her photography.'

'Her photography?' Mel's fingers tightened on the receiver.

'You know that guy Clarence Laughlin? The one who took all those pictures of mansions and double-exposed them? He got famous for that. But she had it all over him. She made him look like he was shooting an Instamatic. I still got some of her stuff in a box, and what she could do with shadows was unreal.'

Mel could not stop the old man, but he listened for most of an hour as Malcolm created the life his sister would have led had she lived. He did not hear what he wanted to hear, that Leland was a nice guy, that the newspaper was wrong about him when it said he pleaded at the rail of the steamer for five minutes for someone to catch the camera he was holding. Then he remembered something. The official statement issued by the Coast Guard had stated that the old wooden boat had parted and capsized in less than one minute after the collision, the same thing Captain McNabb had told him in the rest home. He listened to Malcolm until the old man had made himself sleepy with talk, and then he thanked him and hung up.

Mel was holding a three-ring binder, standing next to a mooring cleat at the foot of Canal Street, when the girl walked up warily and looked past him, into the Mississippi. Downriver a hundred yards, a ferryboat discharged vehicles, and upriver a gaudy floating casino rolled on the swells of a passing ship. The girl's eyes were red, as though she had a cold. She was nervous, and her fingernails were stabbing her palms. 'So this is where it happened,' she said. 'My mom would kill you if she knew you'd asked me here.'

'I'm sorry you saw that article about your grandfather.'

'So am I.'

'Real sorry. I even checked into the story some more and found your grandmother's brother.'

She stepped up onto the timber at the edge of the wharf, her toes over water. 'I thought I knew him so well.'

Mel stepped back. 'Look, you better come away from the edge.'

'I'm okay,' she told him.

'Well, I wanted to tell you that article wasn't right. The facts, I mean. I've been checking.'

She put one foot out over the river twenty feet below. 'Still, he didn't save her.'

He moved next to her as slowly as he could, and he opened the binder. 'Now, look at her face in these photos. She was looking at your grandfather. What do you see in her expression?'

The girl peered into the binder, turned three plastic-covered pages of photographs, leaning away from the river. 'She really liked him.'

'Liked him?' Mel ducked his head. 'She was glowing. She was crazy about him. That type of expression feeds off of another's, don't you think?' He put a finger onto an eight-by-ten photo. 'Look what's here. In her hand.'

The girl bent her head. 'What is that?'

'It's an old Weston light meter. I noticed that for the first time last night. She was reading off settings for him.'

The girl brushed her hair out of her eyes. 'So *she* was the photographer in the family?'

'Her brother says she was an artist. He told me that she worked as a part-time secretary for ninety cents an hour and saved enough for the Rolleiflex, the best camera in the store in those days. She must have waited years for it.'

The girl put a hand on a photograph. 'Was this the first time?'

'I imagine the roll we removed might have been the only one ever put in it. And you see this last picture?' He told her about the deaf-mute then. As she sat down and dangled her legs over the waves, he bent with her, his tie going over her shoulder. 'I'd bet anything she had just turned from the rail when that last shot was taken. Who knows what was going through her mind when she realized what was about to happen? Maybe she shouted something like "The camera," or "Toss the camera to the dock."'

The girl's mouth opened a little. 'And he turned his back for one second, and then it was over.'

Mel closed the binder and squatted on the wharf, his leather lace-ups protesting. 'Your grandfather was what you thought he was. You can see it in *her* face.'

The girl shaded her eyes with her hand and looked across to the Algiers side. 'I don't know. If he were alive, I could jump into the river and he could save me. That would prove something.'

Mel suddenly looked south, where the current was threading. He realized that he had one chance to say the right thing. Finally, he told her, 'Yes, it would prove something, but he's not here, and these photographs are.'

She shook her head. 'I don't even know if he could swim.' Suddenly, she looked up into his face. 'The pictures. Can I have them?'

'Of course,' he said, standing.

She put a hand up to him. 'Do you think they'll be enough?'

He helped her to her feet. 'Just look at everything in them – objects, shadows, even the blurry parts.' He walked her toward the noise and dusty light of Canal Street. 'You'll see.'

Good for the Soul

Father Ledet took a scorching swallow of brandy and sat in an iron chair on the brick patio behind the rectory, hemmed in by walls of privet stitched through with honeysuckle. His stomach was full from the Ladies' Altar Society supper, where the sweet, sweet women of the parish had fed him pork roast, potato salad, and sweet peas, filling his plate and making over him as if he were an old spayed tomcat who kept the cellar free of rats. He was a big man, white-haired and ruddy, with gray eyes and huge spotted hands that could make a highball glass disappear. It was Thursday evening and nothing much happened on Thursday evenings. The first cool front of the fall was breezing through the pecan trees on the church lot, and nothing is so important in Louisiana as that first release from the sopping, buggy, overheated funk of the atmosphere. Father Ledet breathed deeply in the shadow of a statue of Saint Francis. He took another long swallow, glad that the assistant pastor was on a visit home in Iowa and that the deacon wouldn't be around until the next afternoon. Two pigeons lit on Saint Francis's upturned hands as if they knew who he was. Father Ledet watched the light fade and the privet darken, and then he looked a long time at the pint of brandy before deciding to pour himself another drink.

The phone rang in the rectory, and he got up carefully, moving inside among the dark wood furnishings and dim holy light. It was a parishioner, Mrs Clyde Arceneaux, whose husband was dying of emphysema.

'We need you for the Anointing of the Sick, Father.'

'Um, yes.' He tried to say something else, but the words were stuck back in his throat, the way dollar bills sometimes wadded up in the tubular poor box and wouldn't drop down when he opened the bottom.

'Father?'

'Of course. I'll just come right over there.'

'I know you did it for him last week. But this time, he might really be going, you know.' Mrs Arceneaux's voice began to sound teary. 'He wants you to hear his confession.'

'Um.' The priest had known Clyde Arceneaux for fifteen years. The old man dressed up on Sunday, came to church, but he stayed out on the steps and smoked with three other men as reverent as himself. As far as he knew, Clyde had never been to confession.

Father Ledet locked the rectory door and went into the garage to start the parish car, a venerable black Lincoln. He backed out onto the street, and when the car stopped, he still floated along in a drifting crescent, and he realized that he'd had maybe an ounce too much of brandy. It occurred to him that he should call the housekeeper to drive him to the hospital. It would take only five minutes for her to come over, but then, the old Baptist woman was always figuring him out, and he would have to endure Mrs Scott's roundabout questions and sniffs of the air. Father Ledet felt his mossy human side take over, and he began to navigate the streets of the little town on his own, stopping the car too far into the intersection at Jackman Avenue, clipping a curb on a turn at Bourgeois Street. The car had its logical movement, but his head had a motion of its own.

Patrolman Vic Garafola was parked in front of the post office, talking to the dispatcher about a cow eating string beans out of Mrs LeBlanc's garden, when he heard a crash in the intersection behind him. In his rearview, he saw that a long black sedan had battered the side of a powder-blue Ford. He backed his cruiser fifty feet and turned on his flashers. When he got out and saw his own parish priest sitting wide-eyed behind the steering wheel, he ran to the window.

'You all right, Father?'

The priest had a little red mark on his high forehead, but he smiled dumbly and nodded. Patrolman Garafola looked over to the smashed passenger side door of a faded Crown Victoria. A pretty older woman sat in the middle of the bench seat holding her elbow. He opened the door and saw that Mrs Mamie Barrilleaux's right arm was obviously broken, and her mouth was twitching with pain. Vic's face reddened because it made him angry to see nice people get hurt when it wasn't their fault.

'Mrs Mamie, you hurtin' a lot?' Vic asked. Behind him, the priest walked up and put his hand on Vic's shoulder. When the woman saw Father Ledet, her face was transfigured.

'Oh, it's nothing, just a little bump. Father, did I cause the accident?'

The patrolman looked at the priest for the answer.

'Mamie, your arm.' He took his hand off the policeman and stepped back. Vic could see that the priest was shocked. He knew that Father Ledet was called out to give last rites to strangers at gory highway wrecks all the time, but this woman was the vice president of the Ladies' Altar Society, the group who polished the old church, put flowers on the altar, knit afghans to put on his lap in the drafty wooden rectory.

'Father, Mrs Mamie had the right-of-way.' Vic pointed to the stop sign behind the priest's steaming car.

'I am dreadfully sorry,' Father Ledet said. 'I was going to the hospital to administer the Anointing of the Sick, and I guess my mind was on that.'

'Oh,' Mrs Barrilleaux cried. 'Who's that ill?'

'Mrs Arceneaux's husband.'

Another cruiser pulled up, its lights sparking up the evening. Mrs Barrilleaux pointed at it. 'Vic, can you take him to the hospital and let this other policeman write the report? I know Mrs Arceneaux's husband, and he needs a priest bad.'

Vic looked down at his shoe. He wasn't supposed to do anything like that. 'You want to go on to the hospital and then I can bring you back here, Father?'

'Mamie's the one who should go to the hospital.'

'Shoo.' She waved her good hand at him. 'I can hear the ambulance coming now. Go on; I'm not dying.'

Vic could see a slight trembling in Mamie's silver-laced curls. He put a hand on the priest's arm. 'Okay, Father?'

'Okay.'

They got into the cruiser and immediately Vic smelled the priest's breath. He drove under the tunnel of oak trees that was Nadine Avenue and actually bit his tongue to keep from asking the inevitable question. When they were in sight of the hospital, Patrolman Garafola could no longer stop himself. 'Father, did you have anything to drink today?'

The priest looked at him and blanched. 'Why do you ask?'

'It's on your breath. Whiskey.'

'Brandy,' the priest corrected. 'Yes, I had some brandy after supper.'

'How much?'

'Not too much. Well, here we are.' Father Ledet got out before the patrol car had completely stopped. Vic radioed his location, parked, and went into the modern lobby to find a soft chair.

The priest knew the way to Clyde Arceneaux's room. When he pushed open the door, he saw the old man in his bed, a few strands of smoky hair swept back, his false teeth out, his tobacco-parched tongue wiggling in his mouth like a parrot's. Up close, Father Ledet could hear the hiss of the oxygen through the nose dispenser strapped to the old man's face. He felt his deepest sorrow for the respiratory patients.

'Clyde?'

Mr Arceneaux opened one eye and looked at the priest's shirt. 'The buzzards is circlin',' he rasped.

'How're you feeling?'

'Ah, Padre, I got a elephant standing on my chest.' He spoke slowly, more like an air leak than a voice. 'Doris, she stepped out a minute to eat.' He motioned with his eyes toward the door, and

Father Ledet looked at Clyde's hands, which were bound with dark veins flowing under skin as thin as cigarette paper.

'Is there something you'd like to talk about?' The priest heard the faint sound of a siren and wondered if gentle Mrs Barrilleaux was being brought in to have her arm set.

'I don't need the holy oil no more. You can't grease me so I can slide into heaven.' Clyde ate a bite of air. 'I got to go to confession.'

The priest nodded, removed a broad ribbonlike vestment from his pocket, kissed it, and hung it around his neck. Mr Arceneaux couldn't remember the last time he'd been to confession, but he knew that Kennedy had been President then, because it was during the Cuban missile crisis, when he thought for sure a nuclear strike was coming. He began telling his sins, starting with missing Mass 'damn near seven hundred fifty times.' Father Ledet was happy that Clyde Arceneaux was coming to God for forgiveness, and in a very detailed way, which showed, after all, a healthy conscience. At one point, the old man stopped and began to store up air for what the priest thought would be a new push through his errors, but when he began speaking again, it was to ask a question.

'Sure enough, you think there's a hell?'

Father Ledet knew he had to be careful. Sometimes saving a soul was like catching a dragonfly. You couldn't blunder up to it and trap it with a swipe of the hand. 'There's a lot of talk of it in the Bible,' he said.

'It's for punishment?'

'That's what it's for.'

'But what good would the punishment do?'

The priest sat down. The room did a quarter turn to the left and then stopped. 'I don't think hell is about rehabilitation. It's about what someone might deserve.' He put his hand over his eyes and squeezed them for a moment. 'But you shouldn't worry about that, Clyde, because you're getting the forgiveness you need.'

Mr Arceneaux looked at the ceiling, the corners of his flaccid mouth turning down. 'I don't know. There's one thing I ain't told you yet.'

'Well, it's now or never.' The priest was instantly sorry for saying this, and Clyde gave him a questioning look before glancing down at his purple feet.

'I can't hold just one thing back? I'd hate like hell to tell anybody this.'

'Clyde, it's God listening, not me.'

'Can I just think it to God? I mean, I told you the other stuff. Even about the midget woman.'

'If it's a serious sin, you've got to tell me about it. You can generalize a bit.'

'This is some of that punishment we were talkin' about earlier. It's what I deserve.'

'Let's have it.'

'I stole Nelson Lodrigue's car.'

Something clicked in the priest's brain. He remembered this himself. Nelson Lodrigue owned an old Toronado, which he parked next to the ditch in front of his house. The car had a huge eight-cylinder engine and no muffler, and every morning at six sharp Nelson would crank the thing up and race the engine, waking most of his neighbors and all the dogs for blocks around. He did this for over a year, to keep the battery charged, he'd said. When it disappeared, Nelson put a big ad in the paper offering a fifty-dollar reward for information, but no one came forward. The men in the Knights of Columbus talked of it for weeks.

'That was about ten years ago, wasn't it? And isn't Nelson a friend of yours?' Nelson was another Sunday-morning lingerer on the church steps.

Mr Arceneaux swallowed hard several times and waited a moment, storing up air. 'Father, honest to God, I ain't never stole nothin' before. My daddy told me thievin' is the worst thing a man can do. I hated to take Nelson's hot rod, but I was fixin' to have a nervous breakdown from lack of sleep.'

The priest nodded. 'It's good to get these things off your chest. Is there anything else?'

Mr Arceneaux shook his head. 'I think we hit the high points. Man, I'm ashamed of that last one.'

The priest gave him absolution and a small penance.

Clyde tried to smile, his dark tongue tasting the air. 'Ten Hail Marys? That's a bargain, Father.'

'If you want to do more, you could call Nelson and tell him what you did.'

The old man thought for just a second. 'I'll stick with them little prayers for now.' Father Ledet got out his missal and read aloud over Mr Arceneaux until his words were interrupted by a gentle snoring.

Vic sat in the lobby, waiting for the priest to come down. It had been twenty minutes, and he knew the priest's blood-alcohol level was ready to peak. He took off his uniform hat and began twirling it in front of him. He wondered what good it would do to charge the priest with drunken driving. Priests had to drink wine every day, and they liked the taste in the evening, too. A ticket wouldn't change his mind about drinking for long. On the other hand, Father Ledet had ruined Mrs Barrilleaux's sedan, which for twenty years she had maintained as if it were a child.

A few minutes earlier, Vic had walked down the corridor and peeked into the room where they were treating her. He hadn't let her see him, and he studied her face. Now he sat and twirled his hat, thinking. It would be painful for the priest to have his name in the paper attached to a DWI charge, but it would make him understand the seriousness of what he had done. Patrolman Garafola dealt with too many people who did not understand the seriousness of what they were doing.

The priest came into the lobby and the young policeman stood up. 'Father, we'll have to take a ride to the station.'

'What?'

'I want to run a Breathalyzer test on you.'

249

Father Ledet straightened up, stepped close, and put an arm around the man's shoulders. 'Oh, come on. What good would that do?'

The patrolman started to speak, but then he motioned for the priest to follow him. 'Let me show you something.'

'Where are we going?'

'I want you to see this.' They walked down the hall and through double doors to a triage area for emergency cases. There was a narrow window in a wall, and the policeman told the priest to look through it. An oxygen bottle and gauges partially blocked the view. Inside, Mrs Barrilleaux sat on an examining table, a blue knot swelling in her upper arm. One doctor was pulling back on her shoulder while another twisted her elbow. On the table was a large, menacing syringe, and Mrs Barrilleaux was crying, without expression, great patient tears. 'Take a long look,' Vic said, 'and when you get enough, come on with me.' The priest turned away from the glass and followed.

'You didn't have to show me that.'

'I didn't?'

'That woman is the nicest, the best cook, the best—'

'Come on, Father,' Vic said, pushing open the door to the parking lot. 'I've got a lot of writing to do.'

Father Ledet's blood-alcohol content was well over the legal limit, so the patrolman wrote him a ticket for DWI, to which he added running a stop sign and causing an accident with bodily injury. The traffic court suspended his license, and since he had banged up the Lincoln before, his insurance company dropped his coverage as soon as their computers picked up the offenses. A week after the accident, he came into the rectory hall drinking a glass of tap water, which beaded on his tongue like a nasty oil. The phone rang and the glass jumped in his fingers. It was Mrs Arceneaux again, who told him she'd been arguing with her husband, who wanted to tell her brother Nelson Lodrigue that he had stolen his car ten years before. 'Why'd you tell him to talk to Nelson about the stealing business? It's got him all upset.'

The priest did not understand. 'What would be the harm in him telling Nelson the truth?'

'Aw, no, Father. Clyde's got so little oxygen in his brain, he's not thinking straight. He can't tell Nelson what he did. I don't want him to die with everyone in the neighborhood thinking he's a thief. And Nelson . . . well, I love my brother, but if he found out my husband stole his old bomb, he'd make Clyde's last days hell. He's just like that, you know?'

'I see. Is there something I can do?' He put down the glass of water on the little phone table next to a small white statue of the Blessed Virgin.

'If you would talk to Clyde and let him know it's okay to die without telling Nelson about the car, I'd appreciate it. He already confessed everything anyway, right?'

The priest looked down the hall toward the patio, longing for the openness. 'I can't discuss specific matters of confession.'

'I know. That's why I gave you all the details again.'

'All right, I'll call. Is he awake now?'

'He's here at home. We got him a crank-up bed and a oxygen machine, and a nurse sits with him at night. I'll put him on.'

Father Ledet leaned against the wall and stared at a crucifix, wondering what Christ had done to deserve his punishment. When he heard the hiss of Clyde Arceneaux's mask come out of the phone, he began to tell him what he should hear, that he was forgiven in God's eyes, that if he wanted to make restitution, he could give something to the poor, or figure out how to leave his brother-in-law something. He hung up and sniffed the waxed smell of the rectory, thinking of the sweet, musky brandy in the kitchen cupboard, and immediately he went to find the young priest upstairs to discuss the new Mass schedule.

On Saturday afternoon, Father Ledet was nodding off in the confessional when a woman entered and began to make her confession.

After she'd mentioned one or two venial sins, she addressed him through the screen. 'Father, it's Doris Arceneaux, Clyde's wife.'

The priest yawned. 'How is Clyde?'

'You remember the car business? Well, something new has come up,' she whispered. 'Clyde always told me he and the Scadlock kid towed the car off with a rope, and when they got it downtown behind the seawall, they pushed it overboard into the bay.'

'Yes?'

'There's a new wrinkle.'

He put down his missal and removed his glasses to rub his eyes. 'What do you mean?'

'Clyde just told me he stored the car. Been paying thirty-five dollars a month to keep it in a little closed bin down at the U-Haul place for the past ten years.' She whispered louder: 'I don't know how he kept that from me. Makes me wonder about a few other things.'

The priest's eyebrows went up. 'Now he can give it back, or you can give it back when your husband passes away.' As soon as he'd said this, he knew it wouldn't work. It was too logical. If nothing else, his years in the confessional had taught him that people did not run their lives by reason much of the time, but by some little inferior motion of the spirit, some pride, some desire that defied the simple beauty of doing the sensible thing.

Mrs Arceneaux protested that the secret had to be kept. 'There's only one way to get Nelson his car back like Clyde wants.'

The priest sighed. 'How is that?'

Mrs Arceneaux began to fidget in the dark box. 'Well, you the only one besides me who knows what happened. Clyde says the car will still run. He cranks it up once every three weeks so it keeps its battery hot.'

The priest put his head down. 'And?'

'And you could get up early and drive it back to Nelson's and park it where it was the night Clyde stole it.'

'Not no,' the priest said, 'but hell no!'

'Father!'

'What if I were caught driving that thing? The secret would get out then.'

'Father, this is part of a confession. You can't tell.'

The priest now sensed a plot. 'I'm sorry, but I can't help you, Mrs Arceneaux. Now I'm going to give you a penance of twenty Our Fathers.'

'For telling one fib to my daughter-in-law?'

'You want a cut rate for dishonesty?'

'All right,' she said in an unrepentant voice. 'And I'll pray for you while I'm at it.'

After five o'clock Saturday Mass, Father Ledet felt his soul bang around inside him like a golf ball in a shoe box, something hard and compacted. He yearned for a hot, inflating swallow of spirits, longed for the afterburn of brandy in his nostrils. He went back into the empty church, a high-ceilinged Gothic building over a hundred years old, sat in a pew, and steeped himself in the odors of furniture oil, incense, and hot candle wax. He let the insubstantial colors of the windows flow over him, and after a while, these shades and smells began to fill the emptiness in him. He closed his eyes and imagined the housekeeper's supper, pushing out of mind his need for a drink, replacing the unnecessary with the good. At five to six, he walked to the rectory to have his thoughts made into food.

The next evening, after visiting a sick parishioner, he was reading the newspaper upstairs in his room when the housekeeper knocked on his door. Mrs Mamie Barrilleaux was downstairs and would like to speak with him, the housekeeper said.

The first thing Father Ledet noticed when he walked into the downstairs study was the white cast on the woman's arm.

'Mamie,' he said, sitting next to her on the sofa. 'I have to tell you again how sorry I am about your arm.'

The woman's face brightened, as though to be apologized to was a privilege. 'Oh, don't worry about it, Father. Accidents happen.' She was a graying brunette with fair skin, a woman whose cheerfulness made her pretty. One of the best cooks in a town of good cooks, she volunteered for every charity work connected with a stove or oven, and her time belonged to anyone who needed it, from her well-fed smirk of a husband to the drug addicts who showed up at the parish shelter. While they talked, the priest's eyes wandered repeatedly to the ugly cast, which ran up nearly to her shoulder. For five minutes, he wondered why she had dropped in unannounced. And then she told him.

'Father, I don't know if you understand what good friends Clyde Arceneaux's wife and I are. We went to school together for twelve years.'

'Yes. It's a shame her husband's so sick.'

Mrs Barrilleaux fidgeted into the corner of the sofa, put her cast on the armrest, where it glowed under a lamp. 'That's sort of why I'm here. Doris told me she asked you to do something for her and Clyde, and you told her no. I'm not being specific because I know it was a confession thing.'

'How much did she tell you?' The priest hoped she wouldn't ask what she was going to ask, because he knew he could not refuse her.

'I don't know even one detail, Father. But I wanted to tell you that if Doris wants it done, then it needs doing. She's a good person, and I'm asking you to help her.'

'But you don't know what she wants me to do.'

Mrs Barrilleaux put her good hand on her cast. 'I know it's not something bad.'

'No, no. It's just . . .' He was going to mention that his driver's license was suspended but realized that he couldn't even tell her that.

Mamie lowered her head and turned her face toward the priest. 'Father?'

'Oh, all right.'

He visited Mrs Arceneaux on a Wednesday, got the keys, and late that night he sat outside on the dark rectory patio for a long time, filling up on the smells of honeysuckle. The young priest walked up to him and insisted that he come in out of the mosquitoes and the dampness. Upstairs, he changed into street clothes and lay on the bed like a man waiting for a firing squad. Around midnight, his legs began to ache terribly, and the next thing he knew, they were carrying him downstairs to the kitchen, where the aspirin was kept, and as his hand floated toward the cabinet door to his right, it remembered its accustomed movement to the door on the left, where a quart of brandy waited like an airy medicinal promise. The mind and the spirit pulled his hand to the right, while the earthly body drew it to the left. He heard the drone of an airplane somewhere in the sky above, and he suddenly thought of an old homily that told how people were like twin-engine planes, one engine the logical spirit, the other the sensual body, and that when they were not running in concert, the craft ran off course to disaster. The priest supposed he could rev his spirit in some way, but when he thought of driving the stolen car, he opted to throttle up the body. One jigger, he thought, would calm him down and give him the courage to do this important and good deed. As he took a drink, he tried to picture how glad Nelson Lodrigue would be to have his old car back. As he took another, he thought of how Mr Arceneaux could gasp off into the next world with a clear conscience. After several minutes, the starboard engine sputtered and locked up as Father Ledet lurched sideways through the dark house looking for his car keys.

At one o'clock, he got into the church's sedan and drove to the edge of town to a row of storage buildings. He woke up the manager, a shabby old man living in a trailer next to the gate. Inside the perimeter fence, Father Ledet walked along the numbered roll-up doors of the storage areas until he found the right one. He had trouble fitting the key into the lock but finally managed to open the door and turn on the light. The Oldsmobile showed a hard shell of rust and dust and resembled a million-year-old museum egg. The door squawked when he pulled on it, and the interior smelled like the closed-in mausoleum at the parish graveyard. He put in the key, and the motor groaned and then stuttered alive, rumbling and complaining. Shaking his head, the priest thought he'd never be able to drive this car undetected into the quiet neighborhood where Nelson Lodrigue lived. But after he let it idle and warm up, the engine slowed to a breathy subsonic bass, and he put it in reverse for its first trip in ten years.

The plan was to park the car on a patch of grass next to the street in front of Nelson's house, the very spot where it had been stolen. The priest would walk into the next block to Mrs Arceneaux's house, and she would return him to his car. He pulled out of the rental place and drove a back road, past tin-roofed shotgun houses and abandoned cars better in appearance than the leprous one that now moved among them. He entered the battered railroad underpass and emerged in the better part of town, which was moon-washed and asleep. He found that if he kept his foot off the accelerator and just let the car idle along at ten miles an hour, it didn't make much noise, but when he gave the car just a little gas at stop signs, the exhaust sounded like a lion warming up for a mating. The priest was thankful at least for a certain buoyancy of the blood provided by the glasses of brandy, a numbness of spirit that helped him endure what he was doing. He was still nervous, though, and had trouble managing the touchy accelerator, feeling that the car was trying to bound away in spite of his best efforts to control it. Eventually, he turned onto the main street of Nelson's little subdivision and burbled slowly down it until he could see the apron of grass next to the asphalt where he could park. He turned off the car's lights.

One of the town's six policemen had an inflamed gallbladder, and Patrolman Vic Garafola was working his friend's shift, parked in an alley next to the Elks Club, sitting stone-faced with boredom, when a shuddering and filthy Toronado crawled past in front of him. He would have thought it was just some rough character from the section down by the fish plant, but he got a look at the license plate and saw that it bore a design that hadn't been on any car in at least five years. Vic put his cruiser in gear, left his lights off, and rolled out into the town's empty streets, following the Toronado at a block's distance past the furniture store, across the highway, and into little Shade Tree Subdivision. He radioed a parish officer he'd seen a few minutes earlier and asked him to park across the entrance, the only way in or out of the neighborhood.

Even in the dark, Vic could see that the car's tires were bagged out and that it was dirty in an unnatural way, pale with dust – the ghost of a car. He closed in as it swayed down Cypress Street, and when he saw the driver douse his lights, he thought, Bingo, someone's up to no good, and at once he hit his headlights, flashers, and yowling siren. The Toronado suddenly exploded forward in a flatulent rush, red dust and sparks raining backward from underneath the car as it left the patrolman in twin swirls of tire smoke. Whoever was driving was supremely startled, and Vic began the chase, following but not gaining on the sooty taillights. Shade Tree Subdivision was composed of only one long street that ran in an oval like a racetrack. At the first curve, the roaring car fishtailed to the right, and Vic followed as best he could, watching ahead as the vehicle pulled away and then turned right again in the distance, heading for the subdivision exit. When Vic chased around the curve, he saw a white cruiser blocking the speeding car's escape. The fleeing vehicle then slowed and moved again down Cypress Street toward the middle of the subdivision. Vic raised a questioning eyelid as he watched the grumbling car drive off the road and finally stop in front of Nelson's Lodrigue's brick rancher. The patrolman pulled up, opened his door, and pointed his revolver toward the other vehicle.

'Driver, get out,' he barked. Slowly, a graying, soft-looking man wearing a dark shirt buttoned at the top button slid out of the vehicle, his shaking hands raised high.

'Can you please not yell?' The old man looked around at the drowsing houses.

Vic stared at him, walked close, and looked at his eyes. He holstered his revolver. 'Why'd you speed away like that, Father?'

The priest was out of breath. 'When you turned on those flashers, it frightened me and, well, I guess I pressed the accelerator too hard, and this thing took off like a rocket.'

Vic looked at the car and back to the priest. 'The tag is expired on your vehicle, and it doesn't have an inspection sticker.' He went to his patrol car and reached in for his ticket book.

'Could you please turn off those flashers?'

'Have to leave 'em on. Rules, you know,' Vic said in a nasty voice. 'You want to show me your proof of insurance, driver's license, and pink slip?' He held out a mocking hand.

'You know I don't have any of those.'

'Father, what are you doing in this wreck?'

The priest put his hands in front of him, pleading. 'I can't say anything. It's related to a confession.'

'Oh, is this a good deed or somethin'?'

The priest's face brightened with hope, as though the patrolman understood what this was all about. 'Yes, yes.'

Vic leaned in and sniffed. 'You think it's a good deed to get drunk as a boiled owl and speed around town at night?' he hollered.

'Oh, please, hush,' Father Ledet pleaded.

Vic reached to his gun belt. 'Turn around so I can cuff you.'

'Have some mercy.'

'Them that deserves it get mercy,' Vic told him.

'God would give me mercy,' the priest said, turning around and offering his hands at his back.

'Then he's a better man than I am. Spread your legs.'

'This won't do anyone any good.'

'It'll do me some good.' Just then, a porch light came on, and a shirtless Nelson Lodrigue padded out to the walk in his bare feet, his moon-shaped belly hanging over the elastic of his pajamas.

'Hey. What's goin' on?'

Other porch lights began to fire up across the street and next door, people coming out to the edge of their driveways and looking.

'It's Father Ledet,' Vic called out. 'He's getting a ticket or two.'

Nelson was standing next to the car before his eyes opened fully and his head swung from side to side at the dusty apparition. 'What the hell? This here's my old car that got stole.'

Vic gave the priest a hard look. 'Collections been a little slow, Father?'

'Don't be absurd. I was returning Nelson's car.'

'You know who stole my car?' Nelson lumbered around the hood. 'You better tell me right now. I didn't sleep for a year after this thing got taken. I always had a feeling it was somebody I knew.'

'I can't say anything.'

'It came out in a confession,' Vic explained.

Nelson ran his hand over the chalky paint of the roof. 'Well, charge him with auto theft and I'll bet he'll tell us.'

Two ladies in curlers and a tall middle-aged man wearing a robe and slippers approached from across the street. 'What's going on, Vic?' the man asked. 'Hello, Father.'

The priest nodded, hiding the handcuffs behind him. 'Good evening, Mayor. This isn't what it appears to be.'

'I hope not,' one of the women said.

Other neighbors began walking into the circle of crackling light cast by the police car's flashers. Then the parish deputy pulled up, his own lights blazing. Vic looked on as the priest tried to explain to everyone that he was doing a good thing, that they couldn't know all the details. The patrolman felt sorry for him, he really did, felt bad as he filled out the tickets, as he pushed the old head under the roofline of the patrol car, and, later, as he fingerprinted the soft hands and put the holy body into the cell, taking his belt, his shoelaces, and his rosary.

Father Ledet had to journey to Baton Rouge to endure the frowns and lecturing of the bishop. His parish was taken away for two months, and he was put into an AA program in his own community, where he sat many times in rusty folding chairs along with fundamentalist garage mechanics, striptease artists, and spoiled, depressed subdivision wives to listen to testimonials, admonitions, confessions without end. He rode in cabs to these meetings, and in the evenings no one invited him to the Ladies' Altar Society dinners or to anyplace else. Mrs Arceneaux never called to sympathize, and pretty Mrs Barrilleaux would not look at him when he waved as she drove by the rectory in her new secondhand car. The first day he was again allowed to put on vestments was a Sunday, and he went in to say the eleven o'clock Mass. The church was full, and the sun was bleeding gold streamers of light down through the sacristy windows behind the altar. After the Gloria was sung by the birdlike voices of a visiting children's choir, the priest stood in the pulpit and read the Gospel, drawing scant solace from the story of Jesus turning water into wine. The congregation then sat down in a rumble of settling pews and kicked-up kneelers. Father Ledet began to talk about Christ's first miracle, an old sermon, one he'd given dozens of times. The elder parishioners in the front pews seemed to regard him as a stranger, the children were uninterested, and he felt disconnected and sad as he spoke, wondering if he would ever be punished enough for what he had done. He scanned the faces in the congregation as he preached, looking for forgiveness of any sort, and fifteen minutes into the sermon, he saw in the fifth pew, against the wall, something that was better than forgiveness, better than what he deserved, something that gave sudden light to his dull voice and turned bored heads up to the freshened preaching. It was Clyde Arceneaux, a plastic tube creeping down from his nose and taped to his puckered neck. He was asleep, pale, two steps from death, his head resting against the wall, but at least he had finally come inside.

Easy Pickings

He drove into Louisiana from Texas in the stolen sedan, taking the minor roads, the cracked and grass-lined blacktop where houses showed up one to the mile. The land was overrun with low crops he did not recognize and was absolutely flat, which he liked because he could see a police car from a long way off. He was a short man, small of frame, tattooed on the neck and arms with crabs and scorpions, which fit his grabbing occupation of thief. In the hollow of his throat was a small blue lobster, one of its claws holding a hand-rolled cigarette. He thought of the woman in Houston he'd terrorized the day before, going into her kitchen and pulling his scary knife, a discount bowie he'd bought at the KKK table at a local gun show, and putting it to her throat. She'd wept and trembled, giving him her rings, leading him to her husband's little stash of poker money. The day before that, he'd spotted an old woman in Victoria returning alone from the grocery, and he'd followed her into the house, taking her jewelry, showing the knife when she balked, and getting the cash from her wallet. He'd robbed only these two women, but it seemed that he'd been doing it all his life, like walking and breathing, even though he'd just gotten out of jail the week before after doing two years for stealing welfare checks. He looked through the windshield at the poor, watery country. Anyone who would live out here would be simple, he thought, real stupid and easy pickings.

His name was Marvin, but he called himself Big Blade because the name made him feel other than what he was: small, petty, and dull.

He noticed a white frame house ahead on the right side of the road, sitting at the edge of a flooded field, clothes on the line out back. Big Blade had been raised in a trashy Houston subdivision and had never seen clothes dried out in the open. At first he thought the laundry was part of some type of yard sale, but after he stopped on the shoulder and studied the limp dresses and aprons, he figured it out. Across the road and two hundred yards away was a similar house, an asbestos-sided rectangle with a tin roof, and after that, nothing but blacktop. Big Blade noticed that there were no men's clothes on the line, and he moved the car toward the driveway.

Mrs Landreneaux was eighty-five years old and spoke Acadian French to her chickens because nearly everyone else who could speak it was dead. She came out into the yard with a plastic bowl of feed and was met at the back steps by Marvin, who pulled out his big knife, his eyes gleaming. Mrs Landreneaux's vision was not sharp enough to see the evil eyes, but she saw the tattoos and she saw the knife.

'Baby, who wrote all over you? And what you want, you, wit' that big cane cutter you got? If you hungry, all I got is them chicken *labas*, and if you cut off a head, throw it in the bushes at the back of my lot, and pluck them feather over there, because the wind is blowin' west today and—'

'Shut up, and get inside,' Big Blade growled, giving the old woman a push toward her screen door. 'I want your money.'

Mrs Landreneaux narrowed her eyes at the man and then hobbled up the back steps into her kitchen. 'Well, I be damn. Ain't you got nobody better to rob than a ol' lady whose husband died twenty-nine years ago of a heart attack in a bourrée game holding ace, king, queen of trumps? The priest told me—'

Big Blade began to seethe, his voice hoarse and low. 'I will kill you if you don't give me your jewelry and money. I'll gut you like one of your chickens.' The old lady stopped speaking for just a second to bring him into focus.

'You with the crawfish drew on you throat, you trying to scare me wit' a knife? Like I ain't use to death? I break a chicken neck three time a week and my brother, he got shot dead next to me at the St Landry Parish fair in 1936 and all my husband's brother got killed in that German war and that Lodrigue boy died with his head in my apron the day the tractor run over him, course he was putting on the plow with the damn thing in gear and even the priest said it wasn't too bright to get plowed under by your own plow and—'

'They call me Big Blade,' Marvin thundered.

'My name's Doris Landreneaux. I used to be a Boudreaux before—'

Marvin slapped the old woman, and her upper plate landed on the Formica dinette table. With no hesitation, she picked up her teeth and walked to the sink to rinse them off. Grabbing the incisors, she slid her dentures back in place. 'Hurt?' she yelled. 'You want to hurt a old lady what had seven children, one come out arm-first? Look, I had eight major surgeries and a appendix that blowed up inside me when I was first marry, made me so sick, I was throwing up pieces of gut and the priest gave me Extreme Unction nine time.'

'Shut up,' Marvin yelled, raising his hand over her fluff of hair.

'Oh, you kin hit me again, yeah, and then I'm gonna drop on the floor, and what you gonna do with me then?'

'I can kill you,' Marvin hollered.

'But you can't eat me,' Mrs Landreneaux shrilled back, wagging a knobby finger in Big Blade's befuddled face.

In the other house on that stretch of road, old Mrs Breaux realized with a gasp that she was not going to take a trick in a bourrée game and would have to match an eighteen-dollar pot. The third trick had been raked off the table when Mrs Breaux turned up her hearing aid with a twist of her forefinger and began begging, 'Oh please, somebody, don't drop you biggest trump so I can save myself.'

'I can't hold back, *chère*,' Sadie Lalonde told her. 'I got to play to win. That's the rules.' Mrs Lalonde's upper arms jiggled as she snapped down a trump ace.

Mrs Breaux's eyes got as small as a bat's, and her mouth turned into a raisin. 'You done killed my jack,' she yelled, following suit with her card. 'I'm bourréed.'

Mr Alvin crossed his legs and sniffed. 'You bourréed yourself, girl. You should know better to come in a game with the jack dry.' Mr Alvin shook a poof of white hair out of his florid face and carefully led off with a four trump, followed by Sadie's ten and a stray diamond by Mrs Breaux, whose little cigarette-stained mustache began to quiver as she watched the money get raked off the table.

'You done it,' Mrs Breaux hollered. She shrank back in her wooden chair and searched over her ninety years of evil-tempered earthly existence for the vilest curse words she'd ever heard, and none of them packed the power she wanted. Finally, she said, 'I hope you get diabetes of the blowhole!'

The other three widows and one never-married man laughed out loud at Mrs Breaux and fidgeted with the coins in their little money piles, digging for the next ante. Mrs Guidroz pulled her aluminum cane off the back of her chair to get up for a glass of tap water.

'There's ice water in the fridge,' Sadie offered.

Mrs Guidroz shook her tight blue curls. 'I wasn't raised to drink cold water. That stuff hurts my mout'.' As she drew a glassful from the singing tap, she looked out of the window and down the road. 'Hey. Doris, she got herself some company.'

'If it's a red truck, it must be her son Nelson,' Sadie said. 'Today's Tuesday, when he comes around.'

'*Non*, this is a lil' white car.'

'Maybe it's the power company,' Alvin suggested.

'*Non*, this is too little for a 'lectric company car. Where would they put their pliers and wire in that thing?'

Sadie Lalonde hoisted herself off the two chairs she was sitting on and wobbled to the window, putting her face next to Mrs Guidroz's. 'That's either a Dodge or a Plimmit.'

'What's the difference?'

'I think they the same car, but they label the ones with ugly paint Plimmits.' Sadie looked over her glasses. 'Doris don't know nobody drives a car like that.'

Alvin came to the window and wedged into the women. 'You sure it ain't a Ty-ota? One of her two dozen granddaughters drives one like that.'

'Nanette. I think she sold that, though.'

Alvin shook his head. 'Oh, no, she wouldn't. You know, them little yellow fingers make them Ty-otas and they don't never wear out.' He looked through the window. 'But that's one of them little Freons.'

'Is that a Chevrolet?'

'No, it's a cheap Dodge with a rubber-band motor. Only a Jehovah Witness would drive something like that.'

'Aw, no.' Mrs Guidroz stamped her cane on the linoleum. 'You think we ought to call over there and see if she needs help runnin' them off? Them Jehovah Witness like cockleburs on corduroy.'

From the card table behind the group at the sink rose Beverly Perriloux's voice. She had lit up a Camel and was talking out the smoke. 'Y'all come back and play some cards before Mrs Breaux catches herself a little stroke.' She took another intense drag, all the tiny warts on her face moving in toward the center.

'Damn right,' Mrs Breaux complained. 'I got to win my eighteen dollar back.'

Alvin dusted off his chair and sat down, and Mrs Guidroz gulped two swallows of water while Sadie reached for her wall phone.

Big Blade looked around Mrs Landreneaux's kitchen at the plywood cabinets, the swirling linoleum, which popped when he stepped on it, at a plastic toaster that was a clock and out of which a piece of plastic toast slowly arose every ten seconds. It occurred to him that he was trying to rob the wrong woman.

'I want your wedding rings,' he announced.

She held her hand out toward him. 'I stopped wearin' one when Arthur told me to.'

Big Blade wiggled his knife. 'Arthur?'

'Yah. Arthur-ritis.'

'Where is it?'

'It wasn't but a little silver circle and I gave it to a grandbaby to wear on her necklace. Oh, I had a diamond up on some prongs, too, but it used to get plugged up with grandbaby shit when I'd change diapers, so I gave that away, too.'

The phone rang and Big Blade stepped toward it. 'Answer and act normal. One false word and I'll cut you open.'

Mrs Landreneaux gathered her arms vertically in front of her, her fists under her chin, feigning fright, and tiptoed to the wall phone.

'Hallo,' she yelled. Then turning to Big Blade, she said, 'It's Sadie Lalonde from down the road.' Speaking back into the receiver, she said, 'No, it ain't no Holy Rolly; it's some boy with a sword trying to rob me like the government.'

Big Blade reached out and cut the phone cord with a swipe. 'I ought to kill you where you stand,' he said.

Mrs Landreneaux grabbed the swinging cord and gave him a savage look. 'And then what would you have?'

He blinked. 'Whoever called better not cause no trouble.'

Mrs Landreneaux put a thumb over her shoulder. 'Sadie and that gang playing bourrée. You couldn't blow 'em out that house with dynamite.'

The man looked around as if he was considering gathering up the worn-out contents of her kitchen and packing them into the stolen car he'd left idling out front in the grass. 'You got to have some money around here somewhere. Go get it.'

She raised a hand above her head and toddled off toward the hall. 'If that's all it takes to get you out my hair, you kin have it, yeah.' Abruptly, she turned around and walked toward the stove. 'I almos' forgot my chicken stew heatin' on the burner.'

'Never mind that,' he growled.

Mrs Landreneaux rolled up an eye toward him. 'You hungry, you?' She lifted a lid, and a nimbus laden with smells of onion, garlic, bell pepper, and a medium nut-brown roux rose like a spirit out of the cast-iron pot.

'What's that?' Big Blade sniffed toward the stove, his knife drifting.

'Chicken stew. You eat that over some rice and with potato salad and hot sweet peas.' She looked at the boy's eyes and stirred the rich gravy seductively. 'You burglars take time to eat or what?'

'Oh, Jesus, Mary, and Joseph,' Mrs Lalonde sang, holding the dead receiver to her ear and looking out of her little kitchen window with the four other cardplayers. 'I don't know what to think.'

'She's probably being nasty to us,' Mrs Guidroz said, tapping her cane against Alvin's big soft leg. 'She wants us to worry.'

'That woman says some crazy things,' Beverly agreed. 'She spends so much time cooking, I think she's got natural gas on the brain.'

Mrs Breaux lit up a Picayune with her creaky Zippo. 'Hot damn, let's play cards. Ain't nobody can put nothin' over on Doris Landreneaux.'

'Somebody's over there intrudin',' Sadie protested.

Mrs Breaux sniffed. 'She'll talk the intrudin' parts off their body, that's for true.'

'Well, her phone won't answer back. Somebody ought to go over and see who's there with her.'

The old women turned toward Mr Alvin, a tall, jiggly old man with pale, fine-textured skin who was built like an eggplant. His pleated gray trousers hung on him like a skirt on a fat convent-school girl. 'Why me?'

'You a man!' Mrs Guidroz exclaimed.

Mr Alvin's eyes expanded as though the information were a surprise. '*Mais*, what you want me to do?'

Sadie turned him toward the screen door. 'Just go look in her kitchen window and see if everything is all right.'

'I shouldn't knock on the door?'

Mrs Guidroz shook her tiny head. 'If there's a bad man in there, you gonna tip him off.'

Alvin hung back. 'I don't know.'

'Dammit, Alvin,' Mrs Guidroz said, 'I'd go myself, but it's been raining, and last time I walked to Doris's from here, my stick went down in her lawn a foot deep, yeah, and I couldn't get it unstuck, and Doris wasn't there, so I had to limp all the way back and call my son to come pull it out.'

'Go on, Alvin,' Sadie said, putting a shoulder to his back and nudging him out the door.

Alvin looked down the road to Mrs Landreneaux's house as he walked the clamshell shoulder trying to seem inconspicuous. An old pickup truck passed, driven by what seemed to be a twelve-year-old boy, and Alvin did not return the child's wave. He walked the grassy edge of Mrs Landreneaux's driveway and took to the spongy lawn, circling around to her kitchen window. He stooped and walked under it, the way he had seen detectives do in the movies. When he raised his eyes slowly past the window ledge, he saw a strange man at Mrs Landreneaux's table waving a murderous-looking knife at the old woman while chewing a big mouthful of something.

'You don't watch out, I'm gonna put you in that stew pot,' the man said, and Mr Alvin lowered himself slow as a clock's hand and began to slog through the deep grass toward the highway, where he heard something like a steam engine puffing as he walked along, realizing that it was his own breath. He thought about running and tried to remember how to do it, but his heart was pounding so hard that all he could do was swing his arms faster and paddle the air back to Sadie's house.

The women were at the window, watching him hurry back. 'O *mon Dieu*,' Mrs Guidroz sang, 'look how fast Alvin's moving. What's it mean?'

Mrs Breaux cackled. 'It's probably just his Ex-Lax working.'

They opened the door and pulled him into the room by his flabby arms.

'There's someone there holding a knife on Doris,' Alvin gasped.

'Ai yai-yai!' Sadie shouted.

'Call Deputy Sid,' Beverly announced from the card table, where she was refilling her butane lighter from a miniature canister of gas.

Sadie shook her head. 'It'll take him a half hour to get out here.' She straightened up and looked around. 'Maybe one of us ought to go over there with a gun.'

Alvin put up his big hands. 'Oh no, I went already.' He walked over to the phone and dialed the sheriff's office.

Mrs Breaux threw down a pack of cards in disgust. 'What kind of gun you got?'

Sadie reached into the next room to a little space between an armoire and the wall, retrieving a double-barrel shotgun with exposed hammers. 'This was Lester's daddy's gun.'

Mrs Breaux walked over and figured out how to open the action. 'They ain't no bullets in this thing.'

Sadie walked over to her dresser, her perfume and lotion bottles clinking against each other on the vanity, and pulled out the top drawer. 'Does this fit?' She handed Mrs Breaux a tarnished .38-caliber cartridge. She dropped it into the gun, but it rattled down the barrel and tumbled out onto the linoleum.

'It's not the right size,' Mrs Breaux complained, peering into Sadie's outstretched hand and plucking two high-brass cardboard shells labeled with double O's.

'Here you go.' She plunked in the shells and snapped the action shut.

The parish had only one settlement to the south, Grand Crapaud, and south of that a few miles, the highway came to an end. The center line of the road led up to the steps of a twelve-by-twelve-foot asbestos-sided building on piers, the office of the South End deputy.

Deputy Sid was a tall black man wearing a cowboy hat with a gold badge on the crown and an immaculate, freshly ironed uniform. He sat at his little desk filling out a report about Minos Blanchard letting his Dodge Dart roll overboard at the boat ramp next door. The phone rang, and it was the dispatcher from the parish seat.

'Sid, you there?'

'I'm here all right.'

'Mrs Lalonde out by Prairie Amer called in that Doris Landreneaux has an intruder in her house right now.'

'That's those peoples always playin' cards?'

'And the one that's always cookin'.'

'How does Mrs Lalonde know they's somebody in there?'

'There's a strange car in the yard.'

'Did she say what kind it was?'

'She said it was a Freon.'

'They ain't no such thing.'

'I know that. Mr Alvin looked in the window and saw the intruder.'

Deputy Sid pushed back his hat. 'What's Mr Alvin doing looking in a *woman's* window?'

'Can you get out there?'

'Sho.' He hung up and in one step was at the door.

Mrs Landreneaux watched Big Blade finish one overflowing plate of chicken stew, and then she fixed him another, providing him all the while with French-dripped coffee laced with brandy. 'You better think where you put your money,' Big Blade said through a mouthful of potato salad.

'You ain't had some dessert yet,' Mrs Landreneaux cooed. 'Look, I foun' some bread pudding with whiskey sauce in the fridge.'

Big Blade took a tentative taste of the dessert, then a spoonful, eating slowly and with one eye closed. By the time he'd finished everything on the table, he was stunned with food, drowsy, dim-witted with food. He had been eating for a half hour. When he saw movement at the back screen door, he ignored it for a moment, but when the form of a uniformed black man imprinted itself on his consciousness, he jumped up, holding his knife in one hand and the old lady's bony arm in the other.

Deputy Sid stepped in smiling, moving easily, as though he'd lived in the kitchen all his life and was walking through his own house. 'How you doin', Mrs Landreneaux?'

'Hey, yourself, Deputy Sid. They's fresh coffee on the stove.'

'Freeze,' Blade barked.

Deputy Sid stopped the motion of his hand above the range. 'I can't have no coffee?'

The little plastic slice of toast peeked out of the clock and Blade jumped. 'Ahhh.'

'What?' Deputy Sid looked to the windowsill.

'It's that damn clock,' Mrs Landreneaux said. 'That crazy thing scares the hell out of me, too, but my sister give it to me, and what can you do? I come in here at night sometime and that little toast rises up like a rat sticking its head out a cracker can and—'

'Never mind.' Big Blade was looking at the deputy's staghorn-gripped, nickel-plated revolver. It was angled toward him on the policeman's narrow hip. 'Give me your gun or I'll cut the old lady's throat.'

Deputy Sid considered this for a moment. 'Okay, man. But hold on to Misres Doris, 'cause she fixin' to take off.' The deputy popped his safety strap, lifted his revolver with two fingers, and placed it on the table. Blade held on to the old lady with one hand, reached to the table, still holding the big knife, and realized that he would have to put it down to retrieve the gun. The second he put his finger into the trigger guard of the pistol, Deputy Sid moved his hand over and picked up the knife.

'Hey,' Blade told him, pointing the shiny weapon at his head.

'You don't need this no more.' Deputy Sid dropped the knife behind the refrigerator.

'I want my knife.'

'You better get on out of here while you got the upper hand.'

Big Blade glanced through the screen door. 'Yeah. I bet you got buddies outside just waiting.'

Deputy Sid shook his head. 'No, man. It's just me. But let me give you some advice. You on a dead-end parish highway. The open end got a roadblock right now. South here is marsh and alligators.'

'And then what?'

Deputy Sid screwed up an eye to think. 'Cuba, I guess.'

'Shit. What about north?'

'Rice fields for five miles.'

'That little car I got will get me through the roadblock.'

'I don't know. You left the motor running and it idled out of gas. You can get in it, but it won't go nowhere.'

Big Blade's eyeballs bounced back and forth for a few seconds. He waved the gun. 'Handcuff yourself to that oven door and give me the keys.'

Mrs Landreneaux pointed. 'Careful you don't scratch nothin'. The last thing my husband did before he died is buy me that stove, and it got to last me a long time. He told me—'

'I'm taking her with me. So if you got partners outside, you better call to them.'

'I'm the onliest one back here.'

'Is your cruiser idling?' Big Blade asked with a wicked smile.

The deputy nodded slowly.

'Hah, you people are dumb as dirt,' he said, backing out of the kitchen with the old lady in tow.

Deputy Sid watched them walk out of his line of vision. He looked at the stove, reached and felt the side of the coffeepot, and then stretched to the cabinet to get himself a cup.

The cruiser was eight years old and Big Blade had to clean out clipboards, digital adding machines, dog-eared manuals on report writing, apples, candy bars, chewing gum, magazines, and empty cans of Mace before Mrs Landreneaux would fit into the front seat. She buckled her safety harness, and he climbed in on the driver's side. The old white Dodge's transmission slipped so badly that it would hardly back out onto the road, but soon they were spinning along the highway, going west. After five miles, he could see one police car in the distance parked across the flat road, and he knew he could make the escape work. All he. had to do was hold the pistol to her head and let the officers see this. They would let him roll through like a tourist. Just then, Mrs Landreneaux crossed her hands over her breastbone and announced in a strangled voice, 'I'm having me another heart attack.' Big Blade stopped the car as the old woman's face got red for five seconds, and then she coughed once, her arms falling limp at her side and her upper plate tumbling from her mouth and bouncing once on the floor mat. He looked ahead to what he could now see were two police cars waiting with their flashers swatting the flat light rolling off the rice fields. Feeling with great dread the flesh of the woman's neck, he could find no pulse, and suddenly everything changed. He imagined himself strapped to a gurney in a Louisiana prison, waiting for the fatal charge to come along the tube into his arm. He looked into his rearview and then turned the car around, the old woman's head rolling right. Maybe there would be a boat at the end of the road and he could escape in that.

The Dodge stuttered and groaned up to thirty, forty, forty-five as he headed in the other direction. Soon Doris Landreneaux's house was rolling up on the right, and on the left he watched the only other house in the area, with a mailbox out front and a bushy cedar growing next to it. As soon as he passed that mailbox, his peripheral vision snapped a picture of five old people crouching in a line, hiding behind the cedar. At once, he heard a huge detonation and the car began a drunken spin, metal grinding on the blacktop, the tires howling until the cruiser stopped sideways in the road. Big Blade shook his head and fell out of the front seat, holding Deputy Sid's revolver. He saw a skinny old woman in a print dress walking up and holding a shotgun toward his midsection. One hammer on the gun was down, and the other was up like a fang ready to drop. He stood and raised the nickel-plated revolver and pulled the trigger, aiming at her legs, but all the weapon did was go *tik-tik-tik-tik-tik-tik*.

'Get on the damn ground,' Mrs Breaux hollered in her creaky voice, 'or I'll let the air out of you like I did that tire, yeah.'

Big Blade lay down in the road, and then he heard a cackle from the front seat of the cruiser as Mrs Landreneaux unbuckled herself and climbed out with her upper plate in her hand. 'Ha-haaa, I foolt him good. He tought I was dead and he ran from them other cops.'

Along the shoulder of the road came Deputy Sid, a sea-green oven door under his arm. He bent down, retrieved his revolver, and loaded it with six shells dug out of his pocket. 'I got him now, ladies, Mr Al.'

Mrs Landreneaux sidled up to him. 'You got some more police coming?'

'Yeah. I called 'em from your bedroom phone. Then I called your neighbors here.'

Mrs Breaux lowered the hammer on the shotgun. 'Hot damn. Now we can get back to the game. Doris, you want to play?'

She waved her hand above her white hair as if chasing a fly. 'Nah, me, I got to go clean up my kitchen.'

'What about you, Deputy Sid?'

He looked at his blasted front tire and the pellet holes in the fender. He let the bottom of the oven door rest on the ground. 'It gon' take me a week to write all this up. Maybe next time ya'll play, you can give me a call.'

Sadie lumbered up out of the grass, followed by Alvin. 'Don't bring that gun into the house loaded,' she said.

Mrs Breaux opened the action and plucked out the good shell, chucking the empty into a roadside ditch. She handed the weapon to Alvin, who took it from her with his fingertips, as though it might be red-hot. Mrs Breaux grabbed a handful of Alvin's shirt and let him tow her off the road and across the soft lawn. Suddenly, she wheeled around. 'Hey, you,' she called to Big Blade, who was squirming under the barrel of Deputy Sid's revolver.

'What?' He had to look through the window of the oven door to see her.

'If you ever get out of jail, I want you to come play cards with us.' She threw back her head and laughed.

'Why's that?' he asked. 'What's she mean?'

'Just bring lots of money, boy,' she said as she looked down the road toward an approaching parade of flashers and the warbling laugh of a siren sailing high over the simple rice fields.

The Piano Tuner

The phone rang Monday morning while the piano tuner was shaving, and he nicked himself. The strange lady was on the line, the one who hardly ever came out of her big house stuck back in the cane fields south of town. The piano tuner told her he'd come out, and then he wiped the receiver free of shaving cream and blood. Back at the lavatory, he went after his white whiskers, remembering that she was a fairly good-looking woman, quite a bit younger than he was, in her mid-thirties. She also had a little money, and the piano tuner, whose name was Claude, wondered why she didn't try to lose some of it at the Indian casino or at least spend a bit cheering herself up with a bowl of gumbo at Babineaux's Café. He knew that all she did was sit in a 150-year-old house and practice pop tunes on a moth-eaten George Steck upright.

Claude gathered his tuning kit, drank coffee with his wife, then headed out into the country in his little white van. He made a dozen turns and got on the clamshell road that ran by Michelle Placervent's unpainted house, a squared-off antique thing set high up on crumbling brick pillars. Behind the house were gray-wood outbuildings, and behind those the sugarcane grew taller than a man and spread for miles, level as a giant's lawn.

As he pulled his tool kit out of the van, Claude recalled that Michelle was the end of the line for the Placervents, Creole planters who always had just enough money and influence to make themselves disliked in a poor community. Her mother had died ten years before, after Michelle had graduated with a music degree and come home to take care of her. He looked up on the gallery, stopping a moment to remember her father, a pale, overweight man with oiled hair, who would sit in a rocker and yell after cars speeding in the dusty road, as though he could control the world with a mean word.

The piano tuner remembered that Mr Placervent had begun to step up his drinking after his wife died, and Michelle had to tend him like a baby until he dropped dead in the yard yelling at a postman about receiving too many advertisements from Kmart. From that point on, it was just her, the black housekeeper, the home place, and a thousand acres the bank managed for her. Then the housekeeper died.

It had been a year since she had called him for a tuning. He stopped under a crepe myrtle growing by the porch, noticing that the yard hadn't been cut in a month and the spears of grass were turning to seed. The porch was sagging into a long frown, and the twelve steps that led to it bounced like a trampoline as he went up. He knocked and Michelle turned the knob and backed away, waving him in with a faint hand motion and a small smile, the way Placervents had been doing for two hundred years to people not as good as they were, but Claude didn't hold it against her, because he knew how she had been raised. Michelle reminded him of one of those pastries inside the display case down at Dufresne's Bakery – pretty, but when you tried to handle them, they fell apart, and your fingers went through to the goo inside. She was bouncing on the balls of her feet, as if she expected she might float off at any minute. He saw that she'd put on a few pounds and wasn't carrying her shoulders well, but also that there was still a kind of graceful and old-timey shape to her hips and breasts. Her hair was dark and curly, and her eyes were the brown of worn sharps on an old upright. A man could take an interest in her as long as he didn't look in those eyes, the piano tuner thought. He glanced around the house and saw that it was falling apart.

'I'm glad you could come so soon,' she said. 'C above middle C is stuck.' She pointed over to an ornate walnut-cased vertigrand, and he remembered its rusty harp and dull, hymning soundboard. It would take three hours to get it regulated and pulled back up to pitch. He saw an antique plush chair, faded, with the imprint of her seat in its velvet, and he knew she would sit there until he was finished. Claude usually talked while he did regulations, so he chatted as he unscrewed the fall board, pulled off the front, and flopped back the lid. After a little while, he found an oval pill wedged between two keys and fished it out with a string mute. When she saw what it was, she blushed.

'This one of yours?' he asked, putting it on a side table.

Her eyes followed his hand. 'You remember Chlotilde?'

He nodded. 'She sure could cook, I heard.'

'She called it a "happy pill." She told me that if things got too much for me to handle, I could take it.' She glanced up as though she'd told a secret by accident, and her eyes grew round. 'I never took it, because it's the only one.'

Claude stole a look at her where she sat in front of the buckled plaster wall and its yellowed photographs of dead Placervents. It occurred to him that Michelle had never done anything, never worked except at maintaining her helpless mother and snarling old man. He remembered seeing her in town, always in stores, sometimes looking half-dead and pale, sometimes talking a mile a minute as she bought food, medicines for the aged, adult diapers, coming in quick, going out the same way, enveloped in a cloud of jasmine perfume.

'You know,' he said, 'you could probably go to a doctor and get another pill or two.'

She waved him off with two fingers. 'I can't stand to go to doctors. Their waiting rooms make me want to pass out.'

'There,' he said, running a trill on the freed ivory. 'One problem solved already.'

'It's good to get rid of at least one,' she said, folding her hands in her lap and leaning forward from the waist.

'What problems you having, Michelle?' He put a tuning hammer onto a pin and struck a fork for A. His tuning machine was being repaired at the factory, so he'd gone back to listening, setting temperament by ear.

'Why, none at all,' she said too brightly and breathlessly. Claude thought she spoke like an actress in a 1940s movie, an artificial flower like Loretta Young who couldn't fish a pill from between two piano keys to save her soul.

He struck the butt of the fork on the upturned lid and tuned A 440, then the A's above and below that, and set perfect reference notes in between, tuning by fifths and flatting strings until the sounds in the steel wires matched the sounds in his head. He then tuned by octaves from the reference notes, and this took over an hour. Michelle sat there with her pale hands in her lap, as though she had bought a ticket to watch. The piano's hammers were hard, so he gave them a quick grind with his Moto-Tool, then massaged the dampers, which were starting to buzz when they fell against the strings. He went over the tuning pins again. 'I don't know if this job will hold perfect pitch, Michelle, but if a note or two falls back, give me a call and I'll swing by.'

She nodded. 'Whenever you're out this way, you can stop in. If something's wrong with the piano, I'll be glad to pay to get it fixed.' She smiled a little too widely, like someone desperate to have company, which the tuner guessed she was. He sat down to play a little tune he tested instruments with, but then stopped after half a minute.

What the tuner remembered was that he'd never heard Michelle play. Judging from the wear on the hammers, she must have practiced all the time, so he asked her. She stood, fluffed her skirt, and walked over with a goosey step. Claude expected she might wring the notes out more or less in time, the way most players do, but after about ten measures of 'As Time Goes By,' he could hear that she had a great natural touch, making old George lay the hammers against the strings like big felt teardrops, building note words that belled out into the room. The piano tuner was moved by what she was doing with his work. Next, she surprised him by playing something that sounded like Mozart. Claude had hung around kiddie recitals enough to know a little about classical music, though he'd seldom heard it out here in the cane fields. He watched her long fingers roll and dart.

When she began a slow, fingertippy introduction to 'Stardust,' he had to sit down. He'd heard the song played by everybody and their pet dog, but her touch was something else, like Nat King Cole's voice made from piano notes, echoey and dusty. She used the old bass sustain pedal to milk the overtones out of the new tuning job, and Claude closed his eyes and saw the notes floating slowly around the room.

The piano tuner was the kind of person who hated for anything to go to waste and thought the saddest thing in the world was a fine instrument that nobody ever touched, so it made him uneasy that someone who could play like this lived alone and depressed in an antique nightmare of a house ten miles from the nearest ear that knew what the hell her fingers were doing. When she finished, he asked her how she spent her time.

She folded her music and glanced at him out of the corner of her eye. 'Since my father's gone, there's not much to do,' she said, turning on the bench to face him. 'Sometimes the different people who lease the land come by to talk. I have television.' She motioned to a floor cabinet model topped by an elaborate set of rabbit ears.

'Lord, why don't you get a satellite dish?'

She turned over a hand in her lap. 'I really don't watch anything. It just keeps me company when I can't sleep at night.' She gave him a kind of goofy, apologetic smile.

He began to set his tuning forks in their felt pockets. 'As good as you play, you ought to get a decent piano.'

The corners of her little mouth came down a bit. 'I tried to get Lagneau's Music to bring out a new upright, but they said the old steps wouldn't hold a piano and moving crew.' She placed an upturned hand on George's yellowed teeth. 'They told me they'd never get this big thing off the porch. We're seven feet above the ground here.'

'You can't take it out the back?'

'The steps are worse there. Rotted through.' She let the fall board drop over the ivories with a bang. 'If I could get a new instrument, I'd push this out of the back door and let it fall into the yard for the scrap man.' She passed a hand quickly above her dark hair as though waving off a wasp.

He looked up at the rain-splotched plaster. 'You ever thought about moving?'

'Every day. I can't afford to. And anyway, the house . . . I guess it's like family.'

Claude picked up a screwdriver. 'You ought to get out more. A woman your age needs . . .' He started to say she needed a boyfriend, but then he looked around at the rotting curtains, the twelve-foot ceilings lined with dusty plaster molding, and then back at her trembly shoulders, realizing that she was so out of touch and rusty at life that the only man she should see was a psychiatrist, so then he said, 'A job,' just because he had to finish the sentence.

'Oh,' she said, as though on the edge of crying.

'Hey, it's not so bad. I work every day, and I'm too busy to get blue.'

She looked at his little box of mutes and felts. 'I can't think of a thing I know how to do,' she said.

At supper, Claude's wife was home from her little hole-in-the-wall insurance office, and he asked if she knew Michelle Placervent.

'We don't carry her,' she said, going after a plate of red beans and rice and reading a pamphlet on term life.

'That's not what I asked you.'

She looked up and the light caught in her bottle-brown hair. 'Is she still living out in that little haunted castle?'

'Yeah. The whole place shakes just when you walk through it.'

'Why'd they build it on such tall piers? Did the water get that high before they built the levees?'

'Beats me. You ever hear anything about her?' He handed her the hot sauce and watched her think.

'I heard she was depressed as hell, I can tell you that. Boney LeBlanc said she had a panic attack in his restaurant and had to leave just as the waitress brought her shrimp étouffée.' Evette shook her head. 'And Boney makes dynamite étouffée.'

'She can play the hell out of a piano,' he said.

'Seems like I heard that.' Evette turned the page on her pamphlet. 'Sings, too.'

'She needs to get a job.'

'Well, she knows how to drive a tractor.'

'What?'

'I heard that her father forced her to learn when she was just a kid. I don't know why. Maybe he was mad she wasn't born a boy.' Evette took a long drink of iced tea. 'I heard if a field hand left a tractor by the gate and a rain was coming up, he'd send Michelle out to bring it under the shed. Wouldn't even let her change out of her dress, just made her climb up on the greasy thing and go.'

'Damn, I wouldn't have thought she could operate a doorbell,' Claude said.

His wife cut her eyes over to him. 'It might surprise you what some people can do,' she told him.

Two weeks later, Claude was sitting in his recliner, his mind empty except for a football game playing in it, when the phone rang. It was Michelle Placervent, and her voice struck his ear like the plea of a drowning sailor. She was crying into the receiver about how three notes on her keyboard had soured and another key was stuck. The more she explained what was wrong with her piano, the more she cried, until she began weeping, Claude thought, as if her whole family had died in a plane crash, aunts and cousins and canaries.

He interrupted: 'Michelle, it's only a piano. Next time I'm out your way, I'll check it. Maybe Monday sometime?'

'No,' she cried, 'I need someone to come out now.'

Uh-oh, he thought. He hung up and went to find his wife. Evette was at the sink peeling onions, and he told her about Michelle. She banged a piece of onion skin off her knife. 'You better go fix her piano,' she said. 'If that's what needs fixing.' She looked up at the piano tuner's gray hair as though she might be wondering if Michelle Placervent found him attractive.

'You want to come for the ride?' he asked.

She shook her head and kissed him on the chin. 'I've got to finish supper. When Chad gets home from football practice, he'll be starving.' She picked up another onion and cut off the green shoots, her eyes flicking up at him. 'If she's real sick, call Dr Meltier.'

Claude drove out there as quickly as he could, sorry he'd ever tuned the worn-out piano in the first place. Giving a good musician a fine tuning is always a risk, because when the first string starts to vibrate, he gets dissatisfied and calls up, as if one little note that's just a bit off ruins the whole song.

She was dressed in faded stretch jeans and a green sweatshirt, and her hair was unbrushed and oily. The house was as uncombed as she was. Claude looked at her trembly fingers and her wild eyes, then asked if she had any relatives or friends in town. 'Everybody is dead or moved far away,' she told him, her eyes streaming and her face red and sticky. He watched her, feeling suddenly tired and helpless. He tried to think what Evette would do for her, and then he went into the kitchen to make her some hot tea. The cabinets looked as though someone had thrown the pots into them from across the room. The stove was a first-generation gas range that should have been in a museum, and it was listing, the floor sagging under it. The icebox was full of TV dinners, and the pantry showed a few cans of Vienna sausage and beanie-weenies. Claude realized that he would be depressed himself if that was all he had to eat.

When he brought the tea, she was in a wing chair leaning

to one side, her shoulders rounded in. Sitting on the bench, he carefully checked the keyboard by unisons and fifths, and he found nothing out of pitch, no stuck key. At that moment, he knew that when he turned around, he would have two choices: to say there was nothing wrong, get in his van, and go on with his life, or to deal with her. He inspected the alligatored finish on the George Steck's case for a long time, examined the sharps for lateral play. Even while he was turning on the satiny bench, he didn't know what he was going to say. Then he saw her eyes, big with dread of something like a diagnosis. Claude felt as though he were slipping off into quicksand when he opened his mouth.

'Michelle, who's your doctor?'

Her eyes went to the dark, wax-caked floor. 'I'm not going.'

'You got to. Look at yourself. You're sadder'n a blind man at a strip show.'

'I just need a little time to adjust. My father's been gone only six months.' She put a hand on her forehead and hid her eyes from him.

'You need a little something, all right, but it ain't time. You got too *much* time on your hands.' Then he told her what her doctor could do for her. That her depression was just a chemical thing. She could be straightened up with some medicine, he told her. He said many things off the top of his head, and he convinced her to make an appointment with Dr Meltier. He talked with her a long time in her cold living room. When a thunderbolt lit up the yard and a storm blew in from the west, he helped her put out pots to catch leaks. He held her hand at the door and got her calm so she wouldn't call him out of his warm bed in a few hours, telling him that her piano had gone up in pitch or was playing itself.

A month or so passed, and Claude was cutting grass when suddenly he saw Michelle's old black Lincoln charge up the drive, and she got out, smiling too widely, wearing a navy cotton dress that was baggy and wrinkled. He asked her to come in for coffee, and he listened to her talk and talk. The doctor had given her some medications to test for a couple of months, and her eyes were bright. In fact, her eyes showed so much happiness, they scared him. She asked if he could help her find a job playing the piano.

'When you're ready, I'll help.' For years, Claude had tuned pianos for places that used lounge pianists, and he knew all the managers.

She put four spoons of sugar in her coffee with steady hands. 'I'm ready right this minute,' she said. 'I've got to make my music go to work for me.'

The piano tuner laughed at that, thinking the poor thing was so cheery and upbeat, he should call Sid Fontenot, who managed the lounge in that big new motel over in Lafayette. 'Sid's always trying out pianists,' he told her. 'I'll give him a call for you.'

When he got off the phone, she asked, 'How do you play in a lounge?' and Claude tried to keep his face from screwing up.

'There's nothing to it,' he said, sitting down with her and frowning into his coffee cup. 'You must know a thousand show tunes and ballads.'

She nodded. 'Okay. I play requests. I play what they ask me to.' She adjusted a thin watchband and then looked him in the eye.

Claude got up and put their cups in the sink. 'Sid asked me if you can sing. You don't have to, but he said it would help. You get a lot of requests for old stuff in a classy motel lounge.'

'I was good in voice,' she said, clasping her hands until they went white. And then he thought he saw a weakening of the mood flash through her eyes, a little electrical thrill of fright. 'How do I dress?'

He lathered up a dishcloth and looked at her hair, which was short, coffee-brown. He regarded the white skin on her face, the crow's-feet, the dryness. 'Why don't you go to Sears and buy a black dress and some fake pearls. Get a little makeup while you're at it. You'll be the best-looking thing in the lounge. Sid says he'll try you tomorrow night in the bar at nine o'clock. It's the big new motel on the interstate.'

Claude's wife had often told him that he invented reality by saying it, and he was thinking this as he talked to the medicated hermitlike woman seated in his kitchen. He was also thinking that the last place on earth he would want to be was in the piano bar of a Lafayette motel at nine at night. And naturally, the next question to come out between Michelle Placervent's straight teeth was, 'Can't you please come with me this first time?'

Claude took a breath and said, 'I'd be glad to,' and she clapped her hands like an organ-grinder's monkey. He wondered what she was taking and how much of it.

He almost convinced Evette to come along with them, but their seventeen-year-old boy came down with the flu and she stayed home to nurse. She made her husband wear a sport coat, but he refused to put on a tie. 'You want to look good for your date,' she told him with a smirk.

'Get out of here.' He turned red in the face and walked onto the porch to wait in the night air.

Michelle picked him up, and he had to admit that she looked blue-blood sharp. He imagined she must have bought a girdle along with her velvety black dress. On the way to Lafayette, the Lincoln drifted above the narrow, flat highway through the sugar-cane, and Claude got her to talk about herself. She told him that she had been engaged twice, but old man Placervent was so nasty to the young men, he just ran them off. Her grandfather had wanted to tear the old house down 'from bats to termites' and build a new place, but her father wouldn't hear of it. She said he'd worn the building like a badge, some proof that he was better than anyone else. 'The only proof,' Michelle said. 'And now I'm trapped in it.' The piano tuner didn't know what to say, other than that she could look forward to hurricane season, but he kept his mouth closed.

The lounge was a long room, glass walls on one side and a

long bar with a smiling lady bartender on the other. He introduced Michelle to Sid, a bright-looking man, savvy, dressed in an expensive suit. Sid smiled at her and pointed out the piano, and the next thing Claude knew, Michelle was seated behind a rebuilt satin-black Steinway playing 'Put On a Happy Face,' her high-heeled foot holding down the soft pedal. After a while, the room began to fill with local oil men and their glitzy women, plus the usual salesmen sprawling at the tables, and even a couple of cowboys who lit like dragonflies at the bar. A slim, tipsy woman in tight white jeans and spike heels approached the piano and made a request, putting a bill into a glass on the lid. Michelle stared at the money for a moment and started 'Yesterday,' playing for six minutes.

Claude sat at a tiny table next to the window overlooking the swimming pool and ordered a German beer. He'd never done anything like this and felt out of place. When he did frequent a bar, it was the kind of place with Cajun music on the jukebox and a gallon jar of pigs' feet on the counter. Michelle finished the tune and looked over at him, and he gave her the okay sign. She smiled and sailed into another, then tickled off a half dozen more over the next forty-five minutes. At one point, she walked to Claude's table and asked how she was doing. He could see, even in the dim light, that her eyes were too intense, the way a person's eyes get when she's having too much fun.

The piano tuner wanted to say, Lighten up on the arpeggios. Slow your tempo. But she was floating before him as fragile as a soap bubble, so he gave her the thumbs-up. 'Perfect. Sid says you can have a hundred dollars for four hours, plus tips.'

'Money,' she squealed, bouncing back to the piano and starting 'The Pennsylvania Polka,' playing with a lot of sustain pedal. A brace of oil men looked over briefly, but most people just leaned closer to talk, or patted their feet. Claude signaled her to quiet it down a bit.

For an hour and a half, he watched as Michelle played and grinned at people coming to her tip glass. She sang one song through the microphone over her keyboard and drew a moderate wave of applause. She was a good-looking woman, but she had never learned how to move around people, and Claude got the feeling that folks who studied her close up thought she was a little silly. He sat there wishing there was a regulating button on the back of her head that he could give just a quarter turn.

Eventually, the piano tuner became drowsy and hungry in the dim light of the lounge, so he walked across the lobby to the restaurant and treated himself to a deluxe burger basket and another cold bottle of beer. He sat there next to the plant box full of plastic flowers and worried about Michelle and whether he'd done the right thing by turning a Creole queen into a motel-lounge pianist.

As soon as he left the restaurant, he could tell something was not exactly right. A young couple walked out of the lounge with quick steps, and then he heard the music: Hungarian Rhapsody no. 2. Sid appeared at the lounge entrance and waved him over. 'Michelle's really smoking our Steinway,' he said, putting his mouth to the piano tuner's ear. 'You know, this crowd thinks classical music is something like Floyd Cramer's Greatest Hits.' Claude looked into the room, where customers seemed to bend under the shower of notes like cows hiding from a thunderstorm. Some of the loud salesmen had stopped selling mud pumps and chemicals to listen, and the drunk cowboys, who had picked up two women, were trying to jitterbug.

Sid put a hand on Claude's shoulder. 'What's going on? She's got to know that's not the right music for this place.'

'I'll talk to her.'

He glanced over his shoulder. 'She's smiling a lot. Is she on something?' Sid knew musicians.

'Depression medicine.'

He sniffed. 'Well, I guess that music'll drive you off the deep end.'

After the big rumbling finale, the cowboys let out a rebel yell, but no one applauded, and Claude walked over and put his hand on her back, bending down. 'That was good, Michelle.' What else could he say to her?

She looked up at him and her eyes were wet, her skin flushed and sweating. 'You don't fool me. I know what you're thinking. But I couldn't help it. I just got this surge of anger and had to let it out.'

'What are you mad at?' He saw that her shoulders were trembling.

She didn't say anything at first, and then she looked up at him. 'I've been sitting here thinking that I would have to play piano five nights a week for twenty-three years to pay for the renovation of my house.' She straightened up and looked over the long piano at the bartender, who had both hands on the bar, watching her. 'What am I doing here?' She ran a palm down her soft throat. 'I'm a Placervent.'

Claude pushed her microphone aside. 'Your medications are maybe a little out of adjustment,' he said in a low voice, wishing he were anyplace on earth other than where he was. He looked over at Sid. 'You ought to finish this set.'

'Why? I can survive without the money. I mean, I appreciate you getting me this job, but I think I'm ready to go home.' She seemed angry and out of control, but she didn't move.

He was sure his face showed that he was getting upset himself. She stared down at the keys until finally one of the cowboys, really just a French farm boy from down in Cameron Parish, wearing a loud shirt and a Wal-Mart hat, came up and put a five in her tip glass. 'Hey, lady, can you play any Patsy Cline?'

An injured little smile came to her lips. She straightened her back and started to say something to him, but instead she looked at Claude, at his embarrassed and hopeful face. Her mouth closed in a line, and her right hand went down and began picking out an intro. Then, to his amazement, she started to sing, and people looked up as though Patsy Cline had come back, but without her country accent, and the whole room got quiet to listen. 'Crazy,'

Michelle sang, soft as midnight fog outside a bedroom window, 'crazy for feeling so lonely.'

He didn't see her for a long time. At Sid's, someone spilled a high-ball into the Steinway, and when Claude was over there to straighten it out, the manager told him she was still playing on weekends, and off and on at the Sheraton, and a little at the country club for the oil-company parties. He said that she had gotten her dosage pretty regulated and she played well, except toward the end of the night, when she would start singing blues numbers and laughing out loud between the verses as though she were telling jokes in her head. Laughing very loudly. The piano tuner wondered if she would ever get on an even keel. People like Michelle, he thought, sometimes their talent helped them fix themselves. Sometimes not. Nobody could predict.

In the middle of December, she called him to come tune a new console she'd bought. She'd finally gotten a carpenter to put knee braces under the front steps so Lagneau's Music could bring a piano into the house. They'd told her they didn't want George as a trade-in, though, and that they wouldn't take the big vertigrand down into the yard for a million dollars. It was built like a wooden warship with seven five-by-five back braces, and it weighed nearly eight hundred pounds. When Claude got there, the entry was open, the dark giant of a piano at the head of the long hall that led to the back porch. As he stepped in, he saw the new piano in the parlor, a cheap, ugly blond-wood model. He couldn't believe she'd chosen it. Michelle appeared at the far end of the hall, looking wild-eyed, her hair falling in loose, dangly ringlets. She was wearing rust-smudged tan slacks under a yellow rain slicker and was lugging the end of a half-inch cable in her cotton gardening gloves.

'Claude,' she said, shaking her head. 'You wouldn't believe the trouble I've had this morning. I had Lagneau's crew push the old piano into the hall, but the rollers on the bottom locked up. Just look what they did to the floor.' She swept a hand low. The floors were so covered with two-hundred-year-old divots brimming with cloudy wax that he couldn't spot much new damage. 'They managed to get it up on this old braided rug, and I figured I could tow it off the back porch and let it fall into the yard.'

He looked in her eyes to see what was going on. 'You gonna skid this thing down the hardwood on this rug? We can't just push it ourselves?'

'Give it a try.'

He leaned on it, but he was a small man, and the piano didn't budge. 'I see what you mean.' He looked down the hall to the open rear door. 'You think it'll slide onto the porch and fall through the back steps?'

'They have to be replaced anyway. Mr Arcement said he would cart away the mess next week.' She ran the cable under the keyboard and around the back through the handholds, completing a loop and setting the hook. When she passed by the piano tuner, he smelled gasoline on her clothes, and he walked to the back door to see what she'd hooked the cable to. Idling away in the yard was a John Deere 720, a big two-cylinder tractor running on propane.

'God Almighty, Michelle, that tractor's the size of a locomotive.'

'It's the only one out in the barn that would start,' she said, dropping the cable's slack into the yard.

He looked out at the rust-roofed outbuildings, their gray cypress darkening in the drizzle. She began picking her way down the porous steps, which didn't look like they'd support his weight, so he went out the front door and walked around to the back. He found Michelle standing on the right axle housing of the tractor, facing backward, looking into the hall at the piano. The machine's exhaust was thudding like a bass drum. He remembered that older John Deeres have a long clutch lever instead of a foot pedal, and she was easing this out to take up slack in the cable. A tire rolled up on the septic tank's lid, and the front end veered sharply. Claude didn't know exactly what she was trying to do, but he offered to help.

'I've planned this through. You just stay on the ground and watch.' She sat in the seat, found reverse gear, backed the tractor closer to the house, snugged the steering wheel with a rubber tie-down so it wouldn't wander again, then eased forward in the lowest gear until the cable was taut. With the slack out of the line, she put the lever all the way forward and the machine began to crawl. Claude walked way out in the yard, stood on tiptoe, and saw George skidding down the hall, wandering from side to side but looking as though it would indeed bump out of the house and onto the back porch. About three feet from the door, the piano rolled off the rug and started to turn broadside to the entryway. Michelle stopped the tractor and yelled something. He couldn't understand it over the engine noise, but she might have been asking him to go inside and straighten the piano. She stepped out onto the axle again, leaned forward to jump to the ground, and the piano tuner held his breath because there was something wrong with the way she was getting off. Her rain slicker caught on the long lever and he heard the clutch pop as it engaged. Michelle fell on her stomach, the big tractor moving above her. Claude ran over, and when she came out from under the drawbar, he grabbed her arm to get her up. Meanwhile, the tractor had pulled the piano's soundboard flat against the entryway to the house, where it jammed for about half a second. The tractor gasped as its governor opened up and dumped gas in its engine, and, *chak-chak*, the exhaust exploded, the big tires squatted and bit into the lawn, and the piano came out with the back wall of the entire house, three rows of brick piers collapsing like stacks of dominoes, the kitchen, rear bedroom, and back porch disintegrating in a tornado of plaster dust and cracking, wailing boards. A musical waterfall of slate shingles rattled down from the roof, the whole house trembled, nearly every windowpane tinkled out, and just when Claude and Michelle thought things had stopped collapsing, the hall fell in all the way to the front door, which swung closed with a bang.

The tractor kept puttering away toward the north at around

four miles an hour, and the piano tuner wondered if he should run after it. Michelle began to make a whining noise deep down in her throat. She hung on to him and started to swing as if she'd pass out. He couldn't think of a word to say, and they stared at the wreck of a house as though considering putting it back together with airplane glue, when a big yellow jet of gas flamed up about where the stove would be in all the rubble.

'A fire,' she said breathlessly, tears welling up in her eyes.

'Where's the closest neighbor?' he asked, feeling at least now he could do something.

'The Arcements'. About a mile off.' Her voice was tiny and broken as she pointed a thin white arm to the east, so he gathered her up and walked her to the front, putting her in his van and tearing out down the blacktop toward the nearest working telephone.

By the time the Grand Crapaud Volunteer Fire Department got out to Michelle Placervent's place, the house was one big orange star, burning so hot that it made little smoke. The firemen ran up to the fence but lost heart right there. They began spraying the camellias at roadside and the live oaks farther in. Claude had rescued Michelle's Lincoln before the paint blistered off, and she sat in it on the side of the road, looking like a World War II refugee he had seen on the History Channel. Minos LeBlanc, the fire chief, talked to her for a while and asked if she had insurance.

She nodded. 'The only good thing the house had was insurance.' She put her face in her hands then, and Claude and Minos looked away, expecting the crying to come. But it didn't. She asked for a cup of water, and the piano tuner watched her wash down a pill. After a while, she locked her Lincoln and asked him to take her into town. 'I have an acquaintance I can stay with, but she won't come home from work until five-thirty.' She ran her eyes up a bare chimney rising out of the great fire. 'All these years and only one person who'll put me up.'

'Come on home and eat supper with us,' he said.

'No.' She looked down at her dirty slacks. 'I wouldn't want your wife to see me like this.' She seemed almost frightened and looked around him at the firemen.

'Don't worry about that. She'd be glad to loan you some clothes to get you through the night.' He placed himself between her and the fire.

She ran her white fingers through her curls and nodded. 'All right,' but she watched him out of the corner of her eye all the way into town, as though she didn't trust him to take her to the right place. About a block before Claude turned down his street, she let out a giggle, and he figured her chemicals were starting to take effect. Evette showed her the phone and she called several people, then came into the living room, where Claude was watching TV. 'I can go to my friend Miriam's after six-thirty,' she said, settling slowly into the sofa, her head toward the television.

'I'll take you over right after we eat.' He shook his head and looked at the rust and mud on her knees. 'Gosh, I'm sorry for you.'

She kept watching the screen. 'Look at me. I'm homeless.' But she was not frowning.

When the six o'clock local news came on Channel 10, the fifth story was about a large green tractor that had just come out of a cane field at the edge of Billeaudville, dragging the muddy hulk of a piano on a long cable. The announcer explained how the tractor plowed through a woman's yard and proceeded up Lamonica Street toward downtown, where it climbed a curb and began to struggle up the steps of St Martin's Catholic Church, until Rosalie Landry, a member of the Ladies' Altar Society, who was sweeping out the vestibule, stopped the machine by knocking off the tractor's spark-plug wires with the handle of her broom. As of five-thirty, Vermilion Parish sheriff's deputies did not know where the tractor had come from or who owned it and the battered piano.

Claude stood straight up. 'I can't believe it didn't stall out somewhere. Billeaudville's four miles from your house.'

294

Michelle began laughing, quietly at first, her shoulders jiggling as she tried to hold it in. Then she opened her mouth and let out a big, sailing laugh, and kept it going, soaring up into shrieks and gales, some kind of tears rolling on her face. Evette came to the door holding a big spoon, looked at her husband, and shook her head. He reached over and grabbed Michelle's arm.

'Are you all right?'

She tried to talk between seizures of laughter. 'Can't you see?' she keened. 'It escaped.' On the television, a priest was shaking his head at the steaming tractor. She started laughing again, and this time Claude could see halfway down her throat.

A year later, he was called out for four tunings in Lafayette on one day. September was like that for him, with the start of school and piano lessons. On top of it all, Sid called him to fish a bottle of bar nuts out of the lounge piano. He got there late, and Sid bought him supper in the restaurant before he started work.

The manager wore his usual dark gray silk suit, and his black hair was combed straight back. 'Your friend,' he said, as if the word *friend* held a particularly rich meaning for them, 'is still working here, you know.'

'Yeah, I was over at her apartment last month tuning a new console for her.' Claude shoveled up pieces of hamburger steak.

'You know, there's even some strange folks that come in as regulars just to hear her.'

Claude looked up at him. 'She's a good musician, a nice woman,' he said between chews.

Sid took another slow drink, setting the glass down carefully. 'She looks nice,' he said, emphasizing the word *looks*. The piano tuner recognized that this is how Sid talked, not explaining, just using his voice to hint at things. The manager leaned in to him. 'But sometimes she starts speaking right in the middle of a song. Strange things.' He looked at his watch. 'She's starting early tonight, for a convention crowd, a bunch of four-eyed English teachers.'

'What time?'

'About eight.' He took a drink and looked at the piano tuner. 'Every night, I hold my breath.'

That evening, the room was cool and polished. A new little dance floor had been laid down next to the piano, and Michelle showed up wearing round metal-frame glasses and a black velvet dress. The piano was turned broadside to the room, so that everyone could watch her hands. She started playing immediately, a nice old fox-trot Claude had forgotten the name of. Then she played a hymn, then a ragtime number. He sat there enjoying the bell quality of his own tuning job. Between songs, she spotted him, and her eyes ballooned; she threw her long arms up and yelled into the microphone, 'Hey, everybody, I see Claude from Grand Crapaud, the best piano tuner in the business. Let's give Claude a round of applause.' A spatter of clapping came from the bar. Claude gave her a worried glance, and she made herself calm, put her hands in her lap, and waited for the applause to stop. Then she set a heavy book of music on the rack. Her fingers uncurled into their ivory arches, and she began a slow Scott Joplin number with a hidden tango beat, playing it so that the sad notes bloomed like flowers. Claude remembered the title – 'Solace.'

'Did you know,' she asked the room over her microphone during the music, 'that Scott Joplin played piano in a whorehouse for a little while?' Claude looked out at all the assembled English teachers, at the glint of eyeglasses and name tags and upturned, surprised faces. He understood that Michelle could never adjust to being an entertainer. But at least she was brave. 'Yes,' she continued, 'they say he died crazy with syphilis, on April Fool's Day, 1917.' She nodded toward the thick music book, all rags, marches, and waltzes. 'One penicillin shot might have bought us another hundred melodies,' she told the room. 'That's kind of funny and sad at the same time, isn't it?'

She pulled back from the microphone, polishing the troubling notes. Claude listened and felt the hair rise on his arms. When she finished, he waved at her, then got up and walked toward the lobby, where he stood for a moment watching the ordinary people. He heard her start up a show tune, and he turned and looked back into the lounge as three couples rose in unison to dance.

The Pine Oil Writers' Conference

He was a Presbyterian minister, a tanned little man who'd always wanted to write something more significant than sermons. He was seated in the first session of the Pine Oil Writers' Conference, held at a tiny junior college built in the shadow of an abandoned turpentine mill outside of Pine Oil, Louisiana. At the front of the classroom, three panelists and a moderator had already begun to argue about how to put together a novel. The minister, Brad, thought they were fractious and rude, and so they must indeed be intellectuals, especially Charles Lamot, the long-haired, sixty-five-year-old gentleman in the turtleneck sweater. He was Pine Oil Junior College's most famous creative writing teacher, and at the moment was railing against the idea that a novel had to have a plot, as though the concept were a regressive plan thought up by Republican senators. When the old professor turned his head, Brad could see a grapefruit-sized bald spot in the middle of a wreath of gray hair, and he imagined the teacher sitting in a coffeehouse in San Francisco back in the sixties, wearing a black turtleneck and laboring over his manuscript, accompanied perhaps by an undernourished woman with straight blond hair who hovered next to him, smoking and studying the middle distance. 'Nowadays, people expect to be entertained when they buy a book,' the professor complained. 'No one wants to *think* anymore.' He looked away from the audience as though unable to bear the expectant, middle-class faces. 'It is so boring to be entertained,' he said with an arthritic wave of the hand.

Brad had received the conference flyer in the mail, and he spread it out now on the creaking student desk and saw that the professor had published one novel in Canada in the 1970s. He wondered if the likes of Charles Lamot could supply what he was looking for, that magic, holy thing all writing hopefuls sought: The Answer. Brad imagined that locked up inside him somewhere was a novel that would dazzle the world, or at least create a few sparks in his hometown of Mandeville, Louisiana, and he'd decided to come to the meeting, to hear someone stand up and say, *To put the magic that is in you down on the page, you must listen to this – The Answer.* He worried that he might have a talent that he was wasting, and that he could be called into account for this in the next life, that God might be someone like his burly uncle Ralph, who had given him a circular saw twenty years ago and who never failed to ask, 'Hey, boy, you makin' something with that saw I give you? You keeping oil on it?'

Sometimes he felt close to discovering how to write really well. A year ago he was having stomach problems, his wife was thinking of divorcing him, and he had just been transferred to a smaller church; he got up early one morning to empty his bladder, and he felt a similar liquid weight in his soul. He sat down in the quiet lakeside balcony of his apartment near the edge of Lake Pontchartrain and wrote a story on his laptop about a man quitting his job and buying a motorcycle to escape the South. He wasn't sure whether the story was any good, but after buying a copy of *Writer's Market*, sending his manuscript all over, and getting rejected thirty-one times, a little magazine in Ohio, *The Rust-Belt Muse*, bought it for two contributors' copies. When he received the acceptance in the mail, he felt elevated, as though he'd set foot on the first step of the stairs to the Palace of Fame. He'd gone on to publish four more stories in journals with better reputations. His wife began to find him a little more interesting, gave him new word-processing software, and he set up a little study off the rear viewing deck of his place, where he spent hours looking over the wind-whipped lake, or watching the screen saver on his computer. He wrote a little, and his wife seemed satisfied to see him at home doing something of purpose.

The chirping voice of another panelist politely agreed with the professor. Millicent Winespoor was a romance novelist, a large soft-looking lady dressed in a flowered silk blouse and floppy hat. 'There's no reason to get action rolling too soon,' she sang out to the room. 'A nice long section of description of the novel's setting will—'

'Nothing,' the third panelist interrupted, a sharp-voiced stick of a woman with enormous glasses, 'nothing will shoot a novel in the forehead like a vomity clot of useless description on the first page.' She was spare, older, wearing a denim dress and looking as tough as barbed wire. Brad looked to his brochure and saw that Faye Cooker had published ten novels at university presses and had taught for thirty years. She had the dogged look of a classroom veteran, one of those academic martyrs long-tortured by students' outrageous questions and assumptions about writing.

'Well,' Millicent began, 'I only meant that lulling the reader into a locale—'

'If you believe for a minute that a reader wants to be lulled, I think you should cut back on your estrogen supplement,' Faye snapped. 'A novel is a story, and a story is like an airplane. You get the damned thing off the ground as soon as you can.' She leaned over and gave Professor Lamot a wide smile. 'That means you start the plot.'

A snowstorm of bickering followed for fifty minutes, during which many of the potential writers began to look out the window at the rust-red conveyors and towers of the turpentine mill, the boilers wreathed in Kudzu, giant steam engines exposed by collapsed walls. Some drew stars or torsos in their notebooks. Brad, however, listened to every word, wondering if some fact in the harangue could point him toward The Answer.

That evening he lay on his lumpy cot in the cinder-block dorm trying to read an inscrutable and depressing story in a literary quarterly. His roommate was forty-year-old Butchie Langanstein from Cincinnati, a beef cow of a stockbroker with a crew-cut head made like a butcher's block. He wore a poplin khaki sport coat that was much too small for him, and when he moved, his shoes creaked like overburdened saddles. Brad studied him a moment, then asked, 'What do you expect to get here at the conference?'

Butchie gave him a sly look. 'I'd like to, you know, find out how to fix up my novel a bit.'

'You're a novelist?'

The big man rocked back on the bed. 'I got a few chapters under my belt.'

'You have anything published?'

'Nah.' Butchie waved him off. 'I sent out a few things, but most of the time the bastards never sent anything back. That's one reason I'm here, you know. To make some connections. It's mostly connections that gets you published. I don't think you got to be Faulkner anymore.'

'Are you happy with what you write?'

Butchie cocked his head. 'Hell, I don't know. I like to do it, though. I figure if I write until I die, I'm bound to get some better.'

'I mean, do you think your stuff is any good?'

'My mom likes a couple things I did. How do you know if you're good, anyway? Just because somebody tells you? Well, the next guy might tell you different.' He jerked at his tie as if he were trying to hang himself. 'Hey, you going out tonight?'

Brad turned a page in his book and made a face. 'After the last panel discussion, I'll be pretty tired. I'd like to read a lot while I'm here.'

'There's unattached writing women around. You might get lucky. Did you see that fox that sat next to me at the panel discussion?'

Brad looked at the ceiling and decided not to tell Butchie that he was a minister. 'That old lady?'

'Oh, she ain't so old. There's motion left in those bones.'

Brad sat up. 'She's old enough to be your mother. I took the timber industries bus tour with her and listened to her talk to and from the plywood plant. She's an atheist who has a crucifix collection. She has a pet conch shell that gives her stock tips.'

Butchie ran his hand over his crew cut, which sprang back up like a vegetable brush. 'Yeah, well, you just don't know what's important. Me and the conch lady are going out for drinks after supper.' He announced this as though he had just landed a date with a movie star. 'She said she was gonna help me with my character motivations,' he said, winking.

After the evening meal, Brad went to hear a man read a short story. It was science fiction, set in the future in a coal-mining town in Pennsylvania. Everybody was dressed in self-deodorizing aluminum clothes and lived in vinyl houses. They never went anywhere because they worked, recreated, and bought what they wanted on their home computers. However, every block in the vinyl village had a tavern where they would drink Rolling Rock beer, dance the polka, and argue over the Steelers games. The story was very creative, Brad thought, as it unrolled futuristic fact after fact, though it had no plot, except something about aluminum absorption causing Alzheimer's disease. It was funny, sometimes, and there were clever metaphors that the author had placed like cherries on a cake. Something was missing, though, and Brad couldn't put his finger on it. When the story was over, Professor Lamot applauded with enthusiasm, and Faye Cooker examined the floor.

There was a mixer in an empty classroom afterward, where a cafeteria table held a Tupperware bowl of bean dip and a shallow platter of chips. Brad approached Faye Cooker and decided to talk to her, he didn't care about what, figuring that just being close to a published writer might bathe him in creative emanations. Up close, she was smaller and grayer, her voice reedy-loud from years of lecturing. He introduced himself, and she smiled and took his hand in a way that said, *I have been paid well to be nice to you.*

'I read one of your books,' Brad offered. '*The Midwife's Bill.* I thought it had a lot of good history in it.'

'Thanks. What do you write?' she asked quickly.

He thought a minute. 'Stories. But I want to start a novel.'

'Ah, that's nice,' she said, nodding, then taking a swallow of a clear drink. 'Do you have any idea what you'll say?'

'Say?'

'I like to think of the novel as a voice.'

He blinked and poured himself a cola from a card table bar. 'I was kind of thinking of a detective story, not just a shoot-'em-up, but serious detective fiction.'

Faye raised an eyebrow. 'That's sort of like serious water-balloon fighting, isn't it?'

'I beg your pardon?'

'If you want to write something good, start with your family, something they did either last year or last century. Something your old man told you, or your grandfather.' She looked at him through her bifocals. 'You knew your grandfather?'

'Yes.' He thought of the old man, who did ship inspections for a maritime insurance company, and who had started out as a farmer. 'But he wasn't very interesting.'

'Thank God for that,' she said.

He absorbed the comment and shrugged it off at the same time. He was a man who appreciated truth by storing it away, like coin collectors who keep their treasures in a bank box and haven't seen them for decades. 'I have to come up with something day after tomorrow for a staff member to consider. Will you read my beginning?'

'Why not?' She raised one hand and let it fall. 'Just remember what I said.'

'You don't like the detective angle?'

She looked at him quickly, started to say something, then seemed to reconsider. 'Are you a detective?'

'No.'

'Anybody in your family a detective? A best friend? An acquaintance? A ninth cousin?' Her voice began to cut like a dull razor.

'Okay, okay,' he said. At this point a large, hopeful-looking woman stepped into the conversation and cut him off with her thick body the way a cowboy's horse cuts a calf out of a herd.

Brad returned to the cinder-block dorm, got out his laptop, and stared at it for fifty minutes. Then he began to type, continuing to rattle the keys until Butchie wobbled in at two A.M. The big man shucked his shoes, dropped his wool slacks on the floor in two gray rings, and fell into bed with his knit shirt on, blowing out air like a porpoise. He held up two fingers and said, 'Second base, dude.'

Brad resumed his typing. 'That old lady has the beginnings of a widow's hump.'

Butchie turned away from the light over Brad's bunk and covered his head. 'I'll show you some hump,' he said, muffled and foggy-drunk.

The next morning early, Brad ate at a big round table with eleven other participants in the Pine Oil Writers' Conference, hopeful that some writer talk would emerge, that maybe one of the participants had found The Answer. He asked a freckled woman wearing a faded peasant dress what she was working on, and she told him she used to write poetry in high school and 'was trying to morph back into the whole creative mind-set.' A man with a round white scar in the middle of his forehead said he'd been wanting to put down his war experiences since Korea but could never remember to get started. He tried to smile at his fellow students, but only half of his face looked happy.

At lunch, Brad was back at the same table with a mostly different group, and he listened to them talk of a good lounge they'd been to, a good restaurant. Millicent, the romance writer, soaked in perfume and troweled with makeup, mingled as was her paid duty. At one point, she put her palms down on the table and asked, 'Okay, 'fess up. Who's had an affair already?'

By the end of that meal, Brad was left with the impression that not many people who'd paid to attend the Pine Oil Writers' Conference had ever written much of anything. They were buying the fantasy of being writers, but as long as the booze and the sad, emotionally famished companions held out, the only things they would ever write would be checks to lower-echelon writers' festivals all over America. Brad looked through a window at the leaning smokestacks of the abandoned mill and thought how this town was once a place where real things, aromatic paint-thinner, rosin for fiddle bows, tar to keep us all dry, came out of the steam and noise of the factory. Clouds of soot once rose into the sky, a black song of production and prosperity. Now he guessed that the only things rising over Pine Oil, Louisiana, were the crippled similes of small-hearted writers.

After the late-afternoon seminar on 'How to Market Yourself as a Writerly Persona,' Brad asked Faye Cooker to dinner. She picked up his left hand, looked at the wedding ring trapped on a brown finger, then let go. 'You want to talk about writing, don't you?'

He pushed his round, wire-framed glasses up his nose. 'Well, not if you're tired of it.'

She looked around at the classroom, at the stragglers who seemed as if they wanted to ask her something but were too shy. 'If you take me someplace where none of the conference types will be, I'll go.'

'I don't know much about the area.' He tried to remember what was along the interstate coming into town.

'Think of somewhere this brie-breath crowd wouldn't be caught dead in.'

'Taco Bell?'

'Or me.'

'Shoney's, then.'

'Brilliant,' she said, putting her skinny arm through his.

During the Italian Feast special, he asked her what she thought of writing conferences, and she said there were two types: one where people wanted to learn to improve their writing, and one where people wanted to get drunk with published authors, overeat, and get laid. 'This here one,' she said, faking a backwoods accent, 'is one of the latters.'

Brad made a face and fished a bit of grilled chicken out of a puddle of tomato sauce. 'So I'm finding out.'

Faye sat upright, as though she'd just understood that Brad was someone important. 'Well, I don't want you to waste your money, friend. You've got me cornered here. You want to yak about what you'd like to write?'

'After we talked yesterday, I started something. I just don't know whether it's any good.'

'It's probably not. You don't know where you're going with it, sort of like a football player who gets handed the ball just as the stadium lights go out.'

'That's about it.'

Faye twirled noodles around her fork. 'Keep writing until you think you know where you could go with the tale, then stop and plan. Then rewrite, rewrite, throw the first thirty pages away, and rewrite again, sentence by sentence.'

He was glad when she filled her mouth with food for fear that more work directions would come out. She started talking again soon, though, and made writing a novel sound like restoring a fifteenth-century mural on a damp cathedral wall, going over the surface with a ten-haired brush, millimeter by millimeter. She ended the lecture with a question. 'Why do you want to write, anyway?'

He stared over at a child sticking his fingers into the Jell-O of the salad bar. 'I want to find out if I can do it well, if it's what I do best.'

She wiped her mouth and looked at him. 'And then what?'

'Then it'll be as though I have a good voice. I guess I should sing.'

'A sense of duty to your talent,' she mused, looking up at a dusty vinyl plant hanging from the ceiling. 'My old preacher used to talk about that.'

Brad took a drink of iced tea and looked away. 'Yeah?'

'He said that those who could do good work but wouldn't created a vacuum in the world that would be filled by those who could do bad things and would.'

He frowned, jealous of the cleverness of the statement. 'Did he really say that?'

'Something like that. A long time ago,' Faye Cooker said, gazing over toward the buffet where people roamed around with empty plates, looking and looking.

That night Brad sat in his stale little room, wondering if fiction was really what he could learn to do best. He was a fair sermonizer, and scores of cheating husbands and alimony dodgers in St Tammany Parish had at least considered reform as proof of his talents. Faye's rules and tasks began to line up like penances in his head. He wondered if he really wanted to write or if he just wanted to know if he *could* write. There was a big difference. He fired up his laptop and began typing at once, not stopping until Butchie tumbled into the room around three o'clock.

The big man sat down on his bed with a whoop. 'Hey, Shake-speare, guess who just scored?'

'You and the little lady from Ohio?'

Butchie ran his forearm back and forth like a locomotive piston. 'Banged me a Buckeye!' He collapsed onto the bed.

For several moments Brad tried to think of something appro-priate to say. Finally he asked, 'You going to have a writing sample by tomorrow afternoon?'

'No problem,' he said slowly. 'I'll turn out something on my old portable in the morning.' After a minute, Butchie began to snore, his legs slanted to the carpet like two logs.

It took Brad a while to get back into his manuscript; he began to worry about the slight, smiling, gray lady Butchie had been with. Maybe this was Butchie's talent, though, to share his steamy teutonic self with the world's superannuated wallflowers. But the woman was so thin, he thought, a whisper of a person, like a veteran librarian. He tried not to imagine Butchie Langanstein's bulk pressing out her brittle little self. It would be like Germany invading Belgium all over again.

* * *

The next morning he got up early to eat breakfast, and Butchie lumbered behind him to the student union, where they joined up with Faye and the lady from Ohio, whose name was Leda. Her eyes were all over Butchie, who spent a great deal of time staring at his runny eggs. She put a hand on his shoulder once, when she asked a question, and Brad noticed that the skin on her hands was pale and clear, but with veins the color of cheap blue ink. Faye looked back and forth between Butchie and Leda until her mouth fell open just the slightest. When they'd left the table, she leaned over to Brad and asked, 'Are those two an item?'

'I guess so,' he said, wincing.

She stared after them as they left the building, shoulder to shoulder. 'She's older than I am. That woman probably doesn't even have ovaries anymore.'

'Yes, well.' He took a slurp of coffee. 'I don't guess they're doing much writing.'

Faye shook her head. 'Lord knows they have something to write about, each of them. Anyway, I feel sorry for big piggy, there.'

He put down his knife. 'What?'

'Can you imagine what she's going to do to him after this conference? Phone calls in the night, postcards with flowers drawn in the margins. That old gal's a loose ship looking for a dock.'

'She seems sort of nice to me,' he said.

'This is about the fifth conference I've seen her attend, Brad.' She dragged out his name the way a mother would, and she reached over and patted his hand. 'Just because a character is old doesn't guarantee they're harmless.'

He looked out of the union windows to the midget trees of Pine Oil Junior College. 'Maybe I should write about her.'

'Not right now,' she said. Then she explained for ten minutes why she'd said that, and he put his head down.

'There's so much I've got to know,' he said. 'But I'd like to find out the single most valuable piece of information a writer has to find out, the thing that will set him off in the right direction.'

'The central truth,' Faye said, deadpan.

'I guess so.'

'Like, insert tab A into slot B and write happily ever after?'

He looked up. 'Is it a ridiculous notion?'

'Like Mother Teresa tap-dancing. Nobody can teach you how to write.'

'What will?'

Faye sat back and puffed out her lined cheeks. 'God and hard work.'

Brad skipped that day's sections on 'Making Stories That Sell' and 'How to Choose an Agent' to hole up in his room, polishing sentences. At one point, he scrolled back to the start and read the very first of what he'd done:

> *The farmer stepped out onto his porch and looked off toward the distant tree line, a fence of green, motionless in the noon heat. The crows were not there yet, and he focused on the tomatoes, a hundred rows staked straight as soldiers in the powdery soil. The pumps needed to be primed and run, but there was no help to go out in the blaze and pull the hoses or open the irrigation gates. He thought he saw someone walking at the far end of the rows, and he moved his head with a hopeful motion, but it was merely an anomaly of his cheap bifocals that manufactured little bands of movement out of stillness at the edge of his vision. The motion in the field was like the ghost of his father, or that of his grandfather, or even of his great-grandfather, a legend he barely remembered as a white and withered figure tapping stakes into hills turned up by horses. Now the farmer's wife was dead, his sons gone west to jobs that would not kill them, and he felt like the period at the end of a long sentence. Four crows sailed up into the far trees like black hats thrown against the wind, and he reached to the porch support for the hand-worn shotgun.*

Brad bit the inside of his cheek and stared hard at the words. Something new was happening.

Around four o'clock, Butchie came into the room with a folder of loose pages stuffed into an armpit. 'Hey, I been over at Leda's using her word processor. Try this on for size.' He thrust a wad of pale dot-matrix lines into Brad's stomach and walked into the bathroom. Brad sat in a vinyl chair and began to read a limping paragraph threaded with clichés and inaccuracies.

> *Maxwell Smilington was the best agent the government had in Brooklyn. When the phone rang on Sunday morning, he was given by the voice on the line the most dangerous assignment he'd had since he'd busted up the Tong gang at Lennox and Seventy-seventh Street. Maxwell pulled out his shiny revolver and admired his reflection in the polished stainless steel, his straight-back blond mane and his pearly eyes. He went down to street level and got a cab at once, riding down to the Dutch Embassy, where he was to meet Hans Toffler, to get the low-down on terrorists planning to blow up the Empire State Building. The cab driver, a voluptuous blond like himself, watched him in the rearview mirror. 'Where to?' she asked, pouting her ruby red lips.*
> *'Dutch Embassy,' he said importantly.*
> *She smiled. 'You have friends in Dutch?' she asked.*

Brad read on until Butchie came out of the bathroom fastening his buckle like a cinch strap. 'What you think?'

The minister looked up and smiled, fashioning a lie. 'If this gets published, it'll really sell,' he told him.

Butchie nodded and grabbed the manuscript. 'I'm turning this in to that Millicent broad for evaluation. She's got connections.'

Brad made up a smile. 'I'm surprised you didn't try to score with her.'

'Yeah, man. She's got so many love handles I'd never fall off.' He slapped Brad on the shoulder, nearly knocking him out of the chair.

That night, the fiction group fearfully turned in their sample chapters and Lamot, Millicent, and Faye scheduled conferences for the following afternoon, the last day of the conference. On the final morning, everyone attended an author's fruit breakfast, and some who had not written a word during the week just packed up and left in cabs, well-fed and entertained. Later, Brad sat in a tiled hallway and talked with two other writers, an old bald fireman and a kid from New Orleans. Down the hall, Butchie came out of Millicent's classroom, his manuscript bunched up in his hands.

'How'd it go, Butchie?'

He seemed surprised to see anyone else in the hall. 'All right,' he said. 'It went all right.' He squeezed his pages as though he was trying to hide them in his mittenlike hands.

Brad got up and walked him out into the sunshine. 'You okay?'

'Oh, yeah. But I had that Millicent pegged all wrong.'

'What'd she say?'

He rocked his big head up and down and expanded his eyes, as though agreeing with something he'd been told. 'She said if a garden slug knew how to use a pen, it would write the novel I was writing.'

'Wow.' Brad took a step back.

'She said everything that could be wrong was wrong. I know I didn't spend a lot of time on it, but jeez.'

At this time Leda came around the corner of the building, walking briskly, her white, shoulder-length hair springing like a girl's. 'Hey, Butch,' she called. 'How'd it go?'

The big man's face bloomed crimson. 'Not so good,' he told her. 'She said it was pretty bad.'

Leda stepped close to him and smiled, closing a white hand on his elbow. 'If it's important to you, I can help you with it.' She sounded as though she would write a whole novel for Butchie in one night, if it would help.

Inside again, waiting, Brad heard the office door open, and he looked up to Faye Cooker's unreadable expression as she motioned for him to come in. The thirty pages he'd submitted to her lay stacked neatly on the desk. He coughed and settled into a chair. She stared at him as though perplexed about what to say.

'You've been waiting a long time?' she asked.

'Not long. I was talking with my roommate and his friend.'

'Ah. Leda and the swine.'

'He didn't get a good review on his story.'

Faye picked up the pages from her desk. 'And you were wondering . . .'

'Was it that bad?'

She shook her head. 'I've never told anyone what I'm about to tell you.'

He crossed his arms. 'Well, let's have it.'

'I think you should quit whatever it is you do for a year and finish this novel. When you've completed it, I'll help you find an agent in New York.' She looked at him directly and pointed a finger at him. 'I'm not doing you a favor by telling you that this is the best thirty pages I've read by a student in as many years.'

Brad began to have a subtle elevation of spirit that he suspected was the result of having come down in the neighborhood of The Answer. He had, with Faye's help, figured something out. At least this time. 'Tell me the things I did wrong,' he said, his voice dry, all his energy going to suppress a building excitement.

'Almost nothing. Let me tell you what you did right, and how to keep doing it for years to come.' And she smiled, showing her coffee-stained old teeth, still straight, still able to signal success, when success comes.

Ten years after that meeting, on a Tuesday, Brad was eating in a new bookstore/café that had opened across the street from the church. Since he'd left the Pine Oil Writers' Conference, he'd never written another word of fiction. He'd come home on fire to create, gone into his new little office, stared out into the sky and watched pelicans for days on end. He felt that he had found The Answer, and ultimately, after a few weeks, The Answer didn't matter anymore. He could write well and so what? He tried to funnel creativity into his sermons, but the congregation remained polite and daydreaming as usual, and as their dry cool hands slipped in and out of his at the door to the church, he wanted to ask, What's not quite right?

His wife knew what Faye Cooker had told him, and she seemed to be waiting for the result. Three years passed, and Brad thought she had begun to look at him like a bad investment: a residential lot that was sinking, a slot machine that would never pay off. Eventually an inscrutable glumness began to stick to her like bad makeup, and she divorced him. One day his uncle Ralph, who was really his wife's uncle, showed up and reclaimed his circular saw.

He still read fiction, and while waiting for a complicated Muffelata to be made in the bookstore/café, he scanned the racks. A new display had been set up, and Brad's eye caught sight of a hardback novel by Butchie Langanstein titled *The Machine-Shop Murders*, and he grabbed it at once, turning to the back cover to read a smattering of noncommital reviews. There he saw a photograph of Butchie, graying and a bit thinner, seated on a big veranda next to old Leda, who had dyed her hair and now looked the younger of the two. Brad felt accused of something and stared hard at the photo, studying Butchie's horny smile and the pouches under his eyes. He thumbed to the front and read that the book was in its second printing. Turning to the first paragraph, which contained a rape and a killing, he found the writing to be coarse, borrowed, and plain. Butchie had not evolved a great deal, and Brad wondered how much of the writing was Leda's. He read nine pages, thinking how much better than this he could have done. He kept reading, with each page his mood sinking down, down. He read on even after the counter girl started to bang her little bell repeatedly, calling out his name to please come on and claim what was his.

Resistance

Alvin Boudreaux had outlived his neighbors. His asbestos-sided house was part of a tiny subdivision built in the 1950s, when everybody had children, a single-lane driveway, a rotating TV antenna, and a picnic table out back. Nowadays, he sat on his little porch and watched the next wave of families occupy the neighborhood, each taking over the old houses, driving up in their pairs of bug-shaped cars, one for each spouse to drive to work. Next door, Melvin Tillot had died, and his wife had sold the house to migrate up north with her daughter. Mr Boudreaux used to watch her white puff of hair move through the yard as she snipped roses. Now she was gone, and there was no movement on his street that had consequence for him. Today he sat and watched the sky for sailing wedges of birds, or an army of ranked mackerel clouds, or the electric bruise of a thunderstorm rising from the molten heat of the Gulf. Sometimes he thought of his wife, dead now eight years. He was in that time of life when the past began coming around again, as if to reclaim him. Lately, he thought about his father, the sugarcane farmer, who used to teach him about tractors and steam engines.

Two months before, Mr Boudreaux had watched his new neighbors move in, a young blond woman, overweight, with thin hair and raw, nervous eyes. The husband was small and mean, sat in a lawn chair in the backyard as though he was at the beach, and drank without stopping, every weekend. They had one ten-year-old, a plain, slow-moving daughter.

Mr Boudreaux could not bear to look at these people. They let the rosebushes die of thirst and left the empty garbage cans sitting at the edge of the street until the grass under them forgot what the sun looked like, and died. They never sat on their porch, and they had no pets that he could see. But after a while, he tried to talk to the wife when she dragged out the garbage bag in the morning. Her voice was thin, like a little squeak against the thumb. She worked somewhere for six hours each day, she told him, running an electric coffee-grinding machine.

One mild afternoon, Mr Boudreaux was going to visit the graveyard, and he rattled open a kitchen window to air the room out while he was gone. Next door, he saw the daughter come into the yard and show her father a sheet of paper. The father curled up his lip and took a swallow from a tall tumbler, looking away. Mr Boudreaux felt sorry for the girl when she placed a hand on the father's shoulder and the man grabbed the sheet from her and balled it up. She put a forefinger to her glasses as if to bring the world into focus. The motion showed practice and patience. She was formless and looked overweight in her pleated skirt and baggy white blouse. Her carroty hair was gathered in a short tail above her neck, her lips were too big for her face, and two gray eyes hid behind glasses framed in pale blue plastic, the kind of glasses little girls wore thirty years before. She stepped next to her father's chair again, getting in his space, as Mr Boudreaux's grandson would say. The father began to yell, something about a damned science project. He waved his arms, and his face grew red. Another child might have cried.

The next afternoon, Mr Boudreaux was on his knees pulling grass by the backyard fence when he heard the school bus grind up LeBoeuf Street. He was still pulling when the father came home at four-thirty and sat in the lawn chair, next to the back steps. The girl appeared behind the screen door, like a shadow.

'It's got to be turned in Monday,' she said. Even her voice was ordinary, a plain voice with little music in it.

The father put his glass against his forehead. 'I don't know anything about it,' he said. 'Do you know how tired I am?'

Her half-formed image shifted at the screen, then dispersed like smoke. In a moment, the mother came out and stepped carefully past her husband, not looking at him until she was safely on the grass. 'I'd help her,' she said. 'But I don't know anything about that. Electricity. It's something a man'll have to do.'

The husband drained his drink and flung the ice cubes at the fence. Mr Boudreaux felt a drop hit the back of his spotted hand. 'Why can't she do something like a girl would do? Something *you* could help her with.'

Mr Boudreaux peered through the honeysuckle. The man was wearing jeans and a white button-down shirt with some sort of company emblem embroidered on the breast, a gay and meandering logo that suggested a bowling alley or gas station.

The mother looked down and patted the grass in a semicircle with her left foot. 'You're her parent, too,' she said. It was a weak thing to say, Mr Boudreaux thought.

The father stood up, and the flimsy chair turned over on its side. He swung around and looked at it for a moment, then kicked it across the yard.

After dark, Mr Boudreaux went out on his front porch with a glass of iced tea and listened, wondering whether the girl's parents ever argued. He had never heard them, but then he remembered that since the coming of air-conditioning, he'd heard little from inside anyone's house. When he first moved to the neighborhood, up and down LeBoeuf Street he could hear the tinny cheer of radios, the yelps of children chasing through the houses, a rare yelling match about money or relatives. But now he heard only the breathy hum of the heat pumps and the intermittent *ahhh* of an automobile's tires on the subdivision's ebony streets. He looked over at his fifteen-year-old Buick parked in the single drive. It embarrassed him to drive such a large old car through the neighborhood, where everyone stood out and washed the dust from their Japanese-lantern compacts. Maybe it was time to trade it off for something that would fit in. Next door, the father came out and walked stiffly to his candy apple car and drove away, dragging his tires at every shift of the gears, *irk, irk.*

* * *

The next morning, Mr Boudreaux came out for the paper and saw Carmine sitting on her front steps waiting for the bus to appear out of the fog. Her eyes were red. He picked up the paper and began walking back toward the porch, telling himself, Don't look. But at his front steps, he felt a little electrical tug at his neck muscles, a blank moment of indecision.

He turned his head. 'Good morning, little miss,' he called out, raising his paper.

'Morning, Mr Boudreaux.' Her low voice was small in the fog.

'How you doing in school?' He unfolded the paper and pretended to read the headline.

'Okay.'

He bounced once on the balls of his feet. He could walk into the house and not look back. 'It's springtime,' he said. 'My kids used to have to make their science projects this time of year.'

She looked over at him, her eyebrows up in surprise. 'You have kids?'

Mr Boudreaux realized how impossibly old he must seem. 'Sure. A long time ago. They're nurses and engineers and one's a policeman way up in Virginia. They all had their science projects. What about you?'

She looked down at a heavy brown shoe. 'I want to do one, but no one can help me,' she said.

He banged the paper against his leg several times before he said anything more. He closed his eyes. 'Is your mamma home? Let me talk to her a minute.'

That's how it got started. After school, she rang his doorbell, and he led her into the kitchen, where he fixed her a Coke float. Carmine smelled dusty and hot, and she finished her drink in less than a minute, placing the glass in the sink and sitting down again at Mr Boudreaux's table, spreading open a spiral-bound tablet. She gave him a blank look of evaluation, an expression she might use on a strange dog.

Mr Boudreaux sat down across from her. 'Well, missy, what

kind of project you interested in? Your momma said you needed a little push in the right direction.'

'What did you do when you had a job?' she asked, pushing her hair out of her eyes.

He blinked. 'I started as a millwright at LeBlanc Sugar Mill, and when I retired, I was a foreman over all the maintenance people.'

She frowned. 'Does that mean you don't know anything about electricity?'

Leaning back, he rubbed a spot over his eye. 'I worked on a lot of motors in my time.'

Carmine scooted her chair closer and showed him her notebook. In it were hundreds of O's drawn with legs, all running into a narrow cylinder and jumping one by one out of the other end of it. 'These are electrons,' she said. Some of the electrons were running through a bigger cylinder and more of them seemed to be coming out the other side. 'The tube shapes are resistors,' she instructed. 'Some let electrons through fast, some slow.' Her short finger led his attention along the rows of exiting electrons, which had little smiles drawn on them, as though they had earned passage to a wonderful place. She told him how resistors control current and how without them no one could have ever made a television or computer.

Mr Boudreaux nodded. 'So what you going to call this project?'

'Resistance.' She said the word as though it had another meaning.

'And we gotta figure out how to demonstrate it, right?' He closed his eyes and thought back to those late-night projects of his children. His son Sid, the state patrolman, had done friction. Friction, the old man thought. That was right up Sid's alley. 'We have to state a problem and show how it's solved with resistors. Then we demonstrate how they work.'

Carmine bobbed her head. 'You *have* done this before.'

The next afternoon, they spent on the rug in the den, drawing and brainstorming. When Mr Boudreaux let the girl out at suppertime, he saw her father standing on the front walk, glowering. The next morning was Saturday, and he and Carmine got into his venerable Buick and drove down to the electronics store at the mall. The girl hardly looked at her list. She spent her time browsing the tall Peg-Board sections hung with diodes and toggle switches, condensers and capacitors, fondling little transistors through the thin plastic bags. Mr Boudreaux tended to business, buying a pack of foot-square circuit boards, little red push switches, eighteen-gauge wire. Earlier, Carmine had brought him a dog-eared book, *Electricity for Children*, and from it he had memorized the banding codes for resistors. With this knowledge, he selected an assortment of plastic cylinders that looked like tiny jelly beans decorated with red, black, and silver bands, an inch of silver wire coming out of each end.

Their purchases stowed in a loopy plastic bag, they walked the mall to the candy counter, where Mr Boudreaux bought a quarter pound of lime slices. Carmine took a green wedge from him, saying nothing, and they walked on through the strollers, teenagers, and senior citizens limping along in running shoes. Mr Boudreaux looked at the children who were Carmine's age. They seemed stylish and energetic as they played video games or preened in the reflections of shop windows. Carmine was mechanical, earnest, and as communicative as a very old pet dog.

When they got back to Mr Boudreaux's house, Carmine's father was standing in their way, wavering in the slim line of grass that ridged the middle of the driveway. The old man got out of the Buick and greeted him.

The other man had been drinking again. He pointed a chewed fingernail at Mr Boudreaux. 'You should have asked me before you took that girl off somewhere.'

'I asked your wife. You weren't awake yet.'

'Well, let me tell you, I was worried. I called up the police and checked you out.' Carmine came around the car and stood between them, staring down the street as though she could see all the way to Texas.

Mr Boudreaux passed his tongue along his bottom lip. 'The police. You called the police about me? Why'd you do that?'

'You can't tell nowadays. Old guys such as yourself and kids. You know?' The father stuck his pale hands into a pair of tight work pants.

The old man looked at the ground. He was embarrassed because he didn't know what to think, other than that nobody used to imagine such things. Not in a million years. 'You think I'm gonna rob your kid or something?' he said at last. 'Look.' He held out the plastic bag. 'I helped her pay for her stuff.'

Carmine's father pointed a finger at Mr Boudreaux. 'She can pay for her own stuff. You keep your money in your pocket,' he said. 'I don't know why you think you got to do this.' He gave the girl a wounded glance and then turned toward his steps.

Mr Boudreaux looked at Carmine. She pushed her glasses up her nose and looked back at him. 'Did you have a little girl back when you were a father?' she asked.

He looked at his house and then back at the child. 'Yes, I did. Her name is Charlene. And I have another named Monica.'

For the first time that day, her expression changed and showed surprise. 'What would anybody need with two girls?'

That afternoon, he watched her write her report; he helped her decide where to put headings and how to divide the information up. After supper, she came over, and they planned the display. Carmine drew out a design on lined paper with an oversized pencil. 'I want those little button switches that work like door-bells here,' she said. 'On the first circuit, I want a straight wire to a flashlight bulb in one of those sockets we bought. On the second line, I want a twenty-two-ohm resistor to the same-size bulb. That'll make the bulb glow dimmer.' She stuck out her tongue and bit it as she drew carbon ribbons of circuits. 'The third button will turn on a line with two twenty-two-ohm resistors soldered together in series, and the bulb will glow dimmer.' She went on to draw in the fourth circuit, which would be an ordinary pencil wired to show how current can pass through carbon, 'which is what resistors are made of,' she told him. A fifth circuit would have a rotary switch controlling a bulb. Carmine drew in the electrical symbol for a variable resistor at this point and put down her pencil.

'Now what?' Mr Boudreaux asked, rubbing his eyes with his long forefingers. Since he'd reached his late seventies, he'd been going to bed around eight-thirty. At the moment, his knees were aching like great boils.

'Now we have to solder this together on the perforated circuit board.'

'Ow. I don't know about that.'

She didn't look up. 'Don't you have a soldering iron?'

'I haven't seen it in years.' They got up and Carmine helped him down the back steps into the moonlit yard. Built onto the rear of the garage was a workshop. Mr Boudreaux opened the door, and the glass in its top rattled. At one time he had spent long hours here fixing the house's appliances or rebuilding bicycles and gas-powered airplanes. Now he came in once or twice a year to look for a screwdriver or to store a box. Carmine found the light switch.

'A workbench,' she sang, going over to a vise and turning its handle around.

Mr Boudreaux looked for the soldering gun while she dusted the maple counter with a rag and spread out the components. 'Here it is,' he said. But when he plugged the instrument in and pulled the trigger, a burst of sparks shot from the vents and a smell of melting Bakelite filled the shop. Holding it by its cord, he unplugged it and then threw it into the yard. The girl looked after the soldering iron sorrowfully.

'Do you have another one?'

'No, honey. And it's too late to go to the store. We'll have to finish tomorrow.' He watched her look to the counter and purse her lips. 'What you thinking?'

'Sundays are not good days,' she told him.

He shook his head at the comment. 'You'll be over here.'

She stared at her blocky leather shoes. 'Mom and I have got to be there, and we've got to stay quiet.' She looked up at him and her face showed that she was smarter than he ever was. 'We've always got to be in the corner of his eye.'

'What's that?' He bent a furry ear toward her.

'He wants us around, but kind of on the side. Never the main thing he looks at.'

The old man searched above his head and on a rusty sixteen-penny nail found his Turner gasoline blowtorch. 'If this thing'll work, we'll try to get our soldering done the old-fashioned way.'

She clapped her hands together once. 'What is it?' She put a forefinger on the brass tank.

'Well, you open it up here,' he told her, unscrewing a plug in the bottom and shaking out a few spoonfuls of stale, sweet-smelling gas. 'Then you put some fresh lawn-mower gasoline in, turn it over, and use this little thumb pump on the side.'

'To make pressure?'

'Yeah. Then you light the end of this horizontal tube and adjust the flame with these old knobs.' He dug around in a deep drawer under the counter, coming up with an arrow-shaped tool with a wooden handle on one end and an iron rod running out of that into a pointed bar of copper. 'You got to set this heavy point in the flame, and when it gets hot enough, you touch it to the solder, which melts onto the wires. That's what holds the wires together.'

The girl grabbed the wooden handle and waved the tool like a weapon, stabbing the air.

In a few minutes, the blowtorch was sputtering and surging, humming out a feathery yellow flame. It had been over thirty years since Mr Boudreaux had used such a torch for soldering, and it took several tries before the first wires were trapped in melted silver. He and the girl strung wire and turned screws into a circuit board, and for a minute, he was a younger man, looking down on the head of one of his own daughters. He felt expert as he guided Carmine's short fingers and held the circuit board for her to thread the red wire through to the switch terminals. He felt back at work, almost as though he were getting things done at the mill.

The girl avoided his eyes, but she did give him one glance before asking a question. 'Why're you helping me with this?'

He watched her fingers pull a wire under the board. 'It just needed doing.'

'Did you really help your children with their projects?'

'I don't remember. Maybe their momma did.'

She was quiet as she turned in a stubby screw. 'Did *you* ever have to do a science project?'

He looked out the workshop window and closed one eye. 'I don't think science had been invented yet.' He checked her face, but she wasn't smiling. Then he remembered something. 'When I was in fifth grade, I had to read a novel called *Great Expectations*. The teacher said we had to build something that was in the book, like an old house, or Miss Haversham's wedding cake, or some such foolishness. I forgot all about it until the night before, and knew I was really going to catch it the next day if I showed up without it.'

Carmine took the hot copper away from the torch and soldered a joint herself. 'What did you do?'

He rubbed his chin. 'I think I cried, I was so scared. My mother would whack me with a belt if I ever failed a course, and I wasn't doing so good in English. Anyway, my daddy saw my long face and made me tell him what was wrong. He asked me what was in the book.' Mr Boudreaux laughed. 'I thought that was strange, because he couldn't read hardly two words in a row. But I told him about Pip, and Pip's father, and the prison ship. That caught his ear, and he asked me about that ship, so I told him. Then he went outside. That night, I went to bed and couldn't sleep hardly a wink. I remember that because I've always been a good sleeper. I go out like a light about nine, ten o'clock, you know?' The girl nodded, then placed a bulb in a socket. 'When I got up for school,

Daddy had left for work at the mill, and on the kitchen table was a foot-long sailing boat, painted black, three masts, all the rigging strung with black sewing thread, deck hatches, gun ports, and a bowsprit. It was all done with a pocketknife, and it was warm to the touch, because my momma said he had put it in the oven to dry the paint so it would be ready for school.'

The girl seemed not to hear him. 'I want the battery tied in with wire,' she said.

'The old man was like that,' Mr Boudreaux told her. 'He never asked me if I liked the boat, and I never said anything to him about it, even when I brought home a good grade for the project.'

When they were finished, all the lightbulbs lit up, as she had predicted. He built a hinged wooden frame for the two posters that held her report and drawings. They set everything up on the workbench and stepped back. Mr Boudreaux pretended to be a judge and clamped his fingers thoughtfully around his chin. 'That's a prizewinner,' he said in a mock-serious voice. Then he looked down at Carmine. Her lips were in a straight line, her eyes dark and round.

The next day was Sunday, and Mr Boudreaux went to eleven o'clock Mass, visiting afterward with the men his age who were still able to come out. They sat on the rim of St Anthony's fountain under the shade of a palm tree and told well-worn jokes in Cajun French, then tales of who was sick, who was dead. Mr Landry, who had worked under Mr Boudreaux at the sugar mill, asked him what he had been doing with his granddaughter at the mall.

'That was a neighbor child,' Mr Boudreaux told him. 'My grandchildren live away.'

'What was she doing? Asking you about the dinosaurs?' He laughed and hit the shoulder of the man next to him.

'She's doing a school thing, and I'm helping her with it.'

Mr Landry's face settled into a question. 'She lives on the north side of you?'

'Yes.'

Mr Landry shook his head. 'My son works with her daddy. She needs all the help she can get.'

'He's a piece of work all right.'

The men broke up and moved away from one another, waving. Mr Boudreaux drove the long way home, passing by the school, along the park, behind the ball field. He felt that by helping with the science project, he had completed something important and that he and the girl had learned something. His old Buick hesitated in an intersection, and he looked at its faded upholstery, its dusty buttons and levers, thinking that he should buy a new car. He could cash in his insurance policy and finally use a little of his savings.

When he got home, even though he felt light-headed, he began to clean out the glove compartment, search under the seats, empty the trunk of boots and old tools. He rested in the sun on his front steps, then decided to change into shorts, get the galvanized pail, and wash the car. He was standing in a pool of water from the hose, looking down at his white legs, when he heard the shouting begin next door. The mother's keening yell was washed away by the drunken father's roaring. The girl ran out as though she were escaping a fire and stood on the withering lawn, looking back into the house. Mr Boudreaux saw a wink of something white at the front door, and then the science project posters flew out onto the walkway, followed by the circuit-board display and the little platform they had made for it. The father lurched down the steps, his unbuttoned white shirt pulled from his pants, his eyes narrowed and sick. He kicked the poster frame apart, and Carmine ran to avoid a flying hinge. She turned in time to see the circuit board crackle under a black shoe.

'Hey,' Mr Boudreaux yelled. 'Stop that.'

The father looked around for the voice and spotted the old man. 'You go to hell.'

Mr Boudreaux's back straightened. 'Just because you can't handle your liquor don't give you the right to treat your little girl like that.'

The father staggered toward him. 'You old bastard, you tried to make me look bad.'

Mr Boudreaux's heart misfired once. The walk was so slippery, he couldn't even run away from the father, who was coming around the car in a wobbly, stalking motion. He looked down at the father's doubled fists. 'You stay in your yard. If you give me trouble, I'll call the cops.' The father gave him a shove and Mr Boudreaux went down hard in a grassy puddle.

'Ow. You drunk worm. I'm seventy-eight years old.'

'Leave us alone,' the father yelled. He raised a shoe, and for a moment the old man thought that he was going to kick him. Then the mother was at the man's side, pulling at his arms.

'Come back in the yard, Chet. Please,' she begged. She was not a small woman, and she had two hands on his arm.

Mr Boudreaux squeezed the lever on the hose nozzle and sprayed the father in the stomach and he stumbled backward against the mother, cursing. He sprayed him in the forehead. 'You rummy. You a big man with old guys and little kids.'

'Screw you, you old bastard.' The father shook water from his hair and tried to pull out of his wife's hands.

'Aw, you real scary,' Mr Boudreaux shouted, trying to stand up. When he finally was able to see over the roof of his Buick, the mother was pulling her husband up the steps, and Carmine was standing under a wilting magnolia tree, looking over at the fragments of her science project scattered along the walk.

Mr Boudreaux's lower back was sore. By eight o'clock, he couldn't move without considerable pain. He looked angrily through his living room window at the house next door. He went out on his porch and watched the light in Carmine's bedroom window. Then he went in and watched television, adjusting the rabbit ears on his set and rolling the dial from station to station, not really paying attention to the images on his scuffed Zenith. He turned the machine off and stared at it a long time, felt the cabinet, and tapped it with his fingers. Then he got a screwdriver, unscrewed the back, and peered in. Mr Boudreaux pulled off all the knobs on the front, slid the works out of the case, and carried it over to his dining room table, placing it under the bright drop fixture. When he turned the works over, he smiled into a nest of resistors. He read the band values, and with a pair of pointed wire snips, he removed several that bore two red bands and one black. Behind the selector were light sockets, and he cut these out, noting with a grimace that the bulbs in them drew too much power.

In the living room was his wife's cabinet-model Magnavox hi-fi. He slowly ran a finger along its walnut top. Then he pulled the knobs off and opened it up with a screwdriver, removing several feet of red and black wire, as well as three light sockets that contained little bulbs of the correct voltage. The volume knob was a variable resistor, he now understood, and he removed that also. He went out to his workshop and took the little steel-tongued toggle switches off his old saber saw, his chain saw, his Moto-Tool. He needed one more and found that in the attic on a rusty set of barber's clippers that had been his brother's. Also in the attic he found his first daughter's Royal manual typewriter. Mr Boudreaux could type. He'd learned in the army, so he brought that down, too. He emptied the new batteries out of a penlight he kept on his bedside table. They had bought extra sheets of poster board in case Carmine made a mistake while drawing the big resistors, but she had been careful. He dug the handwritten first draft of her report out of his trash can and penciled in the revisions he could remember. Then, on paper that was only slightly yellowed, he typed her report neatly, with proper headings.

Next, he drew the images on the posters, big color-coded resistors traversed by round electrons with faces drawn on. His lettering was like a child's, and this worried him, but he kept on, finishing up with instructions for operating the display. He drew in the last letter at two o'clock, then went out into the workshop to saw up a spruce two-by-four to make the poster frame again. He needed hinges, so he had to go to the cedar chest in his bedroom and remove the ones on the wooden box that held his family insurance policies. He mounted the posters with thumbtacks pulled from an old corkboard that hung in the kitchen. The tacks' heads were rusty, so he painted them over with gummy white correction fluid he'd found in the box with the typewriter.

At four o'clock, he had to stop to take three aspirin for his back, and from the kitchen window, he looked across through the blue moonlight to the dark house next door, thinking maybe of all the dark houses in town where children endured the lack of light, fidgeting toward dawn.

In the garage, he found that there was no more gasoline for the old torch, which had whispered itself empty on the first project. On the front lawn, he cut a short length out of his new garden hose and siphoned fuel from his Buick, getting a charge of gas in his mouth, where it burned his gums under his dentures. Later, as the soldering tool heated in the voice of the torch, he felt he could spit a tongue of flame.

He ran the wires as she had run them, set the switches, mounted the light sockets, soldered the resistors in little silvery tornadoes of smoke. He found the bulbs left over from the first project and turned them into the sockets, wired in the battery, checked everything, then stepped back. The posters and display were duplicates of those the father had destroyed. Though the workshop window showed a trace of dawn, and though Mr Boudreaux's legs felt as though someone had shot them full of arrows, he allowed himself a faint smile.

He made a pot of coffee and sat out in the dew on the front porch, waiting for the father to come out in his hurting, hung-over fog and drive away. At seven-fifteen, he was gone, and Mr Boudreaux loaded the project into the backseat of his car, started the engine, and sat in it, waiting for the school bus. Carmine came out and stood by the garbage cans, and when the bus came, its seats stippled with white poster boards, for everyone's project was due the same day, she looked up at the opened door, pushed her glasses up her nose, and got on. He followed the bus out of the neighborhood and down the long oak-shaded avenue as the vehicle picked up kids in twos and threes, science projects at each stop. The farther he drove, the more fearful he became, thinking that maybe the girl wouldn't understand, or would think that he was doing this just to get back at her father, which in part, he admitted, he was. Several times he thought he'd better pass the bus, turn around, and head home. But then what would he do with the project? He wouldn't throw it away, and it would haunt him forever if he kept it.

The bus pulled into the school lot, and he followed it and parked. By the time he got to the covered walkway, children were pouring off, carrying jars of colored fluids, homemade generators, Styrofoam models of molecules. He had the bifold project in his arms, and when she came down the bus steps empty-handed, he spread it open for her. She stepped close and looked, lifted a page of the tacked-on report and checked the second, the third page.

'Where's the display?' she asked, not looking at him.

'It's in the car here,' he said, sidling off to retrieve it. When he got back, he saw she had hitched her bookbag onto her shoulder and had the posters folded and under an arm.

'Give it here,' she said, holding out her free hand, her face showing nothing.

He handed it to her. 'You want me to help carry it in?'

She shook her head. 'No. How do the switches work?'

He clicked one for her. 'Up is on, down is off.'

She nodded, then squinted up at him. 'I'll be late.'

'Go on, then.' He watched her waddle off among her class-mates, bearing her load, then he turned for his car. She could have called after him, smiled, and said thank you, but she didn't.

Because he was out so early, he decided to go shopping. He con-sidered his options: the Buick lot, the appliance dealer's, the hardware. After half an hour of driving around town slowly, he went into a department store and bought two small masonry pots filled with plastic flowers. They looked like the jonquils that used to come up in the spring alongside his mother's cypress fence. He drove to the old city graveyard, and after walking among the brick tombs and carefully made marble angels, he placed a colorful pot on the sun-washed slab of his father's grave. His back pained him as he put down the flowers, and when he straightened up, the bone-white tombs hurt his eyes, but still he turned completely around to look at this place where no one would say the things that could have been said, and that was all right with him.

Sorry Blood

The old man walked out of Wal-Mart and stopped dead, recognizing nothing he saw in the steaming Louisiana morning. He tried to step off the curb, but his feet locked up and his chest flashed with a burst of panic. The blacktop parking lot spread away from him, glittering with the enameled tops of a thousand automobiles. One of them was his, and he struggled to form a picture but could not remember which of the family's cars he had taken out that morning. He backstepped into the shade of the store's overhang and sat on a displayed riding lawn mower. Putting his hands down on his khaki pants, he closed his eyes and fought to remember, but one by one, things began to fall away from the morning, and then the day before, and the life before. When he looked up again, all the cars seemed too small, too bright and glossy, more like fishing lures. His right arm trembled, and he regarded the spots on the back of his hand with a light-headed embarrassment. He stared down at his Red Wing brogans, the shoes of a stranger. For a half hour, he sat on the mower seat, dizziness subsiding like a summer storm.

Finally, he got up, stiff and floating, and walked off into the grid of automobiles, his white head turning from side to side under a red feed-store cap. Several angry-looking people sat in hot cars, their faces carrying the uncomprehending disappointment of boiled lobsters. He walked attentively for a long time but recognized nothing, not even his own tall image haunting panels of tinted glass.

Twice he went by a man slouched in a parked Ford sedan, an unwashed thing with a rash of rust on its lower panels. The driver, whose thin hair hung past his ears, was eating a pickled sausage out of a plastic sleeve and chewing it with his front teeth. He watched the wanderer with a slow reptilian stare each time he walked by. On the third pass, the driver of the Ford considered the still-straight back, the big shoulders. He hissed at the old man, who stopped and looked for the sound. 'What's wrong with you, gramps?'

He went to the window and stared into the car at the man whose stomach enveloped the lower curve of the steering wheel. An empty quart beer bottle lay on the front seat. 'Do you know me?' the old man asked in a voice that was soft and lost.

The driver looked at him a long time, his eyes moving down his body as though he were a column of figures. 'Yeah, Dad,' he said at last. 'Don't you remember me?' He put an unfiltered cigarette in his mouth and lit it with a kitchen match. 'I'm your son.'

The old man's hand went to his chin. 'My son,' he said, like a fact.

'Come on.' The man in the Ford smiled only with his mouth. 'You're just having a little trouble remembering.'

The old man got in and placed a hand on the chalky dash. 'What have I been doing?'

'Shopping for me is all. Now give me back my wallet, the one you took in the store with you.' The driver held out a meaty hand.

The other man pulled a wallet from a hip pocket and handed it over.

In a minute, they were leaving the parking lot, riding a trash-strewn highway out of town into the sandy pine barrens of Tangipahoa Parish. The old man watched the littered roadside for clues. 'I can't remember my own name,' he said, looking down at his plaid shirt.

'It's Ted,' the driver told him, giving him a quick look. 'Ted Williams.' He checked his side-view mirrors.

'I don't even remember your name, son. I must be sick.' The old man wanted to feel his head for fever, but he was afraid he would touch a stranger.

'My name is Andy,' the driver said, fixing a veined eye on him for a long moment. After a few miles, he turned off the main highway onto an unpaved road. The old man listened to the knock and ping of rock striking the driveshaft of the car. Then the gravel became patchy and thin, the road blotched with a naked, carroty earth like the hide of a sick dog. Bony cattle heaved their heads between strands of barbed wire, scavenging for roadside weeds. The Ford bumped past mildewed trailers sinking into rain-eaten plots. Farther on, the land was too soggy for trailers, too poor even for the lane's desperate cattle. After two miles of this, they pulled up to a redbrick house squatting in a swampy two-acre lot. Limbs were down everywhere, and catbriers and poison oak covered the rusty fence that sagged between the yard and cutover woods running in every direction.

'This is home,' Andy said, pulling him from the car. 'You remember now?' He held the old man's arm and felt it for muscle.

Ted looked around for more clues but said nothing. He watched Andy walk around the rear of the house and return with a shovel and a pair of boots. 'Follow me, Dad.' They walked to a swale full of coppery standing water that ran along the side of the property, ten feet from the fence. 'This has to be dug out, two deep scoops side by side, all the way down to the ditch at the rear of the property. One hundred yards.' He held the shovel out at arm's length.

'I don't feel very strong,' he said, bending slowly to unlace his shoes. He stepped backward out of them and slipped into the oversized Red Ball boots.

'You're a big man. Maybe your mind ain't so hot, but you can work for a while yet.' And when Ted rocked up the first shovelful of sumpy mud, Andy smiled, showing a pair of yellow incisors.

He worked for an hour, carefully, watching the straightness of the ditch, listening to his heart strum in his ears, studying the awful lawn, which was draining like a boil into the trough he opened for it. The whole lot was flat and low, made of a sterile clay that never dried out between thunderstorms rolling up from the Gulf. After four or five yards, he had to sit down and let the pine and pecan trees swim around him as though they were laboring to stay upright in a great wind. Andy came out of the house carrying a lawn chair and a pitcher of cloudy liquid.

'Can I have some?' the old man asked.

Andy showed his teeth. 'Nah. These are margaritas. You'll fall out for sure if you drink one.' As an afterthought, he added, 'There's water in the hose.'

All morning, Andy drank from the pitcher, and the old man looked back over his shoulder, trying to place him. The shovel turned up a sopping red clay tainted with runoff from a septic tank, and Ted tried to remember such poor soil. The day was still, no traffic bumped down the dirt lane, and the tinkling of the ice cubes and the click of a cigarette lighter were the only sounds the old man heard. About one-thirty he put down his shovel for the twentieth time and breathed deeply, like a man coming up from underwater. He had used a shovel before – his body told him that – but he couldn't remember where or when. Andy drew up his lawn chair, abandoning the empty pitcher in pigweed growing against the fence. The old man could smell his breath when he came close, something like cleaning fluid, and a memory tried to fire up in his brain, but when Andy asked a question, the image broke apart like a dropped ember.

'You ever been beat up by a woman?' Andy asked.

The old man was too tired to look at him. Sweat weighed him down.

Andy scratched his belly through his yellow knit shirt. 'Remember? She told me she'd beat me again and then divorce my ass if I didn't fix this yard up.' He spoke with one eye closed, as though he was too drunk to see with both of them at the same time. 'She's big,' he said. 'Makes a lot of money but hits hard. Gave me over a hundred stitches once.' He held up a flaccid arm. 'Broke this one in two places.' The old man looked at him then, studying the slouching shoulders, the patchy skin in his scalp. He saw that he was desperate, and the old man moved back a step. 'She's coming back soon, the bitch is. I told her I couldn't do it.

That's why I went to the discount parking lot to hire one of those bums that work for food.' He tried to rattle an ice cube in his empty tumbler, but the last one had long since melted. 'Those guys won't work,' he told him, pulling his head back and looking down his lumpy nose at nothing. 'They just hold those cardboard signs saying they'll work so they can get a handout, the lazy bastards.'

Pinheads of light were exploding in the old man's peripheral vision. 'Can I have something to eat?' he asked, looking toward the house and frowning.

Andy led him into the kitchen, which smelled of garbage. The tile floor was cloudy with dirt, and a hill of melamine dishes lay capsized in the murky sink water. Andy unplugged the phone and left the room with it. Returning empty-handed, he fell into a kitchen chair and lit up a cigarette. The old man guessed where the food was and opened a can of Vienna sausages, twisting them out one at a time with a fork. 'Maybe I should go to a doctor?' he said, chewing slowly, as if trying to place the taste.

'Ted. Dad. The best job I ever had was in a nursing home, remember?' He watched the old man's eyes. 'I dealt with people like you all day. I know what to do with you.'

Ted examined the kitchen the way he might regard things during a visit to a museum. He looked and looked.

The afternoon passed like a slow, humid dream, and he completed fifty yards of ditch. By sundown, he was trembling and wet. Had his memory come back, he would have known he was too old for this work. He leaned on the polished wood of the shovel handle and looked at his straight line, almost remembering something, dimly aware that where he was, he had not been before. His memory was like a long novel left open and ruffled by a breeze to a different chapter further along. Andy had disappeared into the house to sleep off the tequila, and the old man came in to find himself something to eat. The pantry showed a good stock of chili, but not one pot was clean, so he scrubbed the least foul for ten minutes and put the food on to heat.

Later, Andy appeared in the kitchen doorway, wavering like the drunk he was. He led Ted to a room that contained only a stripped bed. The old man put two fingers to his chin. 'Where are my clothes?'

'You don't remember anything,' Andy said quickly, turning to walk down the hall. 'I have some overalls that'll fit if you want to clean up and change.'

Ted lay down on the splotched mattress as though claiming it. This bed, it's mine, he thought. Turning onto his stomach, he willed himself to remember the musty smell. Yes, he thought. My name is Ted. I am where I am.

In the middle of the night, his bladder woke him, and on the way back to bed, he saw Andy seated in the boxlike living room watching a pornographic movie in which a hooded man was whipping a naked woman with a rope. He walked up behind him, watching not the television but Andy's head, the shape of it. A quart beer bottle lay sweating in his lap. The old man rolled his shoulders back. 'Only white trash would watch that,' he said.

Andy turned around, slow and stiff, like an old man himself. 'Hey, Dad. Pull up a chair and get off on this.' He looked back to the set.

Ted hit him from behind. It was a roundhouse open-palm swat on the ear that knocked him out of the chair and sent the spewing beer bottle pinwheeling across the floor. Andy hit the tile on his stomach, and it was some time before he could turn up on one elbow to give the big man a disbelieving, angry look. 'You old shit. Just wait till I get up.'

'White trash,' the old man thundered. 'No kid of mine is going to be like that.' He came closer. Andy rolled against the TV cart and held up a hand. The old man raised his right foot as though he would plant it on his neck.

'Hold on, Dad.'

'Turn the thing off,' he said.

'What?'

'Turn the thing off!' the old man shouted, and Andy pressed the power button with a knuckle just as a big calloused heel came down next to his head.

'Okay. Okay.' He blinked and pressed his back against the television, inching away from the old man, who seemed even larger in the small room.

And then a long, bony face fringed with white hair drifted down above his own, examining him closely, looking at his features, the shape of his nose. The old man put out a finger and traced Andy's right ear as if evaluating its quality. 'Maybe you've got from me some sorry blood,' he said, and his voice shook from saying it, that such a soft and stinking man could come out of him. He pulled back and closed his eyes as though he couldn't stand sight itself. 'Let the good blood come out, and it'll tell you what to do,' he said, his back bent with soreness, his hands turning to the rear. 'You can't let your sorry blood run you.'

Andy struggled to his feet in a pool of beer and swayed against the television, watching the old man disappear into the hall. His face burned where he'd been hit, and his right ear rang like struck brass. He moved into the kitchen, where he watched a photograph taped to the refrigerator, an image of his wife standing next to a deer hanging in a tree, her right hand balled around a long knife. He sat down, perhaps forgetting Ted, the spilled beer, even his wife's hard fists, and he fell asleep on his arms at the kitchen table.

The next morning, the old man woke up and looked around the bare bedroom, remembering it from the day before, and almost recalling something else, maybe a person. He concentrated, but the image he saw was something far away, seen without his eyeglasses. He rubbed his thumbs over his fingertips, and the feel of someone was there.

In the kitchen, he found Andy and put on water for coffee, watching his son until the kettle whistled. He loaded a French drip pot and found bread, scraped the mold off and toasted four slices. He retrieved eggs and a lardy bacon from the refrigerator.

When Andy picked up his shaggy head, a dark stink of armpit stirred alive, and the old man told him to go wash himself.

In a half hour, Andy came back into the kitchen, his face nicked and bleeding from a month-old blade, a different T-shirt forming a second skin. He sat and ate without a word, but drank no coffee. After a few bites, he rummaged in a refrigerator drawer, retrieving a can of beer. The old man looked at the early sun caught in the dew on the lawn and then glanced back at the beer. 'Remind me of where you work,' he said.

Andy took a long pull on the can. 'I'm too sick to work. You know that.' He melted into a slouch and looked through the screen door toward a broken lawn mower dismantled in his carport. 'It's all I can do to keep up her place. Every damn thing's broke, and I got to do it all by hand.'

'Why can't I remember?' He sat down with his own breakfast and began eating, thinking, This is an egg. What am I?

Andy watched the old man's expression and perhaps felt a little neon trickle of alcohol brightening his bloodstream, kindling a single Btu of kindness, and he leaned over. 'I seen it happen before. In a few days, your mind'll come back.' He drained the beer and let out a rattling belch. 'Right now, get back on that ditch.'

The old man put a hand on a shoulder. 'I'm stiff.' He left the hand there.

'Come on.' He fished three beer cans from the refrigerator. 'You might be a little achy, but my back can't take the shovel business at all. You've got to finish that ditch today.' He looked into the old man's eyes as though he'd lost something in them. 'Quick as you can.'

'I don't know.'

Andy scratched his ear and, finding it sore, gave the old man a dark look. 'Get up and find that shovel, damn you.'

Andy drove to a crossroads store, and Ted wandered the yard, looking at the bug-infested trees. The other man returned to sit in the shade of a worm-nibbled pecan, where he opened a beer and began to read a paper he had bought. Ted picked up the shovel and cut the soft earth, turning up neat, sopping crescents. In the police reports column was a brief account of an Etienne LeBlanc, a retired farmer from St Mary Parish who had been staying with his son in Pine Oil when he disappeared. The son stated that his father had moved in with him a year ago, had begun to have spells of forgetfulness, and that he wandered. These spells had started the previous year on the day the old man's wife had died while they were shopping at the discount center. Andy looked over at Ted and snickered. He went to the house for another beer and looked again at the photograph on the refrigerator. His wife's stomach reached out farther than her breasts, and her angry red hair shrouded a face tainted by tattooed luminescent-green eye shadow. Her lips were ignited with a permanent chemical pigment that left them bloodred even in the mornings, when he was sometimes startled to wake and find the dyed parts of her shining next to him. She was a dredge-boat cook and was on her regular two-week shift at the mouth of the Mississippi. She had told him that if a drainage ditch was not dug through the side yard by the time she got back, she would come after him with a piece of firewood.

He had tried. The afternoon she left, he had bought a shovel on the way back from the liquor store at the crossroads, but on the second spadeful, he had struck a root and despaired, his heart bumping up in rhythm, his breath drawing short. That night, he couldn't sleep; he left the shovel stuck upright in the side yard, like his headstone. Over the next ten days, the sleeplessness got worse and finally affected his kidneys, causing him to get up six times in one night to use the bathroom, until by dawn he was as dry as a cracker. He drove out to buy quarts of beer, winding up in the Wal-Mart parking lot, staring out the window of his old car, as if by concentration alone he could conjure someone to take on his burden. And then he had seen the old man pass by his hood, aimless as a string of smoke.

Two hours later, the heat rose up inside Ted, and he looked

enviously at a cool can resting on Andy's catfish belly. He tried to remember what beer tasted like and could sense a buzzing tingle on the tip of his tongue, a blue-ice feel in the middle of his mouth. Ted looked hard at his son and again could not place him. Water was building in his little ditch and he put his foot once more on the shovel, pushing it in but not pulling back on the handle. 'I need something to drink.'

Andy did not open his eyes. 'Well, go in the house and get it. But I want you back out here in a minute.'

He went into the kitchen and stood by the sink, taking a glass tumblerful of tap water and drinking it down slowly. He rinsed the glass and opened the cabinet to replace it, when his eye caught sight of an inexpensive stack of dishes showing a blue willow design; a little white spark fired off in the darkness of his brain, almost lighting up a memory. Opening another cabinet, he looked for signs of the woman, for this was some woman's kitchen, and he felt he must know her, but everywhere he looked was cluttered and smelled of insecticide and seemed like no place a woman should have. The photograph on the refrigerator of a big female holding a knife meant nothing to him. He ran a thick finger along the shelf where the coffee was stored, looking for something that was not there. It was bare wood, and a splinter poked him lightly in a finger joint. He turned and walked to Andy's room, looking into a closet, touching jeans, coveralls, pullovers that could have been for a man or a woman, and then five dull dresses shoved against the closet wall. He tried to remember the cloth, until from outside came a slurred shout, and he turned for the bedroom door, running a thumb under an overalls strap that bit into his shoulders.

The sun rose high and the old man suffered, his borrowed khaki shirt growing dark on his straining flesh. Every time he completed ten feet of ditch, Andy would move his chair along beside him like a guard. They broke for lunch, and at one-thirty, when they went back into the yard, a thunderstorm fired up ten miles away, and the clouds and breeze saved them from the sun.

Andy looked at pictures in magazines, drank, and drew hard on many cigarettes. At three o'clock, the old man looked behind him and saw he was thirty feet from the big parish ditch at the rear of the lot. The thought came to him that there might be another job after this one. The roof, he noticed, needed mending, and he imagined himself straddling a gable in the heat. He sat down on the grass, wondering what would happen to him when he finished. Sometimes he thought that he might not be able to finish, that he was digging his own grave.

The little splinter began to bother him and he looked down at the hurt, remembering the raspy edge of the wooden shelf. He blinked twice. Andy had fallen asleep, a colorful magazine fluttering in his lap. Paper, the old man thought. Shelf paper. His wife would have never put anything in a cabinet without first putting down fresh paper over the wood, and then something came back like images on an out-of-focus movie screen when the audience claps and whistles and roars and the projectionist wakes up and gives his machine a twist, and life, movement, and color unite in a razory picture, and at once he remembered his wife and his children and the venerable 1969 Oldsmobile he had driven to the discount store. Etienne LeBlanc gave a little cry, stood up, and looked around at the alien yard and the squat house with the curling roof shingles, remembering everything that ever happened to him in a shoveled-apart sequence, even the time he had come back to the world standing in a cornfield in Texas, or on a Ferris wheel in Baton Rouge, or in the cabin of a shrimp boat off Point au Fer in the Gulf.

He glanced at the sleeping man and was afraid. Remembering his blood pressure pills, he went into the house to find them in his familiar clothes. He looked around the mildew-haunted house, which was unlike the airy cypress home place he still owned down in St Mary Parish, a big-windowed farmhouse hung with rafts of family photographs. He examined a barren hallway. This place was a closed-up closet of empty walls and wilted drapes, and he wondered what kind of people owned no images of their kin.

Andy and his wife were like visitors from another planet, marooned, childless beings enduring their solitude. In the kitchen, he put his hand where the phone used to be, recalling his son's number. He looked out through the screen door to where a fat, bald man slouched asleep in a litter of shiny cans and curling magazines, a wreck of a man, who'd built neither mind nor body, nor soul. He saw the swampy yard, the broken lawn mower, the muddy, splintered rakes and tools scattered in the carport, more ruined than the hundred-year-old implements in his abandoned barn down in the cane fields. He saw ninety yards of shallow ditch. He pushed the screen door out. Something in his blood drew him into the yard.

His shadow fell over the sleeping man as he studied his yellow skin and pasty skull, the thin-haired, overflowing softness of him as he sat off to one side in the aluminum chair, a naked woman frowning in fear in his lap. Etienne LeBlanc held the shovel horizontally with both hands, thinking that he could hit him once in the head for punishment and leave him stunned on the grass and rolling in his rabid magazines while he walked somewhere to call the police, that Andy might learn something at last from a bang on the head. And who would blame an old man for doing such a thing? Here was a criminal, though not an able or very smart one, and such people generally took the heaviest blows of life. His spotted hands tightened on the hickory handle.

Then he again scanned the house and yard, which would never be worth looking at from the road, would never change for the better because the very earth under it all was totally worthless, a boot-sucking, iron-fouled claypan good only for ruining the play clothes of children. He thought of the black soil of his farm, his wife in the field, the wife who had died on his arm a year before as they were buying tomato plants. Looking toward the road, he thought how far away he was from anyone who knew him. Returning to the end of the little ditch, he sank the shovel deep, put up his hands, and pulled sharply, the blade answering with a loud suck of mud that raised one of Andy's eyelids.

'Get on it, Ted,' he said, stirring in the chair, unfocused and dizzy and sick. The old man had done two feet before Andy looked up at him and straightened his back at what he saw in his eyes. 'What you looking at, you old shit?'

Etienne LeBlanc sank the blade behind a four-inch collar of mud. 'Nothing, son. Not a thing.'

'You got to finish this evening. Sometimes she comes back early, maybe even tomorrow afternoon.' He sat up with the difficulty of an invalid in a nursing home, looking around the base of his chair for something to drink, a magazine falling off his lap into the seedy grass. 'Speed up if you know what's good for you.'

For the next two hours, the old man paced himself, throwing the dirt into a straight, watery mound on the right side of the hole, looking behind him to gauge the time. Andy got another six-pack from the house and once more drank himself to sleep. Around suppertime, the old man walked over and nudged the folding chair.

'Wake up.' He put his hand on a pasty arm.

'What?' The eyes opened like a sick hound's.

'I'm fixing to make the last cut.' Etienne motioned toward the ditch. 'Thought you might want to see that.' They walked to the rear of the lot, where the old man inserted the shovel sideways to the channel and pulled up a big wedge, the water cutting through and widening out the last foot of ditch, dumping down two feet into the bigger run.

Andy looked back to the middle of his yard. 'Maybe this will help the damned bug problem,' he said, putting his face close to the old man's. 'Mosquitoes drive her nuts.'

Etienne LeBlanc saw the strange nose, which had been broken before birth, and looked away with a jerk of the head.

The next morning, it was not yet first light when the old man woke to a noise in his room. Someone kicked the mattress lightly. 'Come on,' a voice said. 'We're going for a ride.'

He did not like the sound of the statement, but he got up and put on the clothes he had worn at the discount store and followed out to the driveway. He could barely hear the ditch tickle the dark and was afraid. Andy stood close and asked him what he could remember.

'What?'

'You heard me. I've got to know what you remember.' The old man made his mind work carefully. 'I remember the ditch,' he said.

'And what else?'

The old man averted his eyes. 'I remember my name.'

Andy whistled a single note. 'And what is it?'

'Ted Williams.' There was a little bit of gray light out on the lawn, and the old man watched Andy try to think.

'Okay,' he said at last. 'Get in the car. You lay down in the backseat.' The old man did as he was told and felt the car start and turn for the road, then turn again, and he hoped that all the turning in his head would not lead him back to a world of meaningless faces and things, hoped that he would not forget to recall, for he knew that the only thing he was was memory.

They had not driven a hundred feet down the lane when a set of bright lights came toward them and Andy began crying out an elaborate string of curses. The old man looked over the seat and saw a pickup truck in the middle of the road. 'It's her,' Andy said, his voice trembling and high. 'Don't talk to her. Let me handle it.' It was not quite light enough to see his face, so the old man read his voice and found it vibrating with dread.

The pickup stopped, and in the illumination from the headlights, Etienne saw a woman get out, a big woman whose tight coveralls fit her the way a tarpaulin binds a machine. Her hair was red like armature wire and braided in coppery ropes that fell down over her heavy breasts. Coming to the driver's window, she bent down. She had a big mouth and wide lips. 'What's going on, you slimy worm?' Her voice was a cracked cymbal.

Andy tried a smile. 'Honey. Hey there. I just decided to get an early—'

She reached in and put a big thumb on his Adam's apple. 'You never get up before ten.'

'Honest,' he whined, the words squirting past his pinched vocal cords.

Her neck stiffened when she saw the old man. 'Shut up. Who's this?'

Andy opened his mouth and closed it, opened it again and said with a yodel, 'Just an old drinking buddy. I was bringing him home.'

She squinted at the old man. 'Why you in the backseat?'

Etienne looked into the fat slits of her eyes and remembered a sow that had almost torn off his foot a half century before. 'He told me to sit back here.'

She straightened up and backed away from the car. 'All right, get out. Some kind of bullshit is going on here.' The old man did as she asked, and in the gray light she looked him over, sniffing derisively. 'Who the hell are you?'

He tried to think of something to say, wondering what would cause the least damage. He thought down into his veins for an answer, but his mind began to capsize like an overburdened skiff. 'I'm his father,' he said at last. 'I live with him.'

Her big head rolled sideways like a dog's. 'Who told you that?'

'I'm his father,' he said again.

She put a paw on his shoulder and drew him in. He could smell beer on her sour breath. 'Let me guess. Your memory ain't so hot, right? He found you a couple blocks from a nursing home, hey? You know, he tried this stuff before.' The glance she threw her husband was horrible to see. 'Here, let me look at you.' She pulled him into the glare of the headlights and noticed his pants. 'How'd you get this mud on you, pops?' She showed her big square teeth when she asked the question.

'I was digging a ditch,' he said. Her broad face tightened, the meat on her skull turning to veiny marble. At once, she walked back to her truck and pulled from the bed a short-handled square-point shovel. When Andy saw what she had, he struggled from behind the steering wheel, got out, and tried to run, but she was on him in a second. The old man winced as he heard the dull ring of the shovel blade and saw Andy go down in a skitter of gravel at the rear of the car. She hit him again with a halfhearted swing. Andy cried out, 'Ahhhhh don't, don't,' but his wife screamed back and gave him the corner of the shovel right on a rib.

'You gummy little turd with eyes,' she said, giving him another dig with the shovel. 'I asked you to do one thing for me on your own, one numbskull job,' she said, emphasizing the word *job* with a slap of the shovel back on his belly, 'and you kidnap some old bastard who doesn't know who he is and get him to do it for you.'

'Please,' Andy cried, raising up a hand on which one finger angled off crazily.

'Look at him, you moron,' she shrieked. 'He's a hundred son-of-a-bitching years old. If he had died, we'd a gone to jail for good.' She dropped the shovel and picked him up by the armpits, slamming him down on the car's trunk, giving him open-handed slaps like a gangster in a cheap movie.

The old man looked down the gravel road to where it brightened in the distance. He tried not to hear the ugly noises behind him. He tried to think of town and his family, but when Andy's cries began to fracture like an animal's caught in a steel-jawed trap, he walked around the back of the car and pulled hard on the woman's wrist. 'You're going to kill him,' he scolded, shaking her arm. 'What's wrong with you?'

She straightened up slowly and put both hands on his shirt. 'Nothing is wrong with me,' she raged, pushing him away. She seemed ready to come after him, but when she reached out again, a blade of metal gonged down on her head, her eye sockets flashed white, and she collapsed in a spray of gravel. Andy lowered the shovel and leaned on the handle. Then he spat blood and fell down on one knee.

'Aw, God,' he wheezed.

The old man backed away from the two figures panting in the

dust, the sound of the iron ringing against the woman's head already forming a white scar in his brain. He looked down the lane and saw her idling pickup. In a minute, he was in the truck, backing away in a cloud of rock dust to a wide spot in the road, where he swung around for town, glancing in the rearview mirror at a limping figure waving wide a garden tool. He drove fast out of the sorry countryside, gained the blacktop, and sped up. At a paintless crossroads store, he stopped, and his mind floated over points of the compass. His hands moved left before his brain told them to, and memory turned the truck. In fifteen minutes, he saw, at the edge of town, the cinder-block plinth of the discount center. Soon, the gray side of the building loomed above him, and he slid out of the woman's truck, walking around to the front of the store without knowing why, just that it was proper to complete some type of circle. The bottom of the sun cleared the horizon-making parking lot, and he saw two cars, his old wine-colored Oldsmobile and, next to it, like an embryonic version of the same vehicle, an anonymous modern sedan. Etienne LeBlanc shuffled across the asphalt lake, breathing hard, and there he saw a young man asleep behind the steering wheel in the smaller car. He leaned over him and studied his face, saw the LeBlanc nose, reached in at last and traced the round-topped ears of his wife. He knew him, and his mind closed like a fist on this grandson and every-thing else, even his wife fading in his arms, even the stunned scowl of the copper-haired woman as she was hammered into the gravel. As if memory could be a decision, he accepted it all, knowing now that the only thing worse than reliving nightmares until the day he died was enduring a life full of strangers. He closed his eyes and called on the old farm in his head to stay where it was, remembered its cypress house, its flat and misty lake of sugar-cane keeping the impressions of a morning wind.

Sunset in Heaven

After Chad Felder had turned forty, he'd begun reading articles about health in the New Orleans newspaper. He knew he shouldn't be doing this. He usually imagined he had or would soon develop whatever malady was described in the medical columns, and Louisiana was a land of such exotic ailments: cholera, pollution-induced carcinomas like coronary and nasal cancer. He enjoyed his job at the accounting firm, but he feared that if he carried too many numbers on his back, his resistance to disease would go down, so he'd asked his employer for Fridays off. His boss did not object; Chad had been a fine CPA for twenty-three years and some of the young guys could carry the load, he was told. He'd planned to exercise and eat healthily on Fridays, but what he mainly did was drink coffee, read the newspaper, and stare at the wrinkles on the backs of his hands.

One Friday morning, he was sitting in his windowed breakfast nook, which overlooked a half-acre backyard and a wall of brush beyond. His two-story brick house was in the rear of a new subdivision that had sprung up north of Lake Pontchartrain, and beyond his lot was a two-mile-thick band of sapling woods that had been cut over by a lumber company five years before, leaving a dense welter of loblolly, pin oak, and stickers. He was reading a column on prostate disease when his ears picked up the whopping sound of what he thought was a helicopter. Glancing out toward the garage, he saw only an empty sky above his gray Volvo. Then, from the corner of his eye, he saw movement in the woods directly behind the house and turned to see the grille and vertical muffler of a rusty tractor poke out of a bank of blackberry bushes.

The doddering tractor pulled straight into his yard dragging a bush hog that was cutting a clean trail behind. It was a tall, bulky tractor, its green paint blistered and eroded, and Chad stood up as it approached his house with a ground-shaking rumble, because it seemed ready to push through the wall and into his breakfast room. In the machine's iron seat was a dried-up husk of a man wearing a khaki baseball cap, a green wing-collar shirt, and gray work pants. He pulled back a lever, and the tractor, a shuddering John Deere that must have been fifty years old, stopped short of the flower bed and rolled back a quarter turn of its muddy tires. The old man killed the engine and stared at the house, shifting sideways to look through a window at Chad, who was holding on to the back of a chair. Then he climbed down slowly, taking pains not to slip, and came to the back door.

Chad liked old people because they were living proof that he could steer around all the horrible diseases in life and last a good while. Young people, especially his own teenaged children, worried him like storm clouds because they were always tempted to drive fast, experiment with chemicals, smoke, drink, and get mashed on dangerous summer jobs. When his daughter would introduce a new girlfriend she'd brought from school, Chad would hold her hand a second longer than was comfortable, worrying about how she would get home safely.

The old man was pounding on the door, so Chad opened it wide and said, 'Hi, what can I do for you?' He thought that the farmer's eyes were like cinnamon balls a child spat out because they were too hot. He must have been ninety.

The old man opened his mouth, failed to say anything, then looked down at his work shoes as if to take time to make something up. Finally, he said, 'I was cutting out my field and was gonna turna back at the fence.' Chad understood that most of the old local farmers were Italian, and he adjusted his ear to the accent. 'But I never found the damned fence. I just kept going and come out in your yard.' He pointed to the John Deere, which sat back on its underinflated tires and hissed. 'I never knew about all these fancy houses,' he said, looking behind him.

'Would you like to come in and sit down? It's already getting pretty hot out.' Here was a chance to study a survivor.

'Yeah, okay.' He walked in and stood by the stove but did not look at Chad in his monogrammed shirt and wing-tip shoes.

The breakfast table was buried under the morning paper and dishes, so they wound up in the living room, where Chad offered the farmer a seat in the lounger in front of the television. The farmer's skin was a well-worn, oiled leather, and his ears were sun-bitten and droopy. Chad offered him something to drink.

'That'sa nice,' he said. 'Water's nice.' He looked around like a man waking up in a hospital emergency room.

After a moment, Chad handed him a glass, and he took the water down slowly, as though it were a particularly fine drink of wine. He looked at his host for the first time. 'I'm Joe Santangelo.'

Chad shook hands, told him his name, and sat down. 'I didn't know there was a farm close by.'

'North Cherry Road,' he said, looking at the television deadpan.

Chad's eyebrows went up. 'That's two and a half miles.'

The old man pulled a handkerchief and wiped his arched nose. 'I been there a long time makin' peppers and strawberries.' He jerked his head up. 'You ever farm?'

'No.' Chad thought of farm chemicals and made a face.

Joe Santangelo suddenly leaned out of the chair and pointed a crooked finger at the television. 'Without people like me, you can eat your big TV sets and shiny cars for lunch, but you not gonna have no son-of-a-bitchin' snap beans.'

Chad faked a smile and took the empty glass. 'That's a fact' was all he could think of to say.

'My daughter couldn't grow a four o'clock in a flowerpot. She says, "Why you work so damn hard? You don't have to. You can watch the television."' He made another derisive gesture at Chad's thirty-one-inch screen. 'All that's bullshit. I don't understand nothing on it.' He seemed to reconsider a moment. 'Friday nights they got the fights.'

'Would you like to use the phone? Maybe call home?' It gave

Chad a sinking feeling to think that the old man had lived through life's accidents and diseases, only to wind up with Alzheimer's. He looked out through French doors to the steaming machine and beyond it to the path cut through the woods. Had he gotten himself lost, so that he had to mow around the brush for hours, finally blundering into the subdivision? What would those several hundred acres look like from an airplane? In Chad's mind, a long, ribbony trail wandered in loopy repetitions, like a life story.

'My daughter said, "What the hell you want to grow vegetables for? You can get snap beans in a can."' He said *vegetables* as four syllables, stressing only the third. 'In a *can*. You believe that? I told her, "Try to get in a store yellow grits that taste like the fresh corn. Try to get fresh, tangy ribbon-cane syrup in a big-ass supermarket."' He put his silver head back and closed his eyes.

'Your daughter, does she live with you?'

Joe didn't move, and his voice softened. 'Sometime that little girl's a bitch, let me tell you. I come in from the garden and she yell about the seed I bought. "How the hell you gonna grow something without seed?" I tell her. All she thinks about is the money.'

Chad sat forward and pinched his lip. He wondered what the old man was imagining, maybe a farm scene – a hundred acres of strawberries – tomatoes to the horizon. 'There you go,' Joe said in a drowsy voice, 'talkin' about the money.'

Chad went into the kitchen and checked the phone book for Santangelos but found none. In the living room, he found the old man sound asleep, his mouth open as if saying, Awwww. North Cherry Road was a string of tiny truck farms interspersed with patches of piney woods. It was only five minutes away, and he could drive along and read mailboxes on the east side of the blacktop, find the old man's house, and probably his unappreciative daughter as well. It would take an hour to get a deputy out to the subdivision on such a call. It would be simpler just to find his daughter and have her come get him. He left a note taped to the inside of the door and left, pushing the smoky Volvo out of the subdivision, then over the three miles to North Cherry Road. He drove slowly past the clapboard and asbestos-sided farmhouses, noting names like Dimaggio, Macalusa, Cefalu, Amato, but no Santangelo. Soon he found himself in the little town of Pine Oil, turning around in the lot of the turpentine plant. The smell made his nose itch, and he rode back out of town with a handkerchief held to his face.

Halfway back down North Cherry, he decided that surely all these farmers knew one another, so he would stop and ask. An old woman wearing a kerchief was digging in her roadside mailbox, so he pulled up next to her.

'Hi,' he said. 'I'm looking for the Santangelo place.'

'The which?' She leaned into the passenger's side window.

'Santangelo. You know where they live?' He raised his voice, noting her hearing aids.

'Santangelo? Why you lookin' for that?'

He studied the face powder trapped in the many wrinkles of her upper lip. 'Mr Joe Santangelo is at my house in Belle Acres right now, and I'm trying to find his relatives.'

The old woman laughed. 'Joe Santangelo's not in your house, mister.'

'What do you mean?' He checked his rearview and watched a log truck swing past him.

'Look, you go talk to Mack Muscarella. Fifth driveway on the right. He'll set you straight.' She stood up and began walking down her drive toward a small brick house as square as a child's block. Chad drove on to a poorer section of the road where the land was low and willow oaks and tallow trees crowded out the pines. The fifth driveway led back two hundred yards to a wooden house set up on brick piers and topped with a rusty tin roof. In the middle of the yard, a gas meter rose up on its silver pipes. Tied to it was a black goat stretching the rope, eating a thistle. An old man wearing overalls sat on the porch swing and waved when Chad pulled into the yard, motioning for him to come up the steps.

'I'm looking for the Santangelo place,' he told him.

'That's it,' he said, jerking a thumb over his shoulder. Chad looked but saw nothing but woods to the east.

'I don't see anything.'

'What you looking for?' He ran a comb through his gray hair, which was wavy and white as wood smoke.

Chad gave him a look. 'The Santangelo place.'

Again, the thumb went over the shoulder. Chad strained his eyes and made out a peeling roof ridge rising above a mob of gum saplings. He jumped down from the porch and walked off toward the brush. The house he found was swaybacked, the beams probably eaten out by termites. The windows sagged at crazy angles, their glasses opaque with a film of dirt, their screens in rags. The place had not been lived in for years. In the rear, he found a cypress barn, a pump house, its door hanging by one hinge, and a tractor shed, the door flung wide. He walked inside and imagined that the cool, damp shade was like a freshly opened tomb. He turned around and followed tractor marks in the soft earth to a bare spot where the rusting bush hog had rested. Beyond that, a five-foot-wide path sliced through the weeds.

He walked back to the old man's porch. 'You saw him, didn't you?'

The white head nodded. 'He come over to borrow two cans of gas, talkin' to me like it was thirty years ago.'

Chad looked back, again unable to see the house. 'How did he start that old tractor?'

A shrug. 'Cleaned the points with a pocketknife and turned the flywheel by hand. It's got a magneto. Don't need no battery. It's simple, like he is.' Mr Muscarella looked over toward the dead house and sniffed. 'Joe raised four children in that place, payin' for everything with bell pepper and strawberry, raisin' the corn and bean. He was okay, you know? Kept his grass down, drained his septic tank to the back, a good neighbor.' Again he put the thumb over his shoulder. 'Every year, he'd make that strawberry wine, and on Saturday him and the wife would ask some of us

353

on Cherry Road to come around and dance in the kitchen. They got a big kitchen in that house.'

Chad brushed privet leaves off his pants. 'He had a record player in the kitchen?'

'Nah. Joe had him a pearl-button concertina, and he'd play that till the wine jug got dry and his wife went to bed, wore out from dancing with us and the kids.'

Chad looked over at his Volvo, which was parked in a sunny spot, heating up. 'You know where I can call one of his children?'

Mr Muscarella folded his hands on his belly and shook his head. 'They all gone from Louisiana. Couldn't find no work, except little Pearl.' He stretched out his bare feet, which were cased in calluses. 'I'm pretty sure he's been livin' with her over in Gumwood.'

'Lord, that's fifty miles. How'd he get back here?'

The old man crossed his legs at the ankles. 'I never thought to ask him.'

'Didn't you worry when he took off on the tractor like that?' He tried to keep accusation out of his voice, and he looked at the goat, who was sniffing the gas meter.

The old man smiled at something complex and private. 'Mister, he got that olds-timer's disease.' He made a twirling motion at his temple with a forefinger. 'That wasn't Joe Santangelo what come by here. That was just his old body.' He pursed his lips a moment. 'Kind of like a movin' picture, but not the real thing.'

Chad pulled at his collar. 'He thinks he's who he is. He told me his name.' He undid one button on his shirt, which was starting to stick to his chest.

'He's doin' things the second time in his head. He told me he was gonna clear two acres for some peppers. Like he did long time ago.' The old man opened a thick hand and looked at the palm. 'Mister, you can't do nothing the second time. It's the first time what count.'

Mack Muscarella gave him permission to use the phone and did not follow him in. The house smelled of furniture oil and cooking and bug spray, and he sat on an old vinyl couch to use the rotary phone to call the sheriff. Then he drove home quickly, to be there before the deputy arrived. He hurried to the living room, but it was empty. In the kitchen, the note was where he'd left it, and his head snapped up to look through the breakfast room window. The tractor was gone.

In the backyard, he closed his eyes to listen, and far off he imagined he heard the whopping exhaust of a big two-cylinder John Deere working under a load. When the breeze shifted, the noise faded away; after a while, it came back like the smell of supper cooking. He wondered what the old man thought he was doing, and he remembered Mr Muscarella's words: 'It's the first time what count.'

Chad stood in the driveway waiting for the policeman, watching his tall, bald image move in the window of his car. He bent toward the reflection and checked his earlobe for a deep crease, a sure sign of heart disease. The crunch of gravel signaled the approach of the deputy, so he walked down his long drive to meet him.

Everything about the officer was big, his shoulders, his pistol, his salt-and-pepper mustache, his mitten hands. His name tag read DRULEY WATTS. He asked why he'd been called, and Chad told him the story.

'Well,' the policeman drawled, 'would you like to help me walk after him through the brush? Maybe we can find him without too much trouble, and I won't have to pull another deputy in on this.'

'Let me change my shoes.'

The policeman looked down at the shiny wing tips. 'Good idea. By the way, do you have any idea how he got to his old place?'

'Old man Muscarella said he just walked in off North Cherry Road.'

'Just a minute.' He held a finger up in the air and turned for his cruiser. After speaking to someone on the radio, he walked with Chad up to the house. 'My dispatcher says a 1969 Chevrolet was found out of gas in the middle of the highway north of Pine Oil. Had 1981 tags on it. That's probably how he got to town.'

In his walk-in closet, he searched for a pair of Bean's woods shoes, finding them under his tennis bag. As he laced them up, he thought of Joe Santangelo's cracked brogans.

A hundred yards into the thicket, they came to a Y and had to decide which leg to take. Already the parish officer was sweating through his uniform. He pulled off his hat and looked to the south. 'I hunted this tract years ago, and as I recall, it gets pretty rough up ahead. The trees are some bigger and too close together to let a wide tractor through. If he gets an axle hung against an oak sapling and that old machine doesn't stall out, it'll go round like a Tilt-A-Whirl at the fair and fling him over a tire.' He started down the south path. 'How old would you say this guy is?'

Chad followed along in the deputy's steps, watching for snakes. 'He's so old, I can't even guess.' He pulled a tendril of dewberry from his shirtsleeve. The peppery smell of the fresh-cut weeds made his nose burn and run.

'Let's pick it up, then. These old ones don't do so good in the sun.' He hopped over a small log.

'You talk as though you've faced this before.'

'Mister,' the deputy said over his shoulder, 'the world's full of people who don't know what year it is. When they stray off, who you think gets called out to find them? One time I found old lady Cotton, who owns the big sawmill, living with a family of Mexicans in the next town. She'd just wandered in and plopped down on their sofa, and they didn't know what to do with her. All she did was watch television and eat, so they let her stay a couple days. When I found her, she thought I was her son and wouldn't leave until after her program was over. What the hell? I ate chili till *The Young and the Restless* went off, then brought her to her daughter at Waxhaw Estates.' Druley Watts shook his head. 'Richest woman in town and all she could appreciate was cheap food and soap operas.'

Chad tripped on the stump of a blackjack sapling. He bent down to lace his shoe, which had been pulled off, and the deputy waited for him, listening. 'I don't hear a thing. Maybe he's run out of gas.'

They walked for fifteen minutes, crossing shallow ditches left over from when the ground had been farmland a hundred years before. The trail twisted back on itself, went around big trees, headed south, then west, then southeast. Beyond a patch of pigweed was an area of washouts near a bayou. The deputy whistled. 'I'm glad he didn't roll off in that direction.' They pushed on into a grove of live oaks, black arms searching wide for sun. Here the undergrowth was sparse and low, the canopy thick. It was a cool, damp room. 'There.' The deputy pointed. 'Oh, damn, damn, damn.'

Chad broke into a run, because he had seen it, too. Fifty yards ahead, the tractor was stalled against a tree and behind it something like a bundle of laundry lay in the cutover poison ivy and swamp iris. It was Joe Santangelo, or a rag doll likeness of him, his head lying over on one shoulder, a blue joint in his neck. Above him was an oak limb as big as a stovepipe. The deputy felt for a pulse and touched the broken neck with a little finger.

'What happened?' Chad was breathing hard, his mouth open. He looked around as if to remind himself where he was and why.

'You okay?' Druley Watts looked at him.

'I'm dizzy,' he said. 'I'll be all right in a minute.' But when he stared down at the body, he felt threatened and sick. With his cap knocked off and his face relaxed, Joe Santangelo seemed younger, and Chad bent close to make sure it was the right man.

The deputy looked up at the tree. 'He must have looked back a minute and the limb raked him off. He probably came down on the mower deck headfirst.' Reaching low with his big hand, he pulled down the eyelids. Chad made a noise in the back of his throat, but the deputy didn't look up. He knelt slowly in the wild grass to examine the body.

Giddy, Chad went down close to him. 'I'm always thinking something like this might happen to me.'

The deputy picked up one wing of Joe Santangelo's collar with a big finger and let it drop. 'Why would you think that?'

The next morning, Saturday, Chad sat at the breakfast table and stared into the woods until his wife shooed him out of the house. He walked to the head of the trail the old man had cut and stared to where it turned in the undergrowth.

Returning to his yard, he set about cutting the grass with the riding mower, then edging the walks and driveway. After lunch, he ate a salt tablet and carried a quart of water out with him as he raked pine straw, trimmed dead branches, poisoned fire-ant mounds. Movement did not allow him to think much, so even after supper, as long as the light lasted, he cleaned the rain gutters and shoveled up a single ten-foot-long row in which to plant late-season tomatoes. That night, his body did not let him think or dream, and even his spirit sank down into bone-tired sleep. But the next day, Sunday, his back hurt, and he worried about it all through church.

That afternoon, he got into his sedan and drove to Cumwood, a gravel-shouldered hamlet of bald red-dirt yards. He had gotten the address from the sheriff's department, and when he pulled into her lot, he saw she lived in a trailer, a clean one, surrounded by low boxwoods and flanked on one side by a neat hand-turned garden. He got out and knocked, looking up into a thunderstorm-haunted sky.

She was about fifty or so, loaded with the padding of middle age. Her face showed too much work, too little money, and so her expression berated him. 'What you need?' she asked.

'My name's Chad Felder. I'm the one who found your father in the woods behind my house.'

'Oh,' she said, nodding in a way that said, Too bad, but at the same time, So what? At that moment, the thunderstorm broke open like a melon, and she told him to come in. The trailer was not as small as he had imagined. Looking around, it occurred to him that he had never been in a trailer. Three very young and somber children trooped past him toward the back; she sniffed loudly and told him to sit down at a little table next to a steaming coffeemaker. 'Them's my grandkids,' she said. 'Cream and sugar?' she asked, as if it would never occur to him to turn down free coffee.

'Yes. I just wanted to come by and see if you had any questions.' He looked at her back as she stretched up to get cups out of a tiny cabinet. He had surprised himself by coming up with a reason for his visit.

She put down the cups noisily, old melamine things that jittered on the Formica table. 'The cops said he hit a tree and broke his fool neck,' she said. He opened his mouth but then closed it again. 'Course,' she continued, 'it's a wonder he didn't run off the road and kill himself before he got back to the old place. That ratty Chevy of his didn't have no brakes to speak of.' She sloshed coffee into his cup, sweetened hers, added powdered creamer from a quart jar, then shoved the sugar bowl at him. 'So you found him, huh?'

Chad took a sip. It was good coffee. 'Yes. A policeman was with me, but I still got pretty upset.' He told her the story, keeping his voice well modulated and respectful. He did not mention that her father had called her a bitch. 'I understand the funeral was yesterday afternoon.'

She nodded, lighting a filterless cigarette. 'Good thing he had a policy. That box cost like hell.'

He watched her eyes. 'Well, I know you'll miss him around here.'

She did not hesitate. 'No, I won't.'

He straightened his back. 'What?' The rain was pelting the trailer like gravel.

'Mister, that old man was my daddy, and he did good for me most times, but he had to be tended like a child. Got to be more of a child every day.' She pulled the cigarette from her mouth and quickly drew a backhanded circle in the air. 'He got to be contrary and mixed up a couple years ago, and half the time he didn't feel good enough to go outside, so I had to live inside and listen to his crap about sugarcane and how they ain't milled good grits in this country since hybrid corn come in style. Mister, day in and day out, that talk is more tiring than a case of the flu.'

Chad looked away at a fake knot in the fake paneling. He was slightly outraged and didn't know why exactly. 'You didn't love him?' he asked.

The woman took a lung-scorching drag. 'I didn't say that.' She looked at him hard and blew the smoke out the side of her mouth, away from the table. 'Now answer me. Did I say that?'

'No.'

'Joe Santangelo was eighty-nine years old. You don't live forever, mister.' She dropped an ash on her cotton print blouse and brushed it off with her hand, pulling the bottom down over her stretch jeans. 'What, you want him to be ninety-five and all stove up with hurting in every joint, not knowing his own children from Adam's house cat?'

He looked down at the table. 'No.' She was right, and he hated it. The three young children came up from the rear of the trailer, opened the door, and tumbled back at a flash of lightning, running down the hall supple as puppies. 'Did he enjoy those kids?'

'Most of the time, except when they got in his little spoonfed garden. Then he give 'em hell. Standing out in that dirt like a crazy man, yelling at those little bitties like they know what they done.' She got up and slammed the door. 'You want some more coffee?'

'I don't think so. I just wanted to tell you that, uh . . .' His mouth hung open. He didn't really want to tell her anything. He had come to hear a life story but was getting just a bitter summation. Chad thought that Joe Santangelo might have left something behind for him. Some clue, maybe, of why he rode the planet for eighty-nine years and then wound up in his backyard. Maybe there were no clues; or the clue was this snorting daughter.

'I appreciate you coming by,' she was saying, 'but the sheriff's men told me everything Friday night.' She sat sideways in her chair and looked out the diamond-shaped window set in the door. 'I'm sorry you had to find him and get all bent out of shape like you are. But you can't let that stuff bother you. He taught me that. Hell, if Joe Santangelo would've found me dead in front the TV, he would've put me in a Hefty bag and set me out on the curb. I'd show up in heaven covered in coffee grounds and cigarette butts.'

Chad made a face and shook his head. 'I wish I could joke about it like you can.'

The daughter regarded him closely, blinking when a lightning bolt came down in the next block. She poured them both another cup. 'Mister, you think the old man's in heaven?'

The question made him move in the chair. 'Why, I'd guess so.'

'What you reckon he's doing there?'

'Doing?'

'Yeah. What?'

He took a swallow of coffee. 'Farming. That's what he liked most, wasn't it?' He imagined Joe Santangelo riding a big John Deere, pulling a set of silver plows in a straight line forever, behind him lines of crumbly black dirt that looked as though they'd been drawn with a pencil and ruler.

'And what'll you do up there?'

'I don't know.'

She tilted her head to one side. 'Would you fish? Hunt?'

A flash popped at the window, a gust of wind rocked the trailer, and the lights blinked, once. 'I guess I'd keep records for the place.'

She raised one eyebrow. 'That's what you'd like to do?'

He turned up a palm to her. 'I'm an accountant. I like to make numbers balance out.'

She straightened up. 'That's it, then.'

'That's what?' He poured himself more coffee and spooned sugar into the tan plastic cup.

'That's what people want to do when they go to heaven. Their jobs. They want to get 'em right.' She lit another cigarette and squinted through the smoke, watching him.

Chad sat back and listened to hail banging down on the roof. He thought about what it would be like to complete an important balance sheet without his usual fear of causing a fiscal disaster. The daughter excused herself to go and check on her grandchildren, and Chad closed his eyes for a moment, imagining a mountain-sized computer monitor gradually lighting up at sunset, its screen covered with rows of amber numerals winking like stars. He walked along the bottom of his columns, which ran as high as night itself, knowing he'd never make a mistake, never be out of balance.

The woman returned to the little kitchen and began gathering up cups and spoons, banging them into the sink and turning on the hot water full blast. 'Hey, mister, that junky tractor of his is still in the woods in back of your place. I'll sell it to you cheap. You can go to raising snap beans.' She looked over her shoulder at him, her tongue making a lump in her cheek.

He thought about this for a moment. 'I like my snap beans from a can,' he told her.

She laughed above the sink's steamy spray. 'Amen to that,' she said.

Rodeo Parole

Four inmates walked out into the hot, powdery dirt of the corral to sit in folding chairs at a neon-orange card table. Where they dragged their boots, the soil smoked. Jimmy, the burglar, was the youngest, a tall, bent rail of a man with scrambled-egg hair and a barbecued, narrow face. He didn't want to sit at the table under the blowtorch sun with his palms down on the flimsy surface, waiting for the pain, but the others had told him that if he stayed with them longest, if they all could just sit there with their hands on the table while it happened, they could win, and the reporters would put their pictures in the statewide paper, where the parole board would see what good Joes they were, brave competitors, winners. Two members of last year's winning team were free already.

Minutes before, Jimmy had leaned over the rough-cut fence and watched what had happened to the other teams. The first foursome to compete had tried not to look. They were veterans. He had watched Rex Ted and Black Diamond and Mollyfish and Ray-Ray sit like statues in a tornado, as though no kind of movement could save them. He'd looked and willed to be like them, draining himself of feeling as he heard the knock of the wood latch, the explosion of breath from the animal, and the ground-trembling plants of the hooves as the bull came on, but he'd turned his head from the arena at the first yell, which was followed by a sympathetic '*Awwww*' from the crowd. Three men had scattered, Rex Ted was rolling on the ground, gored, and the card table had not come down yet. Two trusties came out with a stretcher and carried Rex Ted away, passing by the fence where Jimmy stood looking into the bloody man's face, which bore an expression saying, It finally happened and I'm not surprised one damned bit.

Now Jimmy was in the arena, waiting for the bull to arrive like a decision come out of thin air. Nookey, a hairless older man, who was in for dynamiting a toxic-waste dump, sat across the table. 'Okay,' he said. 'Look at it like this. It's like a judge saying something and you can't stop it or change it.'

Little Claude, an accordionist who had burned down his wife's lover's house, nodded agreement. 'Don't look at that judge; don't look at that bull,' he said, spreading his palms out on the plywood. The fourth was a new man, a murderer who would never get out, not even after death, for no family would claim him, and someday he would be buried in the prison graveyard by the swamp. He was big, with a head of thick black hair combed back and eyes wild as a bear's, a man whom any stupid woman would notice and love at once.

Jimmy spat, and his spit sat on top of the dust like quicksilver. 'Rex Ted's group has the best time. Ray-Ray picked up his hands right before the bull hooked.'

'Let's don't talk about it,' Little Claude said. 'If you talk about it, you gonna try to get out the way. You gonna pick up your hands.'

Nookey closed his eyes just for a moment. 'We got to be still and hope he goes for the table.'

'This is something,' the murderer said, and the other men looked at his eyes, which were open too wide for the strobe-hot sun, as though they were unaffected by light. He had the worst position. His back was to the gate, and behind him a prison guard gave a Brahma repeated shocks with a cattle prod, the animal shrieking and trying to climb the boards.

Jimmy turned to the murderer. 'Why you doing this? We can get out.'

'I can get out,' said the murderer.

'You doing over three hundred years, man,' Nookey said, tilting the white dome of his head so sweat could roll off sideways, missing his eyes. 'They welded the door on you.'

'I can get out,' he said again, looking at nobody.

A little cloud passed over, and the table turned dark. The men looked at their hands on the dusty surface. Jimmy heard the gate latch knock open, and then the cloud uncovered the sun. The wood under his hands glowed with fire.

The bull spun out of the pen like a tornado of angry meat, a gray animal with shadowed black eyes, a lurching hump on his back and, under him, his tortured, swinging bag loaded with electricity from the shock sticks of the howling guards. His hooves kicked up the floury dust, and it seemed for a moment that he had camouflaged the men and their bright table, that the onion eyeballs would not turn on them and the animal would not bolt into their quiet pocket of territory. Jimmy felt the dirt under his boot soles jump each time the animal planted a hoof, but he looked at nothing and willed his mind empty, waiting for whatever fact was about to be proved on him. He saw Nookey's face go blank, Little Claude's lids close. The murderer's eyes got even wider, and he looked over at the bull. 'Easy,' Jimmy said in his direction.

'Easy,' the murderer repeated, with no inflection. Jimmy saw the man's black hair gleam, every strand in place in soft oiled lines like the hair on holy statues, and then the bull whirled and jumped for them, its haunches digging in, its sea of angry muscles directed at something it sought without knowing why, choosing the table and the men as a target with the logic a thunderbolt uses to select a tree or a house or a man walking along with a rake hoisted on his shoulder.

The animal could choose, if they sat still enough, to go for the table, to come in beside one of them and put a horn on the underneath, or even its whole head, and give it a murderous heave out of their hands. If they all kept their palms down, they would do better than Rex Ted's team. Or the Brahma could choose to lay his skull against the table's edge, and then it would go hard for the man on the other side. Or he might lay the barrel of a horn against a man and push them all down like bowling pins. None of the men thought any of this; they were not there, as far as Jimmy could tell. They had drained themselves of feeling and were white and empty.

What the bull did do was lower his head and hit Nookey from the rear, the animal's flat skull battering the chair and the man's backbone together, shoving his chest against the table, which shocked into Jimmy's ribs, the plywood top breaking in two and heaving up in the middle. Little Claude raised his hands right before a horn tip went through his cheek and into his mouth. Jimmy's long arms cracked like a whip over his head when the table hit him, and then he was in the dust, watching a hoof come down next to his face. Two rodeo clowns fell off the fence and distracted the animal as Little Claude dragged Jimmy clear into an opened gate, and a trusty hustled a white-faced Nookey over the fence, where he was put down in fresh manure, his legs kicking as a man with a cross on his shirtsleeve knelt down to blow breath into his flattened lungs. The clowns got to the pen where Jimmy lay, jumping in ahead of the bull, and then Jimmy looked under the bottom board to see the murderer, whom everyone had seemed to forget, sitting untouched in front of nothing, his hands still out flat, palms down, in the center of the ring, his hair flawless, his eyes open. Jimmy wanted to yell, but there was no air in him. The rodeo announcer said something incomprehensible and awful, a squawk of speech, and before the clowns could get back over the fence, the bull ran into the murderer like a train, hitting him so hard that rivets flew out of the folding chair.

Jimmy lay back and robbed his share of the atmosphere in little sips until he could breathe again. He saw arms come under a board and drag out the murderer's body. After a minute or two, a guard holding a shock stick climbed into the pen with Jimmy and told him that Red Tex's group had won the competition.

'That right?' Jimmy rasped.

'They gonna get their pictures in the paper,' the guard told him. He looked at Jimmy as though he almost felt sorry about something. 'We can only have one winner.'

'Well,' Jimmy said, looking under the bottom board to where the bull was trying to kill a clown trapped in a barrel, 'maybe so.'

Dancing with the One-Armed Gal

On Saturday, Iry Boudreaux's girlfriend fired him. The young man had just come on shift at the icehouse and was seated in a wooden chair under the big wall-mounted ammonia gauge, reading a cowboy novel. The room was full of whirring, hot machinery, antique compressors run by long, flat belts, black-enameled electric motors that turned for months at a time without stopping. His book was a good one and he was lost in a series of fast-moving chapters involving long-distance rifle duels, cattle massacres, and an elaborate saloon fight that lasted thirty pages. At the edge of his attention, Iry heard something like a bird squawk, but he continued to read. He turned a page, trying to ignore an intermittent iron-on-iron binding noise rising above the usual lubricated whir of the engine room. Suddenly, the old number-two ammonia compressor began to shriek and bang. Before Iry could get to the power box to shut off the motor, a piston rod broke, and the compressor knocked its brains out. In a few seconds, Babette, Iry's girlfriend, ran into the engine room from the direction of the office. White smoke was leaking from a compressor's crankshaft compartment, and Iry bent down to open the little cast-iron inspection door.

Babette pointed a red fingernail to the sight glass of the brass lubricator. 'You let it run out of oil,' she said, putting the heel of her other hand on her forehead. 'I can't believe it.'

Iry's face flushed as he looked in and saw the chewed crankshaft glowing dully in the dark base of the engine. 'Son of a bitch,' he said, shaking his head.

She bent over his shoulder, and he could smell the mango perfume that he had given her for Christmas. Her dark hair touched his left earlobe for an instant, and then she straightened up. He knew that she was doing the math already, and numbers were her strength: cubic feet of crushed ice, tons of block ice. 'Iry, the damned piston rod seized on the crankshaft,' she said, her voice rising. 'The foundry'll have to cast new parts, and we're looking at six or seven thousand dollars, plus the downtime.' Now she was yelling.

He had let both Babette and the machine down. He looked up to say something and saw that she was staring at the cowboy novel he'd left open and facedown on his folding chair.

'I don't know, Iry. The owner's gonna have a hard time with this.' She folded her arms. 'He's gonna want to know what you were doing, and I'm gonna tell him.' She gestured toward the book.

'Look, I checked the damned oil level when I came on shift. It wasn't my fault.'

She looked at him hard. 'Iry, the machine didn't commit suicide.' She licked a finger and touched it to the hot iron. 'Mr Lanier has been after me to cut staff, and now this.' She closed her eyes for a moment, then opened them and shook her head. 'You need to get away from this place.'

He pulled a shop rag from the back pocket of his jeans and wiped his hands, feeling something important coming. 'What's that mean?'

She looked at him the way a boss looks at an employee. 'I'm going to lay you off.'

'You're firing me?'

'Last time we had a compressor rebuild, we were down for a long time. Come back, maybe next month, and we'll see.'

'Aw, come on. Let's go out tonight and talk about this over a couple cold ones.' He pushed back his baseball cap and gave her a grin, showing his big teeth.

She shook her head. 'You need a vacation is what you need. You ought to go somewhere. Get out of town, you know?'

'A vacation.'

'Yeah. Get your head out of those books. Go look at some real stuff.'

'Who's gonna watch the compressor that's still working?'

Babette took his shop rag from him and wiped a spot of oil from a glossy red fingernail. 'The new man who watches during your lunch break. Mauvais.'

'Mauvais can't operate a roll of toilet paper.'

'We'll just be making party ice after this.' She looked at him. 'At least he's never let the oil get low.'

He glanced at her dark hair, trying to remember the last time he'd touched it.

The next morning, Iry got up and drove to early Mass through the rain. The church was full of retirees, people who had stayed on the same job all their lives. The priest talked about the dignity of work, and Iry stared at the floor. He felt that his relationship with Babette, such as it was, might be over. He remembered how she had looked at him the last time, trying to figure why a good engineer would let the oil run out. Maybe he wasn't a good engineer – or a good anything. After Mass he stood in the drizzle on the stone steps of the church, watching people get into their cars, waved at a few, and suddenly felt inauthentic, as though he no longer owned a real position in his little town of Grand Crapaud. He drove to his rent house, and called his mother with instructions to come over and water his tomato patch once a day. Then he packed up his old red Jeep Cherokee and headed west toward Texas.

After a few miles, the two-lane highway broke out of a littered swamp and began to cut through sugarcane fields. The rain clouds burned off, and the new-growth cane flowed to the horizons in deep apple-green lawns. Iry's spirits rose as he watched herons and cranes slow-stepping through irrigation ditches. He realized that what Babette had said about a vacation was true.

He avoided the main highway and drove the flat land past gray cypress houses and their manicured vegetable gardens. Through sleepy live oak-covered settlements, the old Jeep bobbed along with a steady grinding noise that made Iry feel primitive and adventurous.

On the outskirts of New Iberia, he saw something unusual: A one-armed woman wearing a short-sleeve navy dress was hitch-hiking. She was standing next to a big tan suitcase a hundred yards west of a rusty Grenada parked in the weeds with its hood raised. Iry seldom picked up anyone from the side of the road, but this woman's right arm was missing below the elbow, and she was thumbing with her left hand, which looked awkward as she held it across her breast. He realized that she would only look normal thumbing a ride on the left side of a highway, where no one would stop for her.

When he pulled off, she didn't come to the car at first, but bent down to look through the back window at him. He opened the passenger door and she came to it and ducked her head in, studying him a moment. Iry looked down at his little paunch and resettled his baseball cap.

'You need a ride?'

'Yes.' She was pale, late thirties or so, with tawny skin and dark wiry hair spiked straight up in a tall, scary crew cut. He thought she looked like a woman he'd once seen on TV who was beating a policeman with a sign on a stick. She seemed very nervous. 'But I was hoping for a ride from a woman,' she said.

'I can't afford no sex-change operation,' he told her. 'That your car?'

She looked back down the road. 'Yes. At least it was. A man just pulled off who made all kinds of mystifying mechanical statements about it, saying it'd take three thousand dollars' worth of work to make it worth four hundred. I guess I'll just leave it.' She sniffed the air inside the Jeep. 'It's awfully hot, and I hate to pass up a ride.'

He turned and looked at a large dark spray of oil under the engine. 'That man say it threw a rod cap through the oil pan?'

She gave him an annoyed look. 'All you men speak this same private language.'

He nodded, agreeing. 'You don't have to be afraid of me, but if you want to wait for a woman, I'll just get going.'

'Well, I don't really relate well to most men.' She looked at him carefully for a moment and then announced, 'I'm a lesbian.'

Iry pretended to look at something in his rearview mirror, wondering what kind of person would say that to a stranger. He figured she must be an intellectual, educated in the North. 'That mean you like women?' he asked.

'Yes.'

He pursed his lips and saw the day's heat burning her cheeks. 'Well, I guess we got something in common.'

She frowned at this but wrestled her suitcase into the back-seat anyway, got in and pulled the door shut, adjusting the air-conditioning vents to blow on her face. 'My name is Claudine Glover.'

'Iry Boudreaux.' He turned back onto the highway and said nothing, sensing that she'd begin to speak at any moment, and after a mile or so, she did, breathlessly, talking with her hand.

'I've never hitchhiked before. I was on my way from New Orleans, where I just lost my job, of all things. My car was a little old, maybe too old, I think, and it started to smoke and bang around Franklin. I just need a ride to the next decent-sized town so I can get to an airport and fly home to El Paso, where my mother . . .' She went on and on. Every hitchhiker he'd ever picked up had told him their life stories. Some of them had started with their birth. One man, named Cathell, began with a relative who had made armor in the Middle Ages and then summarized his family tree all the way to his own son, who made wrist braces for video-game addicts with carpal tunnel syndrome. Iry guessed people thought they owed you an explanation when you helped them out.

'We got something else in common,' he told her.

'What?'

'I just got fired myself.' He then told her what he did for a living. She listened but seemed unimpressed.

'Well, I'm sorry for you all right. But you can probably go anywhere and find another icehouse or whatever to operate, can't you?'

He admitted that this was so.

'I am a professor of women's studies,' she said, her voice nipping at the syllables like a Chihuahua's. 'It took me a long time to get that position, and now after four years of teaching, I lost it.' She raised her hand and covered her face with it.

He rolled the term *women's studies* around in his head for a moment, wondering if she was some kind of nurse. 'Aw, you'll find some more gals to teach,' he said at last. He was afraid she was going to cry. It was forty minutes to Lafayette and its little airport, and he didn't want to experience the woman's emotional meltdown all the way there.

She blinked and sniffed. 'You don't know how it is in academics. My Ph.D. is not from the best institution. You've got to find your little niche and hold on, because if you don't get tenure, you're pretty much done for. Oh, I can't believe I'm saying this to a stranger.' She gave him a lightning glance. 'Does this airport have jets?'

'I don't think so. Those eggbeater planes take off for Baton Rouge and New Orleans.'

She did begin to cry then. 'I hate propeller aircraft,' she sobbed.

He looked to the south across a vast field of rice and noticed a thunderstorm trying to climb out of the Gulf. If he didn't have to stop in Lafayette, he might be able to outrun it. 'Hey, c'mon. I'm going all the way through Houston. I can drop you by Hobby. They got planes big as ocean liners.'

She wiped her nose with a Kleenex and put it into a shoulder bag. She looked as though she was willing herself to be calm. After a few miles, she looked out at the open land whizzing by, at egrets stabbing for crawfish. She sniffed and wiped her nose again. 'Where are you going, anyway?'

'I don't know. Just out west. Maybe go to a couple cowboy

373

museums. Look at some cactus. See a rodeo.' He glanced at her worried face. 'What you gonna do when you get home?'

She gave a little mocking laugh. 'Cut my throat.'

The woman talked and talked. Iry stopped for lunch over the Texas border at a roadside café, figuring a meal would stop her mouth for a while. Their wobbly table was next to a taped-up picture window. He drank a beer with his hamburger and she told him that she was originally hired because she was a woman and that her gender helped the college administration meet a quota. 'Well,' he said, wiping mustard off his shirt, 'whatever the hell works.'

'After I'd been there a year, the English Department began considering hiring a black man to replace me.'

He picked up his burger and shook it at her. 'Yeah, I missed out on a job like that once. The company had to have at least one black guy on this oil rig, so they hired this New Orleans dude instead of me and put him on Magnolia number twenty-two with a bunch of them old plowboys from central Mississippi. He lasted like a fart in a whirlwind.'

Claudine raised her head a bit. 'When I produced evidence of my own one-sixteenth African-American blood, they let me stay on.' Iry looked at her skin when she told him this. He'd thought she was from Cuba.

'During my second year, the department brought in other women's studies specialists, and at that point I stopped wearing my prosthesis, to emphasize the fact that I was not only black and a woman but disabled as well.' She waved away a fly. 'But they still tried to get rid of me.'

'Ain't you no good at teaching studying women?'

'My students liked me. I published articles and went to con-ferences.' Claudine nibbled at the cheese sandwich she'd ordered, and put it back on the plate. She looked at something invisible above Iry's head. It was clear that she did not understand what had happened to her. 'They kept trying to let me go.'

'That's a bitch.'

She frowned and narrowed her eyes at him. 'Yes, well, I wouldn't put it exactly in those words. When a search committee member told me they'd received an application from a gay black female double amputee from Ghana, I reminded the committee that part of my childhood was spent in Mexico, and then I played my last card and came out as a lesbian.' She picked up the dry sandwich and ate a little of the crust. Iry wondered if she was afraid that eating a juicy hamburger might poison her. 'But it did no good. The college found someone more specialized, foreign, and incomplete than I could ever be.'

He listened to her through the meal and decided that he'd rather spend eight hours a day with his tongue stuck on a hot pipe than teach in a college.

The two-lane's abandoned filling stations and rickety vegetable stands began to bore him, so he switched over to the interstate. In the middle of a Houston traffic jam, the woman suddenly asked if he was going all the way to San Antonio.

'Well, yeah, I guess.' He felt what was coming and didn't know what to think. The woman talked about things he'd never known: university politics, glass ceilings.

'You could save an hour by going straight through instead of detouring for the airport.' The statement hung in the air like a temptation.

He shrugged. 'Okay.' So she kept riding with him west, out into the suburbs and beyond, entering a country that started to open up more as they glided through Katy and Frydek, Alleyton and Glidden. Claudine found an NPR broadcast and listened to a program of harpsichord music, but soon the weakling signal began to fade, succumbing to slide guitars and fiddles. To his surprise, she brought in a strong country station and listened for a while to a barroom ballad.

Claudine grabbed a fistful of her short hair and turned her head away from him to stare out into the brush. 'When I hear that music,' she began, 'I think of my father and his Mexican wranglers sitting out under a tree in the backyard drinking long-necks in the wind. I think of their laughter and not being able to understand any of it, because I never found one thing to laugh about in that blistered moonscape we lived on.'

'You were raised on a ranch?'

'We raised cows and killed them is what we did. The place was so big, I'd go off on horseback and actually get lost on our own land. One time, I rode out at night, and over a hill from the house there were so many stars and such a black nothing that I thought I'd fall up into the sky. I felt like a speck of dust. The sky was so big, I stopped believing in God.'

'You had your own horse?'

She looked at him, annoyed. 'You are really fixated on the cowboy thing. Let me tell you about my horse.' She held up her nub and her voice took on an edge. 'He was a stallion who was always trying to run under a tree to rake me off his back. The last time I got on him, I was sixteen and had a date lined up for the prom with a nice boy. When I mounted the horse, he was balky and I could tell he didn't want to work that day. I gave him the spur at the corral gate, and he bolted to a shallow gully full of sharp rocks about the size of anvils. He lay down in them and rolled over like a dog, with me in the stirrups. That's how I got this,' she said, pointing at him with her stump.

'Ow.'

'Now, do you have some ruined or missing part you want to tell me about?'

His mouth fell open for a moment, and he shook his head. Iry didn't say anything for a hundred miles. He imagined that she might be unhappy because of her missing arm, but he'd known several maimed and happy ex-oil field workers who drank beer with the hand they had left. He guessed at the type of information she taught in her university. Too much of all that weird man-hating stuff is bound to warp a woman, he thought. But from what she told him, he decided she'd been born unhappy, like his cousin

Ted, who'd won $92,000 in the lottery and yet had to be medicated when he found out about the tax due on his winnings.

The sun went low and red in the face. He drove past Luling and Seguin, where she asked him to stop at a lone roadside table sitting in a circle of walked-down grass. Iry got out and pulled off his cap, pawing at his short dark hair, which in texture resembled a storm-flattened cane field. They walked around the table like arthritic old people until their muscles stretched, and then they sat down on its cement benches. A barbed-wire fence ran fifteen feet from the table, and a Black Angus stepped up and looked at them, pressing its forehead against the top strand. Iry was a town boy, unused to cattle, and he examined the animal's slobbery nose, the plastic tag in its ear. Claudine picked up a rock the size of a quarter and threw it overhand, hitting the cow on the flank, causing it to wheel and walk off mooing.

'I want to drive awhile,' she told him.

They stayed in separate rooms in a Motel Six, and the next morning early, they got up and drove around San Antonio like a tourist couple. She mentioned several times that she wanted to get to El Paso as soon as possible, but he convinced her to stop at a cowboy museum, and they wandered from room to room looking at pictures of pioneer cattlemen, displays of branding irons, six-shooters, and leatherwork. Iry stared at the Winchesters, leggins, badges, and high-crown hats as though he were in the Louvre. At the last display case, Claudine put her ruined arm on the glass. 'This place feels like a tomb,' she said. 'A graveyard.'

He fumbled with the two-page brochure that the woman at the desk had given him. 'I don't know. It's pretty interesting. All these people came out here when this place was like some empty planet. They made something out of nothing.' He pointed at a gallery of mustachioed vaqueros. 'What's the difference between one of these guys and Neil Armstrong?'

'Neil Armstrong was two hundred and thirty-nine thousand miles from home.'

He looked at the gray in her haircut, wondering how much of it was premature. 'What you think it was like in 1840 to get on a horse in St Louis and ride to the Rio Grande, maybe seeing a half dozen guys in between? I bet the feeling was the same.'

'The romance of isolation,' she said, heading for the door. 'A vestige of obsolete paternalistic culture.'

He made a face, as if her language had an odor. 'What?'

She pushed open a glass door and walked out, pausing on the bottom stone step. 'How many images of women are in this museum?'

'A few,' he said. 'I bet not too many gals got famous for roping steers and blowin' up Indians.'

'It could have been their job. Why not?'

He stepped down past her and turned around to look up into her face. He started to say something, but he feared the avalanche of four-syllable words he would trigger down the slope of her anger. Finally, he brought his big thick-fingered hand up, matching it under her thin white one. 'Here's one reason,' he told her. 'The other's this: Women are more family – that is, social-like. They're people people.'

She took back her hand. 'That's a stereotype.'

'Oh yeah? Well, look at us. I'm heading off into the brush to look at stuff, not people, stuff. You going home to stay with Mama.' He expected a scowl, but she looked at him closely, as though he had suddenly revealed another identity to her.

West of San Antonio, they took Highway 90. The weather became hotter, and the villages squatted at roadside, beaten down by the sun. Some towns like Hondo were brick and stucco holdovers from the last century, while some were just low and poor and could have been in southern Illinois except for the Mexicans and the drought. The land seemed to be tumbling away from water as he drove the old Jeep west, passing through broad thickets and then open country, a dry beige world peopled by cactus and mesquite, hotter and hotter as they moved toward Uvalde,

Brackettville, and Del Rio. She talked over the tinny jar of the Jeep, and he listened and looked. West of Del Rio, he stopped and wandered out in the brush to look at the sunstruck plants, and Claudine had to spend twenty minutes pulling needles from his hands.

They stopped at Langtry to see where Judge Roy Bean had presided.

'Now, I've got to concede that here's a real astronaut,' she said, standing on a basketball-size rock at the edge of the parking lot. 'A wild man comes where there is no law and just says, "I am the law."' She motioned with her good arm. 'He staked out his territory.'

Iry pulled off his cap and scratched his head. He was feeling hot and tired. 'Ain't that what professors do? Like what you was telling me in the car?'

She gave him a startled look. 'What?'

'I mean, like, you say I'm going to be the Tillie Dogschmidt scholar. She's my territory because I'm the first to read all her poems or whatever and study what all everybody's written about her. That what you called "carving your niche," right? Some kind of space you claim, just like the judge here did?'

She raised her chin. 'Don't belittle what I do.'

'Hey, I think it's great. You invent yourself a job out of thin air. Wish I could do that.' He thought about something a moment and then pointed at her. 'I read a old book called *Tex Goes to Europe*, and in it they talked about castrated opera singers. I bet if you found out some of those singers wrote stories – you know, about what a drag their life was – you could start up a whole department called Castrated Opera Singer Studies.'

Her eyes opened a bit. 'That's not how it works at all.'

'It ain't?'

She stepped off of her rock. 'No. Can we please get back on the road?'

He pulled open the door to the Jeep and sat down, wincing at the hot vinyl.

379

She got in on her side. 'Am I just not a real person to you?'

He turned up the air conditioner and frowned. 'Am I to you?'

On the other side of Sanderson, he got a glimpse of the Woods Hollow Mountains and sped up, his hands clenching and unclenching the steering wheel. The Jeep began to vibrate.

'They're not going anywhere,' she told him.

'I don't get to see mountains too often.'

'They're like everything else. You get used to them.'

'You got a job lined up when you get to El Paso?'

'Mom knows the head of the English Department at a community college in the desert. I just have to show up and sell myself.'

'How you gonna do that?'

'Tell them how rare a bird I am. How I'll fill all their quotas in one shot. Aw, geez.' She began digging in her bag. 'I need a Prozac. I'm sinking down, down.'

'Hey. We're heading toward the mountains.'

She washed a pill down with a sip of hot diet Sprite. 'You bet.'

'I think you ought to forget about all that quota shit. Just tell them you're a good teacher.'

She seemed to bite the inside of her cheek. 'The world's full of good teachers,' she said.

They dawdled over the Glass Mountains and pulled into Alpine at suppertime. She told him that her credit card had room for one more motel, and they found a low stucco place on the edge of downtown and got two rooms. The place had a lounge and café, and she met him for supper at eight, ordering a margarita as soon as she sat down at a table. He ordered a beer with his burritos and the waitress checked his ID. As the girl tried to read the little numerals in the dim room, he looked around at the other customers and the large hats the men wore. Claudine was wearing blue jeans and a white short-sleeve blouse. He looked at her makeup and smelled her perfume, which was still burning off its

380

alcohol, and felt vaguely apprehensive, as though he were having supper out with his mother.

'You think it's all right to mix booze with your pills?' he asked.

She made a sweeping motion at him with her fingers. 'Let's not worry about that.' Her voice was tight.

'You think you got a shot at this teaching job?'

'Oh, they'll need somebody like me,' she told him.

'You going to say to them that you're a good teacher? You know, show them those records you were telling me about? Those forms?'

'I'm a crippled black woman and a gay feminist.' She put her elbows on the table. 'I'm a lock for the job.'

He shook his head. 'They won't hire you for those things.'

'They'll at least need me to teach freshman English.' She took a long drink. He wondered if she'd taken another pill in her room.

'Why don't you just tell them you're good with the students?'

'You have to be a certain kind of good,' she said, her voice hardening.

'How's that?'

'You can't understand. They don't have people like me in icehouses.'

A man in a wheelchair rolled through the front door. He wore a white cowboy hat, and his belt was cinched with a big buckle sporting a golden music note in the center. He coasted into the corner of the room behind a little dance floor and flipped switches on an amplifier. A computerized box came alive with blinking lights. Iry saw the man pick up a microphone and press a button on the box. The little café/lounge filled with guitars and a bass beat, and the shriveled man in the wheelchair began to sing in a tough, accurate voice that was much bigger than he was. Two couples got up and danced. After the song, the food came, and Claudine ordered another margarita.

By the time the meal was over, she was sailing a bit. He could tell. Her eyelids seemed to be sticky, and she was blinking too much. He began to get sleepy and bored, and he was wondering what was on the cigarette-branded television in his room when she leaned over to him.

'Ivy,' she began, 'it's noisy in here.'

'Iry,' he said.

'What?'

'My name's Iry.'

'Yes. Well. I'm going to get a fresh drink and walk back to my room.' She looked at him for a second or two. 'If you want to talk, come with me.'

'No, I believe I'll check out what's on the tube,' he told her.

'You'd rather watch TV than have a conversation with someone?' Her face twisted slightly, and he looked away.

'No, I mean, it might not look right, me going in your room.' He felt silly as soon as he'd said it. Who, in Alpine, Texas, would give a damn what tourists from a thousand miles away did with their free time?

Claudine's face fell, and she sat back in her chair, staring toward the door. The music machine began playing 'When a Tear Becomes a Rose,' the beat a little faster than usual. When the old man sang, he closed his eyes as though the music hurt. Iry stood up and cupped a hand under Claudine's right elbow, right where things stopped.

'What are you doing?' She looked up at him, her eyelids popping.

'Asking you to dance,' he said, taking off his cap and putting it on the table.

She looked around quickly. 'Don't be absurd.'

'Come on, I bet you used to do the Texas two-step in high school.'

'That was another life,' she said, rising out of the chair as if overcoming a greater force of gravity than most people have to deal with.

For a few seconds, she bobbled the step and they bumped shoe tips and looked down as though their feet were separate animals from themselves, but on a turn at the end of the floor, she found the rhythm and moved into the dance. 'Hey,' he said.

'Gosh.' She settled the end of her arm into his palm as though the rest of her were there, a phantom limb extending up onto his shoulder. The little man did a good job with the song, stretching it out for the six or seven couples on the floor. Claudine wore a sad smile on her face, and halfway into the song, her eyes became wet.

Iry leaned close to her ear. 'You all right?'

'Sure,' she said, biting her lip. 'It's just that right now I'm not being a very good lesbian.' She tried to laugh and reached up to touch her crew cut.

'You ain't one right now.'

'How can you tell?'

'You dance backward too good.'

'That's stupid.'

He turned her, and she came around like his shadow. 'Maybe it is, and maybe it ain't.' About a minute later, toward the end of the song, he told her, 'I've danced with lots of black girls, and you don't move like they do.'

'You're making generalities that won't stand up,' she said. Then the tone of her voice grew defensive. 'Besides, I'm only one-sixteenth African-American.'

'On whose side?'

'My mother's.'

He walked her to their table, his hand riding in the small of her back. He noticed how well she let it fit there, his fingertips in the hollow of her backbone. He pursed his lips and sat down, pointing to her old navy purse. 'You got any pictures of your family?'

She gave him a look. 'Why?'

'Just curious. Come on, I'll show you Babette and my mama. They're in my wallet.' He pulled out his billfold and showed her the images in the glow of the candle. 'Now you.'

She reached down and retrieved her wallet, pulling from it a faded, professionally done portrait of her parents. The father was blond and sun-wrinkled, and the mother lovely and tawny-skinned, with a noble nose and curly hair.

'Nice-looking people,' he said. 'Your mama, she's Italian.'

Her lips parted a little. 'How would you know?'

'Hey, Grand Crapaud has more Italians than Palermo. I went to Catholic school with a hundred of them. This lady looks like a Cefalu.'

'She's part African-American.'

'When I bring you home tomorrow, can I ask her?'

She leaned close and hissed, 'Don't you dare.'

'Aha.' He said this very loudly. Several people in the little room turned and looked in his direction, so he lowered his voice to say, 'Now I know why you really got your butt fired.'

'What?'

'You lied to those people at the college. And they knew it. I mean, if I can figure you out in a couple days, don't you think they could after a few years?'

She stood up and swept the photos into her purse. He tossed some money on the table and followed her outside, where the air was still hot and alien, too dry, like furnace heat. 'Hey,' he called. He watched her go to her room and disappear inside. He was alone in the asphalt lot, and he stuck his hands into his jeans and looked up at the sky, which was graveled with stars. He looked a long time, as though the sky were a painting he had paid money to see, and then he went in to his own room and called her.

'What do you want?'

'I didn't want to make you mad.'

'The word is *angry*. You didn't want to make me angry.'

'I was trying to help.'

There was a sigh on the line. 'You don't understand the academic world. Decent jobs are so scarce. I have to do whatever it takes.'

'Well, you know what I think.'

'Yes, I know what you think,' she told him.

'You're a straight white woman who's a good teacher because she loves what she's doing.'

'You're racist.'

'How many black people have *you* danced with?'

She began to cry into the phone, 'I'm a gay African-American who was crippled by a horse.'

Iry shook his head and told her, as respectfully as he could, 'You're crippled all right, but the horse didn't have nothin' to do with it.' He hung up and stared at the phone. After a minute, he put his hand on the receiver, and then he took it away again.

The next morning, he didn't see her in the motel café, but when he put his little suitcase in the back of the Jeep, she walked up, wearing a limp green sundress, and got into the passenger seat. Five hours later, he had gone through El Paso and was on US 180, heading for Carlsbad, when she pointed through the windshield at a ranch gate rolling up through the heat. 'Home' was what she said, looking at him ruefully. It was the only unnecessary word she'd spoken since they'd left Alpine. 'First time in five years.'

He pulled off to the right and drove down a dusty lane that ran between scrub oaks for a half a mile. At the end was a lawn of sorts and a stone ranch-style house, a real ranch house, the pattern for subdivision ranch houses all over America. Out back rose the rusty peak of a horse barn. Iry parked near a low porch, and as soon as he stepped out, Claudine's round mother came through the front door and headed for her daughter, arms wide, voice sailing. Claudine briefly introduced him and explained why he was there. The mother shook his hand and asked if they'd eaten yet. Claudine nodded, but Iry shook his head vigorously and said, 'Your daughter told me you make some great pasta sauce.' He glanced at Claudine, who gave him a savage scowl.

The mother's face became serious, and she patted his hand. 'I have a container in the fridge that I can have hot in ten minutes, and the spaghetti won't take any time to boil.'

Iry grinned at Claudine and said, '*Prepariamo la tavola.*'

'Ah, *sì*,' the mother said, turning to go into the house.

Claudine followed, but she said over her shoulder, 'You are what is wrong with this country.'

'*Scusi?*'

'Will you shut up?'

After the lunch and salad, he asked to see the barn. The mother had leased the range, but she maintained three horses for Claudine's brother and his children, who lived in Albuquerque. Two of the animals were in the pasture, but one, a big reddish horse, came into a gated stall as they entered. Iry inspected the barn's dirt floor, sniffed the air, and walked up to the horse. 'Hey,' he said. 'You think we could go for a little ride?'

She came up behind him, looking around her carefully, a bad memory in her eyes. 'I'm not exactly into horse riding anymore.' Her voice was thin and dry, like the air.

'Aw, come on.'

'Look, I'm thankful that you brought me here, and I don't want to seem rude, but don't you want to get back on the road so you can see cowboys and Indians or whatever it is you came out here for?'

He pushed his cap back an inch and mimicked her. 'If you don't want to seem rude, then why are you that way? I mean, this ain't the horse that hurt you, is it?'

She looked back through the door. At the edge of the yard was the gate to the open range. 'No. I just don't trust horses anymore.' She turned to face him, and her eyes were frightening in the barn's dark. 'I don't think I ever liked them.'

'Well, here,' he said, opening the wooden gate wide and stepping next to the horse, putting his hand on its shoulder. 'Come tell this big fella you don't like him because of something his millionth cousin did. Tell him how you're an animal racist.' The bay took two steps out into the open area of the barn, toward where she was standing, but before he took the third step, she made a small sound, something, Iry thought, a field mouse would make the moment it saw a hawk spread its talons. Claudine shook like a very old woman; she looked down, her eyes blind with fright, and she crossed what was left of her arms before her. Iry stepped in and pushed the horse easily back through the gate. The animal swung around and looked at them, shook its head like a dog shedding water, and stamped once. Claudine put her hand over her eyes. Iry slid his arm around her shoulder and walked her out of the barn.

'Hey, I'm sorry I let him out.'

'You think I don't know who I am,' she said. 'You think the world's a happy cowboy movie.' She stopped walking, turned against him, and Iry felt her tears soak through his shirt. He tried and tried to think of what to do, but he could only turn her loose to her mother at the door and then stand out in the heat and listen to the weeping noises inside.

Two days later, he was at a stucco gas station in the desert, standing out in the sun at a baked and sandblasted pay telephone. On the other end of the line, Claudine picked up, and he said hello.

'What do you want?'

'You get that job?' He winced as a semi roared by on the two-lane.

'No,' she said flatly.

'Did you do what I asked you to?'

'No. I explained all the reasons why his English Department needed me.' There was an awkward pause, in which he felt as if he were falling through a big crack in the earth. Finally, she said, 'He didn't hire me because there weren't any vacancies at the moment.'

'Well, okay.' And then there was another silence, and he knew that there were not only states between them but also planets, and gulfs of time, over which their thoughts would never connect, like rays of light cast in opposite directions. A full half minute passed, and then, as if she were throwing her breath away, she said, 'Thanks for the dance at least,' and hung up.

He looked out across the highway at a hundred square miles of dusty red rock sculpted by the wind into ruined steeples, crumpled hats, and half-eaten birthday cakes. Then he dialed the icehouse's number back in Grand Crapaud and asked for Babette.

'Hello?'

'Hey. It's me.'

'Where in God's name are you?'

'Out with the Indians in Utah, I think.'

'Well, I've got some news for you. The compressor, it wasn't your fault. Mauvais had put mineral spirits in the lubricator instead of oil.'

'Did the shop pick up the parts for machining?'

'No. The owner is buying all new equipment. Can you believe it?'

'Well.'

'When are you coming home?'

'You want me to come back?'

'I guess you'd better. I fired Mauvais.'

He looked west across the road. 'I think I want to see a little more of this country first. I can't figure it out yet.'

'What do you mean?'

'I met this one-armed gal and she hates it out here.'

'Oh, Lord.'

'It ain't like that.' He looked across toward a bloodred mountain. 'It's pretty out here, and she don't want nothing to do with it.'

'Where's she want to be, then?'

He made a face. 'New Orleans.'

Babette snorted. 'Baby, you're liable to stop at a rest area out there and find somebody from Death Valley traveling to Louisiana to see stuff. Even around here you can't swing a dead nutria by the tail without hitting a tourist.'

An Indian wearing a baseball cap rode up bareback on an Appaloosa and waited to use the phone, staring just to the left of Iry. After a minute, he told Babette good-bye and hung up. The

Indian nodded and got down in a puff of red dust. Iry eaves-dropped, pretending to count a handful of change. He didn't know what the Indian would say, if he would speak in Navaho or inquire about his sheep herd in guttural tones. After a while, someone on the other end of the line answered, and the Indian said, 'Gwen? Did you want two percent or skim milk?'

That afternoon at sundown, he was standing on a marker that covered the exact spot in the desert where four states met. Behind him were booths where Indian women sold jewelry made of aqua rocks and silver. In one booth, he asked a little copper-skinned girl if the items were really made by Indians, and she nodded quickly but did not smile at him. He chose a large necklace for Babette and went back to his Jeep, starting up and driving to the parking lot's exit, trying to decide whether to turn right or left. No one was behind him, so he reached over for the road map, and when he did, he noticed a paper label flying from the necklace like a tiny flag. 'Made in India,' it said.

He looked around at the waterless land and licked his lips, thinking of Babette, and the Indians, and the one-armed gal. The West wasn't what he'd thought, and he wanted to go home. He glanced down at the necklace and picked it up. Holding it made him feel like his old self again, authentic beyond belief.

TIM GAUTREAUX

The Clearing

Byron Aldridge, heir to a timber empire, returns from the First World War a changed man and finds refuge as a company policeman in a rough, backwoods Louisiana sawmill. Soon his younger brother Randolph tracks him down amid the swamps, assuming charge of the mill in the hope of rescuing his former idol. But as the brothers try to understand each other and their wives contend with their own hopes and fears, it is Randolph who starts a feud with the Sicilians who control the whisky and girls, and the future grows fearsome for them all.

'One of the best novels I've read in years'
Annie Proulx, Books of the Year, *Daily Telegraph*

'Astonishingly powerful . . . brilliantly written and the characters in their mire are superbly realised'
Toby Clements, *Daily Telegraph*

'This is a novel so firmly located and vividly realised that you can almost smell the Louisiana swampwater as you read . . . A gripping, action-packed tale'
Jem Poster, *Guardian*

'The relationship between the two brothers is sensitively and brilliantly drawn; the strength of the women in the book, which is at odds with the harsh physicality of a land governed by violence, is deftly depicted . . . *The Clearing* carries an emotional charge far beyond its pages and does what all great fiction does: gives insights allowing us to understand human nature and a distant time and place. I cannot recommend it highly enough.'
Peter Straus, *Literary Review*

'Gautreaux captures the fetid atmosphere of a frontier society poised to join the modern world with great skill, each sentence polished to perfection.'
Steve Jelbert, *Independent on Sunday*

'Confident, absorbing, monumental'
Alan Warner, Books of the Year, *Daily Telegraph*

SCEPTRE

TIM GAUTREAUX

The Missing

1920s Louisiana is the setting for this riveting tale of a kidnapped child and the man on her trail – Sam Simoneaux, who feels honour-bound to help find her. Leaving his stalwart wife behind, he works his passage on a pleasure steamer up the Mississippi, entering a wild world of jazz, moonshine and lawlessness. It is a journey that will lead Sam to confront not only violent criminals but his own past, and to make some hard decisions about the value of vengeance.

'Gautreaux writes action-packed novels that stand out for the extraordinary calibre of their prose . . . As the plot accelerates, readers will be torn between turning the pages to find out what happens next and wanting to savour the language at work.'
Andrew Rosenheim, *The Times*

'Sam is a memorable creation . . . his good luck [is] the ability to hold onto his compassion when everyone around him seems desperate to jettison theirs. It is a quality shared by this remarkable novel's author . . . A rip-roaring adventure novel with a true depth of feeling'
Stephen Amidon, *Sunday Times*

'A dramatic, theatrical meditation on law and lawlessness . . . Despite their wise and knowing humour, Gautreaux's novels seem created out of urgent moral duty, and the importance of reading *The Missing* is to learn that to live without hatred is our only true privilege'
Alan Warner, *Guardian*

'Beautifully written, enthralling . . . a compelling novel whose firm grasp of deviance, responsibility and redemption is buoyed up by a steady optimism'
James Urquhart, *Independent*

'He brings a long-gone era to life in lush, fresh detail . . . this novel about the intricacies of the human heart has a great, beating one of its own.'
Heather Thompson, *Sunday Telegraph*

SCEPTRE